THE KING'S HIDDEN HEIR

SHARON KENDRICK

A TYCOON TOO WILD TO WED

CAITLIN CREWS

MILLS & BOON

First published in Great Britain 2024
by Mills & Boon, an imprint of HarperCollins*Publishers* Ltd,
1 London Bridge Street, London, SE1 9GF

www.harpercollins.co.uk

HarperCollins*Publishers*, Macken House, 39/40 Mayor Street Upper, Dublin 1, D01 C9W8, Ireland

ISBN: 978-0-263-31998-9

03/24

This book contains FSC™ certified paper and other controlled sources to ensure responsible forest management.

For more information visit www.harpercollins.co.uk/green.

Printed and Bound in the UK using 100% Renewable Electricity at CPI Group (UK) Ltd, Croydon, CR0 4YY

THE KING'S HIDDEN HEIR

SHARON KENDRICK

MILLS & BOON

For my darling husband, Pete Crone—
an exemplar of humour, adventure and romance. xxx

CHAPTER ONE

London

HIS BODY WAS bathed in the sheen of the early-morning sun. Every sinew washed with pale gold. A powerful thigh spread carelessly over her hip, anchoring her where she most wanted to be.

With him.

Next to him.

And—at countless points throughout the night—under him.

Her body still warm with the aftermath of pleasure, Emerald's gaze drifted over him, drinking in all that hard muscle and marvelling that a man could be so strong and so beautiful.

'I'm not asleep.'

His accented voice filtered through the air and she blushed, unsure of how to respond, because she'd never done anything like this before. Picking up the mechanics of sex was the easy bit—it was the emotional side which was tricky. Would it be so wrong to relay an unarguable fact? She sighed. 'That was fantastic.'

'Yes, it was,' he agreed.

She stroked her finger over his arm. 'Really?'

'Really.' There was a pause while he removed his leg from her body and suddenly a breath of air rippled in from the open window onto her exposed skin and made her shiver. 'But you should have told me.'

She thought about pretending she didn't know what he was talking about but his tone had suddenly become touched with ice and instinct warned Emerald that a man like this would have no desire for game-playing.

A man like this.

What did she know of a man like this? Very little really, apart from the glaringly obvious.

He was a royal prince. A billionaire hunk pursued by just about every woman with a pulse and yet it had been her he had chosen. It was still difficult to get her head around that. But she hadn't known or cared about his status when she'd first met him, when he'd handed her his exquisite cashmere coat and she'd given him a ticket in exchange, at the gentlemen's club where she put in a few hours here and there to supplement her meagre income. She had just looked into the sapphire glitter of his eyes and totally lost her heart. She hadn't shown it, of course. She wasn't *that* stupid.

'That I was a virgin, you mean?' she ventured cautiously.

'Well, I certainly wasn't referring to my surprise when your debit card bounced,' he said wryly.

Emerald wondered whether that was intended to demonstrate just how different their circumstances were—as if he needed to! But none of it was relevant. He'd already explained this wasn't going to morph into a relationship and she'd told him she didn't care. She'd even convinced herself that she meant it.

Because magic didn't come along very often, did it? And when you got the chance, you needed to grab it fast. So she had. She'd had the most blissful night of her life and now she was going to have to do the most grown-up thing of all and pretend she didn't want to see him again.

CHAPTER TWO

Northumberland, six years later

HIS FACE STARED back at her and just the sight of it was doing strange things to her heart. Twisting it with a pain Emerald hadn't expected to feel, not after six years. Making her mind spin with unwanted images as the screen illuminated his autocratic features. Golden-olive skin and hair as black as a raven's wing. Eyes like splinters of blue glass, courtesy of the powerful Greeks who had invaded his country half a millennium ago, though his sensual lips owed more to the Italians, who had arrived a few decades later.

Feeling as if she'd been punched in the solar plexus, she turned away from the computer as her sister came charging into the small kitchen of the house they shared.

'Have you seen the news?' Ruby demanded.

Emerald huffed out a sigh. A mug of cold tea stood in front of her, next to a slice of untouched toast, which should have been fairly explanatory, given how much she usually enjoyed her breakfast.

She looked up to meet her twin's worried gaze. 'Yes, of course I've seen the news,' she answered quietly. 'The Internet is awash with it. I keep telling myself to turn it off, but somehow I can't seem to look away.'

'No. I get that. The question is, what are you going to do?'

Emerald swallowed as she studied Kostandin's image for the hundredth time and wondered if she would ever become immune to those arresting features.

'Emerald?' said Ruby urgently. 'Did you hear me? I said, what are you going to do?'

Did she actually have to *do* anything? Emerald wondered. Couldn't she just bury her head in the sand and pretend none of it had ever happened? After all, when he'd said goodbye to her on that unseasonably frosty English morning Kostandin had made it clear he had no intention of seeing her again. He hadn't been unkind, but he had certainly been very specific.

'Don't waste a second of your time thinking about me, Emerald. I'm not in the market for a relationship. Understand?'

Of course she had. He was a royal prince and she a humble cloakroom attendant—it was hardly a match made in heaven. Their one-night stand was obviously intended to be just that and she'd told herself she should be grateful for his honesty. But it seemed she had been naïve.

Because several days after their passionate liaison his elder brother had been killed in a hunting accident and Prince Kostandin had become King Kostandin of Sofnantis. That had been a lot to process—but what had happened next had provided the killer blow to her tentative plans. For, with almost indecent haste, and despite having told her he never intended to marry *anyone*, her handsome royal lover had wed his dead brother's fiancée and they were living happily ever after.

Or so she and the rest of the world had thought—judging

by the saccharine-tinted photos of the couple, which were periodically released by the palace and which made Emerald flinch every time she saw them.

But no. The latest news reports were stark. The King and Queen of Sofnantis had recently undergone a quiet and 'amicable' divorce. Was there any such thing? she wondered. The couple had requested 'privacy' and there would be no further statement.

Emerald might have been able to absorb this news in peace and think about whether it should be allowed to impact on her future, but Kostandin was on an official visit to London. He was tantalisingly close, not locked in his glittering palace far away. Wasn't fate offering her a golden opportunity to do what she had intended to do all those years ago? What her conscience was urging her to do, even though she was absolutely dreading it.

Ruby's voice broke into her thoughts. 'If you want my advice, you'll give him a wide berth. He won't want to see you,' her sister added, with hurtful candour.

'No, I'm sure he won't. But that's irrelevant, surely. My feelings aren't really the issue here.' Emerald licked her lips. 'The point is that he has a son. A son he doesn't even know about and I think he has a right to know.'

'And what about your rights?' demanded Ruby. 'Don't your needs count for anything? He's a *king*, for heaven's sake—and one of the most powerful men in the world. He's already shown how heartless he could be by acquiring a wife just weeks after sleeping with you. If you just pitch up there with his son and heir, isn't there a chance…?' She paused, delicately. 'Isn't there a chance he could take Alek away from you?'

'Things don't work like that any more,' argued Emerald staunchly, but she could hear the sudden leak of fear into the words she was saying as much to convince herself as her sister. 'Women don't have their children snatched away by men just because they're powerful.'

'Don't they? Aren't you forgetting something, Emmy? Despite being one of the wealthiest men in the world—what's the one thing he hasn't got? The only thing money can't buy, which is extra important for a king. A son and heir. Don't you think he's going to look at Alek—who we both know is the cleverest and most handsome little boy in the whole world—and decide he wants him, no matter what lengths he has to go to in order to achieve that?'

'Aren't you jumping the gun?' questioned Emerald crossly. 'I don't have to take Alek with me. I was planning to go and see him on my own and work out the best way of telling him. Obviously if he seems like some kind of autocratic control freak, I'll walk away, leaving him none the wiser.'

'But I presume you wouldn't have slept with him in the first place if you'd thought he was unstable?'

Emerald wondered what Ruby would say if she confessed that she'd barely known him when she'd spent that unforgettable night in his arms. She hadn't exactly *lied* about her brief relationship with the devastatingly attractive prince, but she hadn't been particularly forthcoming, either. Wasn't the truth that she felt slightly ashamed of getting pregnant by a man with whom she'd shared little more than engaging banter whenever he came into the posh London club where she worked? Until the night when he'd taken her out for dinner and suddenly the sky had exploded with stars—and her foolish heart with it. She wasn't the first woman to have her head turned by a gorgeous man, nor to have to deal with the surprise pregnancy which had followed, and she wouldn't be the last. Yet though she shared her sister's reservations, she knew she had to tell Kostandin about his boy. She couldn't let this secret burn a hole in her heart for much longer, and didn't she owe it to Alek, too?

Getting close to him was going to be the difficult bit. He wouldn't be able to move around with the ease he had always prided himself on before acceding to the throne. She hovered her mouse over the screen until it reached the page which listed the King's official UK engagements. A state banquet in his honour at Buckingham Palace tonight. A parade of military cadets who were passing out from the Sofnantian Military Academy tomorrow, and security would be tighter than tight in both those places. Her gaze skimmed downwards, until she reached the part which read:

The King will be holding a private party at his old members' club, on London's Strand. The chairman of the Colonnade Club professed himself 'thrilled and honoured' that the monarch was revisiting one of his old haunts.

Quickly, Emerald shut down her computer and carried it upstairs, away from the searching stare of her sister.

The modest cottage she shared with her son and twin was described as having three bedrooms, but even the most optimistic person would have listed hers as nothing more than a boxroom. Alek had the biggest room and Ruby the next biggest. But Emerald was fine with that. She was used to coming last in the pecking order, because she was the one who had thrown their lives into disarray with the unplanned birth of her son. Plus, she relied on her sister for help, though it was much easier now Alek was at school. She closed her eyes and imagined his beloved jet-dark head bent diligently over his books, but hot on this rush of maternal pride came a shiver of apprehension. Her son's life might be about to change out of all recognition, and suddenly she was scared.

Picking up her phone, she scrolled through numbers she hadn't used for years. The first she tried was out of service and nobody answered the second. But then a familiar female voice answered her third attempt.

'Emmy?' said the voice doubtfully. 'Is that you?'

'It sure is. How are you, Daisy?'

'I'm good. What the hell happened to you? One day you were there and the next you were gone... You disappeared like a puff of smoke!'

Emerald's heart began to race. She didn't want to answer questions like that, especially not now. Nobody had known she was pregnant when she'd left London and that was the way she wanted it to stay, at least for the time being. 'Oh, I decided to turn my back on the city and embrace country living, and it was cheaper for my sister and I to start our catering business in Northumberland,' she said truthfully. She hesitated. 'You're not still working at the Colonnade, by any chance?'

'Too right, I am. Got promoted, too. I'm in charge of the staff rota now.'

'No way!'

'Yeah.' There was a pause. 'We missed you, Emmy. All the punters loved you.'

And one punter in particular, thought Emerald—though she doubted he would have used the word *love* in any context other than sex. Or was she being unfair? Kostandin might have flirted with her, but she had flirted right back, hadn't she? If any boundaries had been crossed before they had tumbled into bed together—they had both been complicit in crossing them. She cleared her throat. 'Listen, I'm in London next week. It would be great to see you but...well, I'm a bit strapped for cash. I don't suppose there's any chance of me doing a shift at the club?'

There was a pause. 'There could be,' said Daisy, dipping her voice in the way people did when they were about to tell you something they shouldn't. 'Remember that hunky prince who was a member here before he became a king?'

A mocking face and a hard body swam into Emerald's mind. A powerful thigh slung carelessly over her naked hip. She swallowed. 'Vaguely.'

'Well, he's throwing a big do here. A sort of trip down memory lane, I guess. And he's invited some of the members. We could do with an extra pair of hands for that. Someone we can trust. I can't really organise a last-minute booking through an agency—not when I'm dealing with an actual member of a royal family.'

Emerald's throat thickened, because this kind of opportunity seemed almost too good to be true. Had her luck changed for once—giving her relatively free access to a heavily guarded king?

'I'd really appreciate that,' she said huskily. 'I owe you, Daisy.'

'Sure. Look, why don't you come here around about five on Saturday afternoon and I'll fix you up with a uniform?'

Kostandin glanced around at the mass of people thronging in the columned reception room of his old members' club, each one of them trying to catch his eye. Had it been a mistake to come back? he wondered grimly. To imagine that he might somehow capture a sense of the man he used to be. Because wasn't it here, in London, that he had sampled a tantalising taste of freedom, before the constrictions of royal responsibility had been straitjacketed onto his unwilling shoulders?

He thought back to a lifestyle which now seemed like a distant dream. Those heady days when he'd been able to move around the world with relative anonymity, for he had worn his title lightly. And why wouldn't he, when he had never been intended to rule? The business he had built up through his own endeavours had paid dividends—and his development of induction motors had made him one of the wealthiest men on the planet. And when people enquired why he considered it necessary to work so hard, when his birthright would surely have provided a much easier option, he had shrugged, allowing them any amount of unfounded guesswork.

Because Kostandin knew the truth. He had seen his father ruined by emotional weakness and his brother corrupted by greed and excess. From the get-go it had been a point of honour for him to make his own way in the world, rather than benefit from the supposedly swollen coffers of his royal homeland. He hadn't wanted to be like them—and he hadn't been. Until a cruel fate had intervened and the powerful magnet of royal duty had sucked him back into the fold.

He glanced around, looking at the marble pillars which had given the historic London club its name. The famous establishment provided a discreet base for the wealthy and the well connected, but for Kostandin it was more than a place where you could meet on neutral territory, without fuss. Because it was here that he had met *her*—a woman who had blown away his mind and his body and made him behave so uncharacteristically. Before Emerald, he had only ever associated with women from a similar social stratum—it was easier that way. But he had allowed the foxy cloakroom attendant to disrupt his rigidly compartmentalised life to give him the most sensational night he could remember.

The sassy little blonde who had turned out—unbelievably—to be a virgin.

A virgin.

His body began to harden as he remembered their blissful encounter, when she had offered him her delicious body with a sweet fervour unlike anything he'd ever encountered. He had warned her about his boundaries and she had solemnly accepted them. The fact that he had taken her innocence had briefly haunted him, though he'd wondered if his faint flicker of conscience had simply been a way of justifying his uncharacteristic behaviour. But memories of the curvy little blonde stubbornly lingered, and hadn't he secretly fantasised about another night of no-strings sex with her, to help ease his aching body?

Wasn't that one of the reasons why he'd chosen this venue?

His private secretary, who had been glued to his side

all evening, now made a quiet observation. 'Miles Buchanan and his wife are over there, Your Majesty, and I know they are eager to meet you. You remember, they recently donated a significant sum to your foundation.'

'Yes, yes,' said Kostandin, trying not to sound impatient—because why bother holding this party in the first place if he failed to keep his own boredom at bay? 'Bring them over.'

'At once, Your Majesty.'

Kostandin watched the diplomat making his way towards the attractive couple who were drinking in the corner, but he remained so preoccupied with his thoughts that the voice behind him barely registered and it wasn't until he heard the sound of a woman clearing her throat and saying, 'Excuse me, Your Majesty', that he came back to the present with a start.

Composing his face into the faintly forbidding mask he'd been forced to adopt since news of his divorce had become public—because women on the hunt for a royal husband were nothing if not determined—he prepared to rebuff the unwanted attention of someone who was breaking royal protocol by approaching *him* first. But the cool dismissal died on his lips as he found himself looking into a heart-shaped face and a pair of wide green eyes. At first he thought his mind was playing tricks on him—that his erotically nostalgic thoughts had conjured up an apparition. But then his gaze registered hair of a startling hue. The colour of corn, and sunshine. Thick and silky, it was piled into a neat knot on top of her head but he remembered it best spread over his chest, making it easy for him to weave his fingers through the voluminous strands and pull her face to his, and to…to…

'You,' he said, without thinking—and that in itself was strange, because didn't he usually measure every word he uttered, knowing that the language of kings was analysed for every nuance?

'Good evening, Your Majesty.'

She held her tray towards him but he paid the brimming glasses no heed, his attention caught by the crisp white shirt and form-fitting black skirt which clothed her petite body. Yet the stark monochrome uniform did nothing to disguise the luscious swell of her breasts, or the earthy femininity she exuded. It never had done, he realised achingly as he remembered anchoring those hips with his palms and sliding slowly into her incredible tightness. His heart slammed as he felt the urgent clamour of a hunger he'd denied himself for too long.

'Emerald,' he said abruptly.

'Whew!' A look of relief passed over her face. 'You remembered my name.'

'It wasn't exactly difficult,' he answered acidly, trying to dampen down the powerful shaft of desire which was throbbing at his groin. 'You're wearing a name badge.'

'So I am.' A hint of colour rose in her creamy cheeks as he dragged his eyes away from her lapel.

'And it's a very unusual name,' he observed quietly.

'So is Kostandin,' she said, just as quietly.

It was a definite breach of protocol to call him that in public and all it did was reinforce the reason why she felt she had the right to do so. As their gazes clashed and her cheeks grew even pinker, Kostandin knew the kindest thing to do would be to dismiss her as graciously as possible. He was no longer the same man who had flirted with her every time he saw her in that little cubbyhole they called the cloakroom. And certainly not the same man who had removed her panties with his teeth and made her giggle with exultation. Perhaps she needed a gentle but diplomatic reminder that things were very different now that he was King.

And perhaps he needed to heed that reminder himself. At least, until the time was right.

Because he shouldn't be at the mercy of his senses like this. Hadn't he wondered whether his almost primitive desire for her might have lessened? Because that was clearly not the case. Yet it was no longer appropriate to associate with a woman like her, he told himself fiercely. *It never had been, really.* But suddenly his reservations seemed to crumble away. Hadn't he spent too long denying himself the things other men took for granted, in pursuit of an archaic form of duty? Why shouldn't he catch up with her, for old times' sake if nothing else?

'I'm surprised you're still here,' he observed. 'Weren't you talking about getting out of London at some point?'

'Yes, I was.' Long lashes blinked over her incredible eyes. 'I'm surprised you remember that.'

'Oh, you'd be amazed at how much I remember, Emerald,' he informed her softly. 'How about you?'

He saw her eyes darken. Saw the sudden parting of her lips, which reminded him all too vividly of things he'd tried his best to forget. The touch of her skin and the way she had licked at him until he had spilled his seed inside her mouth. The incomparable sensation of being deep inside her as she cried out his name with uninhibited joy. With her, sex had felt so different and he'd never been able to work out why.

'I'm sure I could easily match your powers of recall, given the chance,' she answered.

'Is that so?' he challenged.

Her eyes darkened with complicit fire and Kostandin's pulse began to hammer, as he began to make excuses for what he was about to do. Surely his whole life shouldn't be spent as a servant to destiny. He stared at a bright strand of blonde hair which had escaped from her hair clip to curve over one smooth cheek. Despite her lowly status, Emerald Baker had proved herself as discreet as he would wish any woman to be and their red-hot night had gone undetected. There had been no hints dropped to any newspaper columnists eager for a royal story—a scoop which would have been extra-controversial in light of his subsequent marriage. The tiny blonde had been the perfect candidate for their brief and very satisfying liaison.

His mouth dried.

How simple it would be to see if she was up for a repeat performance. No promises made. No hearts broken. Two grown-ups who knew what they wanted. Out of the corner of his eye he could see Lorenc making his way towards them and knew he had to act quickly.

'Emerald—'

'Would you like a drink, Your Majesty?' she said politely, extending her tray towards him, as if she had suddenly remembered what she was supposed to be doing.

'No. Not now.' He shook his head—the faintest elevation of his finger silently warning his private secretary not to approach. 'And certainly not here. I'd forgotten just how bad the wine could be.'

'The wine committee would be mortified to hear you say that.'

'But we could meet afterwards,' he continued impatiently. 'Would you like that—or do you have somewhere else you need to be?'

He saw the pleasure which flashed through her extraordinary eyes but it was tempered by something else. Something he couldn't quite compute. Kostandin frowned, but the luscious lines of her lips distracted him from his momentary sense of disquiet.

'No, I'd love that,' she answered. 'In fact—'

With an impatient wave of his hand, he cut her off. 'I have people I need to talk to,' he said abruptly. 'What time do you finish?'

There was a pause. 'I knock off at eleven.'

Kostandin's eyes narrowed as he glanced over at the ornate grandfather clock which predated the club's inception. No way was he hanging around here waiting for her—he had never waited for a woman in his life and didn't intend to start now. He could ask for the library upstairs to be made available and catch up on some of the state papers until she finished her shift. What was it the English said? To kill two birds with one stone.

'My car will be waiting for you at the back of the building. But let's keep it as low-key as possible.' His voice grew silky. 'We don't want to announce our assignation to the world, do we?'

'No, of course we don't,' she said brightly, but he couldn't help noticing that the glasses on her tray were jangling as she quickly turned away, almost as if her hands were trembling.

CHAPTER THREE

EMERALD'S PULSE WAS hammering as she emerged from the staff entrance at the back of the club and spotted the darkly gleaming limousine parked in the shadows, with another car close behind—presumably containing Kostandin's bodyguards. She'd gone through an agony of indecision as she'd changed out of her uniform, wondering if she should have agreed to this late-night meeting, or whether she should have asked to see him in the cold light of day. But most likely he would have refused, because it would have been inappropriate to expect such an important man to fit in with *her* plans. And what would she have suggested anyway, if he had agreed to see her? Arranged to meet him in some anonymous coffee bar or pub? His bodyguards would never have allowed it.

No. Better to get it over with and try not to get distracted. She wasn't here to flirt with him, no matter how easily she seemed to have slotted straight back into that role. Calm and collected was what she should be aiming for. But her mouth was dry as she made her way towards the car, wobbling slightly in her sister's sky-high heels, which she had insisted she borrow. 'Because you can't wear a pair of frumpy trainers if you're going to London to see the King,' Ruby had announced, her blunt statement only adding to the butterfly flutter of Emerald's nerves. 'In fact, you'd better have one of my dresses, too.'

But Emerald had resisted borrowing anything else, because Ruby was fashionable and she was not. And it was important not to feel any more of an imposter than she already did. As a working mum she usually dressed for comfort and tied her long hair back in a plait but tonight, as instructed, she had left it loose, at Ruby's bidding. 'Work it, Emmy—it's your best feature.' Maybe it was, but unfortunately it was now flapping around her face in this unseasonably cold wind and her best jumper and skirt made her look as if she were going on a job interview.

Yet despite all her misgivings, the evening had gone better than expected. It had been the King who had suggesting meeting up afterwards, not her. She hadn't needed to drop any heavy hints, or grovel, or risk getting turned down. Or—worst of all—blanked. That had been her biggest fear, that he wouldn't have a clue who she was. He *had* recognised her, which had come as a huge relief, but Emerald was still scared. Scared of what he might say and how he might react to what she was about to tell him. Scared, too, of the way he could make her feel. Even now. How could a body which she had neglected for six long years, suddenly burst into provocative life like this? Her breasts hadn't stopped aching since the moment Kostandin glanced down at her name badge and then glanced up to meet her heated gaze. How did he manage to make her feel that way with nothing more than a few clipped words and a mocking look?

Sometimes she'd wondered if time might have made her immune to his appeal, but she had got her answer tonight. If anything, he seemed even more charismatic. *That was because he was,* she reminded herself. Power was an aphrodisiac and he had power to burn. These days, he possessed absolute authority over his country and that, coupled with his dark good looks—made him even more irresistible.

When he'd swept into the ballroom at the Colonnade tonight, the whole room had grown silent. Men and women had been assessing him with hungry or openly curious eyes. But Emerald couldn't help thinking how *different* he'd seemed. He looked the same and yet it was hard to recognise him as the same man. In repose, his eyes were cold, his mouth tight and unforgiving. It was as though he was encased in a brittle exterior—as if his new title had cut him off from the rest of the world.

As she made her way across the cobblestones where the chauffeur was holding open the passenger door and she slid onto the back seat, Emerald thought how unreal this felt. Of course it did. She was about to inform a powerful king that he had a son. But she needed to choose her moment carefully and that moment wasn't now. Not when Kostandin was seated so close to her on the plush leather seat, his long legs sprawled in front of him, his features shadowed as he turned to look at her. As she met the narrowed glitter of his eyes, Emerald vowed not to be intimidated. She needed to cling onto her sense of self and be strong, because those were her only assets.

'You came,' he observed softly.

'Did you think I wouldn't?'

He smiled. 'No.'

'Because women don't turn down the offer of a date with a man like you, I suppose?'

'I wasn't aware this was a date.' His gaze became mocking, as if he had noted her sudden rise in colour. 'I was referring to the fact that people are fairly predictable whenever they're dealing with a member of the royal family. And having invitations turned down is something which, frankly, never happens.'

Emerald nodded, trying to shake off her embarrassment and remember the type of thing she would have said back in the day, when she'd had nothing to lose. 'Should I feel sorry for you?'

His lazy smile widened. 'You can feel anything you want to feel, Emerald,' he returned softly. 'We both know that.'

It seemed that their intimate verbal shorthand was still intact and, oh, didn't it feel good? Briefly, Emerald closed her eyes. Because in the lonely nights which had followed their fling, she'd sometimes wondered if she had imagined this *thing* they had between them, or had embellished it to make herself feel better about what had happened.

Her breath caught in her throat as her eyelashes fluttered open to meet his molten gaze and she actually thought he was going to lean over and kiss her. But he didn't. Stupid to feel a crashing feeling of frustration. Not sensible at all. More importantly, she was allowing herself to be distracted and maybe this was as good a time as any to tell him. 'Kostandin—'

But the disembodied sound of the chauffeur's voice interrupted her, filtering through the intercom and speaking in a language she didn't understand. 'Damn,' Kostandin said softly, after a moment or two.

'What's wrong?'

'The paps are waiting.'

'But you must have known that might happen,' she said reasonably. 'After all, the papers published a list of your engagements.'

'Ah, but I wasn't expecting to have a passenger with me,' he observed, his shuttered gaze flicking over her. 'Especially a beautiful, unknown blonde with the ability to send the speculating press into overdrive.'

Beautiful. He had called her beautiful. Emerald forced herself not to get too excited by the throwaway compliment. 'So what's going to happen? Do you want me to get out and take a bus?'

'Don't be ridiculous,' he said. 'You'll need to duck, that's all.'

She looked at him blankly. 'Duck?' she echoed, puzzled.

'I'm not talking about the feathered variety they used to serve in that disgusting orange sauce at the Colonnade—'

'You're so critical of the club, Kostandin, it makes me wonder why you ever bothered being a member there.'

'Perhaps because it had plenty of other things going for it,' he purred.

'Oh?' She knew she was flirting with him but she couldn't seem to help herself. 'Such as?'

'Well, there's its prime position in the centre of London, for a start,' he said, deadpan.

'Yes, of course. There is that. And its easy access to the park, of course.'

'Of course.' His eyes glittered as he shot a narrow-eyed glance to the road ahead. 'What I mean is you're going to have to lie down on the back seat when we leave the club. It's the only way to avoid the cameras. But if the idea doesn't appeal, we could part now. I can have one of my back-up cars drop you off home, wherever that might be. Or you could stick to the original plan and come to the Sofnantis Embassy for a glass of champagne.' The challenge of his smile mocked her. 'Depends how much you want my company.'

She wanted his company very much—but not for the reasons he probably imagined. 'Oh, very well,' she said, as if she could take it or leave it, but the flicker of triumph in his eyes told her she hadn't fooled him one bit as he tapped his fingers on the smoked-glass panel which divided them from the driver.

'Lose them,' he instructed tersely, before turning his gaze on her, his subsequent smile driving every other thought from her head. 'Treat it like a game,' he advised softly. 'It's the only way to survive this strange life of mine.'

'You mean you never really take it very seriously?'

He shook his head. 'It's a little more complex than that. But you have to take your fun where you can.' His eyes glittered. 'Ready?'

'Sure,' she said, because when he looked at her that way she honestly thought she might have agreed to anything. 'Why not?'

The car accelerated and the weird thing was that very quickly it *became* fun—which was the last thing Emerald would have expected in the circumstances. But then, she was more used to hard work than frivolity. She'd spent the last five years bogged down by nappies and routine and, as often as not, with worry. She'd scrimped and saved and juggled work and childcare. She'd baked cakes at night and juggled business plans while Alek was in bed and never, *never* seemed to get enough sleep. She saved all her pennies for her darling son and bought her clothes from charity shops. Sometimes she'd felt old before her time and she was damned sure she looked it, too. But this grown-up version of hide-and-seek felt curiously carefree—as if she was making up for some of the years she'd missed out on.

She crouched down, flattening her torso against her knees, dimly aware of the incandescent flash of bulbs outside the window, the yell of voices and sense of urgency as the car increased its speed.

'Are you comfortable?' he asked.

'Mmm… Blissfully. Can't you tell?'

He gave a short laugh. 'It shouldn't be too much longer.'

'Thanks for the reassurance.' She wriggled a bit. 'But won't they wonder why your lips are moving when you're supposedly alone in the car? They might think you're talking to yourself, or I suppose you could be rehearsing a speech?'

'I don't usually rehearse speeches at this time of night in the back of a car, Emerald,' he offered drily. 'Now stop distracting me, will you? I have a message from one of my aides which I need to deal with,' he told her sternly.

He was the one who'd started this conversation but she wasn't going to say so, not when her senses were so aroused by him. By everything, really. By the way they had slipped so easily into that light and teasing wordplay and the weird contradiction of feeling more relaxed with him than with any other man she'd ever met, despite his royal status and her being at the opposite end of the social pecking order.

She could smell leather and the subtle scent of sandal-wood she had always associated with him, but most of all she was aware of his proximity. She had taught herself not to remember the intimacy she had experienced with him because the memory was unbearably bittersweet—but now it was impossible to keep those forbidden images at bay. How dangerously easy it was to recall the memory of his warm skin against hers. His hardness thrusting deep inside her. The way she had choked out her disbeliev-ing joy when he'd made her come, over and over again.

And nothing had changed. She still wanted him, she realised—and that was a distraction she really didn't need. She had to stay focussed and remember why she was here. *The only reason she was here.* She closed her eyes and stayed motionless, until he brushed his finger-tips over her shoulder—a featherlight touch which made her tremble and silently she cursed the sudden warm beat of blood to her breasts.

'It's okay, Emerald. You can get up now.'

Missing that brief physical contact, she sat up, smooth-ing down her mussed hair to gaze out of the window, but the only thing she could see was the red and white glare of slowly moving London traffic, bumper to bum-per. 'Where have they gone?' she questioned, looking in vain for a swarm of paparazzi.

'We've lost them. My bodyguards deployed a decoy car. They're very good at doing that. Mind you, the press are remarkably easy to confuse.'

Emerald studied the set of his profile. 'Is it always like this?' she ventured curiously.

'The very nature of the job is bizarre and isolating.' He shrugged. 'But it's particularly bad at the moment.'

She forced herself to say it. To overcome the tight knot of hurt which was knotted in her stomach, reminding herself that of course he hadn't betrayed her. How could you betray someone you were never supposed to see again? 'Because of the divorce, I suppose?'

'You could say that.'

Emerald nodded, knowing that once she told him about Alek they were probably going to have these kinds of grown-up conversations all the time, during the 'civilised' handover which would take place on neutral territory. The polite small talk which meant nothing other than a useful disguise for the messy churn of emotion. She was dreading her perceived future of possible shared parenthood, but she'd better get used to the idea.

'Was it very bad?' she asked, in the kind of understanding voice she'd heard TV therapists use.

'I don't want to talk about it.'

'No. No, of course not. It's none of my business.'

'You're right,' he snapped. 'It's not.'

Suddenly his voice had become hard and unfriendly and the implications of that troubled her. Did that mean he was hurting badly after his divorce? Had the love of his life shattered his heart? People said emotional pain was the worst kind of pain of all and Emerald could vouch for that. And now she was going to have to tell him something which had the potential to shatter his world even more—and she was dreading that, too.

Soon the luxury car was turning into one of the quiet side roads abutting Regent's Park—a pair of tall, wrought-iron gates opening and shutting behind them to enclose them in a shadowy, tree-lined compound where she could see the occasional flash of a torch and the gleam of a dog's eyes.

'Welcome to the Sofnantian Embassy,' Kostandin said.

Emerald scrambled out of the car and looked up at the Palladian mansion. 'Wow,' she said.

'You like it?'

Who wouldn't like it? she thought. But it was so *big*. So elegant. A different world, and a daunting environment in which to deliver her bombshell news. She'd never really glimpsed the royal side of his life before and as she stepped onto the gravel path, she suddenly felt out of her depth. 'Will there be er…servants?'

'That depends. If you want servants, I can have legions of them at your disposal. All the pomp and ceremony you require can be yours for the taking, Emerald,' he drawled. 'All you have to do is say the word.'

She wrinkled her nose. 'I'll pass on that if you don't mind.'

Kostandin successfully hid his surprise, because most people were turned on by the trappings of his ancient title and all the paraphernalia which went with it. The palaces. The jewels. And the power… That was the biggest turn-on of all.

But not for Emerald, he recalled. That side of him had never been part of the deal. She had known he was a prince, yes—but had treated him as a man. The night they'd spent together had been unplanned, but she had been content to spend it incognito. Their room at the Granchester Hotel had been fairly ordinary by his standards, probably because he'd told her to book it in her name. In fact, that had been the only blip during their brief encounter—when she'd confided that her debit card had been declined because she didn't have enough money in her account to pay for it. He remembered the way she'd flinched when he'd slid his credit card towards her, and for a moment he'd thought she was going to refuse it.

He led the way up the marble steps but, despite having instructed his private secretary to make no fuss, it was Lorenc who opened the door for them, his gaze falling with assessment on the tiny blonde. How would his private secretary view her? Kostandin wondered idly. Would he disapprove of the fact that her pale blonde hair was mussed and untidy from crouching down on the back seat of the car and perhaps jump to the conclusion that the King had been running his fingers through it?

If only.

Would he disapprove of her cheap little jumper and skirt, or shoes which were higher than the ones he remembered her wearing?

'Lorenc,' he said huskily. 'I'd like you to meet Emerald—'

'Baker,' she filled in quickly, as if she was worried he'd forgotten—which, in truth, he had. 'Though lots of people call me Emmy.'

'Indeed,' said his aide thoughtfully. 'Your face seems very familiar.'

'That's because it is,' she said chattily. 'I served you a drink at the Colonnade Club earlier. A tomato juice, as I recall—since you told me you never drank alcohol when you were working.'

Kostandin almost laughed out loud to see the expression on the other man's face because, like most diplomats, he disapproved of instant familiarity between strangers.

'I am delighted to make your acquaintance, Miss Baker,' Lorenc announced formally.

Kostandin held up his hand to truncate the laboured introductions. 'Just have some champagne brought up to the Plavezero suite, will you?' he said, turning to find the petite blonde sniffing at the lavish display of lilies which adorned the entrance hall. 'Are you hungry, Emerald?'

His use of her name seemed to startle her because as she drew away from the flowers and looked up, a dark flush entered her creamy cheeks. 'Er, no, thanks.'

Kostandin's heart missed a beat. Did she have any idea how enchanting she looked when she blushed like that? It made him think about his delicious discovery of her unexpected innocence and how his disbelief had turned into the most intense pleasure he'd ever experienced. Suddenly he found himself wondering how many men Emerald Baker had slept with in the intervening years, unprepared for the savage burst of jealousy which flooded through him. Her sexual history was irrelevant, he reminded himself. It was the present which mattered and he was eager to explore all the possibilities of that.

He ushered her into the Plavezero suite, which was named after his country's capital and studded with its most precious artefacts. Most of the furniture was crafted from the rare blackwood trees which grew in the northernmost forests of Sofnantis, and the cavernous space was softened by the faded hues of ancient silken rugs. It was an undeniably beautiful room, especially when lit by firelight flickering in the huge grate, as it was tonight. But Kostandin had never been dazzled by the accoutrements of royal life, even as a child.

Especially as a child.

He gave a bitter smile as he thought back to the chaos of the past, and the timeline which had brought him to this place. The monarchy he had accepted because there had been no other choice and which inwardly he had railed against, long into the nights which had followed. But he had done his duty. He had stepped up to the plate and embraced the concept of service. Under his reign, Sofnantis had entered a new and golden age—because he was a man who would accept nothing less than success.

But now the tank was empty and he had nothing left to give. He had played the sovereign role to the best of his ability, but his heart had never really been in the task. Many of his nation's cartoonists portrayed him as grim-faced and unsmiling, and in all honesty he couldn't disagree with them. Which was why things were going to change. And soon. He thought about his cousin. Didn't the people of Sofnantis deserve a ruler who actually *enjoyed* being King, instead of someone who saw the role as a burden?

But those plans were for another day. Tonight, he was going to put all that out of his head and focus on Emerald Baker. A servant entered the room with a tray of drinks, before noiselessly leaving. Kostandin gestured for Emerald to sit on one of the sofas but she shook her head, her expression suddenly clouding. She turned away from him, her shoulders set and tense—and although it was a massive breach of protocol to turn your back on a member of the royal household, and would have appalled Lorenc, Kostandin quickly sought to put her at ease.

'It's all a little overwhelming, I know,' he said. 'Rather too much clutter for my liking.'

She turned back to face him, her shoulders still tense. 'Kostandin,' she said.

There was an odd note in her voice, but he was too

distracted by the fire-splashed fall of her hair to heed it. 'So few people call me by my first name any more,' he reflected.

'Because of your elevated position, I suppose?'

'Well, yes. There is that, of course.' He paused. 'But nobody ever says it the way you do.'

'Oh?' She looked startled. 'And how's that?'

'Seriously?'

White teeth dug into a soft bottom lip. 'Uh-huh.'

'Soft and sweet and tender.' He slanted her a mocking look as she blushed. 'You said it that way just before I kissed you for the first time.'

'D-did I? Fancy you remembering that.'

'Oh, I remember a lot about that night.' There was a pause and his voice grew husky. 'You were looking at me then, just like you're looking at me now...'

'How?' she whispered as his words tailed off.

'As if you wanted me to touch you. As if you were longing to have sex with me again.'

She drew in a sharp breath, his candour seeming to surprise her—though nobody could have been more surprised by his words than himself.

'Or am I mistaken?' he questioned silkily.

CHAPTER FOUR

EMERALD FROZE AS Kostandin's silken question reverberated around the room. Even though that incredible chemistry was still fizzing between them, she hadn't expected him to come out and *acknowledge* it like that, as if talking about sex were as normal as talking about the weather. He was throwing down a challenge and she knew exactly how she should respond. Shut it down, right now. It was wrong on so many levels and her big secret was still burning a hole in her heart. She had come here to tell him about his son and that was supposed to be the only thing on her mind.

But when he looked at her like that. With hunger in his eyes, yes, but with something else, too. Something which flickered behind the darkening sapphire and resonated with the emptiness which had existed inside her for so long. He had implied that being crowned King had isolated him and she had witnessed that for herself. Amid all the celebratory hustle at the Colonnade Club tonight, he had seemed remote and apart from everyone else and here, in the magnificent setting of his embassy, he cut just as lonely a figure.

But the waves of desire radiating from his body were almost tangible. All he was doing was subjecting her to that smoky stare and yet it was turning her on unbearably. Suddenly, it was difficult to breathe properly and the heat in her core was distracting. She could feel her nipples hardening beneath her blouse. And he had noticed. His eyes were fixed on the rapid rising and falling of her breasts and she saw the effort it took for him to drag his gaze away to study her face, his eyebrows raised in question.

Would it be so wrong to do this? she wondered achingly. Wouldn't it make telling him easier if they were as close as a man and woman could be, before she uttered words which would inevitably change both their lives? If she could remind him of the mutual pleasure they'd once shared and the wonderful if unexpected gift which had resulted from that passionate night together?

'No, you're not mistaken,' she said slowly.

He didn't move. His body was motionless as if it had been carved from marble and Emerald wondered if he was regretting his words—or maybe even preparing to retract them. But then he smiled and the slow curve of his lips was making her heart thunder.

'Come here,' he commanded softly.

In the breathless excitement of that moment, Emerald felt past and present blending together—like butter and sugar when you were mixing a cake. And suddenly she was back in that place where she'd felt curiously equal to him. Equal enough to answer back and make herself prolong this deliciousness for as long as possible—no matter how much her hungry body was urging her to rush straight into his arms. She met his heated gaze. 'And if I don't?'

'If you don't...' The gaze was growing more speculative by the second—filled with an incandescent blue fire which blazed through her. 'Then I might be forced to conclude that you'd like me to come over there and show you exactly how much I want you.'

Emerald blinked. It was the most unashamedly alpha statement she could have imagined, and it was turning her on even more. He might be a king, but in that moment he sounded more like a caveman and the contrast of that was irresistible. Perhaps she needed to approach this with caution and tell him there were things they needed to discuss first. But when you had denied yourself pleasure for as long as she had, rational thinking wasn't easy. In fact, it was darned near impossible, when your body was on *fire*.

She tilted her chin and her hair swayed against her back. 'Go ahead, then,' she said boldly. 'I'm not stopping you.'

He moved toward her, sinuous and graceful as a jungle cat, his dark gaze fixed on her. 'No, you're not, are you?' he murmured as he pulled her into his arms and that first sweet contact made her shiver. 'In fact, the light you're giving me right now is as green as your incredible eyes.'

Emerald felt dazed as he bent his head and touched his lips to kiss her—a kiss she'd never thought would happen again.

Her brain cleared.

Because he'd married another woman. He'd spent the last five years living in a golden palace with Luljeta, his beautiful, high-born queen, and presumably had been kissing her just like this.

But even that cold swamp of reason wasn't enough to make Emerald hold back, murmuring her approval as he slid his tongue inside her mouth, and the intimacy of that contact sent a wave of need jack-knifing through her pelvis.

'Oh!' she gasped.

'You like that?'

'What do you think?'

'This is what I think,' he growled, levering her even closer.

'Oh!' she gasped, for a second time, because now she could feel the imprint of his erection straining against the fine material of his suit and that blatant demonstration of his arousal sent her pulse-rate soaring even higher. And all the while her core was melting. Her body was growing liquid with need, and maybe she communicated her frustration to him, because when she instinctively circled her hips in silent entreaty, he pulled his mouth away from hers and gave a low laugh.

'Tell me what you want, Emerald,' he commanded huskily. 'Tell me.'

'You!' she declared, the words rushing from her lips. 'I want you.'

And suddenly he was exploring her with urgent fingers. His palms were skating hungrily over the nipples peaking beneath her sensible blouse, then moving down to cup her buttocks, luxuriously kneading her fleshy bottom.

'You're so tiny,' he growled as he started undoing her blouse, his long fingers making swift work of the buttons. He gave a husky moan of approbation as it fluttered open and he peeled it from her shoulders. And now he was sliding her skirt down over her hips, every touch of his fingers making her tremble. He was so gorgeous and she should have felt shy as she stood before him in nothing but her modest bra and pants, yet when he looked at her like that—his face tense with an almost savage hunger—she was filled with a sense of her own sexual power and an idea she couldn't shift.

That maybe this was meant to be.

Was it? she wondered as he tore off his own clothes and hurled them on top of hers. Was it possible that when she told him her news, he might actually receive it gratefully? He was isolated now, as King, but all that could change when he found out about Alek and realised how gorgeous he was. Ruby was right. He needed an heir. Who was to say they couldn't be a *family*? Princes met girls in bars and made them their princesses. Fairy tales happened sometimes, didn't they? *Didn't they?*

'Now let's get you out of this damned lingerie,' he growled, with hungry intent.

Which sounded like no fairy tale *she'd* ever read, but when he was making her feel like this—who cared?

'Yeah. Let's,' she agreed.

With unsteady fingers Kostandin unclipped a bra which was doing little to contain the magnificent breasts which spilled out into his waiting fingers like two pieces of ripe fruit. He sucked on an engorged nipple and heard her playful yelp before she bent her head to do the same to him. For a while he let her, but when her fingers tip-toed towards his groin, he reared back like an unbroken stallion. If she touched him there, he couldn't guarantee what would happen. Or rather, he could...

Kicking off his shorts, he freed his erection and her corresponding little gasp made him want to plunge straight into her. But one thing he never forgot, no matter how great the provocation, was protection. His mouth tightened. Because no child of his would ever be entering this world.

Retrieving a condom from his trousers, he put it within easy reach and sucked in a ragged breath as he gathered her in his arms. He felt so hard it was almost unendurable. But maybe that was understandable. It had been a long time. But even so. Was she intuitive enough to realise that nothing had changed?

'Tonight,' he groaned.

'Wh-what about it?'

'You know what this is, don't you, Emerald?' he demanded urgently. 'It's amazing but it's physical. That's all. Just like last time. Do you understand what I'm saying?'

His words were a warning, Emerald knew that—but it was one she had no intention of heeding. She couldn't seem to stop herself, especially now he had taken her knickers off. Her breasts felt heavy and tight. Her core was soft and thrumming. Because hadn't she longed for this, in those rare moments when desire had crept up on her unannounced—when she'd remembered that she was a woman, as well as a busy working mum?

'Yes, I understand,' she moaned as his hand slid between her thighs.

'You're wet like silk. Like honey. Like cream,' he purred, his finger quickening against her slick flesh.

His sensual commentary was turning her on even more. 'A-am I?'

'Mmm.' Suddenly his voice was urgent. 'And I want to be inside you.'

'So do I,' she whispered, dimly aware of him opening a condom—before he moved over her and she was angling her hips, eager for his thrust. But this time there was no pain, only heart-wrenching pleasure, and Emerald gasped as he filled her with his hardness.

Was that why he drove his lips down on hers? Were his bodyguards listening outside the door? she wondered wildly. But she was happy to be silenced by the sweetness of his kiss as he slowly moved inside her, and soon she was aware of nothing other than the sensual overload of her body as she gave into the most incredible orgasm of her life.

CHAPTER FIVE

DAWN WAS BREAKING when he woke and instantly Kostandin knew he was in an unfamiliar place. His eyelashes flickered open. The floor of the embassy's grandest salon, to be precise. Which was a first, he thought wryly.

Slowly, he acclimatised himself to the pale light which was filtering in through the unshuttered windows. The fire in the grate must have died some time ago, because the room was colder—a fact slammed home by the fact that they were both naked and lying on the floor, with Emerald snuggled up next to him, fast asleep. At least they were covered by a soft, cashmere throw—wrenching that from one of the nearby sofas had been the last thing he'd done before slipping into a blissful form of unconsciousness and having the best night's sleep in years.

He turned his head to look at her. The dark shadows under her eyes he'd noticed earlier must have been there for a reason because it seemed her need for sleep was as great as his—but then he guessed that sex like that took it out of you in more ways than one. Hell, yes. Despite the fierce hunger which had ambushed him, the first time had been slow and utterly...*perfect*—the second time even better. He stretched luxuriously. Her blonde hair was spread out over the rug like a gleaming cloth of pale gold satin. Her breathing was steady, her cheeks gently flushed, and her body...

Man, her body.

He felt another shaft of lust, his attention captivated by one rosy nipple peeping out from the blanket, and couldn't resist reaching out to glide his thumb over it, feeling the flesh grow pert beneath his questing fingers. As his groin began to thicken, he bent his head to flick his tongue against the puckered tip and heard her soft moan of appreciation.

'Oh,' she murmured, pouting a little in her sleep.

He grew even harder. But that was hardly surprising, was it? He'd been in a non-stop state of desire since she'd shimmied up to him in her waitress uniform, and since this was a limited window of opportunity, shouldn't he be making up for lost time? He pulled her close and as her tiny body melted into his, a deep sigh of satisfaction left his lips. He felt free. Deliciously free—and gloriously sated.

It hadn't been a false memory after all. Emerald Baker—as he had now discovered she was called—remained the best lover he'd ever had, as well as the most discreet. Was it that which filled him with an inexplicable desire to wake her up and tell her what was on his mind? To confide in her in a way in which it would be impossible to do with anyone else—even his closest advisors.

'Emerald, I'm thinking of abdicating in favour of my cousin. I want out of this life, for good.'

His pulse slammed. Even acknowledging the truth to himself made him feel as if he were engaged in an act of treason. Lately his discontent had become harder to ignore and he knew it was something he needed to address very soon. But not now. Not with temptation lying right next to him. Why waste time in speculation when he could be losing himself inside her again, before calling for a car to take her home?

Sliding his hand between her thighs, he ran a featherlight fingertip over her rapidly engorging bud. Still half asleep, she began to moan as he slid his finger up and down in slick and delicious rhythm—her trembling body so responsive that he sensed she was going to come very quickly.

'Kostandin,' she murmured, her fingers reaching out to knead his shoulders, her lips whispering against his in a breathless kiss. 'Please.'

He needed no further entreaty. Pausing only to grab a condom, he rolled on top of her and thrust deep inside her, his hardness filling her, and she gave a small moan as he began to move. His prediction of how close she was to orgasm had been uncannily accurate, because within what seemed like seconds her muscles began to clench around him. Her body arched like a taut bow before spasms of pleasure dragged her under and he could hold on no longer. Surrendering to the siren call of her warm flesh, he choked out his fulfilment as she sucked every drop of semen from his body and he'd never felt quite so empty and yet so completely full, all at the same time.

Lost in the sweet aftermath like never before, he tangled his fingers in the split silk of her hair, his breathing ragged as he attempted to drag oxygen into his starved lungs. But then her eyelashes fluttered open and Kostandin was momentarily taken aback, because her expression wasn't what he might have anticipated in that split second of emotional transparency which always occurred when a woman was soft and sated with pleasure.

All he could see was a sudden shadow clouding her features as she let her arms fall from where they'd been clutching his shoulders, to suddenly wriggle away from him. There was something in her face he didn't recognise, though he noticed the sudden goosebumping of her skin, as if she were nervous. But analysis was inevitably tedious, so he didn't enquire about the cause of what looked like discomfiture, just stared into the emerald fire of her eyes instead.

'That was fantastic,' he murmured, echoing the words she'd spoken to him so long ago.

'Yes,' she agreed, her voice low. 'It w-was.'

But she seemed *strained*, he thought—and light years away from the woman who had demonstrated her physical desire for him so enthusiastically just a few minutes earlier. Before his marriage, the only complaint expressed to him by lovers was that he didn't really *talk* to them. Was it conversation she was feeling deprived of? he wondered, as a sense of unexpected indulgence crept over him.

'You know, I wasn't really expecting to see you last night,' he said, with a lazy yawn. 'I thought you would have moved on by now. Yet there you were. Still working at the club. Still wearing that black and white uniform. It is sometimes comforting to realise how little in life changes,' he observed. 'Particularly when so much of my own has altered beyond recognition.'

'Yes.'

Her lashes had fluttered down to conceal her eyes and when she opened them again, he could see that same disquiet lurking in their green depths. Was it embarrass-ment? But if so, *why*?

She cleared her throat. 'Actually, I don't work there any more.'

He frowned. 'But—'

'I blagged myself an extra shift.'

His frown deepened as unease began to whisper over his skin. 'Because you knew I'd be there?'

A long pause followed and beneath the soft blanket, she shifted her weight a little.

'Yes.'

Kostandin's lips curved. Of course. No wonder she was looking embarrassed. It was a pretty bold thing to do. So did that mean she was stalking him, or should he take her impudence as a compliment? In the wake of such intense sexual satisfaction, how could it be anything other than the latter—and why not make the most of it?

'I'm flattered,' he murmured. 'More than flattered. In fact, it's a pity we aren't able to spend a little more time together, but I have to fly to Paris later this morn-ing.' There was a pause. 'But there's no reason why we can't put something in the diary. I'm back in London at the end of the month. I'm sure we could fit in another meeting, just like this. If that's something which would appeal to you,' he added, his careless shrug morphing into another lazy smile.

But the delight he was expecting did not materialise, because she was shaking her head, like someone who'd been driving on autopilot and suddenly realised they'd taken the wrong road.

'Look… I should have told you sooner.' She swal-lowed. 'And there's no easy way to say this.'

'Don't worry, Emerald,' he replied acidly. 'I would be surprised if you refused, but it won't break my heart.'

She was biting her lip in a way which was making warning bells ring loudly inside his head when suddenly she sat up, all that hair streaming down over her shoulders, like liquid gold. She looked like a goddess, he thought achingly, when her next words drove every other thought from his head.

'You have a son, Kostandin.'

What she said didn't compute. In fact, she'd taken him so completely by surprise that Kostandin almost told her the truth. That he'd never had a child, nor wanted one. His determination never to procreate was his get-out-of-jail-free card. He felt the beat of a pulse at his temple. Because what good was a king without an heir?

'Wrong man, honey,' he drawled. 'You must be mixing me up with somebody else.' But then he noticed her expression. The trepidation which had shadowed her features. And the guilt. His eyes narrowed. Yes, definitely guilt.

Suddenly his heart was hammering with an emotion he didn't recognise as he sprang to his feet, pulling on his discarded trousers and turning his back on her as he zipped them up. It was a deliberately distancing movement—which also hid the betraying hardness of his body—so that when he turned to face her, it was with an element of his habitual, steely control. Because he must have misinterpreted what she'd said. Either that, or she was attempting to manipulate him. Mistake, he thought grimly. Big mistake.

'What the hell are you talking about?' he questioned coldly.

Emerald tried not to wince as she met his icy gaze, be-

cause he was looking at her as if she were a stranger—
or an enemy—and she had only herself to blame. She
had weakened her position by having sex with him, she
realised. Why on earth had she done that, without telling him first?

Because you couldn't resist him.

You never could.

She forced the words out as succinctly as possible. It
wasn't as if she'd never rehearsed them, was it? But having a conversation inside your own head was completely
different from being naked on the floor of a posh embassy with a man looking down at you as if you had just
crawled out from beneath a stone. With unsteady fingers
she tugged the blanket further up her breasts, noting the
reluctant flicker of his eyes as he followed the movement.

'You have a son,' she informed him and, instinctively,
her voice softened. 'A five-year-old boy called Alek, who
is the most gorgeous little—'

'That is *enough*!' His furious command cut her off
mid-flow, before he lowered his voice into a deadly whisper. 'Do really imagine you can just walk into my life
and start making unsubstantiated statements like that?
Who the *hell* do you think you're dealing with, Emerald?'

She tried to stay calm even though his words had
shredded through her maternal pride. He was shocked.
Of course he was—and she must make allowances for
that. She'd been pretty shocked herself when she'd stared
at the positive lines of her pregnancy test and had sunk,
trembling, to the floor. 'Obviously, it's not easy to get
your head around the fact that you're a father—'

'Except that I am not. We had sex once, and I took

great care to use protection,' he interrupted, before adding softly, 'I always do.'

Emerald bit her lip. If that last disclaimer had been made with the intention of hurting her by reminding him of how many women he must have had, then he had succeeded. Was it the sudden realisation of how vulnerable she was or his deliberate cruelty which made her want to fight fire with fire? Don't buckle under, she told herself fiercely. And don't let him patronise you.

'Actually, we had sex many more times than just *once*,' she informed him coolly. 'If you remember.'

But he didn't seem to be listening. His eyes had narrowed and he was nodding his head, like a man who had just worked out the answer to something which had been puzzling him.

'So last night was nothing but a set-up?'

She stared at him blankly. 'Excuse me?'

'You concocted an elaborate plan to get close to me—'

'It was hardly elaborate, Kostandin. I made one phone call.'

'Did you deliberately set out to seduce me?' he continued softly. 'Were you hoping I might receive your outrageous contention more sympathetically if we'd just had sex?'

Piercing pain stabbed at her heart. 'Please don't attempt to rewrite history,' she snapped back, all thoughts of staying calm forgotten. 'If there was any seduction—then it was mutual. I was hardly dancing in front of you naked, waving feathers, was I? You were the one who suggested coming here, who requested champagne. And you were the one who started talking about kissing.' She sucked in a deep breath. 'Anyway, none of that matters.

The only thing which is important is what you're intending to do about Alek.'

'I don't actually have to *do* anything,' he informed her imperiously.

'No, of course you don't. And that is, of course, your prerogative,' she said, choosing that moment to stand up. But the deliberate dignity of her words felt at odds with the clumsy way she attempted to conceal her nudity, tugging on her modest underwear and grabbing her crumpled skirt and blouse. Wishing she were in a comfortable pair of sneakers—so she could run away?—she bent down to cram on Ruby's skyscraper shoes and when she'd fastened them, she straightened up and flicked back her hair.

'Okay.' She sucked in a breath. 'Let's forget we ever had this conversation. We can go back to how it was before. I've managed up until now as a single mother and I can keep on managing. Nobody need know. Nobody at all. It won't bother me. I don't need you, Kostandin.' And then she shrugged, even though her shoulders felt as if someone had piled a ton of bricks on top of them, and she wondered if her deep sense of sadness was showing in her eyes. 'Because you're the one who's missing out, and for that I pity you. But at least you know,' she finished quietly as she picked up her handbag.

Still he didn't move, and then—almost as if he had remembered he was bare-chested—he reached for his shirt, his fingers slightly unsteady as he fumbled for the buttons. 'If this is true, then why tell me now? Why not before?'

'I can't believe you've even asked that question,' she breathed, not daring to tell him he'd missed a buttonhole.

'When we…slept together, I knew it was never intended to be more than a single night. You made that very plain. And I was—' She wasn't going to come out and say she'd been happy about that, because obviously she had wanted to see him again. 'I accepted that,' she said. 'Soon afterwards, your brother was killed and I was sorry for your loss,' she added quickly as she saw his mouth harden. 'I would have written to you at the time, only it didn't seem… I don't know…' she shrugged '…appropriate.'

'Why? In case it looked as if you were using the bereavement as an excuse to get in touch with me again? Plenty of women did.'

How hateful he could be, Emerald thought bitterly. But surely his attitude would make his rejection easier to bear. Much better for Alek not to have such an arrogant man in his life. Better for her, too.

'I discovered I was pregnant a couple of weeks later,' she said doggedly. 'But what with your approaching coronation and everything else that was going on, it didn't seem like the ideal time to approach you. I'm guessing that there never would have been an ideal time.'

She drew in a deep breath, trying to iron out the pain and the humiliation from her voice as she remembered how she'd felt when she'd discovered that everything he'd said about not wanting to settle down had been untrue. His assertion that he never intended to marry had been a big, fat lie. His subsequent fairy-tale wedding had been emblazoned everywhere and it had been like a progression of painful blows to her heart to see the darkly handsome groom looking down at his beautiful princess bride—a willowy stunner with hair as black as a sheet of shining ebony.

'And soon after that came the news that you were getting married,' she continued. 'Added to which, your new wife might have become pregnant at any time—so she would have borne you a legitimate heir. You certainly wouldn't have wanted one born out of wedlock.'

Had she been hoping for some shamefaced shrug of admission—some flicker of apology that he'd wed another woman so soon after sleeping with her? Because if so, he wasn't playing ball. Briefly his face tightened as if something she'd said had hurt him, but his eyes remained as cold as glass.

'But that was almost four months later,' he pointed out coolly. 'You had plenty of time to tell me before that.'

She bit her lip. He was right, of course, but she wasn't going to admit to the primeval instinct which had driven her behaviour during those early days. The terrible fear that such a powerful man might attempt to take control of her baby, or worse. Her heart thundered. 'Let's just say that I was very sick during the first trimester,' she said slowly. 'And I couldn't have stomached any kind of drama.'

Kostandin turned away from her. He was a master at controlling his emotions. At keeping them hidden from himself, as well as from other people. But for once it was proving hard not to betray his reaction and not just because Emerald Baker seemed capable of pressing all his buttons. She had ambushed him with this piece of information. Something with the potential to blow his plans for the future straight out of the water. He felt the twist of anger and regret. He didn't want to believe her. Every instinct he possessed was telling him it couldn't be so. Yet he couldn't just walk away, not until he had convinced himself she was lying.

'Take me to him. I want to see him,' he said, turning round to surprise the trembling of her kiss-darkened lips. 'Now,' he added harshly.

Her green eyes were startled. 'That won't be possible.'

'Why not?' he demanded. 'Are you afraid you're going to be caught out in a lie, Emerald? Perhaps I don't really have a son at all—maybe I'm just the richest and therefore the most useful of all your lovers.'

'You really think I would be that mercenary? Do you? Since when did you get so…*suspicious*, Kostandin?' Her lips folded in on themselves. 'Or were you always that way and I just somehow missed it?'

Pretty much, he thought bitterly. A deep distrust of other people's motives had settled on him from the moment he'd discovered that nothing was ever as it seemed. The royal world was one of smoke and mirrors and nobody ever told you the truth. They told you what they thought you wanted to hear. Or what they thought you should hear, in order to protect themselves.

It had been that slow drip-feed of subterfuge which had made him so cynical, though he had hidden that beneath a largely superficial exterior, once he had escaped from Sofnantis and the constraints of royal life. As a businessman he had been able to behave as he pleased. He'd worked hard and played hard, making himself a fortune and acquiring several beautiful homes in San Francisco, Paris and Kahala, in Hawaii. It wasn't until he had been dramatically recalled to the land of his birth to become King that he'd realised flippancy wasn't an appropriate trait for a monarch. It was about the only thing about his accession which had pleased him—the acknowledgement that he could retreat to his emotionally remote default setting and nobody would dare challenge him.

'Let's get a few things straight, shall we, Emerald?' he continued coldly. 'You engineered an opportunity to speak to me, but delayed your grand announcement until after you'd had sex with me. I can only conclude that was done with the intention of making me more...malleable—which is nothing but manipulation honed to a fine art. Yet now you say I can't see him. So why come here at all? What is it you want from me? Money?'

The distress which darkened her eyes was so intense that for a moment he found himself wishing he could retract his bald accusation.

'No, I don't want your damned money,' she explained. 'In fact, I'd like never to set eyes on you again. But this isn't about me. It's about Alek. I'm not stopping you from seeing him, but it isn't that easy and it can't happen at this precise moment.' Her verdant gaze swept towards the mullioned windows, where the pale sun was rising over the park. 'Mainly because I don't live in London. Not any more. My sister and I moved to somewhere much cheaper.'

'Where?' he shot out impatiently.

'Northumberland.'

His eyes narrowed. 'Near Newcastle?'

'You know it?'

'I'm not exactly a stranger to an atlas, Emerald,' he snapped. 'I know it's at the other end of the country, but that won't be a problem.' He glanced down at his watch. 'We'll just have to go by helicopter.'

CHAPTER SIX

EMERALD HAD NEVER been in a helicopter before and the sound of the whirring rotor blades was deafening.

Reaching inside her handbag, she pulled out her phone and met the hostile glitter of Kostandin's blue eyes. 'Can I get a signal here?' she yelled.

'Why?'

Perhaps he would like to confiscate her phone! 'I'd better let my sister know what's happening. I haven't even told her I'm flying in. Certainly not in one of these.' She gave a hollow laugh. 'Or that I'll be back much earlier than expected.'

'I'd rather you didn't speak to her,' he clipped out.

'Are you suddenly policing what I do or don't do?'

'Don't be ridiculous.'

Her eyes narrowed. 'Then why not?'

'Because forewarned is forearmed and I don't want the child gussied up in his Sunday best.' There was a pause. 'I want to see him as he really is.'

Emerald hesitated before dropping her phone back in her bag, trying to convince herself it was a fair point— though she was thinking more from Alek's point of view. He would have a fit if Ruby tried to smarten him up on a Sunday morning at the end of the Easter holidays! And in a way, wouldn't it be better if Kostandin encountered him looking the way he usually did? With mud on his knees and his shirt half on and half off—and that infuriating little lock of black hair flopping over eyes, which were the exact same colour as his father's.

Better for whom? taunted a rogue voice inside her head. Are you secretly hoping the terse King will take one look at his scruffy son and decide to have nothing more to do with him?

'Tell me about him,' he said suddenly.

She should have been prepared for this, but somehow she wasn't—she was too busy imagining how Alek was going to react when Kostandin blazed into his life. The little boy was used to travelling on the bus, or in the beaten-up old car she shared with Ruby. Their idea of a treat was a film at the cinema and an occasional burger and chips. Wasn't there a danger he'd be dazzled by a shiny limousine and bodyguards and a level of wealth which was outside the realm of most mortals?

What had she *done*?

'He's…bright,' she said, dragging her mind back to the question. 'I mean, I know every mother thinks that about their child, but he really is. And he's doing well at school.'

'What's the name of the school?' he demanded.

'You won't have heard of it. It's the local village school, which has an excellent record,' she added defensively, because she certainly wasn't going to start apologising for Ambleton Infants'.

'So what exactly have you told him, Emerald? Does he even know who I am?'

'Of course not.'

'Of course not?' he echoed furiously.

She chewed on her lip. 'It was easier to be vague.'

'Easier for whom? You, almost certainly. You wanted to deny him his father, is that it?'

'No. Not at all. It's not that simple, Kostandin. And it's a bit rich for you to waltz in after all this time and start making judgements about how I've chosen to bring up my son.'

'Since I've only just discovered his existence, I wasn't in a position to do it before, was I?'

'No, you were too busy being married to a beautiful princess!'

'Careful, Emerald.' He gave a short laugh. 'You're starting to sound jealous.'

'I'm not jealous at all,' she lied. 'I'm just stating a fact! Anyway, I thought you didn't believe he was yours.'

'I'm keeping an open mind,' he said steadily.

And something about his quiet declaration took the wind right out of her sails. 'Do you really think I was going to just come out and tell him that his father is a king?' she appealed. 'Can't you see how difficult that would be for an ordinary little boy to understand? What if he started telling his friends in the playground and the teachers and other parents got to hear of it? People might wonder why the son of a monarch was living in a rented house while his mum runs a beach café, and come to the conclusion that he was telling porkies.'

'Porkies?'

'Pork pies. Lies,' she translated, reminding herself that the King of Sofnantis was unlikely to be familiar with Cockney rhyming slang.

'So what changed your mind?' he persisted softly. 'What made you come and find me?'

'I told you.' She licked her lips and tasted salt. 'You got divorced,' she explained baldly. 'And you were also in England, which made it easier to get hold of you…'

'There's something else. Something you're not telling me,' he filled in as her words tailed off. 'Am I right?'

Surprised and slightly impressed by his perception, Emerald expelled a reluctant sigh. 'Just lately, he's been asking me lots of questions about his dad. He's at that age. I didn't want to have to lie to him, but neither did I want…' She met the question which glittered from his sapphire eyes as the helicopter began to make its descent. 'I didn't want him to start fantasising, or hero-worshipping a powerful king who lived in a faraway land, and becoming dissatisfied with the life he's already got.'

Had she told him too much, by making him aware of her vulnerabilities and fears? Because surely that would increase his power over her. But although his expression grew flinty, his only remark as two SUVs with blacked-out windows drove towards them was to ask for her address.

'I'm driving,' he said abruptly as he slid behind the wheel and gestured for her to get in.

Emerald had never been driven by him before but as the car pulled away, it had the effect of making everything seem almost *normal*. If it weren't for the bodyguards following behind, they could have been just an ordinary man and woman heading out into the countryside on an early Sunday afternoon in April, with pale primroses studding the banks of the lanes, and pink and white blossom frothing the trees like foam on a milkshake.

Here, the sky always seemed so big and the air so clean and it had provided a safe haven for her when she'd arrived from London, very pregnant and very scared. She was proud of the café she and Ruby had opened, and the cakes and puddings they made, which were now being bought by some of the hotels in the vicinity. But Emerald could feel her heart thudding with apprehension as they drew closer to Ambleton. What would he think of the place she'd grown to call home? Would he be shocked at its modesty—at the much smaller parameters of her life compared to the dazzling magnitude of his?

'We're nearly there,' she said, as the lightening horizon indicated the nearness of the sea. 'We could stop here, if you like.'

Kostandin cut the engine, seeing nothing but a vast beach beyond the fringes of the sand dunes. 'Where is he?' he demanded, aware of the sudden powerful beat of his heart.

She glanced at her watch. 'Playing football down on the sand, most probably. One of us always takes him on Sundays.'

'*One* of us?' He shifted in his seat to look at her, his voice sharpening as a previously unconsidered scenario suddenly occurred to him. 'And who would that be?' he shot out.

As he met the indignation in her deep green gaze, he acknowledged how powerfully his body was responding to her. She had misled him and manipulated him, yet still he wanted her. How was that even possible when he was so angry and confused? Hadn't he despised his own father for his devotion to a woman who had run rings round him?

'Do you honestly think that I would have had sex with you last night if I were in a relationship with another man?' she demanded, her tiny hands clenching into tight fists on her lap.

Kostandin felt a powerful beat of satisfaction as he registered her furious denial, but he was in no mood to try to placate her. Why should he, when she had used her body like a delicious weapon? 'I have absolutely no idea,' he answered repressively. 'All I'm doing is trying to establish the facts.'

'Well, the facts are these! My sister Ruby helps me with Alek,' she informed him, her voice shaking with rage as she pulled a scarf from her voluminous handbag and wound it round her neck. 'She has done from the get-go. I don't know how I'd have managed otherwise.'

'You don't have parents?'

'No, I don't. Not any more. My mother died a few years ago, when Alek was still a baby.' She gave a short laugh. 'And since my father had never wanted anything to do with us, I was never part of what you might call a traditional nuclear family.'

Maybe that was one thing they did have in common, he thought grimly. 'Go on.'

'When I discovered I was pregnant, Ruby and I moved out of London and came up here. It was much cheaper and we were lucky enough to be able to rent a little café on the beach. We live in a cottage in a village nearby. The café's open every day but someone else does the shift on a Sunday, which means we can always…'

'Always what?' he prompted, his voice unexpectedly softening.

'Oh, you know. It's good for Alek to get some undiluted attention from one or other of us,' she said briskly, lifting her hands to smooth down her hair. 'We're pretty busy the rest of the time. Less so in winter. Ruby does most of the books and I do most of the baking and we sell our wares to local restaurants and hotels. Look—why don't we get out?' She reached for her jacket. 'We could walk across the sand dunes so they won't see us coming.'

'And is that for my benefit?' he questioned slowly. 'Or his?'

'I'm...' There was a pause. 'I'm not sure really,' she admitted.

Kostandin nodded and got out of the car, unprepared for that little note of honesty in her voice as the fierce blast of cold air slashed across his cheeks. But he was even more unprepared for what he saw in the distance as he narrowed his eyes against the pale glare of the sun. A small boy, chasing a plastic ball, which kept being whipped away from him by the wind. Nearby was a woman with hair the same shade as Emerald's and she was laughing, until she looked up and saw them, and then suddenly she wasn't.

Did her body language alert the child to the presence of his mother? Because at that moment the ball was forgotten and the boy came hurtling across the beach towards them, his features becoming more defined with every step he took. At last he skidded to a halt in front of them, his expression alive with interest, and as he glanced at his mother Kostandin could see that his eyes were as bright as jewels.

As sapphires.

Kostandin felt the sudden squeeze of his heart. He didn't need the verification of various gushing profiles which had been written about him over the years, which inevitably described the intense blueness of his gaze, to know who he was looking at. Because it was like staring into a mirror and seeing a younger version of himself.

My boy, he thought.

Now the squeeze of his heart became tighter and he couldn't work out the origin of the feelings which were sweeping through him, like the waves which were rising out at sea. He felt dizzy. Elated. Confused. Scared—and he was never scared. His lips hardened.

His son.

His.

But hot on the heels of all this uncommon emotion came the mental clanging of a door as he realised that the possibility of living like a commoner was now closed to him for ever. He was back in his gilded prison, only this time for good. The discovery of an heir had changed everything. *Everything.* His bloodline had been continued, without him knowing, and his succession was now secured. He turned his head to look at the woman who had trapped him by bearing a baby he had never asked for, but the breathless sound of a child's voice meant that she was distracted from his accusing stare.

'Mummy! Mummy!'

His heart still pounding, Kostandin watched as Emerald scooped him up and whirled him round and round. The little boy was squealing with unbridled excitement, but all the time he was aware of those identical eyes surveying him curiously over his mother's shoulder.

The woman with the blonde hair had now reached them and was also giving him the same silent scrutiny, though hers was markedly unfriendlier than the boy's. For a moment Kostandin was taken off-guard because the two women looked so alike. Uncannily so. Were they twins?

he wondered as he stood and prepared for an introduction which instinct told him he should not attempt to initiate.

'Alek…' Emerald's voice was hesitant. 'I'd like you to meet Kostandin.'

'That's a funny name,' said the little boy as he slid down from his mother's arms and stared up at him.

Unexpectedly, Kostandin's mouth twitched. 'Yes,' he agreed solemnly. 'But it is a popular name in my country.'

'Where's that?'

'Sofnantis. Have you heard of it?'

A tousled black head was shaken. 'No.'

'It is a land far away from here where it is very warm and sunny.'

The boy shot a glance up at the leaden sky. 'Can we go there?'

'Alek!'

He could hear the slight desperation in Emerald's voice. 'Why don't we all go back home and we can offer K-Kostandin a cup of tea?' she said, her words stumbling over each other. 'Oh, and—I'm so sorry—I should have introduced my sister. This is Ruby.'

Kostandin extended his hand and after a moment the woman took it, though it was the shortest handshake he could ever remember. 'You're twins?' he questioned.

'Yes.'

'I had no idea that Emerald had an identical twin sister.' The rare smile he offered, which never failed to charm, was clearly failing him on this occasion.

The woman, who looked very much like Emerald, shrugged. 'I'm sure you didn't.' She gave him a long and steady look. 'Emmy said that the getting-to-know-you side of your…er…*relationship* was rather brief.'

'Let's go, shall we?' interjected Emerald hurriedly, the note of desperation in her voice even more pronounced.

And Kostandin knew he needed to take control of the situation. He could not allow the emotions of these two women to orchestrate events which would impact significantly on all their lives. It was for him to do what needed to be done, no matter what lengths he had to go to in order to achieve it. Again, he felt the punch of something unfamiliar as he looked down into startling blue eyes so like his own.

'You've left something behind,' he observed, and as the child followed the direction of his gaze they saw the plastic football being pulled precariously close to the waves. 'Race you!' said Kostandin with a long-forgotten spontaneity as he began to sprint towards the shore.

There was a split-second pause before the little boy joined in and together they ran across the vast expanse of sands. And although Kostandin had never lost a race in his life, for once he was prepared to let it happen and allow the little boy to surge ahead, with a jubilant shout. And in that moment he felt curiously unfettered. The air was clean and cold and fresh and the vast sky was empty and practically nobody knew who or where he was. How long had it been since that had happened? Not since those days of heady freedom he'd been hopeful of regaining and which Emerald Baker had destroyed with her shock announcement.

But his brooding thoughts were interrupted by Alek kicking the ball towards him, accompanied by a disturbingly recognisable grin, and Kostandin kicked it back. An impromptu game of football followed until, eventually, they made their way back across the beach. The two bodyguards had joined the blonde sisters and they were all standing silhouetted against the dunes, watching them. A disparate group, Kostandin thought. Two strands of his life suddenly blending into one. And he didn't want it. He didn't want it at all.

He kept his gaze trained on Emerald. Beside her smartly dressed sister she looked slightly scruffy and anyone less like a queen would be hard to imagine. But she would do, thought Kostandin grimly. She would have to do.

'Is that your car?' asked Alek as they reached the gleaming SUV and he handed the football to his aunt.

'Kind of. It belongs to my embassy.'

'What's an embassy?'

Kostandin shrugged. 'It's a little bit complicated to explain. How long have you got?'

Alek looked up at his mother and Kostandin knew he hadn't imagined the apprehension which made her soft body stiffen.

'Oh, loads of time!' declared the little boy, with a cheeky smile. 'Can I have a ride in your car?'

Kostandin smiled back. 'Of course you can. You can show me where you live,' he said softly. 'That's if it's okay with your mother?'

There was a heartbeat of a pause. 'Of course it is,' she said brightly.

Kostandin walked towards her, his senses firing into life as he grew tantalisingly close. He dipped his head close to her ear, so that nobody but she could hear.

'And after that—' he gritted the words out from between clenched teeth, trying not to be distracted by the tantalising drift of her scent '—you and I need to talk.'

CHAPTER SEVEN

'SIT DOWN,' HE INSTRUCTED, his rich voice harsh.

Emerald was still trying to get used to the sight of Kostandin standing in front of the unlit fire. The house was deathly quiet. Alek was asleep upstairs and Ruby had diplomatically gone out for the evening, leaving her alone with the King in the sitting room of their tiny rented cottage. Beneath her sweater, her skin was icy—her blood frozen by a mixture of emotions she felt too exhausted to analyse. It felt bizarre having him here, in her home, knowing his bodyguards were outside, their huge vehicles practically blocking the narrow lane. She tried to see the room as he must see it, but that only provided another heart-sink moment. She had tidied up as best she could but it was difficult to hide the signs that three people lived here and there wasn't really enough room for all of them.

Kostandin had offered—though he'd made it sound like yet another command—to take her out for dinner so they could talk, but Emerald had declined. The last thing she felt like doing was sitting opposite him and going through the motions of ordering a meal she felt too sick to eat. And where would they have gone? The local restaurant relied too heavily on its microwave and she hadn't wanted to dress up, even if she had anything remotely appropriate to wear. She didn't want him to think she was putting out for him, or trying to get him to seduce her. Which was why she was still wearing the same jeans and sweater she'd put on this morning when he'd driven her back to the London B&B to collect her stuff. She gave a heavy sigh. She was supposed to have spent the night in the cheap room she'd rented overnight—not sleeping with the King on the floor of an opulent embassy.

'I'd prefer to stand,' she told him stiffly. 'And since it's my house, shouldn't I be the one playing host, not you?'

His jaw tensed. 'You should have told me about the boy long before now,' he snapped and then his sapphire gaze narrowed. 'We're going to need a DNA test.'

'If you think I'm going to allow you to stab needles into the skin of an innocent five-year-old, then you are a very foolish man!'

'It doesn't have to be done like that,' he said, his voice growing exasperated. 'It can be a swab on the inside cheek, or a sample of hair—'

'And both are invasive procedures!' she howled, before remembering that Alek was sleeping upstairs and lowering her voice into a hiss. 'Which I wouldn't dream of subjecting him to. Apart from the physical intrusion involved, how would I even go about explaining why we wanted to do something like that to him?'

'Now who's being foolish? We're going to have to tell him *something*, aren't we? Unless you have a better idea.' His sapphire gaze bored into her. 'What did you think was going to happen when you sought me out to tell me I had a son?' he demanded. 'That I would just shrug my shoulders and say "good to know" and leave it at that? That I would walk away and forget all about it? I am a king, Emerald. I have my realm and dominions and palaces to my name. Any progeny of mine is in line to inherit all those things. Didn't you stop to consider that when you sought me out to tell me? Didn't you think that your actions would have consequences for him? For you?' His voice grew heavy. 'For all of us?'

His words were a shock to the system and Emerald found herself sinking down onto the two-seater sofa, afraid her legs might give way. Because the truth was that she *hadn't* given it much consideration. She hadn't been thinking about inheritance—she had just gone on a gut feeling that the time was right to tell the childless King that he had a son. The opportunity had been there and she had seized it.

But that wasn't the whole truth, was it? Hadn't she secretly wanted to see him again?

Of course she had.

She had experienced an almost visceral need to connect with the father of her child which wouldn't be quietened. She'd tried to convince herself it had nothing to do with her and everything to do with Alek, but now she wondered if she had been secretly scripting a foolish romantic dream, which had been further fuelled by the fact that he obviously still fancied her. Should she have stopped to listen to Ruby's advice instead of forging ahead with her plan?

'I'm sure we can work something out,' she prevaricated.

His blue gaze sliced through her. 'How?' he demanded. 'My country will not accept an heir to their kingdom on his mother's say-so. And please don't give me that wounded-puppy expression, Emerald. I'm just stating facts, no matter how unpalatable you might find them.'

'But he looks like you,' she whispered. 'You know he does. He's the spitting image of you. Anyone with two eyes in their head can see that.'

With a ragged sigh, Kostandin nodded, because her claim was irrefutable. Hadn't his empty heart missed a beat when he'd looked into those mirror-image eyes? 'Yes, he does. But Sofnantis is going to require more proof than an uncanny resemblance to its ruler. What if a whole legion of black-haired and blue-eyed boys made their way to the palace claiming I was their father?'

'Why, is that a possibility?' she questioned unsteadily. 'Just how many one-night stands have you had?'

He wondered how she would react if he told her that she had been the only woman who had ever made him behave so incautiously. But why give her the opportunity to misinterpret something which had been nothing more than an overwhelming hormonal rush, triggered by a pair of remarkable eyes coupled with sensational curves? 'My sexual history is nobody's business but my own. We're supposed to be talking about my son.'

'Make your mind up. I thought you didn't believe he was yours!'

He scowled. 'Your vehemence is nothing if not convincing and I could be prepared to accept that you are speaking the truth, if you were prepared to be reasonable.'

She stared at him suspiciously. 'And what would that involve?'

Kostandin felt the bitter curl of resentment. Up until this very morning he had seen the possibility of a new life—and now, in a single stroke delivered by this petite blonde, all his plans were slipping away from him. His eagerly anticipated freedom had crumbled into a hopeless dream. 'It isn't a question of what I want, but what I need. And I need an heir.' His mouth hardened. 'A legal heir.'

Giving her a few moments to mull over his words, he walked over to a far wall, on which hung a montage of black and white photos, all of them depicting Alek at various stages in his young life. There was an early shot as a newborn—scrawny with dark hair—morphing into a plump and smiling baby, a cute toddler and gradually becoming the little boy he had met today with the lock of hair flopping down over one eye. Kostandin's heart clenched and his voice grew husky. 'Did you take these?'

'Yes. It's a hobby of mine.'

'They're good,' he said, with surprise. 'They're very good.'

She blinked. 'Thank you.'

Abruptly, he turned away, not wanting her to see his expression, for he was damned sure she would try to use any softening on his part as ammunition against him. 'Without matrimony, this boy will have no official recognition and no legal status. He will just be seen as the King's illegitimate son.' He paused. 'Some will even call him a bastard.'

'Don't—'

'Why waste time railing against an incontrovertible truth, Emerald?' he questioned, rigidly composing his features before turning back to face her. 'We have a problem which has a simple solution. In order for Alek to benefit from his royal parentage, you will have to become my wife.'

She leapt to her feet with a look of horror which should have been insulting but, bizarrely, it was no such thing. But then, she looked incredible in that moment in all her blazing defiance, Kostandin acknowledged—all life and fire and passion—and he felt the powerful beat of his heart.

'No!' she declared.

'No?' he echoed disbelievingly.

'I can't possibly marry you.'

'Why not?'

'Well, for a start you've only just got divorced!'

'What does that have to do with anything?'

'What will your people think of such indecent haste? Won't it make you look… I don't know…flaky?'

'Flaky?' He glared at her. Was there no limit to the insults she was prepared to let slip from her traitorous lips? 'My people will prefer the security of knowing their king is settled.'

'Well, what about Luljeta, then? How is she going to deal with it?' She sucked in her cheeks. 'No matter how "amicable" your divorce was, no woman is going to be happy to be replaced that quickly.'

Kostandin felt a pulse thudding at his temple and, as she dropped her gaze to the shabby rug, he found himself wondering if news of his surprise marriage had impacted badly on her at the time. He wondered how much to tell her because, despite his default setting of keeping people at an emotional distance, wouldn't the truth help facilitate what he wanted? Or at least, as much of the truth as he deemed necessary. 'Let me tell you something about my marriage.'

'Actually, I'd rather you didn't. I don't need a blow-by-blow account of what happened,' she put in quickly, unable to hide her instinctive flinch. 'I read the reports on the Web, just like everyone else.'

'Just hear me, will you?' he said impatiently and, although she looked displeased at his imperious demand, she went to sit on the window ledge, against a backdrop of snowy white petals from the blossom tree outside. And for a moment Kostandin was distracted. With the sunlight gilding her hair and her eyes as green as the burgeoning leaves, she looked utterly enchanting, he thought, before reminding himself of everything she had kept from him. He could not trust her.

But he needed her to marry him all the same.

'Luljeta was my late brother Visar's fiancée. The Princess of a neighbouring land who had been promised to him at birth. It was a territorial marriage,' he added bluntly. 'And her dowry was intended to bring a long-disputed piece of land back into the domain of Sofnantis.'

'Nice to see your country moving with the times,' she offered sarcastically.

'It is impossible to change centuries of history overnight!' he bit out. 'She was glad enough for the escape route offered to her, and the fact that it would enable her to get away from the influence of her father—a most malicious man.'

Her eyes narrowed. 'Okay.'

'The wedding preparations were in full swing when my brother was killed. He was reckless,' he admitted, unable to eradicate the disapproval from his voice. 'A risk-taker of the first magnitude. The ground was too wet, his horse too skittish and my brother was hungover. The hunt should never have taken place and the accident should never have happened. But it did.' He gave a heavy sigh. 'And his death put Luljeta in a difficult position—'

'Because your country wouldn't get the land if the

wedding didn't go ahead?' she guessed. 'And that was something you weren't prepared to tolerate?'

'I didn't give a damn about the land,' he said, angry at her inference that he was motivated by greed. 'But I did care that my brother's fiancée would be subjected to unbelievable cruelty from her father if she returned to her own land, still a spinster.'

'Still a *spinster*?' she echoed faintly.

'I didn't write the language, Emerald,' he returned coolly. 'I'm just giving you a flavour of what it was like. Luljeta's father was known to be very sick, with only a few months left to live…which is why I offered to marry her in place of my brother. Except it transpired that he wasn't as sick as he'd led people to believe and took a long time to die.' He gave a short laugh. 'Which was why what was supposed to only be a brief marriage ended up lasting almost five years.'

'I guess that's what's known as a marriage of convenience,' she said slowly.

'Well, not really,' he answered acidly. 'It was never intended to be anything other than a marriage on paper. The fact that it overran was extremely *in*convenient.'

'But you adapted?'

He gave a wolfish smile. 'Human beings are by nature adaptable.'

She pursed her lips together, as if the implication behind this last statement was making her uncomfortable. 'And since you're offering me exactly the same thing, this kind of transactional relationship clearly suits your nature,' she added quickly.

'It isn't a question of suiting my nature,' he drawled. 'It goes with the territory. Royal families have been arranging marriages since the beginning of time. It's a safer bet than relying on the vagaries of emotion and so-called *love*. So what is your answer to be?' He narrowed his eyes. 'Will you be my wife?'

Emerald was glad she was sitting down, although the window ledge was hardly the most comfortable of seats. Kostandin had just asked her—Emerald Marigold Baker—to marry him. Not much of a proposal, it was true. No moonlight, or bended knee, or reaching into a little box to withdraw a twinkling diamond—which, in his case, would probably be the size of a small planet. Instead, he had clipped out a functional question and surely she should have clipped out an equally functional thanks-but-no-thanks reply, because what modern woman would agree to such a heartless arrangement with such a heartless man, even if he was the father of her child?

And yet...

She swallowed, forcing herself to acknowledge the thoughts which were buzzing in her head like wasps in a jam jar. There was definitely still *something* between them other than the son they shared. An unfathomable ease in his company for starters, which was bizarre when you considered their difference in status. And neither could she discount the fierce sexual chemistry which burned as strongly as it had ever done. The way he could make her melt inside with nothing more than a blazing gaze. The way he could make her laugh...

A cautious spear of optimism began to nudge at her heart. She'd seen the way Alek had interacted with Kostandin on the beach today. Afterwards they'd come back here and he'd proudly shown his father all his little football trophies. Even in the short time while Emerald had cooked Alek his evening meal, Emerald had heard father and son talking, sensing that a true compatibility could be possible, with her son having what she'd never had. A father. Wasn't it worth putting her fears of getting hurt on hold, for that one thing alone? As long as she kept it real. No more baseless dreams about love, or romance. This wasn't about love—he'd said that himself—it was about making a marriage work. That was the whole point of arranged marriages.

'Okay. In theory, I don't see why I shouldn't marry you,' she said cautiously, unable to hide the beginnings of a smile.

'Good,' he said abruptly, glancing at the watch gleaming at his wrist. 'In that case, we'd better agree a contract as soon as possible.'

Still in its infancy, her smile died. 'A contract?'

'Of course. I will have my lawyers draw something up, before you and Alek come to Sofnantis. It can all be done very quickly. I'd say a maximum of thirteen years together, until he is of age. A fixed-term marriage and then, if you are agreeable, we can dissolve the union.' He paused. 'Leaving you a very rich woman indeed.'

For a few seconds Emerald wondered if she might have misheard him, but the cool calculation on his face suggested otherwise. And how ironic that while she'd been urging herself not to entertain unrealistic dreams, her heart was now plummeting like a lift as she listened to the fine details of his proposal.

He doesn't care about you. You were never intended to be anything other than a one-night fling and now you're nothing but a means to an end. It's nothing but a cold-blooded business arrangement.

But maybe she should be grateful that his impersonal words were allowing her to see the situation clearly. Because she also had skin in this game and Kostandin needed to understand that. She glanced at the blossom outside, bright against the growing darkness. 'As I said, I agree in *theory*.' Her smile was tight. 'Obviously, there will need to be a trial period before I give you my final decision.'

'A trial period?' There was a moment of disbelieving silence. 'I'm not sure I get you.'

'What you're asking is huge, Kostandin.'

'Finding out you have a hidden heir is huge, Emerald.'

She met the ice of his gaze and tried not to let it intimidate her. 'Surely you don't think I'm going to yank Alek out of school and take him to a strange country, without having sussed it out for myself first?'

'Leaving him behind won't work. We have an international school in Plavezero which has an outstanding record, or I can arrange for him to be tutored at the palace.' His voice was emphatic. 'I want you to bring him.'

'I'm sure you do. But ultimately, this is my decision.' She saw his jaw tighten. 'What's the matter, Kostandin— are you used to always having the final say?'

'I'm a king—what do *you* think?' he snapped. 'Bring your sister along to help, if it makes you feel better.'

A flicker of apprehension whispered over her skin because the last thing Emerald wanted was her twin staying at the palace and giving her sometimes brutal advice. 'We have a business here in Ambleton, which can't just be abandoned,' she objected. 'What's going to happen if we're both away?'

'I can have people drafted in during your absence,' he clipped out. 'They can be here by the end of today.'

Emerald tried to imagine how the locals might react to palace staff taking the place of the sisters who ran the place in their own, slightly bohemian style. 'You think throwing money at everything is the answer?'

'It's certainly one of them, in my experience.'

'The answer is still no. Either I come on my own, or not at all.' She glanced at her watch. 'And now I think you'd better go—before Ruby gets back.'

In eyes as blue as cornflowers, she saw a flash of irritation which didn't disguise their underlying smoulder and, despite her inexperience, Emerald knew in that moment he was turned on by her. And the feeling was mutual, no matter how much she tried to deny it. A beat of heat thudded through her. Was Kostandin aware of her desire for him, or was she managing to successfully hide it? She wondered what would happen if he walked across that cramped sitting room and slid his hands around her waist. If he used all that potent sexuality to try to persuade her to his way of thinking, sweeping aside her objections and carrying her off to his land and insisting that Alek accompany them?

And didn't part of her wish he would? Wouldn't that absolve her of all responsibility, so that for once in her life she could let someone else make all the decisions?

But he did no such thing. The fire in his eyes had died and he was now regarding her with features so stony they might have been chiselled from granite.

'I had no idea you could be so stubborn, Emerald.'

'I'm a mother,' she said simply. 'And I will do anything I can to protect my child.'

She wondered what had made his face grow tense like that as he pulled the door open.

'I will be in touch tomorrow,' he said, stepping into the evening.

And then he was gone. Emerald could see torchlight and shadows as she closed the door behind him, but it wasn't until she heard his powerful vehicle reversing down the lane that she slumped down on the sofa, head in her hands.

And that was where Ruby found her.

'Well? What happened?' demanded her sister, looking around as if expecting their royal visitor to materialise out of thin air.

Emerald lifted her head. 'He's gone.'

'Yeah.' Ruby yanked the curtains shut and turned to face her twin sister, expelling a low whistle as she began to unbutton her coat. 'Seeing him in the flesh like that was quite something. I mean, nobody's going to deny he's sexy and powerful and it's easy to see why you did what you did, but you need a man like that in your life like a hole in the head, Emmy. He's got heartbreak written all over him.'

'I know that,' she said dully.

'So how did you leave it?' Ruby tipped her head to one side and a blonde cascade of hair so like Emerald's own shimmered over her shoulders. 'Did he offer money in exchange for a non-disclosure agreement? That's usually what happens in these cases, apparently.'

There was a pause while Emerald dragged her mind back to what had just taken place, but it seemed like a dream. 'He's asked me to marry him.'

Ruby gave a dry laugh. 'And obviously, you said no.'

'I told him I'd be prepared to go to Sofnantis to consider it.'

A long silence followed. 'You are kidding?'

Emerald shook her head. 'I was hoping you might look after Alek for me.'

'You know I will.' Ruby stared at her, askance. 'But why? Have you taken complete leave of your senses?'

Had she? 'Because I owe it to Alek. He needs to get to know his father.' Yet even as she said it, Emerald wondered if she was being honest with herself. Her feelings for Kostandin were complicated and part of her was curious to see if maybe they *could* make it work, as a couple. Would it shock Ruby if she admitted that? To confess that she wanted to break through that stony exterior to see if the man she'd once known still existed? 'How could I possibly explain to him, when he's older, that I wasn't even prepared to give it a try?'

Ruby shot her a sharply intuitive look—the kind which made having an identical twin such a double-edged sword. 'Just be careful, Emmy,' she advised tonelessly. 'That man is dangerous. He could threaten everything—all the happiness we've built together here.'

'You think I don't know that?'

But Emerald was discovering that danger itself was a very powerful aphrodisiac.

And wasn't that the most shameful thing of all?

CHAPTER EIGHT

'THE ROYAL JET has landed, Your Majesty.'

From behind his desk where he was fathoms deep in paperwork, Kostandin raised his head and met the gaze of his private secretary, who was hovering in the doorway of his vast magisterial office like an uninvited guest.

So. Emerald Baker was here.

A deep sense of satisfaction filled him. He hadn't seriously thought she might change her mind about coming but it had always been a possibility, and that in itself was bizarre. Their explosive sexual chemistry made him think of her as a sure-fire bet, but now he was being forced to recognise that the curvy blonde was no walkover. In fact, during their most recent interaction, hadn't her stubbornness been a match for his own? 'Well? Is there anything else, Lorenc?' he demanded impatiently. 'Can't you see I'm busy?'

'Indeed I can, Your Majesty.' Lorenc hesitated. 'I was wondering how you intended the press office to answer the inevitable questions which will arise once word of Miss Baker's visit gets out. A single woman,' he added delicately. 'And a commoner.'

Kostandin put his gold pen down on top of the pile of official documents he'd been signing and leaned back in his chair. 'This is the woman I intend to make my queen, but only you and my head of security are privy to that information for the time being. Are people already in place in…?' He frowned as he tried to remember the name of the village.

'Ambleton?' prompted Lorenc helpfully. 'Yes, Your Majesty. The boy is being well protected.'

'Good. So this is the deal. We keep Emerald's visit as low profile as possible, until such time as wedding plans are announced.'

Lorenc gave a nervous cough. 'In that case we really do need to have a statement prepared, Your Majesty. The biggest risk is the UK tabloid press who are always looking for a royal scoop. What if someone lets slip she's staying here?' He paused delicately. 'Wasn't there some suggestion that Miss Baker might not wish to marry you and if so, what then? It's a diplomatic nightmare, your majesty!'

Kostandin studied his aide through narrowed eyes and felt tension invade his body. He hadn't ever wanted a child—just like he'd never wanted to be King. His own childhood had been as miserable as hell and he had no desire to recreate a nuclear family of his own. But now the die had been cast and there wasn't a thing he could do about it. Did Lorenc really imagine that, having discovered the existence of a hidden heir, he would be prepared to let him be brought up in obscurity in England, with the possibility of other men in situ?

He was just about to reinforce this assertion when he found himself recalling the tiny blonde's look of determination as she had faced up to him, insisting that this trip would be nothing but a probationary period. He had never had a woman oppose his wishes before—they usually went out of their way to accommodate him—but didn't instinct warn him that Emerald Baker might be as fierce as a tiger when it came to her son? What must it be like to have a mother who cared about you like that? he wondered, with an uncharacteristic wistfulness—which he quickly quashed so that he could glare at his aide.

'There will be no such statement,' he said bluntly. 'She might not know it yet, but Emerald Baker will be staying and she will certainly be marrying me. Do you really think any woman would ever turn me down?'

The aide gave a nervous smile. 'Of course not, Your Majesty. That was an extremely foolish suggestion on my part.'

'I couldn't have put it better myself,' Kostandin snapped. 'Have her brought to the Rose Room, will you?'

Lorenc bowed his way out, obviously keen to beat a hasty retreat when his employer was in such a testy mood, and Kostandin was aware that he had been particularly irritable since his return from Northumberland. His initial buoyancy at having persuaded Emerald to visit had been tainted by her decision to leave Alek behind. And yet part of him admired her protectiveness towards the boy, even if it had thwarted his plans.

Making his way towards the Rose Room, past servants who lowered their eyes as he approached, he felt as if the walls were closing in on him. Two sentries stood on guard, saluting as they opened the double doors, but Kostandin waved his hand in dismissal as one attempted to accompany him inside.

'No. Stay out here,' he instructed abruptly. 'I wish to be alone.'

But as the doors silently enclosed him in the famously rose-tinted chamber, it was sobering to acknowledge that he was never alone, not really. At any given moment of the day, the King's whereabouts were documented. Everybody watched him. Everybody listened to him. Rooms fell silent when he walked into them. In a crowded space, it was his company most craved by all. A few words from him were something to be cherished and dined out on—or relayed to grandchildren in reverential tones. For five years he had endured the strictures of ruling a kingdom and, just when had thought he was loosening the ties, the straitjacket was tightening around his chest once more.

Anger flooded through him. Why hadn't Emerald Baker told him about the child sooner? At least then he would have had time to accept the inevitable. Better never to have anticipated the sweet taste of freedom, than have it snatched away from him at the last minute.

Walking over to the French windows, he stared out at the tumble of early roses, liberated at last from the thick forest of thorns which Kostandin had inherited from his neglectful brother. The exquisite palace gardens which had provided a rare place of sanctuary in his father's troubled life had now been restored to their former beauty, and his heart clenched as he remembered the old man's pain and his suffering. He stared at a portrait of the late King which hung above the fireplace, an impressive row of medals gleaming on the jacket of his military uniform. But nothing could disguise the terrible sadness in his eyes—the acknowledgement of his physical courage waning beneath the infinitely more powerful shadow of his emotional weakness. And that was what 'love' did to you, Kostandin thought bitterly.

So deep was he in thought that he failed to hear the knock on the door. It was only when he heard a soft voice saying his name that he looked round and saw Emerald standing in front of him. And although he was prepared for the heavy throb of blood to his groin, he was surprised—and yes, irritated—by the accompanying thunder of his heart. Why was his response to her so intense that at moments it felt outside his control? He prided himself on restraint and the power of his will, yet with Emerald Baker he had broken every rule in the book. Having sex with her was the very definition of bliss—yet wasn't that kind of desire, at times, almost *debilitating*?

As his gaze flickered over her, he felt another beat of irritation. No other woman summoned before the King of Sofnantis would have dared dress in such a manner as this. Her honed arms were bare and through the flimsy material of her top he could just discern the faint curve of her breasts. She wore glittery sandals such as you might see on one of the cheaper market stalls in Plavezero and her hair was woven into a thick plait, which hung over her shoulder like a gleaming, golden rope. Against the exquisite rose-coloured mosaic of the ancient room, she cut an unbecoming figure. But she was beautiful. Very, very beautiful, he acknowledged hungrily as a pulse hammered at his temple. An angel in blue jeans.

'Hello, Kostandin,' she said.

Torn between desire and resentment, he forced himself to respond with the formality now engrained in him and perfected through the countless official visits he performed every year. 'Emerald. How delightful to see you.'

She looked at him cautiously. 'Do you really mean that?'

'Let's pretend I do. How was your journey?'

'Convoluted. And longer than it needed to be.' She glared at him. 'Why on earth did I have to fly to Frankfurt before getting on another plane? I would have thought you were rich enough to afford a direct flight.'

In spite of everything his lips flickered with amusement in response to her outrageous suggestion that he was being unnecessarily frugal. 'It made you more difficult to trace if you flew from Germany. It means the press would be unable to track your flight path. I'm trying to protect you, Emerald—and to protect our son—by keeping your identity as vague as possible.'

But she didn't appear to be in the least bit mollified by his explanation, just hooked her thumb into the belt tag of her jeans and continued to fix him with that faintly mutinous verdant stare.

'And I didn't realise I was going to receive such a rapturous welcome when eventually I touched down,' she continued.

Something in her tone alerted him to mischief and Kostandin frowned. 'Are you being sarcastic?'

'Why, is that not allowed?'

'It is not usual to insult the King in such a way,' he answered carefully, trying not to think about how much he wanted to kiss that stubborn little pout and have her sweet tongue thrusting inside his mouth. 'Especially not within the first five minutes of being in his company.'

'I hope that doesn't mean you're going to drag me off to the dungeons?'

'Please, don't tempt me.'

Tempting him was something she would like very much to do—no matter how unwise a prospect that might be—but Emerald put her bag down on a table which appeared to be encrusted with semi-precious jewels, determined to hang onto the bravado she'd been practising like mad on the way over. It had been an emotionally fraught journey. It was the first time she'd ever been parted from her little boy and she missed him. Added to that was her wariness about the future and what it held, which had contributed to the dry mouth and thudding heart which were currently making her feel so destabilised. But there was no point in coming here if she was going to be intimidated by Kostandin. She mustn't dwell on the possible pitfalls. She had to give it a chance. She had to give *him* a chance—for Alek's sake. And how could that work unless she spoke to him as normally as possible?

Yet nothing in her world seemed remotely normal any more. Her eyes had grown wide with wonder as she'd been driven from Plavezero airport, down roads lined with brightly flowering trees, to a predominately golden palace, situated close to a sparkling blue lake. Everything was huge and glitteringly appointed but it was the sight of the Sofnantian flag—coloured black and rose and green—which gave her the biggest ice-water shock of reality. Because Alek was heir to this incredible country, she thought dazedly as the enormity of what lay ahead really hit home.

She had to get it right.

She *had* to. She'd put so much into building a life for their son in Northumberland—so had Ruby, come to that—and she couldn't threaten that simple, happy existence unless she was certain that an alternative would be best for Alek.

Yet, so far, she wasn't at all convinced there could

be any kind of future for them here. Jolted out of her comfort zone, she had felt somehow diminished from the moment she'd set foot inside the vast building, while Kostandin himself seemed to have grown in stature. She hadn't really known what to expect when she saw him again, though she'd thought of little else in the intervening days. She'd half wondered whether he might be clothed in some kingly concoction of military pomp or flowing robes, but that had been nothing but a stupid fantasy. Sofnantis was a highly developed market economy and its ruler reflected that in his choice of clothes. His immaculate grey suit could have graced any international setting but, despite its corporate overtones, it did zero to disguise the potent masculinity of the man who wore it. But then, Kostandin had once dominated global boardrooms, she remembered, before his sudden elevation to the throne.

With an effort she dragged her attention away from his sartorial elegance to meet the distracting glitter of his blue eyes. 'I thought you might have come to the airport to meet me,' she said, hating her voice for that giveaway croak.

'Traditionally, the monarch does not make special visits to the airport to greet visitors, unless they are also royal, which you, most evidently, are not.' His gaze was cool. 'And please don't look at me that way, Emerald. All I'm doing is pointing out protocol.'

'You don't even make an exception for the woman you say you want to marry?'

'One prefers not to make exceptions to the rules. It avoids setting precedents.'

She had intended to stay calm but now frustration got

the better of her. 'Is this how it's going to be between us from now on?' she questioned. 'Are you going to keep referring to yourself in the third person? 'One' this and 'one' that! When did you start talking like that?'

'When do you think?' he returned heatedly. 'When the weight of the crown was placed on my head and the sceptre in my hand. When I became King!'

'Well, we're supposed to be sizing one another up to see if we can bear to be married, not pulling rank,' she said. 'So if it's all the same with you, from now on I'd prefer if you treated me like a human being rather than one of your subjects.'

She saw the faint flash of incredulity in his eyes. Heard his quick intake of breath. It was a brief chink in his kingly armour and, in that moment, Emerald recognised that speaking the truth was the only way she was going to survive this.

'Very well. In that case, I shall attempt to be more informal.' There was a pause and suddenly his voice was a little uneven. 'How is Alek?'

Maternal pride rushed through her. 'He's okay. Ruby sent me some photos of him going off to school this morning and he looked happy enough.' She slid her hand towards the back pocket of her jeans. 'Would you like to see them?'

'Very well.' He inclined his head. 'If you wish.'

Don't knock yourself out with eagerness, she wanted to admonish—but fished out her phone and clicked onto the first image before passing it to him. 'Here we go. Look.'

He took the phone from her but his features remained shuttered and, try as she might, Emerald couldn't gauge his reaction as he scrolled through the photos. And wasn't the reality that she found his proximity so unsettling she could barely think straight? Was that because he had re-awoken her senses when he'd made passionate love to her on the floor of the embassy and the memory of that night was still too vivid for comfort? It made her want to touch him and kiss him—and everything else which went with it. But they hadn't even discussed what role sex would play while she was here, and it wasn't really the kind of subject you could just bring up in the cold light of day, was it? It might sound a little desperate if she said:

Kostandin, are you planning to sleep with me?

Was it going to become the elephant in the room? The thing they were both thinking about but which nobody dared mention. And wouldn't it be more sensible if they *didn't* have sex?

The bubble of her thoughts burst as he handed the phone back, the brush of his fingers like wildfire against her skin.

'I agree,' he said. 'He looks happy enough.'

Emerald felt a stab of disenchantment at his lukewarm assessment. Most people would have made a polite comment about Alek's general cuteness, even if they were only going through the motions. But Kostandin didn't have to do anything he didn't want to, she realised. He was an all-powerful king who was used to getting his own way and she should forget that at her own peril.

'He must get his sunny disposition from me,' she said airily, but his only response was to reach towards a previously unnoticed golden bell set into one of the richly panelled walls.

'I have work to do,' he said abruptly. 'I will ring for

someone to take you to your rooms, and we can meet for dinner later.'

Unwilling to be dismissed so carelessly, she drew herself up to her full height. 'Or you could take me yourself?' she suggested boldly. 'To make up for your no-show at the airport.'

His expression was incredulous. 'You wish me to play the part of servant by accompanying you to your suite?'

She shrugged. 'Some people might call it being a good host.'

'Such a veiled criticism of the King is unheard of!'

'Even if it's true?' she returned.

Kostandin glowered at her, but his obvious irritation had no effect for she continued to look at him questioningly and, unwillingly, he felt a flicker of admiration. 'Oh, very well,' he conceded reluctantly. 'Come with me.'

He was acutely aware of being watched as he swept along the corridors with the diminutive blonde scurrying beside him, endeavouring to match his long-legged stride. As they headed towards the central staircase, there were lingering gazes from aides whose role was to be unobtrusive and servants who were supposed to melt into the background. But there was no such melting today. Their eyes were almost popping out of their heads and a hint of half-amused rebellion sparked inside him, because Emerald Baker was certainly not what they had been expecting.

Unlike Luljeta.

The thought slammed into his head. Luljeta had been the perfect Queen. Beautiful, high-born and expertly schooled in the art of being royal.

And yet...

Yet…

His footsteps slowed as he halted outside the largest of the palace guest rooms, hearing her soft inhalation of breath as he pushed open the door. Suddenly he found himself recalling the humbleness of her cottage and the personal touches which had made it seem almost *inviting*. The line of small football trophies above the mantelpiece. The black and white montage of a little boy with disobedient hair and blue eyes which were so disturbingly familiar. The remains of a home-made cake on the scratched surface of the table. Kostandin found his heart contracting with an emotion he didn't recognise as he watched Emerald taking in her surroundings.

'Oh, this is beautiful,' she said, and he wondered if she was referring to the many priceless artworks and antique furniture dotted throughout the roomy suite. But she was standing in front of the window and surveying the distant panorama of mountains beyond the lake, as if nothing gave her more contentment than the unspoilt beauty of nature.

But when he stopped to think about it, she was pretty unspoilt herself. There was certainly no artifice about her. No false lashes, nor bee-stung lips or hair which came courtesy of a bottle. Was that why he found her so intoxicating? Why he couldn't seem to tear his eyes away from the perfect symmetry of her tiny frame? The filmy shirt hinting at the strong body beneath. The faded jeans clinging to the delectable curve of her bottom, which the fall of shimmering hair almost touched. He found himself wishing they were naked on that four-poster bed, with him easing himself into her hot, tight heat—and his heart thundered in wild conjunction with the erotic path of his thoughts.

But her physical appeal had never been in any doubt, he recognised as she turned to survey him with those jewel-bright eyes. He should concentrate on the studied secrecy of which she was capable. He should remember that her baby bombshell had delivered the death blow to his dreams—her fecund body the means by which he was now trapped. And she had used that body again, hadn't she? With a calculation which had taken his breath away, she had waited until he was sated with the sweet aftermath of sex before telling him about his son. She had bided her time for a moment of weakness before delivering her *coup de grâce*. And that was the way women operated, he reminded himself grimly. Ruthlessly. Single-mindedly. Selfishly.

Hardening his heart against the soft beauty of her face, he pointed to a recessed golden button by the door. 'When you press this bell, a servant will appear.'

'You mean, like a genie from a lamp?'

'You can ask them for anything you desire, within reason,' he continued, refusing to rise to her flippancy. 'There is a library, a swimming pool and a cinema at your disposal. The grounds are extensive and a member of the horticultural team will show you around the gardens should you require. Dinner with be in the Silver Dining Room at precisely eight p.m. and formal dress is required.' He raised his brows. 'Anything you want to ask me?'

'Where's the Silver Dining Room?'

'Behind the gilded set of doors on that first wide corridor we walked down. But someone will show you.'

'I don't have any formal dress.'

He gave a click of exasperation. 'Why not?'

'Hmm. Let's have a think about that.' She tapped her forefinger against her nose in mock puzzlement. 'Could it be that most people might be a bit challenged if they had to dress up for dinner in an actual palace, with an actual king? Even my fashion-conscious sister agreed it was a big ask.'

He sighed. 'Then I guess you'd better improvise for tonight. But no jeans. Definitely no jeans. Got that?'

'Oh, yes, Your Majesty,' she replied gravely. 'I get it.'

He was about to turn away when something made him ask it, even though he'd been doing his best to push the thought to the back of his mind. Something which hurt his chest as he forced out the words. 'What have you told him?'

'Him?'

'Alek,' he growled.

'He knows I'm here for a week. He thinks I'm having a holiday in the sun—'

'No, not that,' he interrupted impatiently. 'What have you told him about me? Does he know I'm his father?'

'Well, no. Of course not.'

'Of *course* not?' he echoed furiously.

'I thought it was too soon.' Long lashes shuttered her eyes into slivers of emerald and suddenly her expression was wary. 'And that something so momentous would be better coming from both of us.'

'So he hasn't guessed?'

'Kostandin, he's five years old. Do you really think he imagines that every new man he meets is his dad?'

A pause followed and Kostandin couldn't hold back the

words which filled it, even though he knew they would hurt her. Or was it *because* he knew they would hurt her? Because he wanted to wound her as much as she had him, by guarding her news so secretively and destroying all his hopes and dreams? 'I have no idea, Emerald,' he answered stonily, 'just how many men he meets in the course of a week, or in what circumstances.'

Her cheeks became spiked with pink before her lips grew tight with fury. 'Are you...?' Her fingers splayed out over her throat, in an attempt to conceal the blotchiness which had suddenly bloomed there. 'Are you suggesting that I've introduced him to a constant stream of lovers?'

'Pass.' His eyes bored into her. 'Perhaps you'd care to enlighten me?'

Emerald curled her fingers into fists, feeling almost dizzy with anger and hurt. Not just because he was judging her, but because he was devaluing those two nights they'd shared by making out they could be two of many. That *he* could be one of many. Didn't he realise how special he'd made her feel, or was sex so mechanical for him that she had simply been another faceless woman in his bed? And if that weren't bad enough, all the time...*all the time*...he had been married to his beautiful queen. While Emerald had been slumped on the cold lino of the bathroom floor staring in disbelief at her positive pregnancy test, Kostandin had been enjoying sex with his hot new royal bride. How *dared* he take the moral high ground?

He was clearly waiting for an answer and pride was urging her to tell him she wasn't going to play to his one-sided rules. But pride had no place when measured against her son's welfare. It wasn't just her reputation she was defending, it was her lifestyle, too. In the last five years she'd lived a puritanical life and Alek had never witnessed her having an *overnighter*. How could he have done when every man who wasn't this man left her completely cold?

'You know I was a virgin when we met,' she said quietly.

'That's old news,' he answered. 'And not what we're talking about.'

'And since then, there has been nobody.' She bit her lip, because she felt almost ashamed to admit it. 'Except...except for you.'

There. It was out there. Her weakness. Her misplaced loyalty and, most of all, her vulnerability. She didn't *think* she'd told him in order to please him or get him to value her more highly, but maybe she was deluding herself. Because why else would a wave of disappointment wash over her as she watched the tight line of his lips become an ugly slash?

'Why should I believe you, Emerald?'

She stared at him. 'Why wouldn't you believe me?'

'Because women lie,' he said harshly. 'It's woven into their DNA.'

His harsh accusation took her breath away but even her righteous indignation did nothing to subdue her desire for him. Nor stop her from being achingly aware that a few feet away was the biggest bed she'd ever seen, hung with beautiful velvet drapes, embroidered with bees and birds and flowers.

Was he aware of it too? Did he realise that if he pulled her down on top of it and started tugging at her clothes, she would be lost? That in a tussle between mind and body she suspected her hungry body would win every time? Suddenly she knew she had to break the growing tension between them before she did or said something she might later regret.

'Do you know, I feel sorry for you,' she said witheringly.

'Sorry for me?' he repeated dangerously.

'For having such a desperately jaundiced view about women!' she snapped. 'So if you've got nothing else to say, maybe you'd better go, because I'd like to ring my son now.'

She saw his unmistakable irritation at being dismissed in such a cavalier fashion—and by a cheeky little commoner at that—but then the stony mask was back in place. The gleam of his eyes was cold, his mouth hard and unforgiving as he inclined his dark head with imperial hauteur and stalked from the room without another word.

CHAPTER NINE

YES, THIS BIT of corridor looked familiar. And so did that tall marble statue standing at the end. Which meant…

Sucking in a deep breath, Emerald pushed open the door and stepped inside, to be greeted by a diamond waterfall of chandeliers cascading from vaulted silver ceilings. But despite it being in the most beautiful dining room she'd ever seen—obviously—the only thing which truly captured her attention was Kostandin. He was standing by an open set of French doors, his features implacable as he turned to greet her.

'You're late,' he accused.

'Only ten minutes,' she said, trying to keep her voice calm—even though just the sight of him was making her heart slam against her ribcage. She was still brooding over the things he'd said earlier—implying that she was sexually licentious, or that she was *lying*. It seemed hurtful and unfair but it didn't seem to stop her gaze from drinking him in. His height was emphasised by the darkly formal suit and, in contrast, a snowy shirt provided a perfect backdrop for his glowing skin and glittering blue eyes. He was so gorgeous, she thought. And angry. Very, very angry. 'Sorry.'

'Sorry isn't good enough,' he iced out. 'You must realise that it's considered the height of bad manners to keep the monarch waiting.'

'And I keep telling you, Kostandin—I'm not your subject. I'm trying to treat you in the same way I would treat anyone else. Don't make such a big deal out of it. Anyway, I got lost. Big deal. It's a big place. Actually, it's massive. More like a maze.'

'It's a palace—of course it's big! What did you expect? Why didn't you ring for someone to show you to the dining room?'

'Because I wanted to find it for myself. You never learn properly if someone else always shows you the way. Anyway, I prefer to be independent. I've had to be,' she added pointedly, before shrugging. 'And besides, it's very inhibiting having servants around all the time.'

'Then you'll be pleased to hear we're eating in the garden. It's more private and low-key. I think you'll find it more relaxed out there.'

It was an unexpectedly thoughtful gesture and Emerald was touched as she saw that a table had been laid outside, sheltered by a bower of pale roses and resplendent with crisp white linen. Amid the gleam of silver and crystal stood tall, creamy candles, their flames barely moving in the stillness of the warm evening air. As she followed the King outside she couldn't help herself revelling in the heady atmosphere, because the intoxicating perfume of the roses made the scene seem intensely romantic. *And it isn't,* she reminded herself fiercely as they sat down beneath the faint outline of a curved moon, his next words confirming her thoughts.

'You weren't exaggerating when you said you had

nothing formal to wear,' he observed, leaning back and subjecting her to a cool appraisal.

Emerald tried not to bristle. This was her best dress, one of those rarely worn pieces you could sometimes be lucky enough to pick up at a charity shop. Not the most cutting-edge outfit in the world, true, but it was serviceable, clean and a pretty shade of lemon—the exact colour of the primroses which bloomed in England every springtime.

Ruby had tried to get her to borrow some of *her* clothes but, once again, Emerald had resisted. She had wanted Kostandin to see the real her, but now she wondered if such openness had been an error. Maybe he was one of those shallow men her mother used to warn her about, who thought beauty was only skin-deep.

'Do you think you could manage not to be critical at least for the duration of the meal? I'm not in the mood for the sharp lash of your tongue.' She shot him a defiant look. 'Is that the real reason why you've brought me outside, because you're ashamed of people seeing me? Am I better hidden by starlight, rather than beneath the glare of those massive chandeliers?'

'Don't be absurd, Emerald,' he answered and, in the pause which followed, his voice took on a pensive note. 'If you must know, you look…lovely.'

Suddenly all her certainties were turned on their heads. 'I…do?'

'But living in a palace presents extraordinary demands,' he continued briskly, ignoring her need for reassurance. 'You need a new wardrobe and someone who will steer you in the right direction. Lorenc's assistant will be able to arrange for you to go shopping in Plavezero.'

'Whoa!' She put her goblet down, carefully avoiding the battalion of gleaming silver cutlery—she'd never seen so many knives and forks on one table. 'Not so fast. Why bother making any kind of investment until we know whether or not I'm staying?'

'Because you will need to attend official functions while you are here, to give you a flavour of royal life. Isn't that what we agreed?' In the fading light his gaze pierced into her. 'People will be watching and it won't go down well if you are dressed like...'

'Like what?'

'Why don't you stop feeding me opportunities to insult you, Emerald?' he drawled. 'It only creates conflict.'

'You strike me as the kind of man who thrives on conflict.'

'Or maybe you just bring out the worst in me,' he suggested softly.

Their gazes clashed in silent combat underpinned with something else. Something which was making Emerald's breasts grow heavy beneath her cotton dress and suddenly she hated her body's response to him and her failure to control it. Why was it this man—and only this man— who had the power to make her feel this way?

'So how is this all going to work?' she questioned thickly. 'Aren't people going to wonder who I am and why I'm here?'

'Of course—and inevitably, they will be asking questions. But I've been thinking about that, and about the photos you showed me.'

'What photos?' she repeated, her mind a total blank.

'Of Alek.'

Once again, it still felt weird to hear her son's name on

his lips. *His* son, too, she reminded herself. 'The black and white montage?'

He nodded. 'You said it was a hobby.'

'It is. I take my camera everywhere. I like to snap portraits of people. When I have the time,' she added.

'Well, now you have the time.' His long fingers shifted restlessly as he picked up his water glass, as if something was making him uncomfortable. 'For a while now, my PR team have been urging me to update my image,' he confided reluctantly. 'According to recent polls, I am seen as stern and humourless and apparently it's not a good look. Perhaps you can help change the way people view me.'

'I'm not a miracle-worker, Kostandin.'

He smiled and it was like the warm sun breaking through a bank of heavy grey cloud. He often used to smile like that, she thought wistfully, wishing she could have captured it on film.

'Only Lorenc and my head of security know about your real status,' he continued. 'Giving you a purpose here will deflect any unwanted curiosity, even if it doesn't quite eradicate it. Of course, I will own all the copyright on the photos.' His eyes glittered. 'Just in case you thought they might be useful collateral which could be used against me at some point in the future.'

Emerald stared at him. 'What *is* it with you? Why do you have such a negative view of people's motives?'

He gave a cynical laugh. 'Spend some time in my shoes, then ask me the same question.'

Her response was stifled by the arrival of a fleet of servants, carrying delicate silver platters of food. Emerald helped herself to a spoonful of rice and smiled her thanks at the servant. She still knew practically nothing about

Kostandin and, despite the fact that they shared a child, this was the first time they'd eaten a meal together. How crazy was that? 'You were the one who was just talking about questions being asked, so maybe I should ask you a few of my own.'

The barely noticeable raise of his forefinger was enough to make the attendant servants disappear into the indigo shadows of the garden.

'Please elaborate,' he instructed silkily.

'I'd like to know how…well, how you got to where you are today. Where you went to school. That kind of thing. A bit of your life story. You know.'

Kostandin frowned. He didn't know, as it happened, because he was out of practice. Nobody asked him personal questions any more. Even if anyone managed to penetrate his tight circle, unsolicited enquiries like this were strictly off-limits. It was another of the few favourable aspects of his position that it was a disadvantage to let anyone close. But despite his deep aversion to talking about himself, he recognised that for once he couldn't avoid it. He studied her heart-shaped face in the moonlight and felt the sudden hard beat of his heart. Because Emerald had a right to know.

'I was schooled here until the age of eleven,' he began matter-of-factly. 'After that I was sent away to board, in Switzerland.'

'With your brother?'

'No. My mother would never have countenanced that. She loved him far too much to ever let him leave.' He gave a cynical laugh. 'He continued with his schooling here.'

'And what was that like?'

He gazed at her blankly. 'It was an excellent school. I became fluent in French, German and English as well as—'

'No. That's not what I meant. I'm just thinking about what most people say when they go to boarding school. Didn't you miss your parents, and your brother?'

Kostandin resisted the desire to chastise her for interrupting him. If he wanted her, then it seemed he was going to have to put some work in.

And there was no doubt in his mind that he wanted her.

His gaze travelled over her. He had spoken the truth earlier—she really *was* lovely, despite her cheap dress and the absence of jewellery. But the golden cascade of her hair was adornment enough and he found himself yearning to run his fingers through those silken strands. He wanted to tiptoe his fingers up her bare thighs and feel the molten core of her desire. To slick his finger over her moist heat and make her buck and drench and call out his name.

But desire could make a man weak and, with an effort, he tempered it. 'No, I didn't miss my brother, for we were as different as mountains,' he said flatly. 'And neither did I miss my parents. I was glad to get away.'

'Oh?' She speared a slice of avocado. 'Why?'

'Why do you think?' he demanded. 'The relationship was...'

'Bad?' she questioned, into the silence which followed.

'Toxic.'

'Um...' she ventured. 'Were—?'

He waved his hand to silence her stumbled suggestions because wasn't this the perfect opportunity to spell out a few non-negotiable facts? To use the example of his parents as a warning of what she could—and never should—expect from him.

'My mother and father broke the mould of many of

their royal contemporaries and married for love,' he bit out contemptuously. 'Consequently, the marriage was a disaster.'

'Because they were…incompatible?'

Her soft voice was tentative, and her interest seemed gentle rather than prying. As Kostandin stared into her green eyes he realised that, although her timing couldn't have been worse, he could never question her discretion.

'My mother was a very manipulative woman and my father fell completely under her spell. She used her beauty and her body to get what she wanted. You look shocked, Emerald,' he observed. 'Is it such a terrible taboo to criticise your own mother?'

'Well, it is a *bit* of a taboo,' she said carefully.

'Except that in this case it's justified,' he asserted, his voice growing harsh. 'She played him like a fish. She was openly unfaithful with a variety of different lovers and whenever he summoned up the guts to challenge her, she would just turn those great big eyes on him and tell him she loved him. And he would fall for that particular lie, every single time. And all because he was blinded by the foolish stars in his eyes.'

Emerald didn't rise to his bitter remark. She was used to listening to people and knew that if you remained silent it often encouraged them to talk. And Kostandin was on a roll now. The slick handmade suit and gleaming crested cufflinks seemed like a costume. The exquisite gardens and the lighted palace behind looked more like a stage-set than a real home. As if he had just been playing at the part of being King and suddenly the raw, flesh-and-blood man beneath had surfaced.

'A psychologist might cite my parents' example as the

reason for my psychological distance with women, and they'd probably be right,' he continued softly. 'But that would only be a problem if either of us had unrealistic expectations.'

His gaze cut into her—a cold slash of blue with an edge of steel. 'And you and I are under no illusions about our feelings for one another, are we, Emerald?'

'Of course not,' she said.

Did he hear the uncertainty in her voice? Was that what made him feel the need to spell it out for her?

'I'm not looking for a *soulmate*,' he ground out. 'Not least because I don't believe such a thing exists.'

'Okay.'

'But on the plus side, I find your company entertaining.'

'Should I be flattered?'

'I think, if I were in your situation, then yes, most definitely, I would.' His eyes gleamed. 'And nobody could deny our sexual compatibility.'

'But you think I'm sexually compatible with all kinds of men, don't you?' she challenged. 'You implied that I'd had many other lovers. And although I was perfectly within my rights to have done just that, I didn't.' Her mouth tightened. 'I just don't like not being believed.'

He met her angry gaze and nodded. 'I did believe you,' he said roughly. 'I lashed out at you like that because I was angry, and I'm sorry. I believe too that Alek is my son and I will certainly not demand he undertake any form of DNA test.'

'Okay,' she said, slightly mollified by his unexpected apology.

'Listen to me, Emerald,' he continued slowly. 'We both

want the best for our son, which is why I think this marriage could work. We could make it work. Just as long as you understand my limitations and accept me for the man I am.' His shadowed gaze gleamed out a warning. 'And don't ever make the mistake of falling in love with me.'

CHAPTER TEN

EMERALD WOKE UP in a bed the size of a football pitch when her phone began to buzz and she snatched it up, her heart racing when she saw it was an unknown number. What if one of the teachers from Alek's school was ringing, saying he'd fallen over in the playground and had been blue-lighted to the nearest hospital...? Until she remembered that England was two hours behind Sofnantis and her darling son would still be tucked up in his bed.

Pushing away the inherent fears which resided in the heart of every mother, she clicked onto the number. 'Hello?'

'It's me.'

Cursing her heart's racing response to a man whose dismissive words had sent her to bed in a stew last night, Emerald drew in a deep breath. 'Kostandin?' she clarified carelessly.

'You were expecting someone else?' he growled.

'You've never phoned me before. The number came up as caller unknown. Although I suppose it is quite useful to have it,' she added. 'Otherwise, how am I supposed to contact you in this great big barn of a place?'

There was a pause. 'My room is right next door to yours.'

'Is it really?' she questioned, her heart now demonstrating a rapid series of somersaults. 'I don't remember you mentioning that on the guided tour.'

'Maybe it slipped my mind.'

Did she imagine the lick of amusement which coated his deep voice? Was he *flirting* with her, she wondered, secure in the knowledge that he'd made her aware of his boundaries last night? She remembered the brittleness of his words as they cut through the warm air of that rose-scented garden. *'Don't ever make the mistake of falling in love with me.'* During the fitful night which had followed, she had fumed at his arrogance. And longed for his touch.

Yet her heart gone out to him, too—how could it not have done? Her own early life hadn't been easy as their hard-working mum had struggled to make ends meet. They hadn't exactly been reduced to boiling up potato skins to make soup, but Emerald and Ruby had experienced the very real feeling of never having quite enough of anything. Yet despite that constant financial insecurity, the twins had never doubted their mother's feelings for them—they had been loved and wanted.

Kostandin's growing-up sounded a nightmare in comparison, despite the lavishness of his surroundings. Two warring parents who made a mockery of their supposed love-match, and a mother who sounded as if she favoured his older brother and lied constantly to her husband. No wonder he had trust issues around women. She swallowed. No wonder he was so anti-love.

She cleared her throat. 'Was there any particular reason for this call, Kostandin?'

'One of Lorenc's assistants is going to take you shop-

ping.' There was a muffled sound of him talking to someone else. 'She'll be there around ten. That should keep
you occupied for most of the morning.'

'I'm not a dog,' she objected.

He laughed. 'Come to my office later, will you? I'm
meeting a bunch of politicians at two. You can capture
the occasion on film. But first, go and look outside your
door.'

'Why?'

'Just do it, Emerald.'

Filled with curiosity, she cut the call and padded across
the room, pulling open the door to see a white package
sitting outside and she felt a kick of excitement as she
brought it back into the room. The removal of waxy paper
revealed a cardboard box and inside was a camera she
recognised, because it happened to be the most expensive
on the market—though never in a million years had she
imagined she'd ever own one. She gazed at it, her heart
racing like a train. The rudimentary handmade presents
she got from Alek at Christmas and on her birthday she
had kept and would treasure for ever, but she'd never been
bought something so…

Stupid tears began to prick at her eyes. After a mutual
agreement with her twin sister that they were a waste of
money, nobody had bought her a present for years. She
ran her finger over the strap. It wasn't the expense, it was
the thoughtfulness—and she had never imagined that
the sapphire-eyed King could be so thoughtful. Until
she forced herself to look at it rationally and to remove
unnecessary emotion from the equation. Taking photos
was simply a way to disguise the true purpose of her visit
to Sofnantis. How would it look if she pulled out her an-

cient and rather tatty camera and started aiming it at the mighty monarch? Kostandin's gift was merely a device to authenticate her supposed reason for being here.

But no amount of reasoning could dim her suddenly sunny mood and, after a scented downpour beneath the monsoon shower, she dressed and brushed her hair until it gleamed. Feeling a bit of a prima donna, she rang the bell and within seconds a freckle-faced maid called Hana was tapping on her door, offering a dizzying selection of breakfast options in various dining rooms within the palace. But daylight had an annoying habit of accentuating things you'd rather not see and the bright Sofnantian sunshine seemed to accentuate the shabbiness of Emerald's clothes. Did she really want to eat alone in a vast dining room, surrounded by nameless servants who might be questioning her appearance? No, she did not.

'Would it be all right to have my breakfast up here?' she questioned tentatively. 'I mean, I know it's not a hotel, but…'

'It will be my pleasure, mistress,' replied Hana. 'Your wish is my command.'

It was a weird sentence to hear in real life, but the maid's shy smile had the effect of making Emerald feel welcome and the breakfast which followed added to the elevation of her mood. A monstrous, white-cloth-covered trolley was wheeled into the suite and she tucked into creamy eggs and toast and a delicious bowl of lychees, realising she'd eaten very little the evening before. Her senses had been so achingly attuned to the formidable man sitting across the table that conventional hunger hadn't got a look-in.

She'd just put down the phone to Alek—'I'm *fine*,

Mum!'—when there was another knock on the door, and she opened it to find a woman standing there, who, judging by her appearance, definitely wasn't here to remove the remains of her breakfast. She was tall and model-slim, her red hair as sleek as a creaseless green dress, which matched her elegant suede shoes. She carried a notebook and a pen and she looked at Emerald with an enquiring smile.

'Hi,' she said in a smooth American accent, which made her *sound* like a movie star as well as look like one. 'I'm Jessica Jones and I'm Lorenc's assistant.' She gave a faint frown. 'Did nobody tell you I was coming?'

'Yes, they did. The King explained I'd be going on a shopping trip. I just wasn't expecting…' Emerald's words trailed off because she could hardly come out and say she hadn't been expecting someone who was going to make her feel even more scruffy than she already did.

'Then…' Jessica gave her a questioning look. 'If you're ready—we could go?'

'Great.' Emerald grabbed her bag and tried to conceal it as much as possible as they made their way downstairs, where a brightly gleaming car was waiting in the sunshine. Climbing into an interior replete with silken cushions and bottles of iced water, Emerald wondered what exactly Jessica knew. Was her real status common knowledge among the staff?

'It's very good of you to accompany me,' she told the redhead as the car headed off down a tree-lined drive as wide as a river, towards an elaborate set of wrought-iron gates some way in the distance.

'My pleasure. I love clothes,' Jessica confided. 'And I have a degree in design from Harvard.'

'You're American?'

'Yup. I came to Sofnantis on holiday, fell in love with the place and was lucky enough to find a job here. Usually, I'm overseeing the interiors of all the palaces, so this is a real treat for me.' She looked Emerald up and down with an assessing gaze. 'So... I understand you need new everything and you need it, like, *yesterday*?'

Emerald nodded. 'Something like that.'

'Hmm. A highly unusual request, if I might say so. And super-intriguing, too. I mean, I used to accompany Queen Luljeta on shopping trips occasionally, but that was usually to see what the new season had to offer. I asked Lorenc to spill but...' Jessica twisted the grey pearl bracelet at her wrist and sighed '...that man is a closed book. So, why are you really here?'

The last thing Emerald wanted was to pretend to be something she wasn't, but telling the truth was bound to throw up a lot more questions and even if she *did* blurt it out, wasn't it slightly unbelievable—even to her?

I'm mother to the King's child and contemplating whether or not I should become his wife.

Jessica would probably look at her and wonder who the hell she thought she was. Anyway, she didn't have to *lie*, she just needed to be creative with the truth. 'Oh, I know the King from way back and he wants me to take a series of photos of him. Something to do with softening his image. And, as you can see, my current clothes don't exactly make me blend into the background.'

Jessica's brief nod acknowledged the evasion, but she smiled all the same. 'Then we'll just have to see what we can do about that, won't we? Like to see a bit of the city first?'

'I'd love to.'

They drove through the centre of Plavezero, with its creamy buildings, large green squares and complete absence of skyscrapers. It was a beautiful blend of the ancient and modern and Emerald soaked it all in, her gaze captured by a predominantly glass structure, its sharp edges softened by the judicious planting of flowering trees. Outside, a simple marble statue captured the image of a small girl, her head deep in a book. 'Oh, what a beautiful building,' she exclaimed softly. 'What is it?'

'The children's library,' answered Jessica, with a smile. 'Built by the King within the first two years of his reign, along with a new hospital and two new schools and countless other projects which have since been completed.'

'Wow.'

'Wow is just about right,' agreed Jessica. 'He's certainly very different from his brother. He came in and pretty much transformed the country, like a man on a mission. It's why the people love him, I guess—their stern and efficient king.'

There was a stack more questions on the tip of Emerald's tongue and perhaps it was a good thing their arrival at the store meant she couldn't ask them—because if she was seriously considering becoming Kostandin's wife, it wasn't terribly diplomatic to quiz the staff about her future husband, was it?

They were shown into a private room and offered tiny cups of strong coffee, while Jessica shot out a series of requests in fluent Sofnantian and various assistants reappeared, laden down with armfuls of clothes. There were skirts and trousers, dresses and jeans which were light years away from the pair she'd brought with her, and sets of brand-new lingerie which streamlined her curves in a way which was little short of miraculous. Dutifully, Emerald tried them all on. Some looked dreadful, some were too big or too long, but most were…

The full-length mirror reflected back a woman she didn't recognise—as if the old Emerald had been side-lined and replaced with shiny new version. And that was a weird sensation—as if the old her hadn't been good enough. But she went through the motions of gratitude all the same. 'Thanks, Jessica—though I'm not sure that these clothes are really *me*.' She glanced over her shoulder at the rear view of some pristine white trousers which would never normally have strayed near her radar. 'Does my bottom look huge in this?'

'Not a bit of it. The King said you were small but you're *tiny*.'

What else had the King said? Emerald wondered, her heart beginning to race. Was it that which made her blurt out a statement which was really a question she should never have asked? 'Queen Luljeta must have been fun to dress.'

'Oh, she was. She was *adorable*.' Jessica's voice took on the tone of a serial dieter describing a chocolate brownie. 'You know how some women can throw on a piece of sackcloth and it looks like designer?'

'Well, not personally,' said Emerald, wondering, not for the first time, why the marriage had imploded if Luljeta was so perfect. Was *that* why Kostandin hadn't touched her since she'd arrived here, because this palace reminded him of his ex-wife and her extraordinary beauty? Even if the marriage was never intended to be permanent, they must have known each other pretty well during the five years that the union had lasted. An unwelcome stab of jealousy poked at her heart and she was glad of a distraction as Jessica pulled a final garment off the hanger and handed it to her with a flourish.

'Thought I'd go a little off-piste,' the redhead explained. 'This is something designed by one of our most promising young fashion students who could do with the exposure. Here. Try it.'

But Emerald shook her head as she studied the slippery piece of fabric. 'Oh, no, I don't think so,' she said hurriedly.

'Why not?'

Because dresses like this were for women who weren't like her. 'Because…'

'Go on. Just try it,' urged Jessica, her voice suddenly growing kind. 'You know, you're a lot prettier than you think you are.'

And even though she was probably only saying it to be polite, Emerald found herself stepping into the bias-cut gown and sliding her arms through the long sleeves. Cream was a colour she wouldn't normally have worn— close contact with small, muddy fingers would have made such a pristine choice impractical—yet to her surprise, it suited her. It was understated but it made her look sexy, she realised with a shock. It made her *feel* sexy, too— and she didn't want to feel that way. She didn't want to lust after a man who seemed to be keeping her at arm's length. And she didn't want to wear a dress which had obviously been designed for a woman as unlike her as it was possible to be. But despite her reservations, she allowed it to be added to the other purchases and, with an assurance that any necessary alterations would be completed by the end of the day, she was driven back to the palace.

She spent the rest of the morning trying to get her bearings in the royal residence. First, she explored a large section of the gardens and then she tackled the west wing of the palace complex where she found a large library, which contained a surprising number of detective novels. But all the time she kept thinking about the things she'd seen—the hospitals and the schools—and Jessica's remark about Kostandin being a man on a mission. She had implied that he was single-minded, and driven, and Emerald wondered if he would use that single-mindedness to convince her to marry him. Was she just another project? she wondered listlessly. Another goal to be achieved in his striving to be the perfect King and the antithesis of his brother?

Camera in hand, she was waiting close to the King's offices at the appointed time and her heart started racing as she heard his party in the distance. As Kostandin grew closer she could see he was surrounded by people—all men—yet somehow his towering height and darkly autocratic features made them appear as insubstantial as mountain mist. He looked deep in thought as he walked towards her and she wondered if it was the click of the shutter which alerted him to her presence, or the movement she made as she focussed her camera on a face which tensed the moment he spotted her, despite her best efforts to hide behind a tall, potted plant.

Their gazes met in one long and silent moment and instantly, she could feel herself reacting. A shimmer of awareness whispered over her skin and her nipples began to harden. For a split second she registered the smoky smoulder of his eyes but then the shutters came slamming down and, once again, he was all ice and steel.

The men were staring at her with open curiosity and as Kostandin drew to a halt they all followed suit. 'Gentlemen, this is Emerald Baker who is going to be taking a few informal shots of our meeting this afternoon,' he announced, slanting her a mocking look over the heads of the assembled group. 'No need to start sucking in your stomachs or your cheeks in order to look pretty. We aim to keep it real, don't we, Emerald?'

'Absolutely, Your Majesty,' she answered, wishing her face didn't feel so hot. 'Please. Just act like I'm not here.'

Easier said than done, thought Kostandin achingly as the petite blonde followed the delegation into his office and he sat down to begin the meeting. He had been the one to issue the invitation but now he was wondering why the hell he had granted her access to his inner sanctum like this when he was supposed to be working. Because she was distracting. More than distracting. Out of the corner of his eye he was aware of her moving around to capture him from different angles, and suddenly he was having difficulty concentrating.

He had been photographed ever since he could remember. Stiff, studied portraits taken on birthdays, or at Christmas, or—even worse—those dreadful 'informal' shots which were supposed to suggest that they were one big, happy family. These sessions he had tolerated without really thinking about them because they were part and parcel of being a royal, but never had he felt so exposed as he did beneath the lens being directed at him by the tiny blonde.

Last night he had taken her into his confidence and it

appalled him now to recall how much he'd told her. Was it raking over the bitter memories of the past which had unsettled him, or discovering that he'd been her only lover—a fact which had filled him with a deeply primitive satisfaction? But he had deliberately fought against the powerful tug of his senses, sending her off to bed with a chilly warning about his emotional incapacity, only to spend the rest of the night lying awake thinking about her—an irritation for a man to whom uninterrupted sleep had always been a given.

He had woken this morning feeling distinctly out of sorts, with an ache at his groin which refused to be eased by the hardest of early morning horse-rides, or iciest of showers. The only consolation was that never had he felt quite so much in control. He had demonstrated—to them both—that he was capable of resisting her. And that gave him a perverse sense of pleasure.

'Do you have any thoughts on the matter, Your Majesty?'

Lorenc's polite intervention punctured his frustrated thoughts and Kostandin glanced up to find himself looking into the lens of her camera, feeling his body tense as he forced himself to contribute to the discussion. He was relieved when the politicians were eventually herded out of the office by his aide, who remained beside the open door, his expression bland.

'Would you like me to accompany Miss Baker back to her suite, Your Majesty?'

'Miss Baker will be staying,' Kostandin announced.

The faintest of frowns creased Lorenc's brow. 'You haven't forgotten your appointment with the Petrogorian King in fifteen minutes?'

'I'm hardly likely to do that when it's written on the piece of paper lying in front of me, am I?' Kostandin snapped. 'Just stop fussing and leave us, will you?'

Lorenc's obsequious head was lowered. 'Your Majesty.'

The door closed and suddenly he was alone with her, as he had longed to be throughout that interminable meeting. She stood on the opposite side of the room, her camera resting redundantly in her hands, and, despite the sophisticated new clothes, in many ways she looked almost demure. Sweet and simple—like a handful of daisies strewn over soft grass. Siren she most certainly was not, yet right now she was the most provocative woman Kostandin had ever seen. Surely the simple parting of her lips shouldn't be enough to make his groin ache like this, as if it were about to explode. And why was he finding it so difficult to stop thinking about licking his way over the luscious mounds of her breasts? Frustration flooded through him, but he offered nothing but a careless smile.

'Well?' he questioned. 'Did you get what you wanted?'

'I got loads of photos, if that's what you mean. Oh, and thank you very much for the camera, by the way. But...'

'But?' he shot out.

She hesitated. 'May I be frank?'

'Why change the habit of a lifetime?'

She gave a slow-motion shrug. 'If that session was supposed to be a charm offensive then I'm afraid it failed on just about every level.'

He narrowed his eyes. 'What's that supposed to mean?' he demanded.

'You said you wanted to dispel your stern image and then proceeded to scowl throughout the meeting. I don't think I got a single shot of you smiling. You just looked deadly serious the whole time.'

'The environment is a serious issue,' he ground out.

'Nobody's denying that, Kostandin.'

'Particularly when the minister in question seems unable to convince people in rural areas that rewilding the forests doesn't necessarily mean that wolves are going to be howling at their doors at every damned hour of the day,' he snapped.

'Yes, I understand all that. But you're still coming over as...' she shrugged her shoulders '...tight-lipped.'

'Tight-lipped?' he repeated dangerously.

'Well, yes.' She hesitated. 'You were before the meeting even started. You looked like you would rather be anywhere else but here.'

The irony of her words did not escape him and he gave a hollow laugh. 'Do you realise how deeply you insult me, Emerald?'

'That wasn't my intention. I'm just saying what I think. There's no point in me being here unless we're prepared to be honest with one another, is there? It's a difficult enough situation as it is, without me having to be polite to you just because of your position. What I'm trying to say is...' She looked at him with faint frustration. 'Well, I just don't remember you ever being like this before.' She hesitated. 'I mean, obviously I didn't know you that well—'

'Well enough,' he commented wryly.

A flush of colour rose in her cheeks as she acknowledged his words. 'But back then you seemed almost... carefree.'

Carefree? Was that really how she had seen him? Of

course it was. It was how he had seen himself. He nodded. 'I was a different man back then.'

'So what happened to change you?' She put her camera down on the desk. 'To make you seem so...stern? Was it just the enormity of becoming King?'

His instinct was to clam up. To hide behind the veneer of royal privilege and berate her for insubordination. But maybe she was right. If their marriage was to be one of expedience, then why not at least be honest with her? If she was to become his wife, he must be able to tell her the truth, even if at times it might hurt her. Not just about his emotional coldness and all the things he didn't want from a relationship, but all the other things—which he did. And he needed their son more than anything, he reminded himself fiercely. Without Alek she would not be here.

And neither would he.

'What I am about to tell you must go no further.'

'This is completely off the record. For heaven's sake, surely I've proved that I'm not a gossip. Can't you just trust me, Kostandin?'

Her voice was soft and pleading but an instinct born of many years made him fight against it. 'I find it difficult to trust anyone,' he admitted gruffly.

'If you're hoping to persuade me to give up a life in England and come and live here with Alek, then you're going to have to try.'

'Is that an ultimatum, Emerald?'

'It's a fact.'

'Your insubordination is not appropriate,' he growled.

But she didn't appear in the least bit chastened by his admonishment, she just continued to stare at him with those curious green eyes. Abruptly, he stood up and went over to the window, staring at the tamed beauty of the rose garden and all that it symbolised. When he turned round she had perched on a velvet seat and, though he knew it was unreasonable for the mother of his child to ask permission to sit down, he still had to bite back his instinctive irritation that she hadn't done so. For all his complaints, how quickly he had adapted to the privileges of monarchy, he acknowledged wryly.

A ragged sigh left his lungs. 'When I became King, I discovered that things in Sofnantis were not as they seemed. The idyllic paradise was collapsing, because theft had been committed on a grand scale—'

'Theft?' she interrupted incredulously.

'Large-scale fraud by first my father and then my brother, who had used the country's reserves as their own personal bank account before bleeding them almost dry. My father in an attempt to win back the love of my faithless mother—and we all know how that turned out.' He gave a short laugh. 'And my brother because he was an addict.'

He waited for shock. For judgement. But her face remained implacable.

'What kind of addict?' she questioned softly.

'Gambling. Alcohol. Drugs.' He shrugged. 'Take your pick.'

She absorbed this in silence. 'And did he go into rehab?'

'No, Emerald. Rehab is for people who want to get better, not for people who want to get high.' His voice was bitter. 'By the time Visar died, the national debt was astronomical and Sofnantis was sinking into terminal decline. I used some of my own fortune to develop the lithium mines which have been our country's saviour, and I've been working non-stop for almost six years to undo all the damage inflicted. Perhaps that might explain why I acquired such a *stern* demeanour along the way.'

There was a pause while she considered his words. 'But surely you must let your guard down sometimes?'

He thought back to that night on the embassy floor, before she had shattered his world with her words—and a night six years before that. Both times had been the ultimate in erotic pleasure and both times it had felt as if she had torn away a layer of his skin, leaving him raw and vulnerable. And he'd wondered how it was possible to enjoy something yet fear it, all at the same time.

'Rarely,' he answered repressively. 'A good king needs to be strong. A figurehead of resilience and power.'

'That's a pretty punishing standard to live up to.'

'I don't deny it.'

'And don't forget…' her voice was gentle now '…that a good father mustn't be stern all the time, because that's quite scary for a child.'

It was something he'd never even considered and perhaps his answer might have bordered on the defensive had she not chosen that moment to lean back against the wall, so that a shaft of sunlight transmuted her hair into a stream of purest gold which melted away his uneasy thoughts.

'So, how do you relax?' she questioned.

It was such an alien concept that for a moment Kostandin struggled to come up with an answer. 'I ride,' he said eventually. 'We have a stable of fine thoroughbreds here at the palace.'

'Perhaps I could come and watch you some time?' She hesitated. 'You know. To take your photo. Searching for that elusive smile.'

Kostandin felt his body tense. She was doing it again. Staring at him with green eyes which had darkened like the night sky—provocation oozing from every pore of her tiny figure. Mocking him and teasing him and making him want to hold her. To rock that perfect little body beneath his. To feel her heat and possess her.

But that wasn't going to happen until the time was right. A time of *his* choosing—and only when she had agreed to marry him and his son was here at the palace. There was a price to be paid if she wanted sex with him again, and he would make her pay for it. She would learn that he would not be manipulated by her, nor swayed by her powerful sensual allure. To wait would be to test his resolve, and he *liked* to be tested. If nothing else, it reassured him that the steely control on which he had relied so heavily all his life remained intact.

But right now he could feel that control slipping away—like the tide being dragged out from the shore. The air was thick with desire. Her body was soft with promise, while his was hard with need. He could see a pulse flickering wildly beneath the blonde hair at her temple and, although temptation was licking at his skin, somehow he managed to refocus, and block it.

'Certainly you can come and watch me ride,' he agreed carelessly. 'I'll text you and let you know when I'll be there.'

She nodded and he found himself transfixed by that glorious cascade of hair, shimmering down over the generous swell of her breasts, and he flicked a glance down at the light which was flashing on his desk, knowing he needed to get her out of there before he changed his mind. 'And now, if there's nothing further, I really must get on.' His voice was deliberately impatient. 'My next appointment is due and I'm expecting the King of Petrogoria, a notoriously private man who I suspect wouldn't take kindly to the presence of a photographer, no matter how much I might vouch for her discretion.'

'Of course,' she said stiffly as she grabbed her camera and headed towards the door. 'I certainly didn't mean to outstay my welcome.'

'Emerald?' he questioned suddenly.

She stilled, like an animal caught in the target of a hunter's gun. 'What?'

'Will you speak to the boy?'

'Yes, of course. I'm going to phone him when he's finished school.'

'Tell him…' His words died away and, for once, Kostandin wasn't sure how to continue, for he did not know how to speak lovingly to a child.

He did not know how to speak lovingly to anyone.

'Say hello from me,' he finished gruffly.

CHAPTER ELEVEN

SHE COULD SEE him in the distance—dark and fast and fluid.

Emerald's breath caught in her throat as she stood in the shadows of the stables and watched the rider putting the horse through its paces. She supposed it was inevitable that he should be astride a gleaming black stallion which seemed bigger and more powerful than any horse she'd ever seen. The man's ebony hair was tinged red by the fire of the rising sun, close-fitting jodhpurs emphasised the long, muscular legs and his white shirt billowed in the whip of the wind. Sometimes, she acknowledged wryly, the reality of Kostandin really did surpass the fantasy.

Was that his intention? Was he deliberately allowing her close, but not *too* close? Allowing her to witness from a distance his power and magnetism as he went about his day in a way which few other mortals would ever experience. Or was he flagging up the reality of this life which would also be her life, if she became his queen? She'd watched him opening a paediatric hospital with—for her—the heartbreaking sight of him holding the small baby which had been thrust into his arms. She'd attended lunches and dinners which sometimes she was allowed to photograph before sitting down to eat, while at others she would be told by Lorenc that there was a privacy issue. She was the woman on the edges of the room who nobody was quite sure how to treat.

Yet behind the fantasy figure of the King was a man whose brother had been an addict and his father a spendthrift. A king who had married a beautiful young princess to save her from the wrath of her cruel father. His whole life seemed to have been governed by malign forces outside his control. No wonder he was such an enigma. She remembered the expression on his face when he'd asked her to say hello to Alek the other day. The emptiness which had clouded the brilliance of his eyes, when he had seemed almost...*lost.*

She wondered what might have happened were it not for the arrival of the Petrogorian King, which had forced her to beat a hasty retreat. Would she have had the courage to reach out and comfort him, as she had been longing to do? But she hadn't seen him for the rest of the day, and she suspected that had been deliberate. He had sent a message via one of the servants that he was having a private dinner with the prime minister, so what could she do? She could hardly gate-crash a meal with the head of state!

The morning sun was high in the sky now, bathing the stable yard in a rich, red light. Already the air was soft and warm as she watched Kostandin negotiate a series of jumps and she was so lost in the visual beauty of his riding that she completely forgot to record it.

Did he notice her suddenly reach for her camera and notice the sunlight flashing on the lens? Was that why he slowed the horse into a canter, before easing it into a steady trot and making his way across the yard towards her? She raised the camera and started to shoot, grateful that her suddenly unsteady hands had something to hold onto. And for the first time in her very amateur photographic career, she became aware of the camera's ability to make voyeurism acceptable. It gave her licence to stare at him and keep staring and she wasn't going to deny the pleasure that gave her. She zoomed in on his face, so that only his strong, slashed features were in focus. The patrician nose and sensual lips. The chiselled cheekbones and hard curve of a shadowed jaw, framed by tendrils of damp, dark hair. He jumped to the ground, giving the horse a quick pat on the neck, before a groom appeared to lead the animal away.

'Emerald,' he observed softly. 'This is a surprise.'

'You told me you rode every morning and were supposed to text and let me know. Remember?' She gave an exaggerated sigh. 'But alas, there was no text to be seen. As it happens, I heard you walk past my room earlier.' She met his challenging gaze with one of her own. 'Footsteps can sound very loud along that echoey marble corridor.'

He frowned. 'But I was extremely quiet.'

'And I'm a very light sleeper.' Something made her want to explain why. Was it a need to illuminate something of her own past, so that he might understand her a little more? Or was she hoping it might ease the residual ache in her heart from seeing him hold someone else's baby and realising that, because of her, he had missed the chance of ever doing it with his own son? 'Alek was a very colicky baby. He used to wake up in the night and I was always listening out for him, so in the end it becomes a habit which is hard to break.'

There was a pause. His eyes were hooded. She was afraid he might turn away. Please don't turn away, she thought.

'Do you miss him?'

She nodded. 'Yes, I miss him. I miss him like mad. I'm used to him being there morning and night, and all day at weekends and holidays. It's weird being here and having to communicate by phone all the time.' A lump rose in her throat. 'We've never had to do that before.'

He absorbed this in silence, nodding his head so that little droplets of sweat shimmered in the glow of the early morning light. 'What was it like?' he questioned suddenly. 'Those early years?'

The flare of hope inside her grew stronger. He'd never asked anything like this before. It felt like a step forward and she knew her answer was as important as the question itself. 'Having a new baby is always difficult,' she said carefully.

'Are you saying that to spare my feelings, Emerald?' he questioned wryly.

'No. It's the truth. The adjustment is a massive shock for everyone. They even call it baby shock. But I was lucky because my mum was there, at least for the first couple of years. And then, just when she should have been enjoying her retirement and her grandson, she caught some awful pneumonia and died.'

Her voice became a little hoarse at the memory and she cleared her throat. 'At least, I still had Ruby and she was absolutely brilliant. Money was tight, but we managed.' In fact, the hardest bit had been the realisation that every time she looked at her growing child, she was going to be reminded of the man who had sired him. The man in the damp shirt who stood before her, his face tight with an emotion she couldn't work out.

'You should have come to me,' he said roughly.

'Even though you were married?'

'Yes, even though I was married.'

'I was afraid,' she admitted.

'Of me?' he verified incredulously.

'Of the situation I found myself in. You see, my mum got pregnant by a man who was married to someone else and he did everything he could to get her to...to...'

As the stumbled implication of her words became apparent, his face grew tight. 'And you think I would have done the same?' he demanded furiously. 'That I would have told you to get rid of our child?'

'I thought not. I prayed not, but I couldn't be sure. How could I? You're a very powerful man, Kostandin, and sometimes that kind of power is difficult for a person like me to comprehend.'

For a moment it seemed as if he might contest her assertion, but he didn't. And perhaps some of her confusion showed in her face because suddenly he reached out and brushed his fingers down her cheek.

'You should have come to me,' he repeated.

His words pierced at her heart, filling her with a sadness and regret as she thought about those wasted years. All that time when he could have got to know Alek, and vice versa. Did he consider her selfish in keeping the two of them apart—as if she cared about nothing more than the need to protect her own heart? But as she met the sapphire blaze of his eyes, she saw no judgement there, just the unmistakable smouldering of desire. She froze—too scared to move or speak in case she broke the spell—wondering if her eyes were conveying how much she wanted him to touch her again. Please, she thought. Just kiss me.

And suddenly he was levering her back into the gloomy light of the stable, pushing her against a bale of straw where even the stab of a few stray strands sticking into her back wasn't enough to puncture her hunger for him. He stared at her for a long moment before bending his head to kiss her, with an intensity which took her breath away. Her eyelids fluttered to a close as his mouth pressed down on hers and the urgency of his kiss seemed to match her growing frustration. Her fingers splayed greedily over his damp shirt, untucking it from his jodhpurs and burrowing her hands underneath and he gave a moan as she encountered the slick, bare flesh. As she tweaked his nipple between finger and thumb, he groaned again—as if she had wounded him.

'Hell, Emerald.'

'Or heaven?' she parried softly.

She could feel the thunder of his heart as he pulled her closer, as if to imprint the hardness of his body against hers. His erection was large and proud against his close-fitting jodhpurs and she gave an instinctive gasp of delight as she felt its outline.

'Kostandin,' she breathed.

'Can you feel me? Can you feel what you do to me?'

'Hmm. Not sure,' she managed, her teasing words having exactly the right effect, because he circled his hips against her very deliberately.

'Now can you feel me?'

'Yes.' Her voice trembled. 'Oh, my God. Yes.'

With a triumphant laugh he started kissing her neck

and as the stubble of his unshaven jaw grazed her skin, she wondered whether it might leave a mark and stupidly, she wanted that. He began to unbutton her shirt and warm air rushed over breasts which were straining against the satin and lace of her new bra.

'And what's this?' he murmured, his fingertip outlining the proud thrust of a nipple.

'Oh,' she moaned as he dipped his head and nipped the silk-covered tip with his teeth.

His hand moved towards her jeans and helpfully she sucked in her stomach to allow him to slide it inside, his palm making contact with her bare belly before inching towards her drenched core, which was screaming for his touch. And just when she thought he might actually drag her behind the hay bale, or at least propose a breathless assignation back inside the palace, he dragged his lips away from hers.

'No,' he said roughly, wrenching his hand out of the front of her jeans.

'No?' Her word was husky and confused as she looked at him blankly.

'We are not going to do this, Emerald. Not here and certainly not now.' Quickly, he regained his composure as he tucked his shirt back into his jodhpurs and slanted a stern look in her direction. 'The King of Sofnantis will not be caught *in flagrante* in the stable block with—'

'A common little cloakroom attendant?' she questioned furiously, buttoning her shirt back up with shaking fingers.

'With a woman who is not his wife!'

She sucked in an unsteady breath, trying not to think about aching flesh and how much she wanted him to carry on touching her. 'Is this your not very subtle attempt to manipulate me into marrying you, Kostandin? By making me so frustrated that I'll agree to anything?'

'I am simply stating facts,' he said coolly. 'You wouldn't need to be an expert in the ways of royal protocol to realise how inappropriate it would be if we were discovered by one of the grooms. Think about it. At the moment you have no real status here, Emerald. You're just an Englishwoman on some spurious mission to take my photos.'

'It's not spurious—it's real!' she declared. 'I'm very proud of the photos I've taken, if you must know—even if you look miserable in ninety per cent of them!'

As if to contradict her, he offered the briefest flicker of a smile. 'But if you were my wife-to-be, your position would change. It would confer on you instant respectability and status,' he continued softly. 'And then we could do what the hell we wanted.'

'This is nothing but manipulation!' she howled. 'I told you. I'm not agreeing to anything until I'm certain.'

'You're just enjoying the power of keeping me waiting for an answer, is that it?'

'It's not particularly enjoyable to find myself in this curious state of limbo,' she admitted. 'But perhaps it's a good thing to make you wait, Kostandin—since I don't imagine it's ever happened to you before.'

'And what exactly are you waiting for, Emerald?' he challenged softly.

'Isn't it obvious?' she challenged. 'Let's just say I'm information-gathering. I'm not making any decision about the future until I'm as sure as I can be that it's the right one.'

A flicker of what appeared to be grudging admiration lightened the sapphire depths of his eyes, but with Kostandin you could never be sure.

'I'm flying down to the southern peninsula this morning,' he said carelessly. 'I assume you're coming with me?'

'Lorenc said he wasn't sure if there was going to be room.'

He gave the ghost of a smile. 'Oh, there's room,' he said.

Despite the low-grade throb of frustration which still plagued her, the day which unfolded was more enjoyable than Emerald had anticipated, on so many levels—because for once Kostandin kept his aides and bodyguards at a distance. She wasn't going to deny the buzz it gave her to travel in the royal helicopter—particularly when it was being piloted by the King himself, his usual stern expression replaced by one of very sexy concentration.

Emerald watched the reaction of the crowds who surged forward when they touched down and it made her heart do weird and twisty things when she saw their reaction. Jessica had been right, she realised. They really *did* love him—in spite of his stern demeanour. He moved with such grace and elan that suddenly she found herself wishing Alek could be here, to witness his dad making old ladies swoon and young sea cadets swell with pride. Wouldn't he adore it? Of course he would. But any little boy was bound to be dazzled by this and that had the potential to be dangerous. She mustn't let the glittering veneer of royal life blind her to the reality of the substance beneath.

Back in the cockpit, he slanted her a sideways look. 'I think we'll have lunch at my summer residence,' he said, before pulling on the headphones.

'Are you showcasing your property portfolio in order to impress me?' she questioned mildly, and he glittered her a smile.

'Trust me, it's worth a look,' he promised softly.

It certainly was. Standing in expansive grounds of lush, beautifully maintained gardens, the gleaming white villa was situated at the very tip of the peninsula, in a sheltered bay which protected it from the coastal winds. Just before landing, Kostandin hovered the helicopter over the entire property so she could get a bird's eye view and from here she could see the silver glitter of a private beach, a vast aqua-tinted swimming pool, as well as two tennis courts set into the sprawling grounds.

Beneath the shade of a vine-covered canopy, the resident staff served lunch on the terrace and Emerald tucked into figs, local goat's cheese and delicious salads, washed down with half a glass of an award-winning Sofnantian wine. When she'd finished, she leaned back in her chair and cast her gaze towards the sea, experiencing a moment of pure relaxation. 'I wish I'd brought my swimsuit with me.'

Kostandin didn't respond to the longing in her voice, cursing the erotic pictures which began to play out in his mind as he pictured her in a tiny bikini. He knew of a sheltered cove which would have provided complete privacy and where they could have swum naked. A curve of bay with deep, transparent waters and smooth rocks on which to dry out unobserved.

He used to come here as a teenager, during those unbearable months when there was no school. Eager to escape the tensions at the palace, he had spent long days here—always with a different girl in tow—engaging in long sessions of sex which now seemed anatomical and mechanical.

How he had changed, he thought wryly. It would have been beyond easy to take Emerald to one of those hidden places. To have stripped off their clothes and slipped into the sea—the water silky against their heated flesh as they joined together in the most fundamental way of all, knowing that with her it would be dynamite.

His throat tightened. But it wasn't going to happen. Abstinence felt like his only weapon in this strange battle which was waging between them. She might call it manipulation, but he preferred to think of it as a method of getting what he wanted, from a woman who was proving to be very stubborn.

'We need to head off back to the palace,' he drawled. 'I have some work I need to do before tonight's reception.'

As soon as they got back Emerald cooled off with a swim in the slightly underheated palace pool and afterwards phoned Alek. They talked about his day at school—one of the boys had broken his tooth in the playground and Aunty Ruby was making cupcakes for tea. But his next question was a curveball.

'How's that man, Mummy?' he asked. 'The King man?'

Emerald's fingers tightened around the phone. Had she naïvely thought her son might have forgotten the intriguing stranger who had burst into their lives one cold afternoon and whisked his mother away?

'He's…' Her sentence tailed away. No suitable answer sprang to mind. She knew what she could have said. That she was as confused as hell. That her feelings for Kostandin were deep and complex, yet she had no idea what he thought about her. Sometimes his gaze was stony and remote—while at other times he looked as if he would like to devour her. How could you tell a child that sometimes grown-ups played games with each other and you had no idea what the outcome might be? She swallowed.

'He's very well, thank you, darling. He's busy being a king, and kings have quite a lot of work to do.' She smoothed her fingers back through her hair, still damp after her swim. 'He has a big country to look after. Today, he flew me in his helicopter—'

'He *flew* you?'

She heard the unmistakable note of hero-worship. Why hadn't she missed that bit out? 'And we went to his summer residence,' she said hastily. 'Which is lovely.'

'What's a summer residence?'

'It's a posh way of saying holiday house.'

'Is it by the seaside?'

'Yes, it is. I'll send you a picture.'

'And is he playing football?'

'Football?' Alek's random query puzzled her until she remembered him kicking a ball around on the beach with a man who looked exactly like him, the chill Northumbrian wind whipping through two heads of dark hair, in a scene so deceptively normal that now it seemed to mock her.

And suddenly, she found herself wishing they were back there, away from all this glamour and glitz. She found herself wishing that her son's father weren't a king with untold wealth and power at his fingertips and all the baggage which came with that. If he'd been an ordinary man, mightn't they have had a better chance at happiness? she wondered wistfully. Or was she in danger of rewriting history just to suit her own narrative?

'When are you coming home, Mummy?'

The simple question floored her. He sounded so young. So lost. Was it that which made another shimmer of fear whisper down Emerald's spine? Because she hadn't really stopped to think about the consequences of her solo trip to Sofnantis, had she? She'd thought that coming here alone would protect Alek from the King's powerful influence, but maybe she had been naïve. Because that influence wasn't going anywhere. She couldn't and shouldn't deny Kostandin access to his son.

She stared out of the window, at the gleaming lake, acknowledging all the potential repercussions which were waiting in the wings. Because if she *didn't* marry the King, she was going to have to spend long periods apart from her little boy. Alek would be proclaimed as the heir and learn to live as a prince, and his life in England would seem very dull in comparison. As his world filled with crowns and horses and unimaginable wealth, there was the possibility she could be permanently side-lined—an unimportant woman who lived her life in the shadows.

A lump rose in her throat. Could she really take that risk? Could she bear to settle for a life of snatched and unsatisfactory telephone conversations and seeing her son being whisked away in a luxury car as he joined his father for half-term?

She stared at the oil painting on the wall, barely registered the bucolic landscape of the Sofnantian countryside. Yet if she *did* marry Kostandin… If she accepted the cold-blooded terms of his thirteen-year marital contract, wouldn't that provide the most secure framework—for all of them?

'I'll be back at the end of the week, darling,' she told Alek slowly. 'Not very long now.'

As she ended the call, she thought about Kostandin's behaviour towards her. He had granted her limited access to his company—a few meagre crumbs here and there—enough to take the edge off her appetite but not to satisfy it. He had kissed her passionately in the stables and then pulled away. Why, when his desire had been glaringly apparent to them both? Was it because of his need to control and manipulate, or was Luljeta's shadowy presence too profound to allow any other woman a rightful place here? He'd never spoken of his former queen—she'd only heard Jessica's breathless admiration for her. Emerald swallowed. No wonder she felt so small and insignificant in comparison to the willowy ex-wife who had graced so many magazine covers. Yes, insignificant.

But she was never going to discover the truth or take their relationship on to the next step if she continued to let Kostandin dictate all the terms. Despite protesting that she wasn't one of his subjects, she had still allowed him to summon and dismiss her at will, hadn't she? What had happened to the woman who used to banter with him in her cloakroom booth, who could give as good as she got? Who had so willingly given him her innocence because she hadn't been able to contemplate the alternative.

She took the memory card from her camera and slotted it into her computer and the photos she had taken of him began to appear on the screen, one by one. Kostandin the ruler, walking down a corridor with his advisors, his face so stern and cold. Kostandin the horseman, astride his gleaming black stallion, all strength and grace. And Kostandin the man, walking among the adoring crowds, his face occasionally breaking into a rare smile which transformed those autocratic features into a face of heart-breaking beauty.

She turned off the computer, knowing that her future depended on whether she was content to be passive—or whether she was prepared to assert her own needs and stop acting like his tame lapdog. She had to ask herself what she really wanted.

Her heart missed a beat.

She wanted him.

Not as a king, but as a man.

And not at some cold-blooded time of *his* choosing.

She wandered over to the wardrobe, her gaze lingering on the creamy dress Jessica had encouraged her to accept. She had rejected it as unsuitable but suddenly she found herself looking at it with different eyes. Such a grown-up piece of clothing could be a game-changer, she realised, if only she had the courage to wear it. Tonight there was going to be an official reception and it was going to be a proper dress-up occasion.

Could she slither into this slippery piece of finery and walk into a crowded ballroom? *Should* she? Her heart began to pound. Because no way would she look insignificant in this.

CHAPTER TWELVE

KOSTANDIN WAS USED to being the centre of attention. His royal status made people stare at him, obviously, but he wasn't hypocritical enough to deny that his physical attributes inevitably commanded the gaze of others, especially women. But although social invisibility was something he often yearned for—he now found himself intensely irritated by it. Or rather, by her. The diminutive blonde who had just entered the ballroom—late, he noted sourly—a camera held insouciantly in one hand and a small sparkly bag in the other. He was even more irritated by the throng of dignitaries who were all staring at her, as if a golden star had just fallen to earth. Kostandin tensed. How dared she be late in his presence and... what in God's name was she wearing?

His heart thudded out a primitive thunder as his gaze drank her in and he suddenly realised that this wasn't an Emerald he was familiar with, but a sexy and sophisticated stranger. Yet her dress wasn't especially revealing, certainly not compared to some of the others on display tonight. It wasn't low-cut and the floor-length sweep, which allowed only the occasional peep of a satin shoe, was positively demure. But the pale material which clung to her generous curves made her body appear to have been dipped in cream and the hair cascading down her back shone like liquid gold. She dazzled. She glowed. She drew the eye inexorably and suddenly he was filled with a potent desire which was incompatible with being in such a public arena.

He raised his brows in silent command for her to approach, his irritation compounded when she did no such thing—just slanted him a sunny smile as she raised her camera and began to focus the lens on his rapidly tightening features. And since he had invited her to do exactly that, he could hardly accuse her of invading his privacy, could he? Deliberately, he turned away, his mouth hard with displeasure. Let her photograph his back and see if she found *that* interesting! If she wanted to capture an image of the face she claimed could be so stern and forbidding, then let her first come and seek his permission!

But no such permission was sought and he was forced to endure a conversation with a new and very earnest ambassador from Khayarzah, who could hardly believe his luck in having the King to himself. A princess from a nearby country rather boldly introduced herself, but Kostandin was curt in response to her suggestion that he might visit her palace soon, because he certainly wasn't interested in the assignation she was hinting at.

The evening dragged on predictably, with people hovering in his vicinity, eager to shake his hand. And still Emerald did not come—until eventually, he was forced to turn around to look for her, feeling as if he had lost some kind of silent combat by having to capitulate like this. His gaze sought her out like a heat-seeking missile, unprepared for the sudden jerk of his heart when he failed to locate her. Had she gone? he wondered incredulously. Had she actually left the reception before the monarch himself, and committed yet another glaring error of protocol?

Finally, he spotted a movement on the terrace outside—a pale cream shape outlined against the lushness of the flowers and foliage—and he was unprepared for the sudden clench of his heart as he turned to Lorenc, who was hovering nearby.

'Ensure that I am not disturbed,' he instructed curtly.

'Certainly, Your Majesty.'

He began to walk across the ballroom towards the French windows and as he stepped onto the terrace the powerful scent of flowers invaded his starved senses. She stood with her back to him, a series of pale curves, photographing the roses in the dying light of the sun, seemingly absorbed in her work.

Small groups of people were standing nearby, enjoying the sunset as they drank from goblets of champagne, and he wondered if his demeanour was especially forbidding because they quickly began to move back inside the ballroom once they saw him. And all at once he was alone with her. Well, as alone as two people could be with a couple of hundred others close by. His heart was hammering, his groin aching like a teenage boy's and he was filled with the sense of something he couldn't begin to understand.

'Emerald,' he said abruptly.

Slowly, she turned around, her eyes veiled by her long lashes. 'Good evening, Your Majesty.'

Her voice was tinged with a note he didn't recognise and his brain was too befuddled by her presence to work out what that might be. She dropped into a deep curtsey, which suddenly became an exquisite form of torture because it accentuated the faint wobble of her silk-covered breasts. Was that deliberate? he wondered savagely. Yet women had flaunted their bodies at him countless times in the past and it had never made him feel like *this*.

'Get up,' he said, his abrasive tone proving an ineffective antidote to his sudden overwhelming sense of powerlessness. 'What are you doing out here alone?'

Obediently, she rose to her feet, a look of caution on her face, as if correctly identifying the pugnacious tilt of his chin. But her steadfast air didn't waver. There was a new strength and determination in her gaze tonight, he thought, which only added to her glowing beauty.

'The light in the palace gardens is so exquisite that it seemed foolish not to capitalise on it,' she answered equably. 'I've got some amazing shots of the roses, with that statue in the background. Would you like to see them?'

'I don't want to look at your damned photos. Why didn't you come over to greet me when you arrived?'

'Because you were glaring at me.'

'Was I?'

'You know you were, Kostandin. In fact, you're glaring at me now.' In the fading light her huge eyes looked as dark as polished jade. 'I never seem able to please you, do I?'

For a moment he was tempted to articulate his frustration at being trapped in a situation he'd been so close to leaving—and since she was the unwitting cause, wasn't it reasonable to rage at her? But he could feel his anger draining away and with it, his resolve— vanquished by the creamy thrust of her breasts and gentle curve of her hips.

Why prolong the inevitable and, with it, all his aching frustration? Why ruin the evening with the bitter truth and risk driving her away? His throat tightened. Too many times he had turned away from the longing in her eyes in an attempt to contain the way she made him feel. Yet who was the supposed beneficiary of all this self-denial? he wondered bitterly. Nobody. Least of all him. Surely he had demonstrated to them both by now that he didn't actually *need* her.

'Did you choose to wear that dress tonight knowing that every man in the room would be staring at you?' he questioned.

Emerald registered the smoky glint of his eyes and recognised that something between them had changed. She'd known from the minute she'd walked into the ballroom and their gazes had clashed, the dark fire in his eyes making her feel so heated that she had been forced to seek refuge outside. But even the cool evening air was having little effect on her stinging nipples and she wondered if he had noticed.

Of course he had. Someone looking down from space could probably see their pebbled outline.

'There was only one man I wanted to stare at me,' she admitted softly.

His eyes flashed an unmistakable glint of satisfaction. 'Well, your wish has come true, because here I am.'

'Who said I was talking about you?' She hid a smile and relented when she saw his outraged expression. 'Of course it's you.'

There was a pause. 'Does that mean you're going to marry me?'

'That's a bit of a leap, Kostandin. I haven't decided. The jury's still out.'

'Is there anything I could do to hurry your decision along?'

'You could stop pushing me away.'

'I've already told you the reason why,' he grated.

'In which case, there's nothing more to be said, is there? We seem to be at a bit of an impasse.'

He stared at her with what looked like a mixture of impatience and incredulity until, at last, he gave a sigh of resignation. 'Okay, Emerald. You win.'

'I win? You're making it sound like some sort of battle.'

'Which it is. And while it's an undoubted turn-on to engage in this kind of verbal sparring, I suspect that any minute now one my aides is bound to come looking for me, telling me that a very important person craves my attention. And since I am loath to have this fascinating discussion interrupted, I suggest we continue it upstairs, where we will not be disturbed.'

Emerald felt her pulse skitter because, even though this was exactly why she had worn the slippery dress in the first place, suddenly she was nervous at having her bluff called. 'But…you're in the middle of an official reception. Surely you can't just leave?'

'I am the King,' he drawled. 'I can do anything I damned well please. And it is winding down now anyway. What would please me most right now would be to take you to bed and put us both out of our misery.'

'Misery?' she echoed indignantly.

'Frustration, then, if you prefer. Isn't that what you want, Emerald?'

Emerald ran her hands over her dress, feeling the softness of her hips beneath her clammy fingers. Not really.

She wanted so much more than that. She wanted him to whisper sweet words of longing and then kiss her passionately on the sunset-flooded terrace. To pull her into his arms and crush her against his hard body. To seduce her into such a state of mindless desire that she would go with him, wherever he asked—not to imply in that almost conversational way that they should have sex again. If it seemed impersonal that was because it was, she reminded herself fiercely. This whole marriage proposal was little more than a business arrangement.

But refusal was an option she couldn't contemplate. She didn't want to play games or act proud. She wanted to hold him and kiss him. To show him with her body what she didn't dare express in words. A mother's instinct told her he would be a good father to their son, but she wanted to get to the bottom of why he was so remote and forbidding—and how could she do that if he kept pushing her away? For once he seemed so gloriously accessible and surely she would be mad to turn down an opportunity like this.

'Yes,' she said, as carelessly as she could. 'That's exactly what I want.'

Still he didn't touch her as they set off through the grounds. There were no linked hands or a tender arm around her shoulder, but somehow that only added to the tension mounting inside her as Emerald followed him through the darkening gardens, where the scented blooms made the setting seem even more romantic. But romance was nothing but an illusion, she reminded herself. This was all about sex—plain and simple—and it would just have to do for now.

As they entered through one of the gilded arches she

wondered what the servants would make of it if they were seen together, or even worse—the rather terrifying Lorenc—but a series of secret passages and quieter stairways shielded them from view, until they found themselves on an upstairs corridor she recognised.

'Your place?' she questioned tentatively. 'Or mine.'

'Yours, I think,' he growled softly.

As he pushed open the door of her bedroom, Emerald felt another sting of disappointment. She'd been dying to see his kingly quarters—perhaps with a view to eying them up as a future marital boudoir—and couldn't help wondering why he didn't take her there. Was he thinking about Luljeta? Was he unwilling to use the same bed where he'd spent so many nights with his former queen? Theirs might have been a marriage of convenience, but that didn't mean they hadn't enjoyed passionate sex. Maybe he was afraid he might use the wrong name at the crucial moment.

'You look nervous,' he murmured, noticing her flinch.

'I am a bit,' she admitted. 'Aren't you?'

Kostandin shook his head, luxuriating in the heady pulse of anticipation as he took a step towards her. 'All I can feel is desire,' he husked.

'Can we turn the light off?'

'Why would I want to do that?' he queried softly. 'When you look so damned beautiful?'

For a wordless moment they stared at one another until suddenly, he could wait no longer. Hadn't he demonstrated more restraint than it was reasonable to expect? He had shown her that he was capable of icy control when the need should arise and she would do well to remember that. The lesson had been taught and now it was time for play.

But he couldn't hold back the groan which erupted

from deep in his lungs as he started to kiss her. She tasted of honey and roses and trembling sexuality. He loved the way she shivered as he reacquainted himself with her petite frame, stroking her breasts with rapt preoccupation until she made a little moan of assent.

His palms cupping her buttocks, he brought her up hard against his pelvis and suddenly her hands were running frantically through his hair as she came at him with an enthusiasm which was as provocative as it was untutored. She was almost clumsily thrusting her hips against his and the frustration of having the barrier of their clothes between them was perversely delicious. With a low laugh he gently propelled her backwards, his hands guiding her until she was pressed against the wall, the firm surface allowing easier access for his questing fingers.

'Oh,' she moaned as he skimmed his hand over her belly.

'Are you going to let me rip your dress off?' he drawled. 'I've been fantasising about doing that all night.'

She opened her eyes and blinked, her earlier nervousness replaced by sass. 'No way. This is far too beautiful a garment. It would be an insult to the designer.'

'Correct me if I'm wrong, but he isn't actually in the room with us.'

'She,' she emphasised. 'The designer is a she.'

He laughed at this before his expression grew serious, his jaw tightening as he located the concealed fastening. Sliding the zip down, he slipped the gown from her body until she was standing before him in nothing but some extremely hot lingerie, her generous curves coated in satin and lace—and that was when he lost it.

'I want you, Emerald Baker,' he rasped hungrily, unclipping her bra with unsteady fingers so that her breasts came tumbling out into his waiting hands. 'You are so damned...irresistible.'

'Really?' She wriggled appreciatively beneath his touch. 'Yet you seem to find it quite easy to resist me.'

'Not easy at all.'

'So why do it?'

'It doesn't matter. Stop talking and undress me,' he commanded.

She was obviously a novice but her faltering movements pleased him, though he grew impatient when she took so long to remove the stiffened collar of his shirt, as well as all the other formal paraphernalia. Before long his clothes lay in careless disarray by their feet and all he wore was a pair of boxers, while she was barely covered by the scrap of lace at her thighs.

'If only you knew just how much I want you,' he groaned, peeling away her moist panties from the cluster of pale blonde hair which whorled so seductively at her groin.

'I think I can tell,' she offered shyly as she carefully removed his boxer shorts.

The rush of air to his heated skin added yet another layer of stimulation to his already overloaded senses and Kostandin, driven by a desire which she alone could rouse in him, picked her up and carried her into the bedroom to tumble her down onto the bed. He moved over her, her body warm beneath his, the soft rise and fall of her breasts only inches away. He stared deep into her eyes and suddenly all that teasing flirtation evaporated.

'What is it you do to me,' he questioned unsteadily, 'that makes me feel so damned primitive?'

She bit her lip and all at once she looked sweet. Uncertain. And that made him want her even more.

'The same that you do to me, I guess,' she whispered.

He felt the thunder of his heart. The hot rush of heat to his groin and he was grateful for the wild hunger which drove the nag of unfamiliar questions from his mind. Eager to lose himself in the infinitely less threatening domain of her body, he lowered his head to reacquaint himself with her skin. He drifted his mouth to her neck. To the damp path between her engorged breasts. To the faint softness of her belly. And then...

'Kostandin!'

Her cry was ecstatic as his dark head came to a rest between her thighs, his tongue delving into the silken folds and making her quiver, feeling in control once more as he orchestrated her pleasure until she was begging him for release. He feasted on her for as long as it took her flesh to convulse around his mouth and then, when he could bear no more, he moved on top of her. But as he encountered her warm flesh beneath his, her eyes opened—her beautiful, green eyes—and she was staring at him with an expression he didn't recognise. Was it trust, or was it tenderness which was making the sudden clench of his heart almost as distracting as the hard throb of hunger at his groin? And why the hell was he feeling so helpless?

'Emerald,' he said, sliding into her slick heat and hearing her murmur his name, like a prayer. She gasped with pleasure as he filled her and Kostandin realised that this was different. Different from every other time he'd ever had sex and why the hell was that? But it was good. Oh, yes... So. Damned. Good. He tried to make it last, even after she'd shuddered out her pleasure again and again, but suddenly he couldn't hold back any longer. As hot and as hard as he had ever been, the spill of his seed shattering—the cry torn from his lips, incomprehensible.

Half dazed, he felt her hand slide around his waist, her fingers resting comfortably on the jut of his hips as if they were perfectly at home there and all at once he felt...

What was it?

Safe?

As if he'd wandered into a place where he'd never been before and was being given the opportunity to stay there, if he wanted?

His eyes snapped open as he chased the elusive thought before it disappeared, and perhaps he conveyed something of his disorientation. Was that why she snuggled even closer, until he wasn't quite sure where her skin began and his ended and instead of being two, they were one? It felt as close as when he'd been having sex with her only he was no longer inside her. So what was going on? Suddenly the feeling of safety—if that was what it was—felt claustrophobic.

Choking him.

Trapping him. Just as she had trapped him once before.

'Kostandin,' she murmured again.

But as he heard the emotion in her voice, he lay perfectly still, regulating his breathing until it was deep and even. Until her hand slipped away. And although he heard her sigh, he steeled his heart against that wistful sound.

Because whatever it was she wanted to say right now, he didn't want to hear it.

CHAPTER THIRTEEN

IN THE MORNING, he was gone.

As she lay amid the rumpled sheets, her body aching with remembered pleasure, Emerald should have been prepared for the clench of disappointment, but somehow she wasn't prepared at all. Still half asleep, she sat up and looked around, as if searching for proof that Kostandin had actually been there, but the only sign of last night's passion was a pair of crumpled cream panties, lying discarded on the bedroom floor. The ultimate flag of surrender, she thought, slumping back against the pillows and staring at an oil painting of a man on a horse, positioned right opposite the bed.

Their lovemaking had been sensational. No surprises there. He had taken her to the stars and back. That feeling of being in his arms again had made her lose every one of her inhibitions. It had felt different. *Special.* As if it had been about more than just physical satisfaction. Or maybe that was just wishful thinking on her part. Was that the reason why she had started whispering his name afterwards—with several soppy words of affection close to slipping from her lips as she'd snuggled up beside him? But either he'd been asleep or been feigning

sleep because she'd never got the chance to say them—
and maybe that was best.

So now what?

The knock on the door had her tugging on a robe and
running into the salon, unable to wipe the smile from
her lips—though when she stopped to think about it afterwards, why on earth would the King bother to *knock*?
Because it was Hana who stood there, the servant politely
wondering whether she would like breakfast served in
her room, since the hour was so late.

Emerald glanced up at the ornate face of the clock.
How could she have lain undisturbed until almost eleven
o'clock?

You know how.

It had been the best night's sleep she'd had in ages.
Well, pretty much ever, really. While they'd been making love, all the questions and the tension had just seeped
away and everything in her world had felt exactly as it
should do. Okay, so the intimate pillow talk she'd been
hoping for hadn't materialised—but maybe she should be
empowered by what had happened, rather than wondering why he hadn't bothered to say goodbye this morning.
Maybe he hadn't wanted to disturb her. Wasn't that what
men always said in films?

You looked so beautiful I didn't want to wake you.

Shouldn't she build on all the good bits, going forward,
rather than focussing on the negative?

'No, thanks, Hana, I'll come downstairs,' she said before cautiously testing the ground as a potential wife
with a domestic enquiry. 'I suppose the King will have
already eaten?'

Hana looked startled. 'The King never eats breakfast.'

Emerald frowned and not just because the maid's answer made her feel a bit stupid. Now certainly wasn't the time to fanfare the nutritional benefits of starting the day with a proper meal and setting a good example to Alek in future. Actually, today might be the day when they did a joint video call with her son... *Their* son. She felt a warm flicker of anticipation. Maybe Kostandin could do a virtual tour of the palace stables and introduce him to all his horses—what a thrill that would be for the little boy back in Northumberland.

She showered and dressed with extra care, determined to look the part as she pulled on a floaty lemon dress and a pair of espadrilles, before setting off downstairs. En route to breakfast, she decided to make a spontaneous detour. She would call in and say hello to her lover, because wasn't that the sort of thing a future queen was allowed to do?

In the King's outer office she found Lorenc, working industriously at his desk, and though the aide was nothing but courteous as he rose to greet her, his face wasn't exactly what you'd call *friendly*.

'Good morning, Miss Baker. How can I help you.'

'Good morning, Lorenc.' She smiled at him. 'I wondered if I could have a quick word with Kostandin? I'm wondering what's in his diary for today and whether there will be any good, er...photo opportunities.'

I'm afraid that won't be possible.'

Something about his tone made the smile freeze on her lips. 'Oh? Why not?'

'The King has already left for a meeting at the Sofnantian parliament.'

Don't ask it.

Definitely don't ask it.

She asked it. 'Did he…did he leave a message for me?'

Lorenc's eyes narrowed and she wondered if he looked almost *regretful*. 'I am afraid not. He really is exceptionally busy today, Miss Baker,' he informed her smoothly, walking towards the door before holding it open for her. 'But I will certainly tell him you were looking for him.'

She didn't know what made her peer across to the opposite side of the office—only that her heart started slamming when she saw the portrait lying on top of a large, unoccupied desk. An oil painting of a woman whose face she knew so well, even though they'd never met. A woman with a fall of jet-dark hair and eyes the colour of bright amber. Luljeta.

She opened her lips to demand to know what it was doing there, before shutting them and wondering if she'd taken complete leave of her senses. Why abandon her dignity by displaying jealousy and risk being regarded with pity, or scorn? She doubted Kostandin's fiercely loyal aide would tell her anyway, even if he knew. Which left her with no choice but to smile politely and make her way to the dining room, where—for all her supposed enthusiasm about eating breakfast—Emerald could do little more than disconsolately stir the pistachio-flecked yoghurt round and round in its little golden bowl.

Had Kostandin instructed his aide to be as obstructive as possible? she wondered bleakly. Suddenly it was difficult to keep her destructive thoughts at bay, because why had Luljeta's portrait made such an untimely appearance—had the King been gazing on it with nostalgia, perhaps?

She stared out of the window, where the roses dancing in the bright sunshine seemed to mock her suddenly deflated mood. Of *course* he had been feigning sleep last night—deep down she'd known that. She had sensed his instant retreat the moment he'd orgasmed. And there was her, imagining that it had been in some way special. How could it have been when he'd rushed away afterwards—creeping out some time in the night when she was still asleep?

Her throat grew dry as agitation prickled over her skin. Was this how he intended it to be, going forward? No real change in his behaviour at all? A scrap of affection offered here—and then instantly retracted, so she never knew whether she was coming or going.

What had she said to herself about being passive?

As she made her way back up the sweeping staircase, she was aware of having every kind of conceivable entertainment at her fingertips for the day ahead. Being here was like the ultimate five-star holiday, all expenses paid. She could swim in the pool, or walk around the beautiful grounds and take photos with her brand-new camera, or ring for someone to take her into Plavezero, but… Suddenly the prospect of any of those things felt so empty. Just as this place—this *palace*—felt empty. As if the heart had been ripped out of it, leaving nothing but a gaping hole behind.

Was that what had happened when Luljeta had left the marriage—had she left a broken man in her wake? He had explained that it had been a marriage of convenience but nobody had forced him into it, had they? It wasn't as if a son and heir had been driving his proposal, as it was with Emerald. Perhaps Kostandin had grown to love his beautiful queen along the way. Did that explain his often icy demeanour towards Emerald, and reluctance to take her to bed until last night? Until she had dressed up like some cut-price siren and practically dragged him there! But to *her* bed, she remembered bitterly, not his...

Her footsteps slowed as she passed Kostandin's chamber, unable to stop the cold serpent of curiosity from uncoiling inside her. She looked around but there was no sign of any servants and she wondered what she had been expecting. A couple of armed guards, standing sentry outside his room, perhaps? This was his *home*, for heaven's sake—even if right now it didn't feel like one. Her head still spinning with indecision, she came to a halt. She should walk straight past. But even as she thought it, her fingers were closing over the gilded handle and, pushing open the door, she quietly let herself inside.

For a moment she just stood there, acclimatising herself to the atmosphere of the vast salon. It was completely silent, all sound muffled by rich velvet drapes and heavy brocade, and it was much darker than the room she'd been given. Deep, masculine shades of red abounded, with exquisitely carved dark furniture and a rather menacing-looking sculpture in one corner. Her heart was crashing against her ribcage as she walked from the salon through to the bedroom, not really knowing what she was looking for.

Yes, you do.

You're seeking out the ghost of the woman who came before you.

But she found nothing to pin her fears onto. There were no photos or portraits of Luljeta in here. In fact, there was no evidence of a woman's touch at all in this dark and forbidding room. It was like a lavish version of one of the bedrooms at the Colonnade Club—completely anonymous, and soulless.

'What are you doing?'

The voice was icy and Emerald whirled round, the crashing of her heart intensifying when she saw Kostandin standing there. She hadn't heard him enter and as she met the quiet fury in his eyes, suddenly she was scared. Because there were unspoken rules when you lived in a palace and she had probably just broken the most fundamental of them all. You didn't enter the King's private bedchamber without invitation, even if he'd asked you to marry him. You were supposed to know your place. To sit back and admire all his kingly accomplishments and do whatever he or one of his aides suggested. The would-be bride auditioning for a role the King had no real stomach for, something which was becoming glaringly apparent. Emerald felt the familiar twist of pain in her heart. Even when he let her close, he ended up pushing her away—as if she were a toy he could play with, until he grew bored.

'I said, what are you doing?'

Somehow Emerald managed to meet the ice in his eyes without flinching. And maybe this was a conversation which couldn't have been started in any other way because, inevitably, he would have cut it short. She wasn't going to insult either of their intelligence by prevaricating and saying she'd wanted to see the colour of his drapes. Or behave like a burglar, caught in the act, even if his cutting blue gaze was making her feel that way.

'I wanted to see your bedroom.'

'Well, now you've seen it.'

'And? *And?*' She balled her hands into fists. 'Aren't

you going to ask me why, or are you just not interested? No, I can see you're not. No change there, then!'

Kostandin tensed, sensing the showdown which was near and, though he loathed the kind of ugly exchange which was all too reminiscent of the atmosphere in which he'd been raised, maybe it would clear the air once and for all. And make her understand that boundaries really did mean boundaries.

'Tell me, then,' he drawled. 'If it makes you feel better.'

'Oh!' The fists were curling like claws against her yellow dress. 'Do you have any idea how patronising you can be at times? I wanted...' She sucked in a deep breath. 'I wanted to see if you had created some sort of shrine to Luljeta and if that was the reason why you didn't want to bring me here last night.'

'A shrine to Luljeta?' He furrowed his brows and the confusion in his voice sounded genuine. 'Why would I do something like that?'

'Because there's a damned portrait of her currently sitting in your aide's office!'

His mouth hardened. 'It was one of her favourite portraits, which she has requested be returned to her.'

'Oh.'

'But I should not need to explain my actions to you, Emerald,' he continued, his voice just as icy. 'And nor do I intend to. I do not need to answer to *you*.'

For a moment Emerald couldn't speak. She felt winded—as if the world had briefly become blurred, and when it came back into focus it looked like a different place. 'Even if I were prepared to overlook the sheer arrogance of that statement, I would still be left with the conclusion that a marriage between us isn't going to work.' She sucked in a shaky breath. 'I've tried to be understanding, Kostandin. I really have. Because you've had a difficult upbringing, which probably didn't encourage you to talk very much on a personal level—'

'Every cloud has a silver lining,' he interjected sardonically.

'Although I recognise that you've probably told me more than is usual for you.'

'So what's your beef?' he demanded.

'I know you only ever planned to have a one-night stand with me and that you've tried to do the right thing ever since—in that rather uptight way you've developed since the time I last saw you. And I suppose I must be grateful for that, because I'm certainly not without flaws myself. Who is? I came to Sofnantis with a view to moving here with Alek and making a real go of our marriage, but I don't...' She swallowed. 'I don't think I can live with a man who keeps shutting me out.'

'You think I was shutting you out last night?'

'I'm not talking about sex, Kostandin. You're brilliant at sex. You know that. But you didn't spend the night with me, did you? You weren't there when I woke up this morning and somehow I wasn't surprised.' She walked over to the window, the silk of her lemon dress rustling like the wind as she moved. 'Maybe you were just preserving decorum, because you're a king and didn't want to make the servants gossip because, as you pointed out yesterday, I don't have any real status.' She hesitated. 'So was your reluctance to spend the night with me governed by the fact that we're not married? And will that change if or when we are?'

Kostandin tensed as a heavy silence followed her question. She looked so vulnerable right then that once again his heart began to ache with something he didn't understand, but he steeled himself against the flare of hope in her eyes. He would *not* engage with her at this level. Not now and not ever. Why give her the opportunity to dissect him and pick him apart as women always tried to do—to get inside his *head* and then spend the rest of her life messing with it? He would not give her that power.

'No, I'm afraid it will not,' he said eventually, trying to keep his words succinct and matter-of-fact. 'Let me try and explain to you why that is, since you obviously know little of royal life—'

'There you go—patronising me again!'

'Having separate bedrooms isn't considered unusual for a monarch,' he continued calmly. 'It helps keep mystique and excitement alive—a benefit to any marriage, surely? Don't worry about it, Emerald. You'll soon get used to it.'

'There! You're doing it again,' she said. 'Deliberately pushing me away. I don't think keeping mystique and excitement alive is what's motivating you, Kostandin, as much as trying to avoid intimacy itself. You pretended to be asleep last night, didn't you? You didn't want to hear what I might want to say. Heaven forbid that I might start murmuring words of endearment.'

'That's enough,' he bit out.

'I don't think it is. Because I confess I'm perplexed. Sometimes you sound as if you're really angry with me and I just don't understand why. So what is it? What have I done that's so wrong? Is it because I didn't tell you that you were a father, even though I explained all the reasons why I kept it quiet? Is it because I'm a commoner and deep down you resent that? Or is it because I have the nerve to speak to you as a man, instead of as a symbol of greatness and power?'

A slow breath left Kostandin's lips. If knowledge was power, then didn't she already possess a large enough armoury which could be used against him at any time? But maybe he needed to say this if she wanted to understand him. It would help her accept why he could never be the man she might want him to be.

'I would no longer *be* King of Sofnantis,' he said savagely, 'if you hadn't brought the boy into my life.'

'What…what are you talking about?'

He shook his head impatiently. 'When I inherited a crown I had never wanted, I saw it as a type of firefighting I needed to do to repair the damage done by my father and brother.'

'And you did a great job, by all accounts. The economy is booming and the people obviously love you.'

He waved away her attempt to placate him. 'But my attitude to being King didn't alter,' he continued remorselessly. 'It was still an unwanted burden and once Sofnantis had recovered economically, I was determined to address my own future. I was divorced by then. I had no plans to remarry and I certainly wasn't going to have children. And that was to be my freedom,' he emphasised.

'I still don't understand.'

'Don't you? Think about it, Emerald.' He gave a bitter laugh. 'Kings need a bloodline, and I never intended to have one. I had planned to abdicate to allow my cousin Namik to be King. He is next in line to the throne, a dutiful and clever man with a delightful wife and young son. He would have been perfect for the role. He still would.

But that can never happen. Not now. Because one day you walked into my life and in the time it took for you to tell me about Alek, my world changed out of all recognition. He is the rightful heir and if I abdicate, Alek will lose out on his birthright. Not only that—but if I abdicate for personal reasons, it will weaken the monarchy and my conscience will not allow me to do that. Now do you understand?'

'Yes, I see,' she said slowly. 'But why do you hate being King so much? Especially when you're so good at it.'

He shook his head impatiently. 'Because I am trapped by the constraints of these gilded chains and by the total lack of freedom! By the way people look at me wherever I go, and listen to whatever I have to say, nodding their heads like obedient dogs at whatever springs from my mouth.' His eyes narrowed. 'Except for you, of course,' he added reflectively. 'You have never been quite so... obedient.'

'And this...this life of restraint—these gilded chains you speak of,' she said, her eyes narrowing. 'Is that what you wish for our son?'

'He needs to be given the choice,' he argued. 'Alek is heir to a great country and a great fortune and he deserves to know that. We cannot hide that knowledge from him, Emerald. Who knows how he might regard his future legacy? He might love it.'

'He might,' she said uncertainly.

Emerald's thoughts were buzzing as she tried to process everything he'd just told her. It explained a lot. The resentment and anger which simmered beneath all that red-hot desire and which had made him push her away so often. These were painful things to hear and she could easily react by showing him she was hurt. But at least he had been honest with her—and didn't she owe him a similar honesty in return?

She thought about the lifestyle and circumstances which had forged him. The unfaithful mother who had never loved him. The weak father and addict brother. She'd seen the anguish on his face when he'd talked about his past. Was it any surprise he'd never wanted to create a family of his own, with that as an example? And while he might be stern and angry at times, he was also brave. And strong. He hadn't wanted the crown but he had worn it well for the sake of his country, and now he was prepared to continue wearing it, for the sake of his son. He was prepared to change in a very practical way.

Couldn't she show him that emotional change was possible too, if only he would let his guard down enough to embrace it? Was she also capable of being strong—strong enough to swallow her pride and tell him how she really felt about him? Didn't a man whose mother had never loved him deserve some kind of acknowledgement that he wasn't an unlovable man?

She cleared her throat. 'You once asked me why I was a virgin when I met you, but I never told you, and maybe it's time I did. You see, after my mum got pregnant, she spent the rest of her life drumming it into me and Ruby that men were bad and you should never trust them.' She shrugged. 'And it doesn't seem to matter how balanced you try to be about relationships, when you reach adulthood some of that indoctrination is bound to sink in. So I was always really, really careful around men. I hardly ever went out on dates and when I did, I was just incredibly bored.' She paused. 'Maybe I subconsciously chose boring men rather than men who did dangerous things to your pulse-rate, thinking they'd be safe. Until I met you.'

'And I was dangerous?' he surmised silkily.

'Of course you were.' She laughed. 'And I can see from your expression what you're probably thinking. You think I wanted you because you were a prince. That women only want you because you're rich and royal, blah-de-blah-de-blah. It has nothing to do with your intelligence or wit, or your knockout body and incredible blue eyes. Yet, despite your lofty position in life, you made me feel like we were equals—even though, patently, we weren't. I'd never thought it could be so easy to talk to a man and fancy him, all at the same time. When you made it clear there was no future for us, I accepted that, even if I didn't want to. If circumstances had been different I would have come to you and told you that you were a father and you now know why I didn't. But I never stopped thinking about you. How could I, when I saw your features in our son every day of my life?'

His mouth remained tight, his blue eyes cold. 'Why are you telling me all this, Emerald?'

It was right up there as contender for the most hurtful of responses to such an emotional declaration, but Emerald forced herself to continue, even though tears were pricking at the backs of her eyes. She had to stay resolute, to show him she meant every word, without scaring him off with the crazy truth. That she loved him. Her pulse thumped. That deep down, she had always loved him. Of course she had—why else had she put herself through all this? And just because he didn't feel the same way about her, that didn't mean it couldn't change. She swallowed. Because wasn't hope the bedrock of love?

'What if I tell you that I think we could be happy together as a family?' she suggested tentatively. 'If you could only stop putting up so many barriers to that happiness. If you could learn to trust us—and yourself. Alek is an affectionate little boy, who would love to shower some of that affection on his dad. Think how wonderful that could be, Kostandin. Because doesn't love give you its own kind of freedom? Our family could provide an escape from all the pomp and ceremony which surround you. It could be a place of real safety and refuge.'

'I think that's a little fanciful,' he answered coolly. 'So let's just keep our expectations real, shall we? I will do my best to be as good a father to Alek as I can, especially since I suspect you will have no qualms about telling me when I'm doing it wrong.' He allowed a flicker of humour to curve his lips, before his features assumed their familiar stony mask. 'To you I can offer affection, respect and fidelity and that will have to be enough. Because, frankly, that's all I have to give.'

She sensed he was making a big concession and maybe if it had been just her she might have accepted his terms, in the hope that he might soften his rigid stance over time. But it wasn't just about her. She had their son to consider and he had to be her number one priority. And even though the words were sticking in her throat like little pebbles, she forced herself to say them.

'I'm sorry, Kostandin, but it's not enough. I don't want a fixed-term contractual marriage, where emotion and love are out of bounds.'

'Are you holding out for romance, Emerald?' he questioned mockingly. 'Is that what this is all about?'

A lump rose in her throat and in that moment she hated him for his perception and yes, his cruelty. Of course she wanted romance. She wanted it all—but she was damned if she was going to let him know that. He might have ripped her heart to shreds, but no way was he going to destroy her self-respect.

'If I'd been holding out for romance I would never have gone with you in the first place!' she declared. 'Maybe you think being a royal means you don't have to make much effort because with you, it's all been terse instructions about what you will or will not tolerate—even on that very first time we slept together. Though at least back then you stayed the night.'

She stared down at the blurred pattern of the silk carpet, blinking her eyes once or twice, and when she lifted her gaze again, she was composed enough to be able to speak without her voice trembling. 'But it's made me realise that, not only do I owe it to our son to turn down your mean-spirited offer of carefully rationed affection and as little emotion as you can get away with, but I owe it to myself, too. Because he and I are worth more than that. Much more.'

'More than what?' he demanded.

'This! This fancy, empty palace of yours!' She sliced her hand wildly through the air. 'I don't want Alek growing up in an environment where he has to spend his time tiptoeing over eggshells in case he does or says the wrong thing. We may not have much in the way of possessions in our little house in Northumberland, but it's spilling over with love and nobody is afraid to express their feelings. I won't stop you seeing him, Kostandin. In fact, I'll make it as easy as possible for you, because that is the right thing to do. If you still want to abdicate, I'll be as discreet as you want. But that's none of my business. I just want out of here. I want to go back to England. I can't stay here in this atmosphere.'

She met his gaze, praying that the last trace of her tears had vanished. 'I want to go home as soon as possible, and you can make that happen for me, Kostandin. Please. Just set me free.'

CHAPTER FOURTEEN

KOSTANDIN PACED UP and down the long gallery, his long strides making short work of the lengthy dimensions of the gilded room.

How dared she?

How *dared* she?

Telling him what she would and wouldn't tolerate from their relationship! Listing a catalogue of complaints against him and then demanding he make his plane ready to have her flown to England as quickly as possible. Why, Emerald Baker was acting as if *she* were the royal and he her humble lackey!

He could have told her no, that she would have to wait until the morning for a scheduled flight leaving from Plavezero airport—and hadn't he been tempted to do that? As if by flexing his undoubted muscle and power he could punish her, as she had tried to punish him. But in the end he'd decided that this intolerable situation should not be extended any longer than it needed to be and had arranged to have his private jet on standby.

'Your Majesty?'

Impatiently, he glanced up as the doors to the first-floor gallery were opened. 'What is it, Lorenc?'

'Miss Baker is just about to leave for the airport and I

wondered…' The aide gave a polite cough. 'Is His Majesty intending to bid her farewell?'

'No, His Majesty most definitely is not intending to bid her farewell,' he bit out. 'Have her gone. I have work to do.'

But once his aide had left, Kostandin found his footsteps automatically straying towards the window—though he took great care to stand to one side, making sure he was hidden from sight by the heavy drapes. The waiting car was gleaming, the royal flag fluttering in the light breeze as the chauffeur stood to attention. And then he saw her, walking down the short flight of marble steps, wearing… He frowned. Wearing the very jeans she'd arrived in, and carrying not just her computer case, but a small and very battered suitcase. He frowned again. Why were the servants not taking it from her? Why hadn't someone provided her with a decent set of luggage? And was she really leaving behind the expensive and updated wardrobe she had acquired since being here?

She looked up then, as if she sensed being watched, the expression on her heart-shaped face impossible to see, and Kostandin felt his heart contract with something which felt like pain as he saw the sunlight bouncing off her golden hair. But better the brief pain of parting than the enduring hurt of something he was fighting with every fibre of his being. He turned away from her distracting image, trying to get his tangled thoughts in order and wondering where they went from here. There were many things they needed to consider—his relationship with Alek, for a start, though that might best be done through professional mediators, once the heat of her departure had died down.

But the conflict raging inside his head showed no sign of abating during the next few days as he went about his busy schedule, trying to distract himself with the customary round of business delegations, receptions and dinners—though he was aware of slamming his office door more often than was usual.

He worked diligently on the routine piles of official papers but at times the words danced and blurred and he could feel the inexorable mount of frustration building inside him. His mind kept returning to Emerald and it didn't matter how hard he tried, he couldn't stop thinking about her.

He let out a heavy sigh as he pushed his pen away. Not just the obvious things—like her beauty or her sensuality, or that she had nurtured such a beautiful son. Her strength and resolve were equally admirable—for she had refused to be dazzled by the trappings of his position, hadn't she? She was willing to turn her back on them all because she wanted the best for Alek. She hadn't demanded money, or power, or an elevated position in society—all she had wanted was honesty and emotion and he had been unwilling and unable to provide them for her. At least he was free of her and her demands, he reasoned. A muscle began to work at his temple. So why the hell did he feel so…empty?

His thoughts were interrupted by a light tap on the door—his barked reply enough to summon into the office Lorenc, who was carrying what looked like a photograph.

'What is it?' Kostandin questioned.

His aide carefully placed the photo on the desk in front of him. 'I was wondering if we might use this to accompany the press statement about your forthcoming trip to Maraban, Your Majesty.'

Kostandin was tempted to snap back that this kind of decision was way below his pay grade, when he glanced at the black and white shot and his heart missed a beat when he realised it was one of Emerald's. He had always been the first to acknowledge her talent but now he found himself picking it up to study the image more closely because… He swallowed. It didn't *look* like him. The stern and occasionally forbidding expression of his formal portraits was nowhere to be seen. His lips were curved in what appeared to be a failed bid to repress a rising laugh and his eyes were…soft… He shook his head in confusion.

As if he was looking at something which pleased him very much.

Or someone.

But he had. He had been looking at her.

Her.

The only woman who had ever been able to make him really smile. He stood up and went over to stare at the roses whose heady perfume was drifting in through the open French doors, and could feel his resistance crumbling. He found himself thinking how different the atmosphere in the palace had been when Emerald had been living there. For the first time the mighty citadel hadn't felt like a cold monument, or the symbol of a position he had never asked for—it had come *alive.*

And he had come alive, too—like a parched piece of ground being sprinkled with sweet water. He *liked* her company, he realised. Her feisty curiosity and stubbornness might have irritated him at times, but she always intrigued him. Her calm questions had made him examine himself in a way he'd never done before—and wasn't it better to confront the darkness she had exposed, than to bury it away again and let it moulder?

His throat dried. She hadn't flinched when he had laid out his unfeeling demands, telling her she must never love him, nor expect any real intimacy. He had implied that he would just carry on exactly as before and she and the boy would be expected to fit in around that. He had offered her marriage but that wasn't a marriage.

Not a real marriage.

He turned away from the sunshine, his head swimming, like someone emerging from a long sleep.

'Sit down, Lorenc,' he said slowly. 'I need you to help me make plans.'

Emerald glanced at her watch as she had been doing for the entire morning. She should be, if not happy, then at least a little bit glad. After all, it wasn't every week that you got two such well-paid jobs on exactly the same day, especially when you were a teeny organisation like hers and Ruby's. Her twin had been delighted to take a big batch of the local stottie cakes to some fancy hotel in Newcastle, where a famous footballer was revisiting his roots, while Emerald was on hand to deal with the somewhat mystifying request to book out their entire beach café for a private function.

She didn't even know how many people were supposed to be attending—in fact, she didn't know anything much at all. Her dealings had been with some posh-sounding woman in central London, who hadn't exactly been forthcoming. At least, the catering side of the booking was mercifully modest, which meant she was able to handle it on her own since the only food requested were two punnets of English strawberries, a tub of cream and some passion fruit. The customer would be providing their own booze as well as their own flowers.

Emerald blinked as she looked around. And what flowers they were. They had arrived in a fancy florist's van earlier. Stacks and stacks of fragrant roses in shades of deep crimson and faded lilac, their rich perfume filling the air. Dozens of blooms were crammed into exquisite crystal vases—which was a bit of a relief as otherwise they would have been destined to be displayed in a few hastily assembled jam jars.

But Emerald had been forced to fake her excitement, despite the jaw-dropping amount of money they were being paid for the gig. All she could think about was Kostandin and how much she missed him, even though she'd been trying her best *not* to miss him. But focussing on his arrogance and emotional rigidity was refusing to ease the terrible ache in her heart, which had been there since she'd left Sofnantis, almost a week ago. She had been evasive with Alek about her trip, she knew she had—but what was she supposed to say?

I'm sorry, darling. I've refused to marry your father because he won't ever be able to love me as much as I love him.

What had seemed to make perfect sense at the time now seemed like an act of complete selfishness—or was she just trying to talk herself into going back to him? And then what? Spend the next thirteen years of their contractual marriage wishing things could be different?

The flash of sunlight on an approaching car had her

straightening her frilly apron, her official smile of welcome dying on her lips when she saw the identity of the tall figure who was unfolding his long limbs from the luxury vehicle. In his faded jeans and a T-shirt which matched the ebony gleam of his hair, he didn't look much like a king—especially not as he was carrying what looked like a cool bag. She screwed up her eyes, wondering if she was hallucinating. A *cool bag*? But her senses were so battered by his powerful presence as he walked into the café and closed the door behind him that any kind of rational analysis was proving impossible.

So she just stood there, surrounded by vases of scented flowers, trying not to show any heartache or regret on a face she hoped was composed—as befitted the mother of the King's child.

'Kostandin,' she said, her voice not quite as steady as she would have wished for. 'What on earth are you doing here?'

Kostandin put the bag on the floor wondering if she would comment on the chinking sound of glass against bottle, but she didn't. Hadn't she worked it out yet? But even if she had, it seemed she wasn't letting on and the cool gaze she was directing at him from between narrowed green eyes didn't look particularly welcoming.

He was a man who had always been renowned for his eloquence and articulation but for the first time in his life, the words were sticking like glue in his throat. Because how did you go about articulating something you'd never said before? Something which experience had made you wary of and you'd spent your whole life avoiding? He swallowed. 'Because I want you to come back.'

'Really?' She arched her eyebrows. 'Is this a power thing?'

'To hell with power,' he said, unable to keep the desperation from his voice.

And then she clapped her palm against her forehead. 'Of course!' she exclaimed. 'It's all becoming clear now. You're the mystery client who booked out the café. Pretty extreme lengths to go to, aren't they? If you'd picked up the phone, I would have agreed to a meeting.'

'But I didn't want a *meeting*,' he ground out. 'I wanted to surprise you.'

'Well, you've certainly done that.' She slanted him a look of defiance. 'The question is, why?'

'You made me realise I'd never shown you any romance,' he gritted out. 'And this is my attempt to make up for that.'

'No, no. I get all that,' she said impatiently. 'But you still haven't told me why.'

She wasn't making it easy for him, he realised. Did she want him to jump through hoops of fire? 'Because I need you, Emerald.'

But still there was no capitulation. Her mouth did not smile. 'Let's get this straight, Kostandin. It's not me you need.' She shook her head, as if to contradict the slight wobble of her voice. 'It's your son and heir. At least be honest—with yourself as well as me. I meant what I said about letting you see Alek as much as possible, but you'd better accept that I'm not coming back in order to secure your succession. I'm sorry, but I can't. I just can't.'

'This has nothing to do with succession,' he breathed urgently. 'And everything to do with you, and the way I feel about you, only I've just been too stupid and too stubborn to acknowledge it before.' She was shaking her head as he spoke, as if she wanted to block out his explanation, even though she had been the one who had just demanded it. 'You once told me that you never forgot me, well, as it happens, I never forgot you either, Emerald. After that first night we spent together, I couldn't get you out of my head. Or my body.' His jaw clenched. 'You wanted to know if there was a shrine to my ex-wife in my bedroom but you saw for yourself there was not. How could there be when she didn't spend a single night there?'

'Yes, you already explained that,' she said, in a bored tone. 'The King's precious bed is never shared with a woman.'

'No, it wasn't that. My marriage to Luljeta was unconsummated and was dissolved on those grounds.' There was a pause as he gazed into eyes which were now widening and he spoke the words slowly and very deliberately, for maximum impact. 'You are the only woman I've had sex with since that night in London, six years ago.'

'I'm not... I'm not sure I believe you,' she said, but a rush of colour had turned her cheeks rosy pink.

'Believe me,' he said roughly. 'Because it's true.'

'But... Luljeta is beautiful.'

'So what if she is? Do you imagine that a man is always controlled by his base instincts?' he demanded hotly. 'I didn't fancy her for all kinds of reasons and not just because she was my brother's fiancée and the thought of intimacy with her felt all wrong. And, just for the record, she didn't fancy me either. Because, by then I had met you and for me, that changed everything. You enchanted me, Emerald, and the spell you cast on me has never faded. Once the abdication had been made official, I had planned to come and find you, but then I happened to be in London and I didn't want to wait. I wondered if you were still working at the club. Why the hell do you think I held my party there when I had a whole embassy at my disposal? It was a long shot...' He paused. 'But there you were.'

'Let me guess.' Her voice took on an odd tone. 'You wanted to have sex with me to try and get me out of your system for good?'

'Perhaps that was what I thought would happen. I don't know.' He saw the way she bit her lip. 'You asked for honesty, Emerald, and that is what I'm giving you. Because when you came back to the embassy with me that night...' His throat thickened. 'It was like the culmination of all my recurring fantasies. Beautiful sex with the woman I'd been obsessed with. And then you told me about Alek. The discovery of a hidden heir gave me reason to mistrust you and I *wanted* that, because mistrusting felt safe. It was a situation I was comfortable with and certainly easier than the alternative, which was...' and now when he spoke it didn't sound like his voice at all '...to love you.'

Emerald sat in silence as his words rippled over her skin like velvet—words she'd never thought she'd hear him say, though she'd imagined them often enough, usually in her wildest dreams. But wasn't it strange how you could long for something and then be paralysed with fear when it came your way? As if she might still be dreaming. As if it might not be real. 'So where does that leave us?'

'I don't want a contractual marriage. I want a real one. Till death do us part. The whole deal. But I don't know how you'd feel about that.' He shrugged. 'Do I?'

She met his gaze, because surely the sincerity blazing from his sapphire eyes was too intense to be anything *but* real. But she needed to be sure. She needed to protect herself, for all their sakes. And, ironically, the only way she could do that was by opening up her heart and telling him how she felt. How she *really* felt.

'I love you, too,' she said slowly. 'I always have—even though I did everything in my power to try and stop myself. But even when you were being your most remote and objectionable, I never stopped loving you. Gosh, it's such a relief to be able to say it at last,' she admitted as he pulled her into his arms and her fingers began to stroke the dark rasp of his jaw.

'And such a relief to hear it,' he said, a deep note of amusement curling his voice. 'Even though deep down I knew.'

'You're so arrogant, Kostandin.'

'Maybe,' he conceded. 'But would you have me any other way?'

'Ask me in a year's time.'

He kissed her then. A kiss which was long and hard and deep. A stamp of possession, but underpinned with a tenderness which tugged at her heartstrings, and when she finally came up for air, she could see that his eyes were as bright as her own.

'Oh, darling,' she said softly. 'Darling, darling, darling.'

'Tell me what you want, Emerald. And I will do everything in my power to give it to you.'

And suddenly it was so simple. As simple as breathing. Her finger was remarkably steady as it reached out to trace the outline of his beautiful lips. She didn't want the things he was capable of giving her. Not palaces, or planes or diamonds—because all those things were replaceable. But this wasn't, this feeling. And he wasn't, this man.

'You,' she said as his lips closed around her finger. 'That's all I want, Kostandin. You.'

EPILOGUE

'READ ME ANOTHER STORY, Papa—please!'

A pair of heavy-lidded eyes were turned upwards and as Kostandin met the gaze of a little boy who was valiantly fighting sleep, his heart turned over with love. 'No more tonight,' he said softly, planting a kiss on his head. 'You've had a busy day and we're going to have an even busier one tomorrow.'

Alek yawned. 'Can we go snorkelling again, Papa?'

'We sure can.'

'And will we see another turtle?'

'We might. But right now you need to go to sleep, young man, and I'm going to have dinner with your mama.'

A pair of dark eyelashes fluttered. 'Do you think she liked her birthday cake, Papa?' he murmured drowsily. 'Had you ever made a cake before?'

'Never,' said Kostandin with a smile. 'That's why it was so lopsided!'

Another quick kiss to the forehead, but the giggling boy was asleep before he'd even left the room and Kostandin just stood watching the soft rise and fall of his little chest before making his way across the terrace to the summer house that looked out over the cove below. Just like last year, they had spent the long vacation in their summer residence and, just like last year, he was happy. Happier than he had believed it was possible to be.

Deeply touched by a congratulatory message from Luljeta, he and Emerald had married in a low-key ceremony—she hadn't wanted comparisons made with his first marriage or to overwhelm their son with more pomp and ceremony than was necessary. But despite the dramatic change to all their lives, the three of them had quickly settled into what felt like unadulterated bliss. Kostandin had bonded with his little boy and had decided not to regret the past, but learn from it. They had become a family, he realised. A real family—not one riven apart by lies and deceit.

And Emerald had been right. Bonded by love as they were, the perceived chains which had bound him to the monarchy seemed to fall away. His position no longer felt like a burden and neither did his feelings. It was as if the woman he loved had shown him that it was okay to show your emotions, even if you'd spent the previous three decades pretending they didn't exist. Between them, they had created a modern royal family and tried to ensure that Alek had as normal an upbringing as possible.

He opened the door of the summer house and surveyed the interior with satisfaction, before dismissing the servant who had just finished lighting the final candle. And then he settled down to wait for her. Heard her light footfall before he saw her and, as always, his heart leapt.

'Kostandin?'

He didn't answer as she stood on the threshold, her filmy dress brushing against the curve of her belly, her hair gleaming in the flicker of the candle flames as she looked around, an expression of delight on her beautiful face.

'Kostandin,' she breathed. 'What is this?'

'Happy birthday, my love,' he said softly, then narrowed his eyes. 'Do you think it's over the top?'

Did she think it was over the top? Emerald wondered dazedly as she breathed in the rich scent of the roses which covered every available surface. Totally. There were white candles everywhere, little points of light glittering like so many indoor stars among all the flowers. At the far end of the summer house, which was relatively modest—one of the reasons she liked it so much—a table was laid for dinner, with a bottle of sparkling elderflower on ice—her favourite tipple throughout this pregnancy.

For a moment she was too choked to speak as her memory took her back to when she had agreed to become Kostandin's wife, and everything which had happened since then. These days he was no stranger to romance—indeed, he demonstrated it at every opportunity. That he was a considerate husband was in no doubt, but he was the most brilliant father, too. She'd watched the careful way he had taken time to bond with his son and relished his gentleness, which she suspected had never been given a chance to flourish before. Just as his kingship had flourished, his gratitude and happiness plain for all to see, making his people adore him even more.

The three of them had become a tight unit, and Alek was flourishing at the international school in Plavezero, while Emerald was rapidly learning how to make her adopted country proud of her. The language she was getting better at and her photos of Kostandin had been exhibited around the country to great acclaim and made into a book, with all the proceeds going to a charity for the homeless. She wanted to use her talent for good, she realised. She wanted to be a queen the King could be proud of.

Jessica had left and gone back to America and, to nobody's great surprise, Lorenc had resigned his post and taken up the Sofnantian ambassadorship in Washington DC. So far, there were no reports of a relationship.

Emerald's only sadness was Ruby's initial reaction to news of her marriage and that she and Alek were moving away from Northumberland. Her twin had explained how genuinely happy she was for her and then promptly burst into tears.

'I mean, I know you've got to go,' she had sobbed. 'But I'm going to miss Alek so much, Emmy. So very much.'

And Emerald had cried too, telling her beloved sister there would always be a place for her in Sofnantis and recognising that she'd been like a second mother to Alek and of course it was going to be hard to let that go. Ruby needed a family of her own, Emerald realised, and wondered whether that would ever happen.

She looked up to meet the loving and watchful gaze of her husband and went into his waiting arms. 'Only a bit over the top,' she said, with a giggle. 'You don't have to keep doing it, you know.'

'Ah, but I like doing it.' He kissed the tip of her nose and drifted his lips towards her cheek.

Emerald elevated her chin to allow him easier access to her neck. 'Don't get me wrong,' she breathed. 'I love all the romance, but it's all the other things you do which count more than anything. The way you nurture and care for me and do everything you can to ensure Alek and I are happy. The way you've cherished me throughout this pregnancy.'

He splayed his fingers over her bump and his voice was husky. 'I'm trying to make up for not having been there the first time round.'

'I know you are.' She touched her fingers to the side of his face, feeling so full of emotion that she thought she might burst. 'And that's one of the reasons why I love you.'

'Give me another reason,' he murmured as her fingertips began to tiptoe downwards.

'How about…*this*?'

Boldly, she reached for the erection which was pressing against his formal trousers and he gave a low laugh of pleasure as she began to stroke him with nimble fingers. And when it appeared that neither of them could wait much longer, he carried her over to the day bed and began to undress her—kissing every inch of the soft skin he revealed, as a silvery moon rose high over the Sofnantian sea.

* * * * *

A TYCOON
TOO WILD TO WED

CAITLIN CREWS

MILLS & BOON

To Jackie,
because writing with you is always so much fun!

CHAPTER ONE

PROUD ASTERION TERAS gazed down at the elegant and diminutive old woman before him in dark, arrogant astonishment, his default expression. "I beg your pardon?"

"You heard me," his grandmother replied. Her gaze was canny and sharp, as ever. She sat in her favorite chair as if it was a throne, but Asterion was not the sort to bend a knee to anyone, not even the matriarch of what was left of his family. Then she said the same astounding thing again. "You need a wife. Badly."

"I can think of nothing I require less, Yia Yia," Asterion replied dryly.

And that should have been the end of the matter, but he knew very well it was not.

He looked across the elegant, airy room that offered views of the island from all sides with the Mediterranean gleaming in the distance. The Teras villa had been the family's prize jewel for generations, sitting on the estate that some glorious ancestor or another had won by finding favor with a long-ago king.

The villa was unofficially known as his grandmother's castle, high on the most sought-after hill with one of the finest views around of the whole of the island kingdom.

And these days, Dimitra Teras was more than happy to consider herself a sort of queen of all she surveyed.

Given that Dimitra was one of the few residents of the island who could boast of a friendship with the actual queen, who was rarely seen in public any longer, no one would dare question her on this.

Not even Asterion, who otherwise questioned everyone. On everything. As if it was his duty.

He sometimes thought it was.

His twin brother, Poseidon, stood by one of the far windows, and Asterion could tell from the set to his twin's shoulders that Poseidon was no more interested in a potential wife than he was. It was a topic of some amusement for the both of them that while newspapers and ambitious strangers were forever intimating that there was strife between the two heirs to the Teras family fortune, the brothers actually enjoyed each other's company.

They were a mere minute apart, after all.

But they preferred not to let the truth get out—not when it was far more entertaining to read reports of their nonexistent enmity instead. The reality was that Asterion and Poseidon had competed for everything because they liked competing. They had each taken to their part of the family empire with the competitive spirit that had marked their relationship since the womb, according to their mother, who they could both remember telling them stories of what she was certain had been brawls while tucked away in her belly.

They'd lost her in the same car accident that had taken

their father and grandfather, too, when the twins were twelve.

Asterion preferred not to think about unpleasant things he couldn't change. Particularly that. Not when he could still recall the jolt of impact. And worse, what came after.

"Both of you," Dimitra was saying, with an unfortunate sort of ring in her voice, as if she was issuing proclamations. "The pair of you are little better than wolves. From day to day, I don't know which one of you has the worst reputation."

At this, Poseidon laughed. "I have endeavored to make certain it was me."

"Nonsense," Asterion responded, lifting a brow. "What are you but everyone's favorite playboy? A mere trinket, to be used and discarded."

"Not all of us take pride in being considered the Monster of the Mediterranean, *ton megalýtero adelfó,*" Poseidon replied with his usual ease.

Poseidon smiled. Asterion brooded. They had been thus since birth.

"I am old," their grandmother announced. Which was a shocking statement from a woman who had previously made it clear that she intended to defy the ravages of age by remaining immortal. Asterion had not doubted her. Now, as both of her grandsons stared at her, she smiled. In a manner that could only be called dangerous. "Death stalks me even now."

"Only last week you made a great song and dance out of the fact your doctors told you that you are healthier than the average thirty-year-old," Asterion said. "Or have you forgotten? Is that the sort of stalking you mean?"

"I wish that I could gracefully recede into the shrouds of a foggy memory," Dimitra replied crisply. "Sadly, my mind is all too sharp. I see the two of you with perfect clarity. I am forced to read about your exploits daily, and I am not a young woman. I have no intention of seeing this family die out simply because the two of you are so useless."

"Useless," Poseidon repeated, with that laugh of his that one tabloid had once called more dangerous than an earthquake, such was its seductive power. "I'm not sure the shareholders would agree, Yia Yia."

"Last I checked," Asterion said in agreement, "Poseidon's Hydra Shipping and my own Minotaur Group far exceed the average annual earnings of any other member of this family. Ever. Not only this year, Yia Yia—every year. But you know this."

"You demand this," Poseidon murmured.

Dimitra pretended not to hear him. "I want great-grandchildren," she replied, waving a hand as if accomplishments in the corporate world mattered little to her.

When Asterion knew all too well that Dimitra Teras had a keen business mind that she never hesitated to use as a weapon, taking her competitors out at the knees.

Where did she imagine he and his brother had learned it?

"Are you well?" he asked, while Poseidon only laughed. They were identical, but no one had any trouble telling them apart. The same dark hair. The same blue eyes the color of the sea all around them. But one of them never smiled. The other never stopped. "Since when have you been domestic?"

"It has nothing to do with domesticity, *paidiá*," their grandmother replied.

Children. As if Asterion and Poseidon were toddlers, clambering about in short pants.

No one else would dare speak to two of the most powerful men in the world in this fashion. No one else ever had. Their exploits and accomplishments were known the world over. Business rivals surrendered rather than attempt to fight them. Women flung themselves at their feet. Since their twelfth birthday, there had only ever been one person with the audacity to suggest to them that they, too, were mortal beings.

And she was laying it on a bit thick today.

"The sad truth I have come to accept is that neither one of you can be trusted to find suitable mates," Dimitra was saying now, in a particularly long-suffering way that suggested she was enjoying herself. "Far too dissolute, the pair of you, for all that you come at it differently." The brothers eyed each other, but could not argue. "Nor can either one of you be trusted to take care of things in a reasonable amount of time. I would like to see my great-grandchildren, if only to ensure that they are brought up properly. This has nothing to do with my severe concerns about your characters, and everything to do with the family legacy."

The brothers gazed at each other once more, then aimed that look at her.

"We are the family legacy," Asterion said quietly.

Dimitra sniffed. "I have given you both many hints over the years, none of which you have appeared to notice. So this time I will speak to you in a language I know you understand." She leaned forward in her chair, clasping her hands together so that her many priceless jewels caught the light and sent it spinning this way and that, as if she controlled that, too. "You will each marry the woman of my choosing, or I will make certain that your inheritance is left to an outsider rather than split between you. An outsider who will then, lest you have forgotten, have a controlling interest in the family trust."

Asterion made a disapproving sound. "We have not forgotten."

"You hate outsiders more than we do," Poseidon reminded her.

"The choice is yours," Dimitra said resolutely.

And smiled, a bit too cat-with-the-canary for Asterion. If it had been anyone but his much-beloved grandmother saying such things to him, he would simply have turned on his heel, left her presence, and set about destroying her. But he loved his grandmother—and not only because he knew too well that she did not make idle threats.

And besides, she was their only weak spot. They had made their own fortunes. They had carved their own paths. She was the only family they had left after the accident and she had cared for them ever since. In her own inimitable way, certainly, but Asterion did not have to consult with Poseidon to know they still felt as they always had.

If Dimitra wanted a legacy, they would give her one. However grudgingly.

She waited, as if she expected explosions. Crockery tossed against walls, fists through walls—but she had not raised them to be so obvious.

Dimitra smiled wider when all they did was wait. "I want to be very clear that this is under my control, not yours. You both must agree to both woo and marry the women I select for you."

Again, the twins looked at each other, communicating without words.

"You say this as if it is some hardship for us to woo women, Yia Yia," Poseidon drawled. "I do not wish to make you blush, but this has not been a great challenge for either one of us. Ever."

"I said *woo and then marry*," Dimitra replied tartly. "I did not say *seduce and then discard*. And these will not be those dreadful cardboard creatures the two of you favor. You need a good woman, each of you. And in the interests of full disclosure, I will share with you that I do not believe either one of you is capable of gaining the regard of a decent woman." There was a glint her eyes, the same blue as theirs. "Given that you never have."

Asterion was frowning. "I don't understand why you would risk the family legacy over something as silly as *wooing* and *marrying*."

"The two of you are miserable, whether you know it or not," she said, and shook her head, even though her eyes yet gleamed. "Too powerful for your own good, too set in your ways, and what do you have to show for it?

Brokenhearted women of low caliber trail about behind you, telling appalling tales of your treatment of them."

"No one complains of the way we treat them," Poseidon said. "Rather that we do not continue treating them that way as long as they would like us to."

Dimitra didn't *quite* roll her eyes. "You are forever in the tabloids, one scandal after the next, and trust me when I tell you that at a certain point you will be considered irredeemable by any decent woman."

Poseidon laughed. "You say that as if it is a bad thing."

"You have responsibilities to this family and its continuing legacy, Poseidon," she shot back. "And at present you are on the verge of being known as little more than a silly whore."

In another family, that might have been an insult. But Poseidon only laughed.

"Never a *silly* whore, surely."

Dimitra turned her glare on Asterion. "Meanwhile, you delight in brooding about like something out of a gothic mystery, when the only real mystery is how any female alive confuses that for anything but the worst kind of narcissism. No one is interested in your pain, Asterion. It is not a personality, it is an affectation."

Asterion lifted a brow at her, ignoring his twin's laughter. "Not all of us are charming, Yia Yia. Some of us must be challenging instead."

"I've made my decision," Dimitra shot back. "And you must decide right now, as death could take me at any moment." She was literally flushed with good health, but neither one of them argued. So she went on. "Either surrender your inheritance entirely, or, for once in your life, do as you're told."

The brothers looked at each other and for a moment, all was still.

But they communicated the way they always had. And Asterion could see his own reaction reflected in his brother's eyes.

How bad could it be? Poseidon asked silently.

Asterion remembered his parents' marriage and knew it could be very bad indeed. Terrible, even.

But he decided, then and there, that while he might acquiesce to the trappings of this farce if it would please his grandmother—and he knew he would always do what he could to please Dimitra, old dragon though she was, and within reason—he had no intention of allowing any of the other things people were always trumpeting on about when it came to marriage to ensnare him. Connection. Intimacy.

He was not built for such things and would not permit them anywhere near him. And as he thought that, he knew it to be true, for there was so far nothing in his life that he could not control. And nothing he did not control, even his grandmother.

For she might think she was getting the upper hand here, but Asterion knew full well she could not force either one of them to any altar.

The fact of the matter was that the Teras legacy needed heirs.

It was all the better that he was to be provided with a suitable bride so he could make that happen and then carry on as he always had, doing precisely as he pleased in pursuit of his goals.

Not that he would tell his grandmother this. She was a Teras, after all. She also liked to win.

As for the potential bride, he was unconcerned. Women were like dessert. Fluffy, sugary, quickly consumed, and easily forgotten.

Asterion had to assume the "decent" ones were too, perhaps beneath a few layers of tedious virtue.

He indicated this, more or less, to his brother. Silently.

He and Poseidon, in perfect accord, nodded. Then they turned back to their grandmother, who sat in her chair looking nothing but serene.

"We will marry the brides of your choice, of course," Asterion said.

Forbiddingly, but that only made Dimitra seem to glow.

"Someone should notify the press," Poseidon added. "As I expect there will be much lamentation. Wailing in the streets, rending of garments—the usual."

But Dimitra Teras only smiled, as if she knew something they didn't.

When surely that was impossible.

CHAPTER TWO

BRITA MARTIS ONLY returned to her father's sad, ruined house that night out of necessity.

That was the only reason she ever went back.

She had spent the better part of this last year camping out in the wildest reaches of the land that her family had stopped pretending to care for generations back. As a child she had crept about the property, looking for the ruins of the old gardens in the tangles of greenery and creeping vines, and trying to find the maze of hedges she'd seen old drawings of in some of the unused rooms.

Even then she had been avoiding her family as much as possible.

These days she preferred to spend her time with the creatures who lived in the wild thickets and dense forests all over the old hills, because she'd always considered them her real family and the woodlands her true home. Brita found fangs and claws and the odd sting significantly more pleasant than spending time with any of the people she was related to by blood, all of whom lived in the old villa—made more of regret and dashed dreams these days than the crumbling, whitewashed stones.

It was late in the evening and she crept in from the

untended sprawl of gardens gone wild slowly. Carefully. Because she had learned that it was far better to know exactly where her father, stepmother, and haughty cousins were than to come upon them unexpectedly or unprepared. That never seemed to go well. It was all slings and arrows, hideous accusations and terrible scenes. She had been heartily sick of the lot of them long ago.

After three years away from her family and their demands, this last year of more contact had been a lot harder than she'd remembered it.

Tonight, she only needed to replenish her supplies and do a bit of laundry. Then she intended to head straight out again, long before dawn. Because she liked to avoid anyone she was related to at all costs and also because she was never happier than when she was sleeping beneath the sky with the wildlife she loved near.

Who needed the questionable ties of her blood relatives when she had all that?

She crossed the wild grass and melted into the shadows at the side of the old villa that had been little more than a shadow of its once resplendent self since well before Brita was born. Something she only knew from the dusty old photographs she'd found in boxes in abandoned rooms here, because it was a fact that no one in her family had taken much care of the place in as long as anyone could remember. *Taking care* of the historic villas of this island kingdom took funds that her family preferred to spend on themselves. The wiring was treacherous if it existed at all, the roof leaked, and there were mice in the walls, but her stepmother drove an aspirational car and could swan about in fashionable clothes in the glitzy beach communities.

The old villa stood, cracked and diminished and largely ignored, as the perfect monument to what had become of the Martis family.

Brita had always related more to the building than her blood. If it was up to her, she would kick out all the parasitical people and give it to the animals she preferred. Sometimes she dreamed she did just that.

The doors and windows were all flung open to let the soft, breezy Mediterranean night inside. Brita knew at a glance that this was not because her father and stepmother, or any of her grasping cousins, had particular affinity for the outdoors. Or cared much for fresh air, for that matter.

It was usually because there was precious little money for air-conditioning, and the house got stifling in the evenings—and they did need to keep the skeleton staff on, lest they be forced to fend for themselves, which meant at least *some* attention to said skeleton staff's well-being. So they opened all the windows and pretended they liked it that way, and far better than noisy machines.

Brita never had to pretend. The sea was *just there*, forever in the corner of everyone's eye no matter where they cared to look, and breezes were plentiful. Especially when she was on one of the cliff tops she considered her very own living room, surrounded by the flora and fauna that were all the family she needed.

And who were also a good deal quieter of an evening. She had learned how to move silently and unseen a long time ago, a skill she used to track wildlife all over the island kingdom these days, the better to rehabilitate the wounded, observe the habits of the healthy, and find her friends. Her own family members were easy game in comparison.

They also made *a lot* more noise.

"Something needs to be done, Vasilis," came her stepmother's voice in the hectoring tone she used all the time but specifically liked to aim at Brita's father. "There is only a month or two left before this trial year of hers is at an end. And then what will become of us? She swans off into a nunnery and we go into the poorhouse?"

As usual, they were discussing Brita.

Out in the dark, she sighed. Quietly.

Had everything gone according to plan—or at least, according to how it had always been since she was a child—they all would have ignored Brita entirely. Her mother had run off from Vasilis when Brita was small and had proven herself unequal to the task of mothering from afar. Or perhaps it was that she had taken her escape when she could, and Brita was simply collateral damage. In any case, she had removed herself from the island and never looked back. Last Brita had heard from her—in a very strange email sometime last year—she was *following her bliss* on a yoga retreat in Indonesia that had so far lasted for *four whole trips around the sun.*

Vasilis had remarried with alacrity. And her new stepmother, the perpetually victimized Nikoletta, had at first wanted to see as little of Brita as possible.

A state of affairs which had suited young Brita just fine.

Brita still thought of those years as glorious, really. She had still been a child and had been left to run about the estate as she pleased. The Martis family, once a part of the aristocracy on this little island kingdom plunked down in the Mediterranean not far from the Greek mainland, had long since lost any of the wealth that had once gone along with their station. So while her father and stepmother and cousins all plotted out various ways to regain it that did not involve lowering themselves to *work* of any kind, Brita had been left to her own devices.

She had greatly enjoyed her own devices.

But then, sadly, it had become more and more clear that she was going to be quite pretty. There had been endless discussions about it. Every time she came in from a carefree tramp about in the woodlands and over the hills she would find them all *peering* at her, but since she considered the lot of them odd—and odder by the day the more she got to know the far friendlier and more approachable wildlife—she'd assumed they'd get bored and stop.

Instead, it got worse. Because as time went on and adolescence enhanced her looks instead of stealing them away into the more typical awkwardness, Brita turned out to be actually rather beautiful.

It had been a disaster.

Overnight, she had been forbidden from roaming the grounds—much less farther afield. She had gone from raising herself as she liked to having an unpleasant committee overseeing her every breath.

Because every last one of her relatives suddenly

needed to rail on about every last detail about Brita and her appearance, from her clothing to her manners to her style of speech. She had been unable to walk three steps without stinging critiques on all sides. It had been as baffling as it was a complete shift from all she knew, and no one had explained it to her.

But soon enough, the reason for this shift became clear.

She'd overheard it in much the same manner as tonight. Because her family liked to sit about tossing back the *ouzo* while Brita preferred to keep her wits about her—and, if possible, from a protected vantage point. Like every other child in all of history, she'd been scolded that eavesdroppers never heard a good word about themselves, but then, she wasn't looking for praise.

Brita was always and ever looking for information, since she was never given explanations. And sooner or later, her garrulous and indiscreet relatives always shouted out the things she wanted to hear when they thought she was tucked away in bed.

It was like a fairy tale, she discovered. The bad parts of the real fairy tales.

Because her family had decided that since Brita was so shockingly and unexpectedly beautiful, all they needed to do to solve their ever-growing financial problems was to marry her off to a suitably rich man. And the more beautiful she got with each passing year, the more wild their fantasies became as they imagined the ways this future wealthy husband of hers would be beholden to the family, a victim to her beauty forevermore.

They were certain they could raise their fortunes from the grave that easily.

The first attempt to hurry up and get her married off had come when she turned eighteen.

On her birthday, her older cousins had produced a selection of suitors, all of them of a certain social class and each less appealing than the last.

Brita had appealed to her stepmother's ambition, taking care to act as if *she* didn't care either way. That was the key, she had learned long ago. The very hint of any emotion and Nikoletta would instantly do the opposite of whatever it was Brita asked, forever on the lookout for ways she could punish her stepdaughter for being the walking, talking reminder of the wife Vasilis liked only in retrospect. And only when drunk.

That time she'd kept her composure and her gambit had worked. She'd been permitted to get an education because, as she'd argued, she needed to learn how to conduct herself in the company of the sorts of great men she knew her stepmother fancied *should* wish to align themselves with the Martis family's spotless pedigree.

The family had skipped her university graduation and, in lieu of the traditional celebration, had presented her instead with the suitor they had chosen for her to wed. This time, they had colluded. Instead of presenting her with a selection, they had all decided that the man in question was the only one who would do.

He was significantly older. Her father's age, if not ten years on. And while he had not been unkind—already an upgrade from the original set of suitors—he had reminded Brita of the sort of unfortunate fish that could only be found deep beneath the sea, walleyed and pasty.

All of which would have made her think twice had she wanted to marry him, but Brita had never had any intention of marrying this man. Or any man. And though she had spent her university years keeping her own counsel, so as not to engage in the unnecessary squabbles her family viewed as sport, she hadn't been able to keep her revulsion in.

One day, while her cousins were sitting around arguing over which famous personages they would invite to the wedding reception, despite not knowing any of them personally, and her father and stepmother were toasting their success, Brita had looked up from her own dinner—made separately in the kitchens by the staff, who she also considered more her family than this lot, because she could not eat the meat of the creatures she cared for—and smiled.

Politely, she had thought.

I will not marry him, she said. Very simply.

Don't be childish, Nikoletta had snapped back at once, slamming her glass down on the scarred surface of the old table, the scene of many an operatic family battle. *You'll do what you're told.*

Brita had made sure to take a moment and look each of them in the eye, one after the next, to make certain they were all paying attention. *I won't.*

They had not taken this pronouncement well.

There had been the usual shouting and screaming, and much damage to objects and walls. There had been threats aplenty. They had locked her in her room, because they knew so little about her that they were unaware that she had been sneaking out into the hills since she was small. They had told her that she would no longer be allowed the *privilege* of the vegetarian food she preferred, and she'd heard them chortling about that cruelty while in their cups, because they had no idea that it wasn't only Brita who viewed the long-suffering staff with great fondness. The staff liked her back. They would never keep food from her. They simply made sure she got it in secret, usually when she crept into the kitchens to eat with them, as she had been doing since she was small. Far better than attempting to digest anything in the midst of the usual nightly battles.

This nonsense went on for a whole summer.

In the end, Vasilis had given her an ultimatum. *You will marry this man or you will become a nun, destined to live out your days in a convent, with nothing to do but pray for deliverance. Do you understand me?*

Brita had packed her bags for the local convent that night.

And rather than being the punishment her father imagined, Brita found her time as a novitiate quite pleasant. She liked the schedule of the days and the solitude of so much prayer. She liked the company and her shared labor with the sisters in the convent gardens and kitchens. There were never any temper tantrums. There were no tedious scenes.

No one was ever drunk and disorderly.

But the best part of the convent was that the sisters were far more interested in who Brita was as a person and what gifts she could bring to bear in her time with them than her family ever had been.

Not one of them seemed to notice or care that she was beautiful.

Instead, they asked her about her dreams. And when she told them that she had always wanted nothing more than to open some sort of wildlife sanctuary here on the island, they hadn't laughed in her face like her cousins, or angrily dismissed her like her father and stepmother.

On the contrary. The sisters loved the idea.

Instead of being a punishment, being consigned to a life of monasticism was the freest Brita had felt around other people since she had been a largely ignored child.

But the order did not allow anyone to take more permanent vows without first making absolutely certain that giving her life to the church in this way was right for her.

I know it's right, Brita had argued, because she would have been happy never to see her relatives again.

But the Abbess had only smiled in her serene way. *You must take this year not to ask what it is* you *know, child. But instead what it is that He requires of you.*

It was that part of her life of piety that Brita found the most challenging. The looking for answers instead of making her own as she went along.

Still, she had gamely gone off to test herself in the world.

That was the point of the trial year, the sisters had all assured her. To go and tempt herself with everything that the world had to offer, all the things she enjoyed that had no part in convent life, so she could decide if this quiet life of contemplation was truly for her.

Brita had spent the year wandering through the wildest parts of the island, taking note of all the animals and birds and assorted creatures who lived there, making friends with some of them and helping those who needed it. It had been a long year, but a good one, and she was looking forward to the life she planned to build in the convent.

She had almost forgotten that her family was opposed to that life. They had expected her to beg them to let her come home, but she never had. Maybe it wasn't really a shock to discover that they were still bound and determined to marry her off anyway, whether she liked it or not.

But out here in the shadows, where she had always been—where she preferred to be—it felt like a rather large shock all the same.

Since she couldn't recall the last time any one of them had bothered to have so much as a conversation with her, how could they be so certain that she would obey them? Why would she want to when they had never been able to even feign a passing interest in her—aside from what her assortment of features could buy them?

"Exactly how much of her input is really required?" one of her older cousins asked in his oily way. "Surely we can slip her a few pills and be done with it. She wouldn't be the first bride in the world who was less than *compos mentis* at her own nuptials."

"This is the modern age," another agreed. "Surely the priest can be bribed like anyone else."

It was probably only that she hadn't heard them talk about her in a while now—a deliberate choice on her part that she underscored by staying far away—that their words landed so hard. Brita sighed a little, shook it off, and then made her way around to the far side of the old house. None of the family ever bothered with this wing of the villa. It had been closed off in her grandfather's day, with sheets thrown over all the furniture that hadn't been sold and bartered away to pay the bills over the years.

This was the part of the villa she liked. This part had always been hers. Where her cousins saw sad old ghosts of lost splendor, Brita saw her happiest memories. Playing tag with the cook. Hiding out with old photographs. Reading her way through every book about the island and its wildlife she could find.

At some point, Vasilis would have to start selling off parts of the Martis estate, and that would break her heart, because to him it was nothing but land, but to her it was worlds within worlds, a universe of memories and comfort, furry friends and feathered things who watched over her when no one else ever had.

Eventually he would have to sell the villa, too, and she was all too aware that no potential buyer was likely to take on such an overwhelming renovation project. They were far more likely to knock the place down and put in condos in this neglected part of the island where tourists never ventured.

Brita didn't like to think about it.

Instead, she called on one of the most important lessons she'd learned from her many, many hours in this abandoned part of the house. That being her encyclopedic knowledge of which windows were never latched. And which were accessible even if they were.

She pulled one open now, hoisted herself onto the ledge, then swung herself inside.

Another skill her childhood had taught her was how to move like a ghost through the house itself, and the staff liked her too much to react to the way she slipped in and out of rooms as she wished, sometimes spooking them when she did. She did a load of laundry, avoided her stepmother tottering down the hallway muttering about *faded glory,* and took a long bath. Then she dressed again, packed up the supplies she needed in her bag, and made her way down to the kitchen with her beloved quiver and bow over her shoulder.

"They've all gone a bit mad tonight," the cook, Maria, murmured when Brita came in. "You know what they're like. Too much *tsipouro* and they think it's a feudal system around here."

"The last time I came home, I suggested that Cousin Panagiota do the marrying," Brita reminded her. Both she and Maria laughed at that notion. "Since she is so big on the idea."

"As if madam would ever submit herself to such an indignity." Maria hooted. "Besides, she still thinks she's going to trade on the Martis name and snag herself one of the few remaining nobles cluttering up the hills."

Brita rolled her eyes and settled in for one of her favorite sorts of discussions—in this case, a philosophical exploration of what nobility even meant on an island like this, where everyone knew that the real power was in the wealth and consequence of men like the mighty Teras brothers, who were known the world over and regularly appeared in flashy events with famous people, or so everyone told her every time their names were mentioned.

She personally wouldn't know a Teras brother if she tripped over one of them.

These days, the island was still a kingdom—but in name only. She couldn't remember the last time the old queen had even bothered to cast an eye outside her fancy palace. Why should she? The island ran on tourism, commerce, and the influx of wealthy businessmen who wanted nothing more than to get in with corporate giants like the Minotaur Group and Hydra Shipping, both Teras family enterprises.

In her more charitable moments, which came along more rarely these days, she thought it was a sad sort of disappointment that her family was so determined to cling to a way of life that had never been theirs in the first place. Not in any of their lifetimes, anyway.

But before she and Maria could really get into what was one of their favorite topics for long nights in this very kitchen, a man appeared.

One moment it was just her and Maria and the villa's old kitchen, where they had spent many an evening together when Brita was supposedly confined to her bedchamber, confident that none of the rest of the family would ever demean themselves by entering a place where grubby scrub work was done by servants.

Brita had hoisted herself up on one of the counters,

and was swinging her feet against the cabinets below her, snacking on a bit of bread and cheese that Maria had slid her way.

But suddenly and without warning the man appeared, and she froze.

And the only thing that had ever felt the way she did in this moment was when she'd been caught out in a storm last summer. She'd miscalculated and had found herself with no cover, but she hadn't panicked.

Instead, she'd been forced to surrender herself to the rain, the wind, the crack of lightning high over the island's hills.

And it hadn't felt like a surrender at all.

She'd felt elemental. Alive.

As if she was a part of the same great upheaval as the storm that crashed through the sky. As if it lived in her.

Some part of her thought it had, ever since, and now she looked at this man in the kitchen doorway and could see that same *immensity*.

That same intense, awe-inducing electricity.

She felt shocked straight through, the way she had when lightning had forked across the sky *just there*—so close she could nearly *touch* it—making her skin burn, but tonight that burning was inside as well as out.

It was all a kind of narrowing spiral, tighter and tighter, and it landed like heat between her legs.

"Begging your pardon, sir," Maria said in a far more polite tone of voice that anything Brita could imagine attempting to get out, even if the old queen herself had appeared before her in all her finery. "But I think you might have lost your way. The family are all gathered in the other part of the house."

But Brita hardly heard her. She couldn't seem to look away from the man before her, who hadn't moved from the threshold, yet still seemed to crowd the rambling kitchen.

Until everything was airless.

Particularly her.

He was so *severe,* she thought. No one to be trifled with.

All he did was stand there, and though the way he held his body should have seemed nonchalant, it wasn't.

Nothing about him is casual, she found herself thinking, the way she would about any wild thing, and no matter that this one wore a dark suit that whispered of wealth and consequence instead of a pelt or some fur.

There was an intensity that rippled within him, and from him.

He gazed at Maria for a long moment, acknowledging her, and then he shifted that gaze to Brita. And held it there.

Lightning struck again, hard and deep.

"I'm not here for the family," he said, and the way he looked at her, Brita thought he knew. She thought he knew every crackle of that lightning that struck her again and again, every kiss of electricity and wonder. "I'm here for you."

CHAPTER THREE

IT WAS WORSE—much worse—than Asterion had anticipated.

And his expectations had been markedly low.

When Dimitra explained to him who she expected
him to marry, he stared at her as if she had taken leave
of her senses at last. He almost said as much. He almost
suggested that time came inexorably for everyone, and
perhaps her razor-sharp intellect was not the weapon it
had once been.

He restrained himself. By a hair.

"I do not understand the resistance," his grandmother
replied, though her dark eyes danced. "Brita Martis is a
young woman of great virtue. You would be lucky indeed
if she were to lower herself to the likes of you."

"She is a nun," Asterion said shortly. "An actual nun,
Yia Yia."

"Best of luck to you then," she replied smoothly. "You
like to consider yourself a god among men, do you not?
Now is your chance to prove that you are equal to the
god she has already pledged to follow."

There had been nothing for it but to seek out the para-
gon in question. And the fact that the woman was an un-

touched saint was not what bothered the decidedly sinful Asterion the most when he set out to deliver the good news to her—that he would be changing her life for the better.

It was that the woman in question wasn't even in residence in said nunnery to receive him or her own great luck. When he had gone there, doing his best to appear the part of the besotted suitor—or really, any man who wasn't him and might therefore do things like seek out women instead of brush them off in droves—the nun who stood in the doorway and denied him entrance told him that Brita was not there.

He had not allowed for that possibility. He had, at first, been unable to take it on board. Surely nuns remained in their nunneries instead of roaming about. That was, as far as Asterion was aware, the purpose of herding them into monastic collectives in the first place.

"Brita is out on her trial year, as it happens," the nun before him told him with an unhurriedness that made it clear she answered to no earthly man, and certainly not to the likes of Asterion. "Her last hurrah, if you will." When Asterion stared back at her blankly, she continued in the same untroubled manner. "It is a whole year in which to immerse herself in all of the world's temptations to see if she can find her way back to the Lord."

He had always imagined that these places preferred to lock the world out forever and hide away from it, fearful that any stray hint of its existence outside their prayers would bring all their devils crashing in with vengeance aplenty. It was fascinating that these nuns went in the opposite direction, but he did not wish to find himself fascinated by a nun. Or any other creature so wholly un-impressed with him. "And if she does not?"

The austere sister eyed him in a manner that reminded him entirely too much of Dimitra. "Then she has a different path to walk than ours, with our blessing. We will pray for her."

Asterion decided this plot twist was a good thing. If she was off kicking up her heels in the sorts of clubs and bars that crowded the beaches here, the places where all the ill-behaved tourists liked to congregate while addled on drink and too much sunshine, all the better. It was always possible his grandmother had been mistaken about this woman's virtue.

Despite what she herself professed to believe and claimed could be easily proven, his grandmother was not, in fact, infallible.

After some investigating, Asterion had not liked finding out that as far as anyone could tell, Brita Martis was some sort of virgin huntress. She was rumored to be as uncivilized as the animals she cared for, roaming the hills of the island like a wild thing with a bow and her arrows. Like something out of a myth.

Not that she hunted animals. It was strongly suggested that said bow and its arrows were entirely for making certain that men did not bother her.

And they did not.

Those were the sorts of stories that were told about her in the villages. That sometimes, on a full moon, you could see Brita roaming the hills, flanked by wolves and deer and all manner of woodland creatures.

Some said they were her friends. Some claimed they were her army.

What everyone agreed on was that no matter how wild Brita might be, she was still better than her family, who lived on top of each other in that falling-down old villa out on the far side of the island, dreaming of glory days past.

Dimitra had always had a wicked sense of humor.

Asterion had never been much for hunting in the wilderness when there were empires to topple instead, though he had to believe the principles were the same. Tonight, he had waited about outside the Martis villa as he had done for nearly a week now. All of the information he and his people had collected had indicated that she returned to the family estate now and again, but none of his sources thought it particularly credible she would march in the front door and interact with her family in the normal way when she otherwise went to such lengths to avoid them.

He'd been beginning to think she was nothing more than a figment of everyone's overwrought imaginations when he'd seen her at last, slipping across the grounds from the untended mess of former gardens that tangled their way off into the hills.

She kept to the shadows outside the villa's windows, pausing briefly before going on around toward the back. He'd followed at a distance, circling until he saw her inside. Nowhere near the reception rooms at the front, where the liquor flowed freely, but in the back with the servants.

He was not one to lurk about now that his quarry was in sight, and so he walked straight in.

Then stopped, as if held in place by an unseen hand.

He might have found that an outrage to be addressed, but he could not focus on it. Because she stared at him, and he stared back.

And that seemed to take a very long while.

Asterion could not wait to ask his grandmother what on earth she'd been thinking.

For Brita Martis was exactly as wild as it had been said she was. Maybe more.

Her black hair flowed all about her, part of it still wet, a mess of unruly waves that fell nearly to her waist. He had expected to find her wearing the hides of animals, dirt and twigs, and so it was a slight disappointment that she was dressed reasonably enough in what looked like tactical hiking trousers, a formfitting tank top, and a button-down shirt that was falling off one of her slender shoulders.

She had obviously just bathed, so perhaps the dirt, twigs, and skins were next on the sartorial agenda, but that wasn't the trouble here.

It wasn't even that she wore her *otherness* like the skins she'd left off tonight, visible in the way she sat, the way she stared back at him, the way she *breathed*.

The real trouble with Brita Martis, which no one had bothered to mention to him, was that she was objectively beautiful.

Just…beautiful. Astonishingly so.

Stunning, to be more precise.

Asterion, who had long prided himself on his cynicism and his immunity to the usual blandishments of attractive women, recognized that he was actually *stunned*.

Nothing could have appalled him more.

Her face was like a work of art, the kind involving oil and paint and old masters, or perhaps the sensual touch of marble. Her hair was black, her eyes were a kind of brilliant bronze and gold, and everything else about her a pageant of symmetry and feminine glory. With sensual lips that made him hunger to taste her, and the hint of supple curves. He had the sudden thought that it was no wonder she would rather spend time with wild animals, because surely every man who gazed upon her became little more than a slavering beast at the sight.

He was close to such a display himself, when Asterion had always been about control. It wasn't a *preference*, it was a *necessity*, because he had seen where letting go led. He had been in the same car that had killed most of his family, and he remembered the fiery, passionate, high-decibel relationship his parents had indulged in that had caused it.

He had vowed that he would never allow himself such a loss of restraint.

He had never imagined that vow would be tested. In all his days and the many women he'd sampled, it never had been.

Which was to say, he had never stared at a woman before as if he'd been cut in two.

As if there was a great divide between all that had come before, and now.

Having seen her.

As if that simple act had changed him, Asterion Teras, who was like the great rock where he'd built his house and started his business—always the same impossibly hard surface, impervious to the attempts of time and weather to alter him in any way.

He felt something roar in him, deep.

As if he was no rock after all but another wild thing, and here she was, the local myth all wild things followed—

But Asterion followed no one. He was only doing his grandmother's bidding at present because it had to do with his fortune. His legacy.

The only things he cared about.

His fortune because he controlled it ruthlessly and made it do what he liked.

His legacy because it mattered to Dimitra, and she was the only woman who mattered to him, or ever would.

He told himself it had nothing at all to do with the heat and ache in his sex and the urge he had to roar out these strange things inside him like the beast he'd never been. To tear down this villa if he had to and carry her off—

But he was not one of the storybook creatures the villagers claimed followed her about adoringly or became her minions every full moon, depending.

Though he thought he would never know how it was he didn't give in to the urge to become one, there in the door to that rumpled, ancient kitchen.

"I need your help," he told her instead, sounding quite pleasant and conversational to his ear. And though he had planned to say that all along, it was a little more close to the truth than he liked. "You are Brita Martis, are you not? The nun who can charm any animal she sees?"

He could see she liked that description. She tilted her head slightly, though her gaze was solemn. "I'm not a nun. Nor an animal charmer. Though I am Brita Martis, all the same. That part is true enough."

"There's something crying on the cliffs near my home," he told her, giving the words the same sort of solemnity. "It's been going on some while. I was told that you might be the one who can find the source of the sound and perhaps save the poor creature, whatever it is."

There were no cries. He was lying—though he preferred to think it not quite a *lie*. It was, instead, a deliberate snare. A little trap, that was all.

"And you tracked me down here?" She lifted her chin. "Most people do not present themselves around the back of a stranger's house in the middle of the night. Or perhaps things are different wherever it is you live, Mr....?"

It had been a long while since someone failed to recognize him on sight. Asterion wasn't sure he believed that it was a possibility, not on this island where his family was more recognizable than the queen, since they actually ventured out into daylight from time to time.

And, of course, everyone knew what had happened to them. And more, what he and Poseidon had made out of that wreckage.

Whether it was a slight or sheer ignorance, he ignored it. "I would have gone to the front door, but there were no lights on. When I followed the sounds I heard around the side, there appeared to be a great many people arguing in one of the rooms." He made an ineffective sort of gesture that felt entirely wrong, which was how he knew that he should lean into it. That had been his grandmother's only advice, such as it was.

Try to be something other than who you are, she had told him. *You catch more flies with honey than with vinegar, child.*

Though he did not think she could possibly know if that was so, having embodied all that was vinegar for the whole of her life. "So I kept going until I found you here."

Some women would blush and stammer. This one did neither. "Who told you about me?"

Asterion was assaulted by the strangest sensation. On the one hand, he was obviously amazed and astonished that she didn't leap to do his bidding like everyone else did without question. On the other, it was reasonable to be suspicious of a stranger turning up as he had.

He decided he was glad that this otherworldly creature, who he must wed no matter what, was not as foolhardy as her actions had suggested she would be, gallivanting about in the hills day and night. By herself, no less.

And so he chose to answer her question. He named several shopkeepers in the biggest village on the island. After a moment, she nodded, and so he inclined his head. "I am sorry we have not had occasion to meet before. I am Asterion Teras."

Then he watched, intrigued, as her face…changed. "Oh," she murmured, exchanging a look with the red-cheeked, yet otherwise poker-faced woman at her side. "You would be. I should have known."

He would have followed that up, that artless *you would be,* but she was sliding off the counter then. And she was landing on the cracked floor with a kind of athletic lithe-ness that made his whole body go tight. Hot.

Asterion was a big man, but she was taller than most of the local women, and he liked it. Better yet, she did not stoop her shoulders as many tall women did when they were not models or the like, trying to make themselves smaller. Her hair was curling as they spoke, making her look even wilder as it tumbled down her back. He had no trouble at all believing that she did nothing with her time but roam up and down the hills of the island, communing with nature at will.

"Come," she said to him and frowned slightly, a good reminder that he could not stand there and stare at her like this. That it would lead nowhere good.

Or at least, not to the sort of *wooing* he knew his grandmother had in mind.

"Let's not delay if something's hurt," she said, clearly not impressed with the fact he wasn't already making tracks.

She exchanged another glance with the cook and then came toward him, making his chest feel tight—but he had taken a step or two farther inside as they'd talked. And so she only moved past him, smelling faintly of rosemary and deep green things he knew he could not name, heading out the door of the kitchen into the darkness.

Leaving him no choice but to follow her.

He chose not to acknowledge that he wanted to follow her. A lot more than he cared to admit.

And having very little to do with Dimitra's demands.

Outside, Brita took to the shadows again and he followed suit. He watched the supple way she covered ground, not seeming to react to the sound of her family's voices. They were harsh and clearly inebriated, pouring out into the night. Polluting it.

But if it bothered her, she did not seem to give a sign except for the wide berth she gave the windows.

When they were at the still dark and forbidding front of the house once more, she adjusted the bow she carried, altered the way the strap of her bag lay over her shoulder, and then made as if to head off into the hills.

"I did drive here," Asterion pointed out. "It seemed a more efficient mode of travel than a great hike through the underbrush. At this hour."

Brita looked at him. But said nothing.

"When, as you say," he continued with great piety, "there could be something hurt awaiting you."

He was not normally given to outright lies. Then again, there *could* be something hurt there. Or anywhere.

She glided beside him as he walked down the drive, then glowered at him in earnest when he stopped beside his low-slung sports car and opened the passenger door for her.

"How did that do on the drive out here?" she asked with a suspicious lack of inflection. "Last I checked, the ruts in the dirt road could swallow a bull or two whole."

"I am an excellent driver," he assured her, though he had already called his staff to make certain the car's undercarriage was checked thoroughly upon his return.

Brita did not respond, though the *way* she failed to say anything felt like a rebuke all its own. Then she slid inside the car so many simply toppled into instead, another hint of that easy physical grace that he could see might very well become intoxicating.

It was impossible not to think about…all the potential applications.

As long as he did so in an appropriately analytical fashion.

He closed the door and was glad of the walk around to his side. He ordered himself back under control.

Not something he had ever need to concern himself with before now.

If it weren't for his grandmother's threats, he would end this right now.

He was sure he would—if he could.

The moon up above them played hide-and-seek with the clouds as he drove them across the island, down the deeply rutted dirt track that eventually led to the more accessible road hugging the coast, always kept in top shape for tourists and their holiday photographs. Then, before hitting the stretch of the most popular beaches, bristling all year round and bright tonight as they drove on the high road above them, he headed up into the hills.

Then, at last, he navigated the car—definitely not sounding its best—out onto the bluff where he'd built the house that he liked to call his labyrinth.

It hugged the cliff in a vertical drop, half in and half out of the rock face, and his own drive wound its way through a bit of wilderness. Beside him, Brita seemed content to remain silent, but she rolled down the window as they drove closer to the cliffs.

It took him a moment to realize that she was listening. Intently.

For the cries he had told her she would hear.

Asterion did not feel guilty about that. He wouldn't know the feeling anyway, he assured himself, so alien was it to him—though he rubbed absently at his chest.

He drove up to the very small part of his house that was actually on the bluff and parked, but this time, she did not wait for him to circle the vehicle to let her out. She climbed out herself and then stood there, her head cocked slightly as she listened to the wind rushing up from the sea far below. Rushing through the trees all around them. Making its own song of wildness and far-off lands as it danced where it liked.

He led her, not down into his house proper, but only on to the great garden terrace at the top that looked almost as wild as the hill behind them. It was extensively landscaped to appear so, except for the glass dome in the center that was, he could admit it, a bit much for a front door.

But Brita did not comment on it.

Unlike every other person who he had ever brought here, she did not spare even a glance for the house.

It was his very own personal feat of engineering, one twisting level after the next, crawling down into the rock and all along the outside of the cliff's sheer drop. It had been written up in too many architectural magazines to count. It was so famous that it was a stop, out in the water, for tourists on their round-the-island boat trips.

He found it…bracing that this woman he'd found in a villa that was already more or less a ruin seemed not to care. Or really even notice.

She followed after him, yet was not paying attention *to* him, and they had walked almost to the other side of the flat garden terrace—beyond which was only the cliff's edge and the sea below—before Asterion was forced to accept that he could not recall, in the whole of his existence, another situation where his mere presence was not enough to send the woman in his company into paroxysms of giddy delight.

In point of fact, Brita hardly seemed to notice that she was in his company at all. She walked beside him, but she was still listening, clearly. For the sound of a creature in distress.

He still did not consider it a *lie*. He was a powerful man used to doing what he must to achieve the results he desired. It was no more and no less than that.

There was no earthly reason why he should keep worrying the fact of it over and over in his head, like he really was this person he was playing. *He* did not waffle about. *He* made decisions, executed the appropriate actions, and dealt with the consequences as they came.

It was all part and parcel of the control he had exerted over himself and everything in his orbit since he was all of twelve.

It was this bizarre woman who was tangling things up inside him, that was all. No one had thought to give her a script. No one had ever explained to her how she ought to act in the presence of a man like him.

Clearly.

"You must know that in the villages people speak of you in tones of awe," he told her when they stopped walking, so she could stand still, continuing to both *listen* and act as if she was alone. "Some think you're a reincarnation of one of the old goddesses. An immortal huntress, worthy of sacrifice. Daily worship. The usual rituals."

He expected her to laugh a bit. Something sparkling, effortless. The way women always did when he spoke, no matter what he said. Though he thought that this, perhaps, was the first time he had ever attempted to offer a statement that was even remotely like a compliment.

Brita did not giggle. She didn't even look at him, then away, eyes glinting, the way some did.

She didn't look at him at all.

"That's very silly," she said instead. "I don't think the sisters at the convent would find that the least bit entertaining."

Then she walked on again, moving ahead of him until she stood at the very edge of his cliff, where there were only smooth, rounded stones, large enough to serve as tables or the odd sacrificial altar, in place of any kind of fence. Brita did not cringe away from the edge, nor did she make the usual comments about the house's steep drop and how dangerous this all was, this open cliff top he called home.

Instead, Brita Martis, virgin huntress and possible myth, jumped up neatly to stand on one of the rocks set there.

Only then did she look all around, taking in the sweep of rocky cliff on either side, and the lights in his labyrinth of a house, twisting its way down the steep drop.

"I can't hear anything," she said after a moment. "Are you certain this is where you were when you heard the cry?"

"I'm certain."

He had thought this the perfect way to begin this farce, but now he was doubting himself, and Asterion had no experience whatsoever with such a state. He was a Teras. He did not doubt himself. He was genetically predisposed to have not a shred of doubt, ever.

But it had not occurred to him that he could bring a woman into his presence and have her…concentrate instead on the task at hand.

It might have been lowering indeed, had he been able to process it.

"There are cats as well as birds that can make a variety of noises that sound a lot like cries of pain or terror, but neither is necessarily the case." She turned back around and gazed down at him, and he was struck, again, by her beauty. As if she truly had loosed an arrow and shot it straight into the center of his chest.

Brita looked like a kind of statue in the moonlight, carved from warm, supple marble and made into a woman by loving hands. Breezes from the hill and the sea caught at her dark tendrils and she didn't seem to mind—or notice—letting them flow about her as her eyes scanned the darkness all around them.

"I'm familiar with the sounds of seabirds," he found himself saying.

"I would think so, with the house perched up here like its own sort of mast. I'm surprised it's not covered in—"

"As the house is an architectural marvel," Asterion found himself saying, as if he was made of a far harder stone than marble, or as if he was the sort of person who allowed himself such base, low, reactive *feelings* in the first place, "we have always felt best to keep it as free of bird droppings as possible." That gaze of hers on his, that combination of gold and silver, felt like another blow and he found himself continuing. "In consultation with all relevant authorities, of course, so as not to disturb the local bird colonies. What do you take me for?"

It was only then, standing so that she towered over him and looked down at him with her arms bare to the night—the wind in her hair, and not the faintest hint of the usual reaction he got from women anywhere visible on her face—Brita, not quite a nun, actually seemed to give him her full attention.

"I know of you," she replied. "I grew up on this island. It would be impossible to avoid tales of you and the rest of your family."

"Unlike tales of your goddess-like immortality, the stories about my family are likely true."

"I have never met a man carved from sadness and stone," she said, in that same matter-of-fact way. There was no coy glance. There was no sideways sort of smile to soften what she was saying. "That's what they say you are. But you don't look so very different from any other man. I hope you don't mind, but it's a bit of a letdown."

Asterion could scarcely credit what he was hearing. "A *letdown*?"

She nodded, but she was already turning away. Her hands were on her hips now, the better to survey the area again. "Think about it from my perspective. I spent my whole life hearing about the Monster of the Mediterranean and then here you are. Perfectly pleasant. Like everyone on this island overdosed on their own overactive imaginations."

"*Perfectly pleasant*," Asterion echoed with all the arrogance and affront he had in him, but it had no effect. Because once again, she wasn't paying him the slightest attention. "I have been called many things in my time, Brita, but never *pleasant*."

"I suppose it's the money," she said in that forthright way, almost as if she couldn't hear the inflection in his voice. As if she was entirely earnest, and deaf to any possible implications. "You have so very much of it that it must inspire people to make up things about you. That you're a monster. That you storm about the planet, ripping fortunes from the hands of anyone silly enough to stand against you, blah blah blah. That's easier to stomach than the truth."

"And what," he asked, because he could not seem to keep himself from it, "is the truth?"

She turned back to him then and tipped her head to one side, the way he already knew she did when she was studying a situation. Surveying it.

He did not know how to process the fact that this half-wild woman was looking at him as if he was the one in need of *explanation*. As if he was the one who made no sense.

"You were born with quite a lot of it, weren't you?" She lifted a shoulder. "Once, a very long time ago, my family also had a lot of money. But they've been spending it ever since, and now there is none. Therefore, it's all that my family talks about. If I had to guess, I'd say that no one in your family talks about money. Why bother? It's assumed to be too abundant to mention, like the sea."

This was accurate, and so Asterion couldn't say why it sat on him so heavily. He should have rejoiced that this woman who would be marrying him, and soon, despite all this nonsense, was able to read him. That she seemed to do so with a careless ease that a great many of his rivals in tense negotiations would likely kill for.

You should rejoice, he ordered himself.

But he did not. He could not, somehow.

"I know of your family," he said in turn, and less... pleasantly. "There have been members of the Martis clan on this island for a great many generations."

"And the last of them are currently hunkered down in that old villa," she agreed briskly. "Waiting for their former glory to be restored. They don't have a concrete plan, in case you wondered. The prevailing hope is that they will wake up one morning and find themselves fabulously wealthy again. And who knows? Stranger things have happened."

"Strange things happen all the while," he agreed, unable, somehow to wrench his gaze from hers. "But generally not where vast fortunes are concerned."

She inclined her head at that, as if in agreement. Then she leaped off the rock and back onto the terrace, making scarcely any sound at all when she landed.

Asterion realized that he was impressed with her.

It was another thing he wasn't sure he'd ever felt before. It moved in him...loudly.

Like an imperative.

"Do you have a mobile?" she asked, and he was beginning to feel weary at how easily she could surprise him. But she wasn't like any other woman he'd ever encountered. For one thing, despite himself, he was the one impressed when it was normally the opposite. And she was bold, unusual, and looking at him now.

Expectantly.

"Yes," he managed to say, horrified that he was not controlling this situation the way he should. The way he controlled every other thing around him without effort. "I have a mobile. Of course I have a mobile." He had several. "Does anyone *not* have one in this day and age?"

She held out her hand instead of answering that, and he had the experience of feeling churlish, like some kind of child in a sulk, while also feeling compelled to obey her. It was another astonishment to add to the lot.

It was not a positive.

He dug in his pocket, pulled out his mobile phone, and handed it to her.

Obediently.

And then stood there, the fearsome CEO of the Minotaur Group, who had never given an inch when he could instead take the entire territory, as she helped herself to a swipe here and a type there, until she handed it straight back to him.

"Spyware?" he asked, perhaps more acerbically than warranted.

Though he would have to instruct his staff to check the mobile as well as his poor car.

"Call me when you hear the crying again," she said,

with only the faintest quizzical look about the eyes to indicate she heard his comment on *spyware*.

He noted that she looked very much as if she hoped he wouldn't call her. This wild huntress who wanted nothing to do with him.

With *him*.

That thought shot through him like another one of her arrows.

"I will," he said, fighting to get back to pleasant-sounding words and vague, indecisive gestures, like the man he'd tried to pretend he was. "I appreciate you coming tonight. But if you'll forgive me, how dire are your family's circumstances? Is it the lack of funds that has you roaming the hills as you do? The rumors I heard in the villages are that you often sleep beneath the stars."

"I could stay in the villa," she said, conversationally enough, as if the state of her family was of little matter to her. Or perhaps, he thought then, it was that its dysfunction was to her what wealth was to him. Unworthy of comment, so obvious was it. He felt an unusual sensation in the region of his ribs, but ignored it, thus proving he could control *something*. "But you see, I only had a year."

"A year?"

Until tonight, he had taken great pride in the fact that he never asked a question in a negotiation unless he already knew the answer.

She looked at him again, all of that dark gold threaded through with bronze, and he felt it like a touch. "I suppose it's a gap year of sorts. I spent three years in the convent, learning how to be a nun. This is the year we take off from all that. We are sent off to rejoin the world, to see if we really, truly want to leave it behind."

"You are not actually a nun," he said.

But he could hardly take stock of the ruckus that caused in him, because Brita smiled.

It was…not better.

It was also glorious.

The smile changed her face as if her very own moon shined down upon her, and he had already imagined too well the things he could do with her. That lithe body. That gorgeous face. The curves he could see there, adding interest to her athletic form.

But now he could imagine nothing else.

He was not sure he ever would, and he certainly didn't know what to do with that. It was nearly poetic. It was not him at all.

It was a nightmare.

Yet he could not wake.

"Almost," Brita told him. "I am *almost* a nun. I only have about two months left before I take the veil."

Then—either unconcerned or wholly unaware of her effect on him—she walked around him, sauntered back through his garden terrace, and melted off into the night.

And she didn't look back.

Not even once.

He knew because he watched her the whole way, until there was only night where she had been, and he was all alone on his cliff top with nothing save the wind.

CHAPTER FOUR

TWO NIGHTS LATER, Brita was sitting at one of her favorite viewpoints. It was high on a rocky outcropping in the hills, far away from the tangle of the touristy villages down below. She liked to sit there most nights, but especially on nights like this one, when she could watch the moon rise over the sea.

The wolf pup she'd saved from a trap the previous winter sat next to her, panting slightly. She called him Heracles, and he whined when she glanced at him, leaning his shoulder against her legs.

Heracles wouldn't let her pet him, proud wolf that he was, but if she sat still enough he would sometimes lean in to show his affection.

She was going to miss this.

For many reasons, but foremost among them the fact she hadn't seen any kind of physical affection in the convent. The sisters prayed. They sang. They cooked food together and ate it together. But in the three years she'd spent there, studying them and their ways, no one had ever leaned in the way this mighty wolf was now.

It was only the creatures she'd spent so much time with who ever had.

The closer it got to the end of her year of temptation, the more bittersweet it all felt. Because so much would be different when she was back in the convent. As supportive as the sisters were about her ideas for a wildlife refuge, and as comforting as she found a sedate life with a predictable routine, it wasn't as if the sisters were going to take to wolf cubs galloping about the convent. Or any of the other creatures that liked to follow Brita about and, sometimes, lean in for a bit of comfort and communion.

You are just like a raggedy, uncouth Snow White, her stepmother had once sneered over an empty bottle of whatever she'd been necking that night.

Brita had taken that as a compliment. *Did you know*, she'd replied, *that animals are far better judges of character than we humans are? They can sense bad intentions from kilometers away. And they never suffer fools*.

She had been sent to her room without any food that day, though sadly it had been Maria's day off, and she still thought it was worth it.

That was life, wasn't it? The peace in the convent came at a price.

Everything did.

That was the one lesson her family had taught her that she had taken to heart, because she knew too well it was true.

"But who ever told you that life was designed to make you happy?" she asked in a low sort of voice, halfway to a croon so that Heracles made a low noise in response.

He was a talker. Between him and the moon and the sea, who could be lonely?

"Why should you not be happy?" came another voice. From behind her.

But Brita recognized it instantly.

Maybe it was more accurate to say that her body responded to it instantly, the way it had done every time she'd thought of him since that first night.

And, for some reason, she had thought about the so-called Monster of the Mediterranean *a lot.*

He had interrupted her sleep. He had given her twisty, dark, aching dreams that haunted her, though they made no sense. They left her wide-awake with too many *feelings* pouring all over her and through her like honey, her body flushed and sensitive and *heavy*—

Brita had been certain she must be ill. Though none of the usual remedies she employed seemed to help.

Heracles growled softly, then loped off. She knew he was finding a new vantage point, where he would stay and watch over her from afar. That was what he did.

And Brita didn't *need* to turn to see who it was who stood some distance away from her on this particular hilltop, but she did anyway. Because, something in her admitted softly, she *wanted* to look at him. How bizarre was that?

Why should the very notion of looking at the man make her feel a rush of that strange sickness all over again?

The first time she'd seen him, he had looked as she expected a man like him would. He'd worn the typical rich man's dark, bespoke suit in a fabric that seemed to hug his body in ways her father's attire thankfully never did. It should have seemed formal and odd, but he had somehow made it seem almost casual.

Or perhaps it had been that he exuded a certain confidence that made it clear that he was as at his ease when strolling into a stranger's kitchen as he was standing out on his personal cliff top. *He* was at ease wherever he went, his whole *person* seemed to whisper, and Brita understood this without having to ask.

In that way, this man was not so different from a wolf.

Though Heracles had never made her feel so inordinately feverish.

Tonight Asterion Teras was dressed in truly casual clothes. He wore a pair of trousers that she hadn't heard from afar, which suggested they were made of a fabric both soft and likely dear. And worse by far for her equanimity, he was wearing a T-shirt.

Brita could not recall ever having a reaction to a *T-shirt* before. She never paid much attention to men and the things they wore. They were not animals who needed her, so unless they were actively repulsive to her—the ones who *gaped* at her, or encouraged her to *smile,* or became irate if she did not respond to them, or wished to marry her at her father's command—she did not see them. She must have been presented with a great number of T-shirts before in her lifetime, particularly as she lived on an island filled with tourists decked out in holiday gear, but it was a shocking truth that she couldn't remember a single one. Not one like this. Not one like *his*.

This T-shirt looked like marble in the moonlight, a sculptural feat.

Brita had seen statues in museums just as she had seen members of her family around the sunken, abandoned pool that hadn't held any water aside from rain in as long as she could remember. She had always thought privately that men's bodies were a bit boring, really, for all they strutted about like pigeons.

But tonight it was as if the sight of him sent her into anaphylactic shock.

Everything was tight. She felt…red. She itched everywhere.

Maybe that explained all this. Maybe this was an *allergy*.

"How did you find me?" she asked, because she was the one who tracked creatures through the hills of this island. He was the one who lived in that marvelously seductive house that had seemed more a dream the cliffside had than any sort of dwelling place. It suggested he was far more wild and starkly uncivilized than she would have imagined a member of the Teras family could be, if she'd thought about it.

Until that night, she had not thought about it. Not really. She had seen the place from afar during her travels, a strange tangle of glass and light and steel that seemed to weave its way into the cliff itself, as if it was an organic thing when it was plainly not. Some nights it gleamed in the distance and she'd had the stray thought that it seemed *alive*.

It had been different up close. The house had seemed elemental.

Maybe he had, too, though that hardly made sense.

"Everyone knows where to look for the goddess of the hunt when the moon rises," he was saying.

Her heart was beating so hard it didn't occur to her to question that, for it wasn't really an answer at all.

"What did you ask me—about happiness?" she asked instead, though she knew. She remembered. *Why should you not be happy?*

It made her feel unsteady, that question. It felt like a detonation, one that kept on and on. One that was even worse than the allergic reaction she was currently suffering through.

He was looking at her almost curiously. Almost, but not quite—there was something deeper there. Darker, maybe. "Isn't that what you said to your dog?"

Brita looked back reflexively, and though she couldn't find the glint of Heracles's eyes in the dark, she knew he was there. She didn't correct Asterion. Wolves were like anything else, she had found. If people wanted to believe they didn't exist, nothing she could say or do could convince them. And it didn't make them any less real. Or any less dangerous.

She couldn't make sense of why her skin prickled the way it did then, instantly covered in too many goose bumps to count, when all she did was look back at Asterion.

"Why do they call you a monster?" she asked him. "As far as I can tell, all you seem to do is worry about lost creatures and moon rises."

"I think you have you and me confused, little huntress."

Something about his cultured voice, with that undercurrent of something rougher, deeper, seemed to abrade her skin where it was already so desperately prickly. She told herself it was allergies again, nothing more. Or those words, *little huntress,* in his mouth like that.

It was a strange thing for a man to say. Especially if he said it like that.

He moved out from the shadows that marked the edge of the trees. Then he came out until he could stand beside her, there in a small clearing that she had long considered her own, for no one else ever ventured here. It should have felt a violation to have him here. To have *anyone* here, she corrected herself, because these were her hills, her views. This was where she came to *escape* people, not entertain them, though no one had ever tested that before. For who else dared trek out this far, through so much dense vegetation, to see a pretty view on an island that had so many?

Yet she did not feel violated in the least when he came to stand beside her. Instead, she realized with a start that some of the dreams she'd been having had been whispering little memories to her all along.

Like the scent of him. She hadn't imagined it. It had been there in the air that night.

It hadn't been that strange sensation in her belly that she'd attributed to standing at the edge of a steep cliff.

It was *him.*

A hint of something like woodsmoke, something brighter woven into it, and a kind of heat she did not understand, but knew was simply him.

She drifted closer and somehow held back from sniffing him the way the wolves did.

For even she knew that was not acceptable behavior.

And besides, it was likely to make her allergies even worse.

"You told me I could call you," he said in that voice again, his gaze out on the moon and the ladder it made across the surface of the sea as it lazily considered rising. "I thought this would be the next best thing."

Brita knew she gave the impression of having, perhaps, been raised by the wolves she liked so much. In some ways, being raised by any of her creatures would have been an improvement over her situation. But she had, in fact, interacted with humans before Asterion. Even she knew that as far as explanations went, this was a bad one.

Yet she couldn't quite bring herself to mind.

"If you've come to tell me that you found something crying again, I'm afraid you've made a bit of a miscalculation," she told him, and though she did not allow herself to look at the T-shirt, she was aware of it. She was *fully* aware of it. "In future, it's better to stay near the wounded thing so it doesn't run off. It is likely to be gone again, like last time."

When he turned his head, she found herself caught as surely as if he had trapped her that way, or possibly between the span of his palms. "My mistake."

And it seemed to cost her something to turn her head back to the moon, the beckoning sea. It seemed to take her too long to stop feeling her breath—all the way in, then out. A little too quick, a little too rough.

She expected something to happen. He seemed the type to make his own weather wherever he went, and she braced for it, for surely a man like this did not simply decide to take a remote hike only to exchange a few words. No one ever had before.

Instead, he stood there beside her, his scent a part of the view, the breeze. The trees at her back, the sea stretching out before them both.

They must have stood there a long time.

But after a while, the moon was high and Brita started to feel itchy again. Feverish. She needed to find a place to camp tonight, and perhaps make herself a poultice from the herbs she foraged as she walked. For the allergies.

She turned and headed back for the trail, the one she'd made herself with her own two feet, and it seemed the most natural thing in the world for him to fall into place beside her, matching his stride to hers.

It felt almost comfortable.

The truth was, Brita did not know a great deal about comfort.

"You can't possibly be committed to your own happiness," she said, aware when he slanted a look in her direction that she'd done that thing she did again. The sisters at the nunnery had explained with great patience that not everyone lived inside her head, and she had to engage in conversation if she wished everyone to know what she was talking about at any given time.

A far kinder approach to that habit of hers, the one she'd developed as a child who spent most of her time inside that head of hers, than the one her family had employed.

But he didn't seem lost. "Can't I?"

"Your brother is the happy-go-lucky one. Too charming to live, they say. His smile could make the Mediterranean dim beside him, according to all reports. And of course, you could look just like him if you wanted, could you not?"

"Our features are identical," he said, which, again, was not exactly an answer to the question she'd asked.

"I only mean that you could be just as bright and shiny if you wished. You clearly don't."

"Does it follow then, that I am therefore forever in the depths of despair?"

She danced over the exposed roots in her way, and let herself swing out a bit off the trail, using the trunk of a young tree to hold her. She wasn't sure why the look on his face was…slightly arrested as she came back to earth.

Or why there was a response inside of her, like a song.

Not a feverish one at all.

"I don't know. Are you in the depths of despair?" Something about *how* he was silent had her hurrying on, suddenly worried that it was possible that he actually was, and she sensed somehow that he wouldn't welcome it if she paused to dig into it. To him. "Maybe you confine all your happiness to places where you can be sure you're in private. That's fair enough. But surely you must know that outside of those places, you are thought of as the grim one."

"We cannot all be my brother, bestowing his charms as freely as he does, to all and sundry." Brita had heard the tales of the great rivalry between the brothers, but Asterion did not sound the way her father did when he discussed those he considered his rivals. Peevish and dark and vengeful. Asterion sounded almost…fond. "Or even my grandmother, who commands a certain kind of attention wherever she goes, and caters to it."

"I've never seen the point of attempting to be someone else," Brita told him matter-of-factly. "And I have been given many opportunities to do exactly that. My cousin Panagiota is five years older than me, and according to my family, possesses every virtue that I do not. Save one."

She looked beside her and he was watching her intently, a terrific way to tumble down the side of the mountain. She nearly told him so, but in her experience, men did not like it when presented with facts they might have overlooked. So she kept that particular fact to herself and supposed she would have to do her best to catch him.

"Why should it matter which one of you is the more virtuous?" he asked.

"It doesn't matter to me." Brita laughed. "But as my father likes to say, usually quite loudly, it's Panagiota who has a face for the nunnery. And me, his cursed daughter, who longs for the nunnery when I have a face that would make Helen of Troy herself jealous."

They walked on, and through a tricky bit, where the trail strayed a bit too close to some hillside erosion. Brita was on alert, but somehow, this expensive man in his *T-shirt* seemed as fleet-footed as a mountain goat.

"I have never heard a woman discuss her own beauty in such a fashion," he said after some while had passed. "It is disarming."

And yet, somehow, Brita knew that was a lie. She

thought there was very little that could disarm this man. And very little that ever had.

Besides, her beauty was an inescapable fact. A fact that seemed to matter to everyone who laid eyes on her, though it had never mattered to her.

But she focused on the conversation they were actually having instead of the various streams of thought in her head. The sisters would be so proud. "My family tells me I am distressingly unfeminine. By that they mean that I ought to blush and stammer and pretend I have imposter syndrome, when I have a mirror as well as anyone else. And it's not as if being in possession of this face has ever done me any good. If I'd inherited the same features as the rest of the women in my family, I would have been left to my own devices long ago. I would not need to join a convent. I could simply do as I liked."

"And what is that, Brita?"

He stopped walking then, turning to look at her. The breeze was sighing through the trees. The moonlight filtered down, dancing through the tree branches, making it all feel like some kind of a dream.

Maybe it was. It was a lot like the dreams she'd been having lately, achy and hot.

"What do I want?" When he gazed back at her, clearly encouraging her to continue, she swallowed. "I want what everyone wants. It is not so special."

"Humor me."

"I want to do what I have always done." And when she flushed then, it was a different wash of color, a different kind of heat. It was half temper and half the little bit of shame her family had managed to put on her despite her best efforts to ignore them entirely. "I want to take care of creatures more helpless than myself. It's not even particularly odd. There are veterinarians the world over. Wildlife specialists. The world is filled these days with more compassionate advocates for animals than not. Did you know that this island has a vast number of indigenous species, some of which can only been found here? On this island only, out of all the islands in the Mediterranean. Apparently this has never interested the crown overmuch, but it interests me."

And, as ever, there was only the sound of her fervent words, hanging there between them. When Brita knew better than that. She'd learned that no one wished to know what she actually thought about anything. Even when—especially when—they asked.

"There are other wildlife advocates here," he said after a moment, a stunned sort of look in his eyes. Usually people she was actually passionate in front of demanded apologies, and Brita understood then that something in her would crack into pieces if he turned out to be the sort of person who needed her apologies. But he didn't. He kept on. "As I told you before, I was required to consult with a number of them when I chose to build a house that some thought disturbed the habitat of native species."

"Yes, and they are marvelous, these advocates," she said. "But I would like there to be an actual wildlife refuge here. Where we could rehabilitate animals in need, release them back into the wild if possible, and if not, let them live out the rest of their days without having to worry about scaring a tourist and being killed for the insult. And I don't need you to tell me that I'm overly emotionally invested," she said quickly, before he could. Because everyone did. "I know I am. My family tells me so all the time. Luckily, once I become a nun in full, the sisters have pledged their support. It might not be the kind of refuge I imagine, but there's no reason why we can't do something." She blew out a breath. "Smaller scale means just what it says. Smaller. Not *less than*."

"Did someone tell you that?"

She smiled at him then, though she could not have said why. "The Abbess. A great many times. Maybe someday it will take."

"You seem resigned to your fate, little huntress."

"I like the convent," she said. He started walking again, and there was a pleasure in it, she found. Matching the way her body moved to the way his did, as if it was a kind of dance, to pick their way down the side of the hill very few ever climbed in the first place. "I was raised in a lot of chaos. A lot of turmoil, I suppose."

And something in her chest seemed to stutter at the look on his face then. As if he knew the kind of chaos and turmoil she would have thought his wealth protected him from. She cautioned herself against reading too much into a look on a man's face in the middle of so many trees doing their best to block out the moonlight.

Still, she wondered.

Yet she continued. "Every day in the convent is the same. The same prayers, the same schedule. The seasons change, as much as they ever do here, but little else does. It feels eternal. Safe. I like that."

She felt the curve of his lips before she looked over to see it. "Surely, Brita, if you're called to a holy life, you must mention your own holiness first. Isn't that the point of it all?"

Bria thought it was such an intimate thing, to walk beside another, surrounded by only dark, trees and all the creatures who lived here. Such an intimate thing to nearly feel the brush of his arm. To feel as if, were he to look at her again, she might so easily stumble and fall all the way down to the bottom of the hill and hardly care at all.

"I think that it is too easy for too many people to confuse things." She found the moon in the sky, though it did not penetrate the trees as well here as before. Still, she knew it was there. "There is very little in this world that is not sacred, if you stop and let it in. And it is not my holiness that I'm seeking. What I'm seeking is a life of service."

A life of *meaning,* she did not say. She knew better than that. Her father had howled with laughter the one time she'd dared say that aloud.

Think of what you can mean to your family, and be still, her stepmother had said waspishly.

While Brita had vowed that she would never waste her life as a bauble on a rich man's arm. No matter what she had to do to avoid it.

She thought that Asterion would pepper her with more questions, because people always did. How could she give up this or that or the other thing—but he didn't ask.

Instead, they walked. In a hushed silence that reminded her of morning prayers. That sacred. That intimate. When they got down to the bottom of the hill, she saw another sports car haphazardly parked beneath the olive trees. She saw the way the olive leaves glinted as silver as the moon, as if they were made as much of moonlight as anything else.

As much moonlight as she could feel inside her, even now.

"I'll call you soon," he told her, and when he moved toward her, she couldn't really say what she thought he was doing, but everything in her surged forward, and upward, and outward, almost as if she wanted—

Yet all he did was brush his thumb over one cheekbone.

She wondered if perhaps one of the overhanging tree branches had brushed her as they walked, if he simply meant to wipe the mark it had left away. It was that quick, that glancing.

Yet they both stood there for a long moment, as if something had changed.

As if in the space between them, now, in the wake of that touch, something had kindled.

And long after his car had disappeared down the winding lane, Brita stayed where he'd left her, staring up at the moon that had witnessed all this.

One hand pressed her cheek, as if he was the one who'd left a mark.

CHAPTER FIVE

"YOUR FAITH IN my abilities is overwhelming, truly," Asterion said dryly, some days later.

But his grandmother was unmoved.

She had summoned him before her yet again, so she could sit on her throne, pretend it was a real one, and wave her elegant hands around as if, were they both to concentrate more fully, they could both see a queenly scepter there. He suspected she did not need to focus at all to envision it.

"I'm not sure what faith would do for me," Dimitra replied in her usual tart way. "I have seen no evidence that you have even approached the girl I chose for you."

"I beg your pardon. I was unaware that you wanted to tag along like some kind of chaperone. Or do I mean a third wheel?"

And he could have told her that, in fact, he had taken to skulking about the hills in order to meet up with the half-wild creature she'd decreed would be his, but he didn't. He told himself that there was no sense in talking about negotiations until they were done. That was sound business strategy, nothing more.

Though there was something in him that wondered if

it was something else. An urge to keep what happened between him and Brita private...

But Asterion dismissed that almost as soon as he thought it. He was not sentimental. He had seen where that sort of thing led and had arranged his life to prevent it. One strange girl could hardly change the habits of a lifetime.

Even sitting in this house brought it back. The shouting from afar, the sounds of splintering glass and sobs. Muffled accusations being thrown with abandon and then, worse, the ones he could hear.

His parents always waved these things away as if they were nothing.

We are passionate, he had heard his father say once, as if that was an excuse.

Asterion did not allow himself to wonder if he would make the same excuse if he'd lived through the accident.

What he did know was that he would never put himself in a position where he would need to make such an excuse himself. To anyone.

He eyed his grandmother and her hand-waving with more stern grimness than he might have, had he not been forced to consider *sentiment* and the worst night of his life in the midst of what should have been a perfectly rational business discussion. "Information that might have been useful, Yia Yia, would have included things like where to actually locate the woman you proclaimed I was to claim as my own. Instead, I was forced to track down a host of rumors and innuendo concerning her. She might not be the typical heiress but nor is she, as I have been led to believe, a huntress of old, stalking the hills of the island to harvest men's souls."

His grandmother's eyes glittered. "You seem very certain of that, dear child."

This was a game, he knew. And Asterion had always been fantastic at games. What were games but another way to practice winning? He had always been exceptionally good at winning.

He felt he was winning now, in fact, but part of that involved keeping the state of affairs, such as it was, to himself. Not only because it would annoy his grandmother, which he felt she had coming to her. But because it made sense to play his cards close to the vest until he had news to share that would make the indisputable fact that he was beating Dimitra at her own game clear.

This was why he did not respond to her the way she likely expected. Instead, he lounged across from her on one of her baroque couches that offended his stark sense of style in every regard—which she knew very well—and only gazed back at her. As close to *idly* as he ever got. "What do you know about the Martis family?"

"The family?" Dimitra let out a sharp bark that was not quite a laugh. "I know too much and none of it precisely awash in glory. The girl's grandfather made quite a name for himself when I was young. He cut a swathe through the local population until he was finally forced to marry by royal decree. At which point he was even more shocking." She gazed off as if into the past, tapping her fingers against her chin. "Brita's father was the oldest son of that unhappy union and has always been particularly unappealing. I have never been quite sure how he ended up married. Twice, no less. The family has been stampeding through the remains of a very old fortune for generations and rejoiced when it became clear that nature had been so kind to Brita."

Her gaze was canny then, as if waiting for Asterion to acknowledge Brita's stunning beauty. He only gazed at her, impassive, until she smiled as if he'd admitted far more than that.

She sounded far too smug when she continued. "They would very much like to marry her off to a man of means, the better to raise the family profile and pay off debt."

It was nothing Asterion didn't know, but he was surprised all the same that she said it out loud. "And you imagine that I am the appropriate man for the job?" He shook his head. "I always thought that your innate snobbery and obsession with the family legacy would inure me forever from fortune hunters of any description."

"Don't be tiresome, child." Dimitra sat a bit straighter in her makeshift throne. "The Martis family is many things, most of them admittedly squalid, but no one can deny the bloodline is one of the oldest and most noble on the island. I have never given Vasilis Martis the time of day, nor acknowledged the existence of his egregious upstart of a wife, and can imagine no reason I ever shall. But that does not change the bloodline. I've done you a favor, Asterion. Brita is all that is innocent and good. She wishes to become a *nun* in this age of astonishing bad behavior and excessive internet nonsense. For all her scampering about the hills, it is quite obvious that she is not only pure and untouched, but somehow otherworldly. And, as it has perhaps escaped your notice, she is the most beautiful woman on this island. You're welcome."

Only because this was his beloved grandmother did he keep to himself his distaste at hearing her discuss Brita as if she was nothing more than a piece of meat hanging in a butcher shop.

"That is great deal of information," he said. "I cannot imagine what made you think you should send me off without sharing it all in the first place. What I don't understand is how she even came to your notice."

"I have my methods." She smiled benignly, when she was nothing of the kind. "Especially when it comes to the production of beautiful great-grandchildren. Why all these questions? Do you find yourself overset by the task before you?"

He had always known that it was his duty to produce children. To provide Dimitra, and even himself, with heirs to all of this. And he had always assumed that, come the day, he would approach the making of them with the cold logic that had defined his life.

Yet thinking of making babies with Brita made him feel as if all the air had gone out of the room.

Because the making of babies turned into the raising of children, and he knew one thing well. He would not repeat his parents' mistakes. Even if that meant he would need to remove himself completely from his children's lives.

Better that than the alternative.

But he had no intention of letting his grandmother see

him worried. He refused to call it worry. He smirked. "Now you insult me, Yia Yia."

Asterion left her after some more affectionate sparring and drove back down her personal hillside to find himself inching through the usual traffic in the seaside villages on the lone coastal road. Here, everyone recognized him and either nodded with respect or turned pale with fright, as was his due. He had earned these reactions. He cherished them. He was not his parents, who had lost sight of their reputations in the heat of their endless love affair and the tempest of it that had consumed them both. And nearly taken Asterion and Poseidon along with them—

But he did not like to think of the accident. It did him no good.

Though he supposed he could understand why his grandmother felt she had no choice but to act in such a typically Teras manner, strong-arming her remaining relatives into expanding the family while she was still around to see it. She had lost more than anyone that night.

He did not appreciate that it had led her here, but he could understand why it had.

Still, he found himself thinking—though he would fling himself from his own cliff before admitting to such a thing, especially to his grandmother—that this was all a little more...unexpectedly difficult than he'd imagined.

Not seeking Brita out, or spending time with her. That was not difficult at all. That was the problem.

He had not expected to *like* her.

Asterion hit a button on his phone and rang his brother in London, who answered on the first ring.

"Not exactly the best time, brother," Poseidon drawled, though if that were true, he would not have picked up the call.

"You like everyone," he said. "Too much, one might say."

"Everyone does say that. Particularly you. With alarming regularity."

Asterion stopped for yet another pack of holidaymakers who streamed across the road, blinded to anything but the beckoning Mediterranean before them. There were people everywhere on a bright day like this, everything a riot of color against the whitewashed walls that were considered a hallmark of this part of the world.

He glared at the tourists. "I find it difficult to understand how a person moves through life, deliberately immersing himself in the company of so many."

There was a rustling bit of noise on the other end of the line. He thought perhaps he heard his brother murmur something, no doubt to one of his many conquests.

But when Poseidon spoke into the phone again, there was no other sound at all. "What exactly are you asking me?"

"I regret the impulse."

"Are you…" His twin sounded delighted. "Are you asking me to teach you how to be charming?"

"I am not." He thought of the look on Brita's face when he'd touched her cheek that first time. Just a brush. Hardly a touch at all. And yet it lived in him still. "I merely wondered what the appeal was. As I have lately heard that I am known as *the grim one*."

"Were you under the impression that you were known as something else?" Poseidon laughed. "Because that would likely require that you stop acting as if you are Atlas himself, hefting the globe on your shoulders at every opportunity and making certain to look aggrieved while you do it."

"I am a man of some intensity," Asterion acknowledged, and he wasn't certain that he liked that he was having this conversation at all. Was this that *self-doubt* he heard so much about from people he did not hire? Or worse, the newly bandied about *imposter syndrome*, which he had never experienced in his life, because he was Asterion Teras and he deserved every single thing that was his and more. "You of all people should understand that it does not make me—"

"The Monster of the Mediterranean?" Poseidon laughed again. "But you are so good at it. You snarl about, dark and brooding, and the poor besotted girls flock to you all the same."

"I suppose I wondered why you bother to charm them at all when I am living proof that there is no need."

"I prefer honey to vinegar, brother," Poseidon said, and unlike their grandmother, Poseidon had at least committed himself to the study of honey. He was famous for it. "Try it. You might discover a whole side of yourself you never knew was there."

"If that is a recommendation—"

"I would never dream of making such recommendations." Poseidon's voice was dry. "After all there's nothing you don't know, as eldest brother of all of one minute. Think of all that you have learned in those sixty seconds you graced this earth without me. What could I possibly have to tell you?"

"I regret that I called," Asterion said darkly, which only set his brother to laughing even more.

He had that ringing in his ears even after he ended the call. And as he navigated his way out of the tourist centers of the beachside villages, heading back into the hills and following the road that curved around and around and eventually became his drive. Once again, he felt unsettled.

Once again, he disliked it. Intensely.

Ever since he had laid eyes on Brita Martis, Asterion had not been...himself. Not quite.

He decided as he drove that it was because he was forced to play this part.

Wooing anyone, a woman or a client or a deal, was not in his nature. Asterion had never been the sort to sell himself. He had never needed to. His reputation preceded him wherever he went and did most of the work for him. Before he had built his own reputation, he'd had his family's.

He had never been the sort to hang about, having pointless conversations with anyone, much less a woman. He had never *walked in the moonlight* without some other, better purpose. There were often women hanging about him, and he indulged himself as he pleased. He was a man of certain means and a great many skills, and he liked a woman who could meet him in all things. Stamina. Imagination.

But most important, he kept his indulgences to the dark hours and did not wish to think of anyone when he woke.

And because he did not wish it, he did not. Such was the iron and steel of his self-control.

It had been his compass all these years.

That was the worst part about this Brita situation. She haunted him. Here it was full daylight, he hadn't even tasted her, and he was thinking about her when he had whole empires to run. It was madness.

He detested it—and yet he could not stop.

Once at his house, he strode down the stairs that led him along the spine of the house so he could make his way to the part set aside for business. His refuge. This was where he had made certain that in one sense, the Teras legacy would last forever. He sat at his desk of stone, built into the cliffside, and yet he could not seem to focus his thoughts as usual.

He had built this house from the depths of his own imagination, had laid many of the stones with his own hands. He had built it to his precise specifications, so this office was deep in the hillside on one end and yet offered an expansive view of the sea on the other, with a wide terrace above the crashing waves where he often took calls.

Usually the only thing he thought of in this space was work.

Yet even now she haunted him.

Even here, he could not escape.

His compass was broken. He blamed her—but he shut that down before it could take root, as it tasted suspiciously like emotion. Passion. These things that were anathema to him.

And grimly—yes, *grimly*—he set himself to the pile of tasks that awaited him anyway.

When night fell, he gave up and took the stairs again, this time back up to his gardens that sprawled out to the edge of the cliff. He considered, then dismissed, the idea of a hard swim in his eternity pool. For there was only one way he truly wished to use his body tonight and it was not available to him.

Because the thought of another woman would not do. He wanted her.

He wanted *her* and that was a disaster.

But when he turned back toward the house, she was there. On the edge of the trees, watching him like a ghost.

Asterion wished he could pretend she was a figment of his imagination, the one he had been unaware he possessed before now, but he could not. She was all too real.

He could *feel* her, from the soles of his feet to his sex to that pounding mess where his heart should have been.

And he knew that this was supposed to be a wooing, not the kind of hard, dark wanting he excelled in. He knew that his grandmother was right. Brita was untried, untouched. An innocent in all ways—

Yet as he drew closer to her, he couldn't find the words to cut this tension inside him. To change that driving need, deep in his blood.

"Asterion," she began as he approached.

But he couldn't help himself. Perhaps he did not wish to help himself, not when there was this unbearable *wanting* that made everything before her seem pale, insubstantial, even something closer to sad.

He moved closer, took her face in his hands, and kissed her.

At last, he kissed her.

Once, then again, Asterion fit his lips to hers, he tasted her heat, and he kissed her even deeper.

Until, to his delight, she kissed him back.

It was like getting sucked into an undertow, a tumble so intense, so overwhelming, that he might have considered it too much to bear if it hadn't also been so deliriously *good*.

Her mouth beneath his was artless. She tasted faintly of herbs and made him think of cool waterfalls and rich, warm Mediterranean nights.

Asterion did not permit himself escapes of any kind that involved women, not work, but Brita tempted him to do more than simply lose his head. She tasted like heat and destiny. She would lead him straight into the kind of oblivion he would never be able to shake, or live without. The kind that could topple great men, raze cities, upend the world no matter whose shoulders it rested upon—

The kind that had killed his parents.

He set her away from him abruptly, though not without the strangest sort of...*tenderness*. He could feel it all over him. In him.

For her.

As if being near this woman made him someone he did not know.

For a moment there was only the tangle of their breath, there in the night, with the trees keeping watch all around them. He could see the gleam of her gaze, gold and silver, sun and moon, twisting around and around inside him, and luring him closer. Luring him—

But this was not the plan. This was not how he intended for this project of his grandmother's to go, and this was certainly not how he permitted himself to behave. Not ever. Asterion was a man of sober contemplation and swift, decisive action.

He did not lose his head. In the moonlight or anywhere else.

He took a step back, and when that did not break the spell, he stepped back again.

Yet the distance did nothing to help. Even then, he was far too taken with her. He was far too...*possessed,* something in him whispered, when that could not be possible.

Because he was a man who had turned his back on anything that even hinted of strong emotion, or anything else he could not control, since the day he had lost most of his family and nearly himself to boot.

He would not allow himself to stray from the standards of behavior he'd set for himself then.

He had never strayed in all this time.

That he was debating this as he stood here, staring at her, sent something in him spinning madly like he was no more than a drunk. When he did not allow himself the mess and muddle of intoxication.

But then that same sensation seemed to *tighten* as if his ribs were closing in on him.

He turned abruptly and stalked back the way he'd come, hardly aware of the ground beneath his feet, so desperate was he to simply get away. To disappear. To put space between him and this woman who was supposed to be an exercise. A challenge.

A game, at best.

Because games were easy for Asterion. He won them without even trying.

He did not understand what this was. What *she* was—

But he stopped short when something *thunked* into the tree directly in front of him, there in the last line of trees keeping him out of sight of his house.

Asterion glared balefully at the arrow that shook there, wobbling slightly in the tree trunk only centimeters from his head.

Scant centimeters at that.

He turned, very slowly, and even though there could only be one explanation, and therefore only one possible image before him—he still couldn't believe it when he saw it. When he saw *her.*

He couldn't make sense of Brita standing there before him, the bow that was normally slung over her back in her hands, drawn back with another arrow notched into place and set to fly.

This time, he suspected she would not miss.

"You shot at me."

It was not a question. It was indignation, pure and simple.

Affront, crystallized now, when he could still taste her on his tongue.

"What was *that?*" she demanded.

"A kiss," he gritted out.

He reached over and wrapped his fingers around the arrow in the tree beside him, his eyes still on Brita, and those two things seem to fuse together inside of him, filling him with a nearly unbearable heat.

Asterion had never felt anything like it.

He told himself it was fury, nothing more, but he didn't quite believe it.

"That was not a kiss," she corrected him, and she was frowning, which should have marred the peerless beauty of her face.

It did not.

If anything, it made her look less like a perfect statue and more like a woman. A flesh and blood woman, that was. Not an object to worship from afar, but a warm, hot human woman who would rub against him, clamp him between her thighs, and ride him until they both cracked wide-open, entrenching him in her soft heat all the while.

God help him, he was as hard as a pike, like the shaft of the arrow he gripped in his hand.

He wrenched it out of the tree trunk and looked down at it. He couldn't think of the last time he'd seen an actual arrow. Much less one with a matching bow. And certainly it had never occurred to him, even in his wildest childhood games with his brother, that anyone would ever dare *aim one at his head*.

"I think, little huntress, that the tales are true. You are untouched."

"Obviously I'm not untouched. For you have touched me."

"And what happens now?" he demanded, though somehow, the affront and indignation had faded. Now the only thing left was that heat. And the blazing thing between them, more gold and silver than even her gaze, seemed to hum in them both. "Will you strike me down for my temerity? Are you so beholden to your own innocence, Brita? That is how those old stories go, is it not? A virgin huntress is beloved by the moon while she remains pure, then is thrust into the unforgiving daylight when she falls into the earthly clutches of unworthy men."

"I think you'll find that's a parable for the fate of all women, in one way or another," Brita said dryly.

"That would make me unworthy." Asterion bared his teeth, though he would not call it a smile. "And I confess to you that I am a great many insalubrious things where women are concerned, but never that."

He couldn't tell if she drifted closer or he did, or maybe they both moved, but when they were nearer to each other, she lowered that bow. And he watched, his own tension growing within him, as she let the tension in the bow go, too.

Her whole body moved with the force of the breath she took in, then blew out.

"I don't understand," she said quietly, her eyes darker than before. "I thought a kiss was supposed to be a little bauble of a thing. Something gleaming and bright, a sweet joy in the moment, and then quickly forgotten. Not...*that*."

He watched her face in the moonlight, able to see the way she trembled—just slightly—and there was no small part of him that exulted in that. And not only because it felt like winning.

But also because that meant that he was not the only one who had spun so far out in all that sensation.

At least there was that.

"Ever since I met you I've felt sick," she said, and he almost laughed, so far was that from his own thoughts. But she was frowning in that ferocious way of hers, and she moved closer to him as she spoke, still gripping her bow, but thankfully pointing the arrow at the ground between them. "Terrible fevers. Aches. And itching, everywhere. I keep thinking I am falling ill, but I never quite fall and it's worse when you are near." Her frown deepened. "But better, too, and then that kiss—"

"I see."

And he did. That odd tenderness washed over him again, but he didn't interrogate it. He reached over and traced an intricate little pattern over her mouth, her full lips with the top one suggesting the perfect bow. To match the one she carried, he supposed. This time, he watched as goose bumps broke out all over her skin, her eyes flashed, and sure enough, a flush rose up all over her lovely cheeks.

Not a fever.

But he knew the cure.

And better still, he knew full well that there was no emotion necessary. Only pleasure.

For the first time since meeting Brita and reeling from his response to her, he felt like himself again. There was no reason to think that this was anything but attraction, and he knew how to handle that.

He knew, at last, how to handle her.

"Good news," he told her then, and no longer minded that he ached, too. "You are not ill, little huntress."

Her lips parted. "What is it then?"

Asterion shifted his weight backward and uncurled his clenched fist, looking down at the arrow. And it took him entirely too long to order the mess of thoughts and the muddle of sensation inside him.

But as he did, the answer became clear. He thought of the things his grandmother had told him. About her family, and her history. He thought of what little he'd seen of that family with his own eyes, shrieking at each other into the night.

Those were reasonable, practical considerations.

And they had nothing to do with the decision he made. He only knew that he could not woo this woman. Not when he wanted her so badly.

Not when she wanted him, too.

Asterion understood that the sooner they burned off this attraction between them, the better things would be. He could control it that way. He could make this work.

But now he looked up from that arrow she'd shot at him and into those eyes of hers, gold and silver, now mixed with wonder.

"It is simple, Brita." He even felt himself smile, slightly, as he said it. A real smile this time. As if he didn't have to pretend to be someone else. As if he wasn't the Monster of the Mediterranean at all, and that should have scared him. That should have made him wish that the arrow in his hand had pierced him straight through. Then again, maybe it had, but he was the one holding it now. "You will have to marry me."

CHAPTER SIX

BRITA DIDN'T MEAN to let out a sigh, but it escaped anyway. She had thought for a moment there that he was about to say something magical, but instead it was this.

The same old bore, and after there had been *kissing*.

It seemed unfair. And right when she'd started to think he was something a bit more thrilling than an *allergy*.

"Once again, that's really very disappointing," she said, after too many moments slid past. During which she was forced to admit to herself that she had not come here in a selfless desire to search for an animal in need. She'd known it the moment she'd seen him.

Brita had come here for this. For him.

And there was something shocking about the way he laughed then. Not only because she was sure that she had heard that he'd never done so in all his days. That he was nothing but a shroud of grim intensity and that all the laughter and smiles were his brother's.

But because his laughter seemed to *ignite* inside her own skin.

"A disappointment?" That word seemed to set him off again, because he laughed more, and it was a dark, rusty sort of sound that seemed to twine its way deep into her bones. "Me? Are you certain?"

"Everyone wants to marry me," she said, scowling at him. "And every time, the notion is presented to me as if it is not only the first time it has ever been mentioned, but is a gift. Something that should make me fall to my knees in praise and pleasure."

He wiped at his face as if his own laughter had made his eyes water. "If you feel moved, do not let me stop you."

She unnotched her arrow from her bow and slid it back into her sheath, then tossed her bow over her shoulder, too.

"When I was at university, all I ever heard the other girls talk about was how little men wished to marry. How they all had to be hunted down like wild game, lured into elaborate traps, and tricked into taking part in the whole enterprise. I have not found this to be so."

"Then you and I are alike," he told her. "For I, too, have received more marriage proposals than I could possibly count."

That made even less sense. Brita puffed out an annoyed sort of laugh herself. "Then you know how annoying they are."

"But I had never offered anyone a proposal myself," he continued in that dark, inexorable way, and suddenly it seemed impossible that there had ever been any laughter at all. "Only think of it, Brita. I can solve all your problems."

That was not the first time she'd heard that, either, though none of the other men who had said such things to her looked the way Asterion did. His eyes like blue midnight, washed with too many vast, dark seas to count. That stillness that made her whole body want to shake. And shake some more.

As if the sickness was spreading.

"My problems don't need solving. Not by you." She sounded cross and didn't do much to make that stop. "I've already solved them myself."

"Have you?" He did not sound convinced, and for some reason, that was the most disconcerting part of this.

"I have done this a thousand times," she told him. "That is only a slight exaggeration. They propose, I decline. They tell me they can make my life better in this way or that, but what they mean is, they are willing to settle my family's debts and expect me to express my gratitude. When I refuse them yet again, they generally become loud and unpleasant and usually quite red in the face. I really can't take my final vows fast enough."

And she knew that was not the wisest sort of speech to make to a man when he'd just done most of the things she'd listed off. But it was like the night he'd asked her what she wanted to do with her life, and she'd told him and had expected him to demand she apologize the way everyone else did. For all her unseemly *passion.*

Brita only knew that if the man who had just kissed her like that, if that could even be called a *kiss,* got garrulous and flushed, it would sour something inside her. Possibly for good.

But he showed no signs of growing red about his face. And when she spoke, he did not sound anything but…

smooth. Dark. *Intense.* "Let me ask you this then, little huntress. How many nuns do you think come alive in a kiss like that?"

And her own heart seemed to work against her, pounding much too hard inside her chest, but she didn't dare reply to that the way she wanted to and launch herself toward him. Even she knew that was a bridge too far. "Perhaps all of them. They have all had their year filled with temptations, perhaps far greater than that."

Though she doubted that very much.

Asterion only watched her, and there was something so knowing in his gaze, so *certain.* It should have made her furious. She should have decried his condescension right then and there.

But that was not, at all, the reaction she had.

Instead, her breath was a shaky thing inside her and she couldn't decide if she wanted to hide it or let him see, because either one seemed equally treacherous just then.

"I need a wife," he said after a while, his midnight eyes gleaming. "And not just any wife, Brita. I need you."

"I have heard that before, too," she informed him, as if her throat wasn't the least bit dry, "and it is never complimentary. Normally it leaves me with the impression that if I were to commission a life-size doll of myself and hand it over in my place, it would serve the same purpose."

She was sure she could feel his laughter inside her again, though she only saw a hint of it in his gaze.

"Many men are collectors," he agreed. "But I am not one of them. The only things I collect are empires, and it has been suggested I already have enough."

"You're very comfortable in your arrogance." That was one way of putting it. Another way was that it made her more *uncomfortable* than it should. "I can say that for you."

His dark eyes gleamed brighter. "Can it be called arrogance when it is nothing less than the simple truth? I do not think so. My grandmother wishes for me to marry, you see. She thinks that it is high time I do something about this reputation of mine. This Monster of the Mediterranean. She is under the impression that a wife will civilize me."

Brita considered that. "I'm afraid that does not sound entirely achievable. No matter who you marry."

"Whether I agree or do not, she has already picked out my bride for me. And I am sorry to tell you that she is the sort of woman who does not permit any deviation from the plans she makes."

Brita also liked a plan, so she nodded at that. But when Asterion only gazed back at her, expectantly, Brita felt that achy heat rush through her all over again.

And this time it was brighter than ever.

"Me?" she managed to ask.

Though there was no reason at all that she should find it difficult to speak.

Asterion only lifted one dark, arrogant brow. "Of course, you."

Another suspicion moved in her, and she let that into her scowl, too, because it felt a bit like armor. And she did not want to think why she needed it, just then, when she had never cared about the things men said. But she did. "There was never any crying creature on your cliff top, was there?"

"That sounds almost poetic." He shrugged, and though it was an arrogant gesture, it was different from before. She was tempted to imagine the great Asterion Teras felt a touch of shame himself. "I'm sure that some poor creature or another has found reason to cry there."

Brita rolled her eyes. "I don't know what makes you think that I would wish to marry an avowed liar."

But the truly strange thing was that she ought to be far more outraged by his games than she was, and she couldn't account for it.

Asterion smiled again, and it was stupid, she thought crossly, that a smile was all he needed to do and she could *feel* it as if he was the one in control of her body, not her. It was an odd new fact she'd discovered tonight and could now file away with the rest. Like the smell of the hills where no one dared walk, right after a rain, like green was a feeling. Like the blue Mediterranean sky above and the sea all around, the color of home.

And now this smile.

He looked at her as if she'd said all of that out loud, and she couldn't be entirely sure she hadn't. "I could wax rhapsodic about each and every one of your attributes, but I suspect you have heard it all before. Tell me, have any of these suitors of yours kissed you?"

She bristled at that. "Certainly not."

"Do you wish they had?"

"Never." She didn't understand why she was flushing then, only that she couldn't seem to stop. "Men are always trying to paw me. That's why I had to learn how to protect myself. The bow and arrow are not my only weapons, you know."

"I should hope not." He reached out, almost languidly. Or more, as if she'd issued him some kind of invitation. As he brushed the backs of his fingers over one hot cheek, then the other, she rather wondered if she had. "You are an adventurer, Brita. You prefer a canopy of stars to any four-poster bed. Your best friend appears to be a besotted wolf." When she looked at him more sharply then, for he was the one who had called Heracles a dog, his eyes only gleamed in that way of his, showing her that private amusement. "There are adventures that I can take you on that I do not think you could have with anyone else."

She considered that. Or maybe what she was considering was that heat beneath her skin and the fact he seemed to know it was there. "I don't know what that means."

"It means that a kiss like that is not ordinary." Again he brushed her cheek, but then his hand moved. This time he slid it over her neck to cup her nape and gently pull her toward him.

It didn't occur to her to do anything but go with it.

She didn't *want* to do anything but that. She thought she would die if she didn't get to see what he was *doing*.

Right now, he was still talking, low and intent. "But a kiss like that, as extraordinary as it is, can only be the beginning. There are worlds to discover, all the many things a man and a woman can teach each other about pleasure. So many horizons to explore. If you dare."

"I'm supposed to enter the convent," she said, but her voice was little more than a faint thread of sound. "Soon."

"Is the convent going somewhere?" Again, all that amusement in his gaze when his face was stern. As if he was honed from this same forge that burned in her. "Surely, if this marriage doesn't suit you, it is always possible for you to return to your solitude and prayers."

She felt suffused with that heat. His hand against her skin was a dark, sinful delight, and she had no doubt that this was the temptation she'd been looking for all along.

That he was.

Because until now, she hadn't really understood the purpose of this year. Until now, she had thought of it as marking time, nothing more. A nostalgic tour of the island, as free as she'd been when she was a small child when no one took the slightest notice of her.

That had been lovely, in its way.

But this was different. This was Asterion Teras with his hands on her body, and that glowing, growing heat between them like a banked flame that could burst into a wildfire at any moment.

He was the sort of sin that was meant to truly tempt her resolve. She understood that.

Brita could still feel the way he had kissed her. As if his mouth on hers had been a brand. And more than that, as if kissing him had plugged her in to the grandest electrical current of all time, when she had considered herself sufficiently *alive* already.

But it was as if she had been calling gray days *bright*

the whole of her life, and only now saw what the world looked like when the sun rose on a blue morning.

And the truth was that while Brita could do without the commentary on her beauty, and all the trouble the fact of her beauty had brought her, she quite loved her body. She loved the things that it could do. The places it took her. She loved how strong she was, how agile. She liked the strength in her arms that let her make her bow sing. And the way her hips moved, as if to a sensual music all their own, when the moon was high.

She had loved all of those things for years now, yet tonight, with the memory of Asterion's mouth on hers and his fingers against her skin, it was as if she was learning her body for the very first time.

And she wanted *more*.

She wanted that sensation. She wanted that fire.

It had never occurred to her that marrying a man could be so easy. That they could do all these lovely things and bask in them. It had always been presented to her as duty and suffering and putting up with something unpleasant for the sake of others—and what could be less appealing than that?

But this was different.

That kiss made her see all of this in a different way. If she married Asterion, it would delight her family. They would get what they wanted and leave her alone. She wouldn't have to join the convent. It had never been her first choice. It had been the better of the choices offered to her, but that wasn't the same thing.

She felt some regret…but only that she didn't feel *more*

regret for a place she'd been quite happy for three whole years.

And best of all, he said that there were worlds to discover, and she thought he meant that.

Brita had never had a fever she didn't bounce back from, the same as before, so why should this one be any different?

And it came with so many other benefits. None of her other suitors had interested her at all, but Asterion did. So much she wasn't sure she'd slept a night through since she'd met him. Marrying him was sure to make all that go away. Even sleeping beneath the stars became familiar over time, no matter how spectacular the shine.

Surely he would, too.

"If I marry you, will there be kissing?" she asked.

Brita didn't entirely understand that indulgent gleam in his gaze then, but it made her feel slick between her legs.

"If you wish."

"Because I've heard my father and stepmother shout at each other about their marriage," she told him, frowning. "And my married cousin is very indiscreet. They all say the same things. They talk of sex a lot, mostly in terms of not having any or using it as currency, but they never kiss." And this time she not only saw that laughter in his gaze, she could feel it in him, as if she was shaking silently with it. "Is that normal?"

"I have never been married, Brita," he told her, as if he was choosing his words very carefully indeed. "But I can promise you that if you marry me, you will have as much kissing as you want and as much sex as I think you can handle."

She didn't like that. "Why do you get to decide?"

And then she watched as Asterion…changed. *Intensified,* rather. She was breathless in an instant, though he didn't move. Yet somehow, she understood that the man she saw before her now was a far realer version of him than any she had seen before. His hand at her nape tightened, though gently.

Gently, it turned out, was like gas on an open flame.

"Because I am a man of vast appetites," he told her. "And when it comes to my pleasure, I am deadly serious. Most women cannot handle me for more than a night. Do you never stop and wonder why it is I'm considered such a monster?"

"I rather thought it was a labyrinth," she said. "And the name of your company. I thought you *wanted* everyone to think of you that way."

"It is because I eat them alive," he said in that dark, intense manner of his, like he was pressing each word into her body. Like it was some kind of dark magic spell.

But it thrilled her.

It filled her up from the inside with a sharp-edged, brilliant glittering she had never felt before. She wanted to die of the joy of it. She wanted to run from him, but only so that she could leap into the air and soar high above the trees, the hills, this sprawling little island that had been her whole world.

Because she could see, now, that the world was so

much bigger and more vast. She could see that touching this man would be worlds within worlds within worlds.

He had said so.

Brita had often wished that she could find that holiness the sisters seemed to access so easily. She had hoped it would come in time. She had prayed that it might.

But now she was fiercely glad that it had not.

"I will marry you," she told him, very matter-of-factly. "But you may not wish to marry me."

"I'm not a man who waffles over his decisions, Brita. You should know this about me from the start." His fingers moved, sending another wave of sensation crashing through her. "I have already said that I wish to marry you."

She had to force herself to focus. "That is all very well, and I'm tempted to hold you to that, but you haven't met my family." One of his dark brows rose, and she sighed. "There's my father to contend with, you see. And he will be a drain upon you forever, demanding money and favors and anything else he can imagine. Then there is his wife, who is worse. That's not even getting into the issue of my cousins. It is easiest if you think of them as one entity, but they are relentless. And if left to their own devices, they will bleed you dry." She waited for him to recoil, but he did not. "I think your grandmother must dislike you very much if she sent you to me."

"My grandmother adores me," he replied with all that confidence of his. "My brother would never admit it, but I am her clear favorite."

"I think you've been much deceived." She shook her

head. "But if my family doesn't put you off, which is astonishing, I do have my own conditions."

He laughed again, and she decided she loved that sound. This man laughing made her...*glad*. It was as if he was like any one of the creatures she tended to out in these hills. Ferocious from afar, but surprisingly tender up close, though he showed no one else.

It made her feel another kind of warm, everywhere, that he showed her.

"By all means," Asterion said, that laughter making his voice richer. Deeper. "Tell me what conditions you have and I will meet them. Perhaps you have not heard, little huntress. I have the means and the will to get everything it is I want."

"I had no intention of marrying any of the suitors my family presented to me," she said. "And I know that they had no intention of doing anything for me. It was always a transaction they worked out with my father first. But the sisters intended to look into the idea of some kind of refuge. That's what I want."

"My family owns more property on this island than anyone else, save the crown." His tone was so offhand that she wasn't sure she followed him. Again, he raised a brow. "It should be no trouble whatsoever to give some of it over to you. You can do as you wish with it."

"The sisters promised to put it to a robust discussion and give it up in prayer." Brita smiled. "But from you, I think I will require it in writing."

"This is what I like about you." Though, as he growled that out, she was not entirely sure that he did. "You're always surprising."

"Well," she said after a moment, aware that she was too hot again, "I suppose I'm glad that I decided not to let my arrow pierce your flesh. That would have been awkward."

Asterion moved closer. The air all around them got thin. "If you wish for me to kiss you more, Brita, now that we are to be married, all you need do is ask."

But all she could do was nod. Mutely.

And this time it was a slow thing, the way he tugged her toward him. The way he tipped her head back and then settled his mouth to hers.

That was a lesson all on its own, that it could be so different. That it could be the same two people, the same mouths coming together.

That it could be called a kiss but be so *different*.

It was as if every shift of his mouth against hers peeled another layer of her skin away. But not her actual skin. It was like layers of her soul.

Brita moved closer, winding her arms around his neck and pressing herself against him because everything in her body urged her on.

He shifted so that he was holding her there, one hand tangled in her hair and the other a small miracle of sensation and heat up and down the line of her spine.

On and on he kissed her, and it felt like too many things at once. Like soaring high in the sky as she'd imagined, and yet as if there was nothing else but this.

As if the whole of the world narrowed down to his lips, his tongue, his teeth.

As if there was nothing left of her but the way it felt

to press her breasts into the hard wall of his chest and try to follow what he did, so he could feel as marvelous as she did, too.

And all the while there was that wild, joyful ache she wanted to go on forever.

For a while it felt as if it did.

But too soon he was pulling back again, and there was something different about his face, she thought. Something different from before.

"Come," he said, his voice gruff. "There is a wedding to plan. And your grasping, social climbing, currently indebted family to appease. Not to mention, you must present yourself before my grandmother. For an inspection, to be clear. Not just of you. But of us."

"She will want to make certain that this is not a trick." Brita nodded. "I'm all for it. I like her already."

And then her breath left her again when he took her hand, winding his fingers through hers.

Something she had never understood the point of, until now. But his fingers moved slightly as they began to walk, and every bit of friction made that ache in her double. Every bit of friction kept her aware and amazed and shivery from her scalp to the soles of her feet.

It was like that until he let her go, so she could find her way to her night's shelter.

And that was why it was not until the next morning, when she woke up in her campsite, with a grin on her face and an edgy need coursing through her body, that the expression he had on his face after that second kiss came back to her.

It was different from the first time. The first time, he had looked stunned. Almost shaken.

The second time, he had looked indulgent. In control.

She could admit that she found both alluring.

Just remembering them made her breath go shallow.

But there was something in her that told her—with a certainty born of a wisdom deep inside her that she could not name, though she found she trusted it implicitly— that the real man was in that first kiss.

That the control was a defense.

And it was up to her to dismantle it, if she dared.

Smiling up at a bright blue dawn, Brita rather thought she did.

CHAPTER SEVEN

THEIR WEDDING DAY dawned bright and beautiful, as if Asterion had ordered it specifically from the gods to honor his name—or to celebrate the fact that he was achieving the very thing his grandmother had dared suggest he could not do. He was marrying a woman of noted and widely known virtue, despite his reputation.

Despite his well-documented *monstrousness*.

He would have ordered a complimentary rainbow or two from all the gods, old and new alike, had he known how to contact them.

His staff had been working at a frenzied pace ever since he'd announced his engagement, racing to cajole by any means necessary the required officials and priests to move more quickly than usual. And much more quickly than they liked. Asterion was fairly certain that his grandmother's favorite church, the setting she would have preferred for the ceremony, had coldly extorted him to bypass the usual restrictions. The bishop himself had come in to grumble and frown and ultimately do as Asterion wished.

Most did.

Their proper engagement had occurred a week after

the night they'd kissed. First he had apprised his staff and sent them off to change the world to suit him. Then he had gone to see the Martis family the very next day.

He had presented himself at the front door of the villa, bright and early. Though he had stood there some while, for it had taken a great deal of knocking and ringing to gain admittance. Then even longer to wait on the family in what must once have been a truly elegant receiving room.

Elegant was not the word for it any longer. The walls were notably cracked. There were indications that paintings had been removed from the walls. The seating arrangements looked as if they had been tossed together, suggesting that whatever elegance had once resided here, it had long since become a bit more of a jumbled collection of odds and ends dragged in from the rest of the sad, old house.

There was no dust. But bitterness seemed to hang over the room just the same, weighing down the beams of sunlight from outside that dared attempt to penetrate it.

This was the very room that boasted the windows he had crept past in the shadows the first night he had met Brita. It was no surprise that it was not a pleasant place.

He had been equally unsurprised at the hollow-eyed, clearly hungover family members who trickled in to greet him—eventually—because their appearances matched the harsh voices he'd heard that night.

There were roughly seven of them in total, assuming no more were lurking about in the villa, unable to rise to the occasion. The man, who he took to be Vasilis Martis.

The clearly vain and overly precious woman at his side, who'd made it clear she was his wife. He saw a woman of about Brita's age, who could only be the cousin she had mentioned, looking haughty and unfriendly. And two other males of the same features, marking them as members of the same clan, one with a sour-faced woman who sat beside him with ill grace.

Asterion disliked them all on sight.

"I cannot say we are normally descended upon at such an uncivil hour," the stepmother said in a querulous voice.

"Forgive me the intrusion," Asterion had said in return, in a tone that made it clear he expected that forgiveness to be a foregone conclusion. "But I come to you with joyful news." He trained his gaze on Brita's father. "Your daughter, sir, has consented to make me the happiest man alive. So it is that I, Asterion Teras, will be taking Brita as my wife, and in so doing, joining your family to mine." He'd inclined his head. "I offer you my felicitations."

Brita had told him exactly what to expect, and he had quickly discovered that she had been right on every score. Down to the surly expressions on each of her relatives' faces at such an early hour. At first they had thought that she might join in this particular scene, but had decided that it would go just as well without her.

Because it wasn't really about her, was it?

And sure enough, the family only looked at each other in astonishment for a few short moments. Then their surprise was quickly overtaken by a far more powerful force.

Greed.

"My daughter is an heiress to the family name and entirely too dear to us," her father had demurred, his gaze alight with dreams of wealth. "I cannot possibly allow *just anyone* to walk in off the street and marry her. Surely you must know that she is in great demand."

"The difference being that she wishes to marry me," Asterion had pointed out silkily.

And it was a mark of how well they all knew precisely who he was, and how little they were inclined to doubt a man with his portfolio, that no one questioned that. Even though Brita had thus far shown no interest in marrying anyone else that had been paraded before her.

There were certainly no calls to bring Brita forth, that she might assure them of the truth of Asterion's claim.

I can assure you, all they need to know about you is that you are...you, Brita had assured him, laughing, though Asterion had found it...significantly less amusing.

And he found it even less so as he witnessed them all behaving precisely as she had predicted.

Her father had leaned forward in his chair, his smile thin, though his eyes still danced. No doubt doing sums in his head and planning his spending. "There are certain considerations," he began.

But Asterion was not an empire builder by accident, even if he was more unsettled by this clinical exchange than he wished to let on. He told himself that it was a good reminder that this marriage would be a contract like any other, and he would control its outcome as he did anything else he chose to sign his name to.

Still, that odd sensation persisted. He was…disconcerted.

Not that he let it show. He leaned back against the nearest mantel, propped himself up as if he was bored, and inclined his head.

"Go on then," he'd said. "Name your price."

And the bargaining had begun in earnest.

Only when that unsavory task was done and the contracts all signed had he brought Brita to see his grandmother.

He had considered putting her in the sort of formal attire that he knew his grandmother preferred, but he didn't. Dimitra was the one who had chosen Brita, and so she could meet the real Brita, in all her glory.

There was ample time to dress her for the role she would need to take on—at least in public—to bring the expected glory to the Teras name.

"Why did you pick me to marry him?" Brita had asked, the moment she and Dimitra had clapped eyes on each other. She hadn't even waited to take a seat on one of the excessively theatrical couches. "I can't imagine why I would be anybody's first choice, and especially not yours."

"You are the only choice," Dimitri had responded, with a cackle. "I rather thought you'd have the good sense to refuse him."

"Well," Brita had murmured, "there's still time."

Asterion supposed that he should not have been surprised that his grandmother found his little huntress delightful. Even though she was nothing like all the heiresses Dimitra had thrown his way in the past, Brita reminded Dimitra of herself. She said so—more than once—and there was no higher compliment his grandmother could bestow.

Once those key meetings were finished, he could get on with the actual engagement.

I suggest you lock that down, his grandmother had told him. *Before she comes to her senses.*

Asterion did not explain to Dimitra that he had a secret weapon. Brita would do almost anything he asked if it would lead to more kissing, and he knew it.

He no longer had any doubt about his ability to control the situation because he controlled the pace. She was an innocent and he was not, and there was no need to worry about *losing himself.* That had been a momentary bit of madness out there in the moonlight—but once they were married, he would not have to worry about such things. They would settle. They would no longer be so *fraught*.

The unsettled sensation would be a memory, nothing more.

Still, he did not tarry. He had talked to Brita about the worlds he would show her, for all of them were at his feet. She had seemed duly unimpressed. And when he asked her where she might like to go, she had named Paris as the city she would most like to see.

She had first named a number of inaccessible wildernesses, to be fair. There were mountains she wanted to climb. Seas she wished to swim. Impossible glaciers she wished to stand upon, for no good reason that he could discern. Yet something about the shiny newness of her enthusiasm got to him. It made him want nothing more than to show her all the things she could imagine, and many more, and explore them all with her and that clear-eyed wonder she brought with her wherever she went.

Another man might have imagined himself besotted.

Asterion, happily, was not another man.

When it came to their engagement, a man of his status had certain expectations attached to him. There were tried-and-true ways that he needed to make certain announcements to the world at large, and a city was needed.

Once again, Brita surprised him. Not only with the choice of Paris, a city many loved the world over but he had not expected she would care for one way or the other, but because she bargained with him there, too.

There were a whole host of museums she wanted to see and cultural monuments she wanted to visit, and only then would she condescend to visit the atelier he had selected to handle the details of her wardrobe.

"I can dress myself," she told him on the flight over, frowning at him over the breakfast the staff had prepared and served them in the cabin of his private plane.

"I do not see the purpose of having a wife if I cannot dress her to my taste," he had replied offhandedly.

She had eyed him. "Like a blow-up doll, you mean."

"Like the man who intends to remove every article of clothing I pay to put on you," he had replied. Just quietly enough.

And had enjoyed very much the shade of pink she took on for the rest of the flight.

That night, he took her out to dinner at a restaurant that

did not take reservations and rarely had seatings—unless a person possessed the sort of name that did not require such pedestrian concerns. Asterion was, naturally, one of them. And it was a deeply pleasurable thing indeed to watch Brita experience new flavors, new culinary artistry, new sensual delights.

Halfway through the meal, he found himself thinking that he would need to make it a priority to introduce her to as many new things as possible, just to watch her immerse herself in these experiences. To be the one sitting with her when she raised her gaze, wide with awe, when something charmed or surprised her.

The way he wanted her would have concerned him, he was sure, if he was someone else. If he had to worry about being unable to control himself.

He had to remind himself that he was Asterion Teras, and he was above such things, no matter what he might find himself feeling in a Parisian restaurant in the company of a woman who only he knew was a wild virgin huntress, like all the myths of old, capable of shooting bows and befuddling men with a single glance.

Afterward, he walked her out into the fireworks display that was the paparazzi waiting for them outside with a ring on her finger that he had put there during the meal. It was a masterwork of a diamond. It was flawless and breathtakingly elegant, yet somehow called to mind the sweet clarity of her hilltops, the moon that had risen before them, and the way she had kissed him, all fire and fury.

"It seems a bit much," Brita had said inside, turning it this way and that.

"I am a bit much, little huntress," he had replied. "And more."

But he had breathed easier than he wanted to admit when she looked at him and smiled.

Rumors of their engagement—or, rather, Asterion Teras's engagement to a mysterious woman in fashionable Paris—made it into the papers before the plane touched down on the island later that same night.

It had been chaotic ever since, and made both worse and better because there were far fewer midnight rambles on the hillsides. Asterion had to be quite stern with himself. Once they were married, he could not allow such security risks. To say nothing of the time commitment. There would have to be no more of such foolishness.

Once they were married, he assured himself, they would have other ways of entertaining themselves.

And now, at last, the wedding day had come. His brother had made an appearance, down from London, which he claimed he preferred to the island. The priests had been appeased and an altar had been set up on Asterion's property, which was ever after to remain a holy place. He had agreed easily enough, for he already considered it holy enough. It was his.

Dimitra had insisted on taking part in the expansive guest list, and so, between her connections and his contacts, it was the breathtakingly sophisticated affair a Teras wedding should be, staged out on the cliffs above his home.

Even Brita's family seemed disposed to behave themselves, no doubt because the wedding itself was the grandest affair any of them had attended in generations.

Dimitra, true to her word as ever, elected to pretend she did not see them.

And finally Asterion stood at the head of the aisle that led to his new chapel, arranged to make sure that anyone watching could not fail to take in the view of the sea that seemed to stretch on into eternity. He could see that more than one guest was duly enchanted.

But he rather liked the vision coming toward him.

Brita on her father's arm in a flowing white dress that was remarkable in its simplicity.

On another woman, it might have been drab. Too plain. She had spent some while discussing the matter at the atelier in Paris and had decided that less was more.

For she was already too beautiful for her own good. Too beautiful for his peace of mind. She did not need adornments and so the dress had none.

She left her hair down and wore a sort of crown of flowers, as if to remind everyone that she was only as civilized as she pretended to be, and only for the moment. Asterion took the message to heart.

But what mattered more was that her eyes were on him.

And then her hands were in his.

Once that happened, he no longer cared about anything else. Only the promise in her eyes and the sound of her voice repeating their simple, ancient vows.

And when he kissed her, making her his wife at last, he felt as if she almost undid him that easily.

When he could not allow himself to be undone.

"We are married," she said solemnly as they walked back down the aisle together.

"Well and truly," he agreed.

And he could not have said why that felt like a storm inside him, rising into full roar.

But the reception was a grand party, and a reprieve. There were people to talk to, a meal to eat, and all the usual speeches, and he told himself he was glad of it all even if he didn't care about any of it.

All he could think about was what would come later.

When he could stand it no longer, he stole Brita away from the people already cozying up to her, the new Teras wife, which might have been amusing if he wasn't so riddled with his need for her. He drew her out onto the dance floor they'd made in his gardens, because it was the next best thing to what he really wanted.

When there were still hours to go.

She swayed with him, lithe and too lovely, tipping her head back so she could study his face.

For once in his life, he had no idea what might be found there.

"How much longer do we have to do all this?" she asked.

And it was easier then. She'd broken the worst of the tension in him and so he could smile.

Better yet, he could pretend that she was the impatient one. "How shocking of you, Brita," he murmured. "All of these people have assembled to celebrate our joy."

"They have assembled to dance attendance on one of the wealthiest men in the world," she replied in her matter-of-fact way that, after so many conversations tonight that were circuitous and treacherous, struck him like a deep breath of good air. "And the strange wild woman he's chosen for a wife."

"Surely you must know that they are attempting to curry your favor as well."

"I cannot be curried," she assured him. Then smiled. "But I do enjoy the attempts. They do not realize that I can only think of one thing."

"Are you so single-minded?" he asked, not quite lazily, though he did not think he should let her know how her words hit at him.

"You know what I want," she told him.

He had signed the documents she'd requested with great flourish, though he made a point to inform her that no one else had ever dared question his word. That his promise to make her the wildlife refuge she wanted should have sufficed.

But he knew that for once, island wildlife was not what was heaviest on her mind.

Not tonight.

"Don't you worry," he told her as they danced, swaying together like a premonition. A glimpse into the future that made him perilously close to embarrassing himself. "I will have my mouth all over you, little huntress. I will make you scream."

And when she kissed him as the song ended, he could feel the hint of her teeth.

"You have your hands full there," Poseidon said idly when Asterion found his brother at the bar, enjoying the attentions of a full rugby scrum of beautiful women. All of whom scattered before Asterion and his monstrous reputation.

He'd had the idle thought that perhaps his marriage would change that, but apparently it hadn't yet.

"I think I'll be just fine," Asterion replied to his brother, smiling in what he could only describe as full elder brother.

"Is it true what they say? She roams the hills, bow and arrow in hand, as one with the wild things?"

Asterion smiled. "Not tonight."

The reception carried on, glittering on into the night, until Asterion began to wonder if it would last forever—trapping him in this strange space where he could never quite touch Brita the way he wished he could.

The way, he could admit now, he had imagined he would too many times to count.

It was becoming too much like that sickness Brita had mentioned. He had never felt its like.

Then again, he had also never denied himself something he wanted for this long.

"And you thought I couldn't do this," he chided his grandmother as he danced with her, something that might have been sentimental in another family.

But they were the last of the Teras dynasty and their dance with so many eyes upon them was a demonstration of power. Marking their legacy and their intention to continue it, just as Dimitra wanted.

"Have you wooed her?" Dimitra asked with too much wisdom in her voice for his liking. As if she was being prophetic. He knew she was only being herself, which was to say, nosy.

"I have wed her," Asterion retorted. "So what does wooing matter, in the end?"

"You," his grandmother said, turning her gleaming gaze on him as they moved across the dance floor, "are a very foolish man."

And Asterion would normally take exception to a statement like that, but he couldn't. Not tonight.

Because *foolish* was the only word to describe how his brand-new wife made him feel, and he did not intend to admit that to anyone.

He could barely admit it to himself.

And just when he was beginning to believe that they were to be stuck in the endless purgatory of this wedding forever, the reception was finally over. His staff ushered the guests out of the gardens, guiding them along with bright lanterns while Asterion and Brita stood before the grand dome that served as the entrance to his labyrinth and waved them off.

Until, at last, they were gone.

His staff melted back around to the cliff side of the house to handle the cleanup, and after all this time, he was alone with his wife.

No staff. No crowd. No one but them.

It felt almost too good to be true.

Asterion hadn't meant to move, but somehow they were facing each other once more, standing there as if they were about to take their vows all over again.

And he could feel his pulse overtaking him, that fire in his blood crowding out his ability to do anything but breathe.

But barely.

The breeze tainted him with that scent of hers that he

knew matched her taste—a little bit herbal, a touch of green. And then the sweetness that was only her.

He thought he ought to say something, for he was the one with experience here. Though at the moment he couldn't recall any of it. Instead, he felt like the callow, overset boy he had never been.

The stars seemed to press in. The dark seemed too thick, suddenly, and far hotter than it should have been this time of year.

And Brita, who should have been the one trembling and beside herself, overcome at what might happen now, smiled.

She took a step back, gave him a speaking sort of glance as she turned, and then melted off toward the trees.

Right before she disappeared into the trees, she looked back over her shoulder and raised her brows in a clear and obvious challenge.

And he was lost.

Asterion was after her without another thought, like the wild animal he prided himself on never allowing himself to become—

Except for tonight.

CHAPTER EIGHT

BRITA WAITED FOR HIM, this brand-new husband of hers, when she had never imagined she would marry unless under the deepest duress, in the soft embrace of the trees.

He was there in a flash, his chest heaving as if he'd run the whole way, when she knew very well he hadn't. She had watched him walk toward her, filled with purpose. She had caught her breath as she waited, and now that he was close, she could see his eyes were dark with the same passion she felt storming inside her.

It was a marvel, that she should like everything about this night.

And about this man.

She liked that her body seemed caught between thunder and lightning, both hitting her at once. She liked how his gaze caught her as surely as any well-aimed arrow, so she felt trapped in the most delicious way possible.

It didn't occur to her to attempt to move.

She would have fought against it if anyone else dared try and move her.

And these were funny thoughts indeed for a woman who had, until so recently, imagined that the only future worth having involved holy orders.

"Husband," she said, testing the word in her mouth. "You're my *husband*."

"And you, little huntress, are my wife," he replied in that same dark, thrilling manner.

She had been there at their wedding. It had been remarkably elegant. She'd spent the better part of it convinced that at any moment, she would shame herself by dumping her food down the front of her white gown, tripping over the hem of it, or otherwise making it clear that she was unequal to the task of becoming a Teras wife.

That was what the papers said. She'd hated it—all those cameras, the endless flashes as if she was caught in a storm again but this time, the lightning hit. And hit. And hit again.

But the true blows had come later, when the papers had opined about her worthiness to marry the scion of the Teras family. They paraded her family's history before the world, and while Brita could not disagree with the conclusions drawn about her father, his wife, and her cousins, she also found she did not care for it when others spoke ill of them.

They called her insulting names. *Like gold digger.*

She wanted to correct them. She wanted to tell the world that actually she alone cared nothing for the man's money and wanted him only for his much-vaunted sexual prowess—but in order to do that, she would have to confess to Asterion that the things the papers said bothered her.

And she couldn't.

She wouldn't.

It had been impressed on her a long, long time ago that

it was always better to be the one who cared less. And that the less she appeared to care, the more she got what she wanted. Like university.

And this time what she wanted was so huge it terrified her.

She would act unbothered—by everything—if it killed her, because the alternative was unthinkable.

Brita was well aware that most of the guests already thought that she was exactly as unworthy of Asterion as the papers had speculated, at great length. Some hadn't even bothered to conceal their sneers.

She had concentrated on the part of her that was tempted to trip *and* stain herself anyway, knowing that whatever shame she felt personally, if she revealed herself to be so embarrassing at such a moment her father would likely leap straight off the side of the cliff before them.

It really had been tempting.

But a wedding was a play that everyone already knew the words to, so that made it both easier and stranger. Brita had been aware of all those eyes on her, but she was used to being stared at. The people in the villages had always made it clear that she was different in ways they didn't quite like, though they had never taken to it with the nasty glee of the gutter press. But the looks from Asterion's posh friends and associates had been far more... assessing. Maybe even intrigued.

And then there'd been the clasping of hands as she'd gazed into Asterion's eyes and the ancient vows they'd recited word for word. The wedding crowns. The three trips around the altar while every member of her family glared at her from the front row.

No doubt they'd been concerned that at any moment Heracles might put in an appearance, or worse, Brita might shame herself—meaning, them—but it had all gone smoothly. Then there had been dinner. Dancing. Endless discussions with people whose names she had no interest in remembering. There had been all the jostling for position and suggestions of influence that she had discussed with Asterion earlier, all of which bored her, but none of that mattered now.

All of that had been for others. The pageantry. The customs. The endless celebrating that had all been for specific reasons, none of them Asterion and her.

But now it was only the two of them, out here in the dark.

Now, at last, they were down to the only things that mattered.

The two of them out in the night with nobody watching, the way it had been at the start or none of this would have happened.

And so it made all the sense in the world that it was here he reached out, drew her to him, and kissed her—

But this time in a way she knew, somehow, he did not mean to stop anytime soon.

It all seemed to hit her the way it always did when he was near. That great flush, that ache, and all the ways she *wanted something* she couldn't define.

It was easy to call it *itchy,* but it felt like something more.

Because as she pressed herself against the wide wall of

his chest, she felt both more and less of all those things. As if he was the cure as well as the disease.

But Brita didn't care what he was. She wound herself around him, jumping up so she could wrap her legs around his waist. Then she sighed a little as he gripped her by the thighs and held her there.

And still he kissed her, on and on, all of it fire.

All of it starshine and moonlight, tangling around inside of her so that all she could do was hold on to him with every part of her that she could think to use, and then see where the storm would take her.

Then, maybe, she would find out what was left of her—if anything—when it blew itself out.

And when he laid her out on the ground, the soft bed she liked best, Brita could hardly tell the difference between the tumble inside her and how it felt to be tipped flat on her back and pressed down.

But she knew she liked that, too.

His hands cupped her face and he kissed her again, deep and wild. Then he tore his mouth from hers and set it to her cheek, her temple, teaching her new ways to burn.

Until she wondered if he meant to turn every last part of her to ash.

And if she would laugh happily into the night while she turned to flame, the way she did now as he went lower still, finding the pulse in her neck, her collarbone.

Then it was as if a great, shattering earthquake overtook them both, because she could feel a trembling within her and in him, too, in every place their bodies touched. In every place he pressed all his strength and heat against her.

In all the places she was soft.

He made a noise that made her think of the wildest things, too wild to let her near, and she felt it echo deep within her.

Something in her whispered, *yes*.

So she indulged herself and let her hands move all over him, finding the astonishing shape of him beneath his clothes, then shoving her fingers through any odd buttonhole she could to find the heat of him and the hard, smooth muscles that made his chest more like a feast than the dinner they'd sat through earlier.

And the more she touched him, the more everything seemed better.

Wilder, yes. Hotter, *yes, please*.

"We must go slow," he warned her, right when she thought she might sink her teeth into him just to see how he would taste. "For you are new and untried, and I fear—"

"I fear nothing," she told him, though she pulled back.

Then paused, her heart a new thunder in her chest, because he looked something like tortured.

But after a considering breath, Brita decided that only made her feel bolder.

She reached down and grabbed the hem of her dress and began to pull it up, baring herself to him.

And was glad she did, because he made another one of those noises, like a wild thing.

Brita didn't need to ask if that was approval. She knew it was.

It was as if she suddenly understood the purpose of

her body in a whole new way. She had long expected it to be able to run. To hike and climb. To dance in the rain and bathe in the moonlight.

But this was something brand-new.

There was that scalding heat between her legs. It made her want to shiver. Maybe she did. And still, all she wanted to do was press herself to him, twine herself around him, and see how much hotter she could get.

When she did, she could feel that thick, hot ridge between his legs, and that made everything inside her seem to *shimmer.*

"Little huntress, you don't understand—" he began.

But she didn't want to understand.

She wanted to follow these sensations, and so she reached out her hand and put it to the front of his trousers. Then she felt for the shape of him, finding herself grinning, then laughing, at the rich, deep sounds he made.

He growled, like any other wild beast, and it was a thrilling sound.

It seemed to fill her up—and then Asterion had her flat on her back.

She didn't even feel him move.

One moment she was laughing, then he loomed over her, on top of her, propping himself up on one elbow as he reached between them. And she did not have to know precisely what he was doing to know exactly what he was doing. Every hair on her body seemed to prickle into awareness.

It was possible she made her own sort of growling noise and got a flash of that midnight blue for her troubles.

But then he focused his attention on the important work of opening his wedding trousers, then taking that great shaft of his and working it all over and through that wetness between her legs.

"You do not wear underthings," he gritted out, as if the knowledge hurt him.

"They seem extraneous," she replied.

And then she forgot about it, because he was *moving*.

It was like magic.

It was extraordinary.

She'd never felt another person's hands on her, much less on her intimate parts, and certainly not *there*.

Asterion dragged himself through all that heat, once, then again, and then suddenly, something seemed to buckle up from within her. She tried to dance in it, like any storm, but she couldn't—

Because before she could find her footing, she was shimmering and burning bright, tumbling out into the universe.

When she was herself again, Asterion was still there, holding himself above her.

She felt the flame start within her all over again.

His eyes were glittering with the dark madness she felt everywhere, and then she watched as he pressed that same part of him into the core of her need.

Everything shook, but she didn't quite *shimmer*—

And then, his eyes on hers, he pushed himself inside her, but only a little.

Then he pulled out again, and the next time, he went a little further—a new need, a new lightning, shooting out from everywhere he touched her, centering deep inside and then fanning out, to light up every last part of her body.

Every limb. Every bone.

Everything she was or ever would be.

And on and on he worked himself inside her, inch by beautiful, treacherous, glorious inch.

Until, at last, he was firmly seated deep within her body.

She heard a high-pitched, strange new sound.

"Breathe," Asterion told her in that dark way of his that she found not even remotely grim, not now.

When she pulled in that breath he'd commanded, she realized that she was the one making that noise. That she was panting wildly, or maybe she was moaning—she didn't know.

But when she bore down on that great, hot length of him inside her, filling her up, pressing her from the inside out, surely too big and too thick to fit—

She broke apart once again,

This time, as she came back down, she heard the sound of his laughter—that dark, not quite musical threat that made everything in her hum with fresh delight.

And then he began to move.

This was not the easing in, then out, from before.

This was different. This was so very different—

But Asterion was in control. He set them a rhythm and did not stray from it.

And all Brita could think to do was hold on to him as best she could, her grip tight and her head thrown back to take in all of it, as he taught her things she never could have guessed about her own body.

About pleasure and desire.

About the kind of passion she had never believed was real.

Again and again, he thrust deep and made her new.

Until finally, she flew apart a third time and he flew with her, catapulting them both out to all the galaxies that spun high above until she couldn't tell the difference between them and her.

Maybe they were all the same.

It was possible she simply disappeared, for a time.

Because she had no memory of him moving away from her, dressing them both in some fashion or another, then swinging her up into his arms. But these things must have happened, because when she knew herself again he was striding back toward that house of his, toward that gleaming globe that rose from the earth, holding her in his arms as if she was some kind of sacrifice.

And Brita had never particularly wished to sacrifice herself for anything, but tonight, she found she did not mind.

She let her head rest on his shoulder and she stared out at the sea as he took her down and then down farther into his labyrinth, down one set of stairs and then another, all of them encased in glass, until he took her into what she assumed must be his bedroom.

He set her on the edge of a very wide, very high bed and then, his eyes glittering once again, he set about stripping her entirely of everything she wore once more—

save the crown of flowers on her head that was only slightly askew.

"You look like a goddess," he told her, his voice rough.

Brita liked that. Every part of her body felt alive and new. The tips of her breasts stood up proudly, begging for his attention. Between her legs, she was softer and hotter than before. That itchiness, that ache—she understood what it was now and she welcomed those sensations as they made her skin feel too tight and yet just right.

And when he knelt down the side of the bed and spread her legs wide before him, she found herself holding her breath.

Then letting it out in a rush as he pulled her thighs over his shoulders, leaned in, and licked his way into her softness.

Where he taught her a whole new way to move, to dance, to rock herself against the wild seduction of his mouth.

When she was sobbing and falling apart, he stood. She could only half watch him, too busy trying to breathe, as he stripped himself of what was left of his own clothes, presenting himself marvelously naked before her at last.

Brita wanted so many things then.

And all of them at once.

That terror of it was almost too much.

She wanted to bury her face between the slabs of muscle that made up his chest. She wanted to follow that trail of hair down to where it ended at that great shaft of his. She wanted to taste him as he tasted her.

But she did none of those things because what he did

was crawl over her, then roll so that she was sitting on top of him, her hair falling between them like a dark, silken curtain that smelled of the things his staff had put in it instead of earth and fire, fresh air and growing things.

Brita did not dislike the scent as much as she thought she should.

And then she stopped caring, because his hands were on her hips, shifting her, and she could feel him pressed into her again.

But this time from a completely different angle.

"Surely you know how to ride," he said, more than a little challenge in his voice.

Brita accepted the challenge. She propped herself up against his chest, pressing the heel of her palms against him, already trembling because it was her turn to move.

And oh, how she wanted to.

So she did.

She lifted herself, then sank down, groaning at the differences in the way he filled her. She writhed against him, following all those longings inside her. She leaned forward and found it was even better when he found her nipple with his mouth and wilder sensations streaked through her like a new way to burn.

She didn't think she could match his rhythm, so she indulged herself instead, making them both dance to a beat of her own making and not stopping no matter how intense it became.

No matter how hard he gripped her hips.

And soon enough, she was catapulting straight for another explosion—

And Asterion took control, hammering into her, making it clear that he knew exactly what every stroke was doing to her—

Until together they ignited, burned like a comet, and then dropped back down into this bed of his.

And the dark of the room swallowed them whole, until, tangled up together, she slept.

At some point he woke her and there were wet cloths and low murmurs she hardly understood.

Still she slept, and when she woke, there were faint notes of peach and orange over the gleaming sea on the far side of the glass, the morning sky a silent symphony stretched out before her. One of her favorite views.

She looked beside her in the wide bed, but Asterion wasn't there.

Brita could admit that there was a part of her that was relieved.

Because she was certain that all of last night was stamped on the skin of her face, or perhaps it had changed the very bone structure she'd had her whole life. She could *feel* it.

All she knew was that she was not the same person she'd been when she'd woken up yesterday.

She was just as glad there was no one else around to see it.

The crown of flowers from the wedding was on the floor beside the bed, and she had no memory of removing it. She was naked, and it was true that she had grown so accustomed to camping, but she did not think that was the only reason that the sheets against her skin felt like a caress.

Nothing in the whole of her life could possibly have prepared her for feeling like this.

For feeling so close, physically and otherwise, to another person.

He had been *inside* her.

His mouth had found parts of her that Brita had never seen with her own eyes. Even now, alone and hours later, she felt shivery all over again—and emotional.

And terrified all over again, and this time worse than before.

Because she had been as innocent as he'd claimed and she'd had no idea that anyone could feel like this.

Vulnerable. Stripped raw. Both wanting more and wanting to run.

As if the emotion inside her was a true fever this time and might burn her alive.

She curled up where she lay, closed her eyes, both shocked and yet unsurprised when moisture leaked from her lashes. And she remembered, almost against her will, the trip she taken to the convent only ten days ago.

Your year is not yet up, child, the Abbess had said when Brita had been brought through to her presence. Though there had been a wise look on her face, as if she already knew what Brita had come to tell her.

I am marrying, Brita had said in her typically blunt way. *But not for the reasons that other people marry. And one day, I think it's entirely possible that I will be back here, hoping to join you once more.*

The Abbess had inclined her head, but when she looked up, she'd only smiled.

Knowingly.

That was all, when Brita had expected a quiet lecture or talk of her duties. Failing that, perhaps a bit of condemnation for straying from the path.

Anything but that smile.

The entire exchange had confused her.

But here in this marriage bed, turned inside out by the man she had married and already desperate for more, she understood.

Too well, she understood.

Everything had changed.

She had changed, inside and out.

He had changed her.

And she could never go back to the girl she had been before last night.

CHAPTER NINE

A MONTH INTO his new marriage, Asterion had to accept that, despite his intentions, which were usually as good as written law where most things were concerned, it was not going to plan.

The evidence had been all around him, but the final straw was an exquisitely exclusive gala event in Monaco.

Brita, as ever, stunned without trying. She wore the simplest of gowns with little to no adornment because none was needed. She was breathtaking as she walked in, catching every eye without seeming to notice that anyone was looking, which Asterion knew could only add to her mystique. The gossipy papers were filled with speculation about the new Teras wife, but he did not have to counsel Brita on how to ignore the tales they spun—she never paid the slightest attention to such things. She treated rumors and gossip and the usual social machinations by the usual people the same way she did everything else. She sailed on by, smiled enigmatically, and then did precisely as she pleased.

Only he knew that she had spent the drive from one of his properties, a villa filled with priceless art and Côte d'Azur sunshine on the water in Cap Ferrat, experimenting with different ways to take him in her mouth.

Yet an hour or so into the event she was nowhere to be found.

This was not unusual, and that was the trouble. Other wives stayed with their husbands, particularly when their husbands were rich and powerful tycoons who did as they pleased in their corporate playgrounds. Staying at or near their husbands' sides was part of their expected marital duties. No point having a trophy, after all, if it couldn't be displayed.

He was certain he had expressed this notion to his errant new wife after the last event, where an acquaintance had slyly pretended not to know that Asterion had married, since there was no blushing bride in evidence. And Asterion hoped the man in question had enjoyed himself, because he'd lost himself and his company a lucrative deal thanks to that tone.

Something he had attempted to impress upon his wife.

But he had looked around some fifteen minutes ago tonight and realized that Brita was nowhere to be found. It wasn't that he worried about her or what she might be getting up to—and not because she was of as little interest to him as other women had been.

Quite the opposite.

Some men might be concerned that a wife so beautiful might be off sharing her charms with others, but Asterion had no doubts on that score. Not a one.

Others might worry that the unscrupulous might attempt to use Brita to get to him in one way or another, but he wasn't worried about that, either.

He did not permit her to carry her bow and arrows into polite society, but he had no doubt that if she wished, his wife could defend herself handily. But there was far too much security in a place like this for that to be a factor.

Asterion exhausted the possibilities in the grand ballroom, found no sign of her, and then asked himself where the least likely place would be for a guest to go. He followed the catering staff in through a set of swinging doors, wound his way through the bowels of the fancy old Château, high on a hillside, and found himself in the kitchens.

Then, following an inkling he did not care to acknowledge closely, he let himself out the back door, walked out into the gardens, and found his wife kneeling there on the ground near a bit of shrubbery.

She looked up at him, but showed no hint of shame or apology.

If anything, she was glowing, there in the dirt.

"I found kittens," she told him, with wonder and joy, as if kittens were a scarce resource in this world. "I think they lost their mama."

"Brita," he began, in tones of admonishment.

Then stopped, because she was paying no attention to him.

To *him*.

Instead, as he watched in astonishment, she gathered up seven tiny, mewling little creatures in the skirt of her gown as if it was no more to her than a rag. She paid no attention to the leaves and dirt clinging to her as she marched all the little kittens inside. She found homes for five of them before clearing the kitchen, and then presented the last two to the host himself, out there in the middle of the exquisitely grand Château.

She was a menace.

It occurred to him that she was also, perhaps, doing what she needed to do to find her own way through the pit of vipers and snakes that was the social circle he moved in. He was sympathetic. He was.

But there was the Teras legacy to uphold.

"You do realize the purpose of attending an event is to actually attend it, do you not?" he asked her as they flew back south toward home, much later that night.

She only looked at him dreamily, no doubt with kittens dancing in her head. "Did you give them an obscene amount of money?" When he only lifted a brow, she laughed. "And why not save a few other lives while you're at it? What is the harm?"

The trouble was, the fact that he could not contain her made him…uneasy. Even if this was just how she'd decided to cope with the demands of her new role.

As the month wore on, it only got worse. He never knew what she would do, and he was sure he did not care for it.

At a wedding of minor, yet well-connected, royals in Europe, she befriended the groom's blind old uncle and made a friend of the watchful royal seeing eye dog, winning her the admiration of two kingdoms without even trying.

"What a coup," his number two man crowed. "We have been trying to get past the insistence both countries have on dealing only with local entities for years. One pat of a dog's head and the doors are now open. She's a secret weapon, sir!"

But Asterion knew better.

She was a loaded weapon, and he was not the one aiming it.

Would he use her to advance his business concerns if he could? He told himself he would, even though that, too, made him uneasy for even more reasons he did not care to excavate. Yet he would never know, because he couldn't *tell* Brita to do the things she did. She simply did them, and *she* didn't care how anyone else responded to those things.

Including him, it seemed.

For at home, no matter how many times he told her it was not appropriate for the wife of Asterion Teras to roam about the hills the way she liked to do, and no matter how many times she nodded sagely as if she agreed, she disappeared into the trees whenever she liked. Not as if she hadn't heard him, but as if he had not spoken on the topic at all.

He found he did not know what to do with the part of him that wanted to ask her if her need to always run for the literal hills was an emotional response to him, to their marriage, to the world he'd thrust her into. Because asking her such a question risked the possibility that she might ask him something similar in return.

And he refused to have *emotions*.

No matter what he felt.

Asterion could not decide what was worse. That for the first time, someone else lived in this house he had built for himself alone and he was aware of her presence, always.

Or the fact that when she was gone, he could feel that, too.

And not like a kind of peace.

He was on edge. He was certain that it was affecting his work—

Though his staff assured him that it was not. By reminding him that he could take the next seventy years off and still increase his annual profits by rote.

It was in this way that Asterion began to find himself behaving like a person he hardly knew.

He waited for her. He *waited up* for her. Sometimes he even roamed about the woods himself, though he never found her.

Making him suspect that she did not wish to be found.

Like she really was a creature made of myth and village lore.

He found himself wondering if it might have been easier if she really had been sneaking out to meet some kind of lover, however little he could imagine a man who could compete with him—and, for once, that was not his arrogance talking.

It was that he knew full well that what happened between them in bed was as shattering for her as it was for him.

Not that he cared to admit, even to himself, *how* intense it was with Brita. How raw. How different from all the shallow games with sex he realized only now he'd been playing his whole life.

He was not at all certain he liked that he no longer wished to play such games—especially because she clearly did.

And he did not ask himself why it was easier to believe she was playing games than to allow for the possibility that there was more to her behavior than simple caprice.

She would melt in and out of his house, always more silently than should have been possible. He would wait for her in the darkened bedroom and turn on the light when she entered like a ghost. He was always expecting her to flinch, offer stammering apologies, look *even remotely* guilty, but she never did.

"I found a nest of blackcaps," she would tell him, chattily, seeming perfectly happy to see him. Seeming not to notice that he was lurking about in the shadows of his own house like the sort of man he had vowed he would never become. The sort of man he had watched behave too much like this when he was a child, and it was not a comparison he cared for. He did not wish to become his father, a victim to every stray passion. He prided himself on having excised such things from his being, deliberately, since the age of twelve. "I had to make sure they were safe from the foxes."

There was always a reason. It was usually an animal in need, or the opportunity to observe another. Sometimes it was the moon over the water again, or the particular beauty of the stars. And no matter how he attempted to make his displeasure clear, she ignored it.

Brita not only ignored it, she would strip out of the clothes she liked to wear to wander the hills in defiance of his wishes. Then she would put out her hands and walk to him, quickly making him forget why he was outraged with her in the first place.

It took him a whole lot longer than it should have to realize that the way she treated him was eerily familiar, and not because it reminded him of his childhood, stuck in the turmoil his parents fed upon like oxygen. Maybe it was because that part of him that wanted her behavior to be a sign of all those deep emotions he should abhor, a sign that she was as overcome by their marriage as he did not wish to admit he was, turned out to be uncannily insistent. Or maybe it took so long because he had become a parody of himself, roaming about his labyrinth like the monster he knew he truly was, deep inside, and counting the hours until she deigned to come home.

That she did so only for sex took him a while to comprehend.

Because one thing was unmistakable. Brita loved sex. She loved every single thing they could do together, her body and his. She was imaginative, inventive, and she adored each and every new thing he'd taught her. There was no *too much*. There was no *enough*.

The only way he could keep her with him was to keep her naked and moaning out her need in his arms.

But even a monster had to sleep, and work, and that

was when she slipped back out into the wilderness as if it was her true lover, not him.

Or because that is where she feels safe, that voice in him whispered.

He ignored it.

It was some six weeks after their wedding day when he sat brooding at the dinner table one night, staring with his usual unacknowledged umbrage at his merry wife.

Who had only appeared moments ago, though he had made a point of telling her that he would prefer that they sat down for the evening meal together on the nights they did not have events.

He had told her when he was deep inside her, the only time he could be certain he had her full and focused attention.

She sauntered in looking like a backpacking university student of some sort, with a torn sleeve, what he hoped was mud and not something more ominous smeared across her cheek, and a look of total nonchalance about her.

As if she was not late. As if she was not clearly in from some more extreme and excessive hiking where she could, at any moment, fall to her death. In remote places where she would never be found, and how would he cope with that?

"This looks lovely." She was beaming down at the platters already crowding the table, all smelling of the sheer local perfection Asterion expected of his personal chef. "I am quite hungry."

It was possible he actually growled. "It would not harm you, I think, to dress for dinner."

Brita shrugged at that. "Or I could undress."

And then she did just that, stripping out of her clothes in that way she had, as if she wasn't attempting to seduce him in any way. As if she simply *preferred* nudity whenever possible and didn't mind if he looked.

She was maddening.

And it was worse when she seated herself at the table in all of her glorious nakedness.

He nearly swallowed his tongue and she barely glanced in his direction.

Asterion had to force himself to concentrate on the extensive list of his grievances, not his enduring lust for this impossible woman.

Because he certainly did not wish to stop and question why it was that his lust for her seemed to have no end. It went on and on, day and night, and only seem to grow sharper, deeper. Bigger. Wider.

Some days it was so large and so intense it was as if he could not breathe through it.

"I would not wish you to mar those perfect breasts by burning them in any way with hot food," he managed to get out with very ill humor. He unbuttoned the shirt he wore and handed it to her, so she could wrap it around her body like a robe.

She looked amused, but she did.

As if any of this was *amusing*.

Then they sat there, staring at each other across the table that had been prepared for them and placed beneath the pergola that was thick with vines not yet in the full bloom and a mess of lights that lit up the whole terrace. Before them was the sea. Behind them, the bedroom they shared and the great tangle of his house, spilling down the cliffside.

But all he could see was her.

Brita smiled at him, all that heat and wickedness in the curve of her mouth, and he wanted to launch himself across the table and get his hands on her. Even as, at the same time, he wanted nothing more than to explain to her why the way she was behaving could not work. Could not be borne.

She must stop this, he told himself, as he often did.

He opened his mouth to tell her so, but stopped himself. Because that eerie realization finally landed, and hard.

All of this was familiar because while *he* was having flashbacks to his childhood and the ways his parents would torment each other, if he ignored that voice inside him, it was obvious that *Brita* was having a different experience entirely.

And he knew that experience well.

She was treating Asterion precisely the way he had always treated his lovers, all throughout his life. She gave her body to him, enthusiastically, delightedly, and without reservation. She talked happily enough about the things she did when she was out there, making her own trail all over the island, much the way he spoke of his work when it was necessary to make polite conversation.

But she did not think about him at all when she was out

there, and when she was with him, she was marking time until they could be lost in the flesh and the fever of it all.

No wonder this felt familiar. This was precisely how he had always behaved, as if the women in his life were exercise equipment, however charming.

This, he finally understood, was why they called him a monster.

Asterion could see the irony. He did not know why it bothered him so much. He only knew it did.

"We have been married for six weeks," he told her, in the same dark tone. "And I have told you, almost daily, what my expectations are. Yet you do not heed them."

Brita sat before her still-empty plate, wrapped in his shirt, somehow even lovelier than usual. He wanted to wipe the dirt from her cheek. He wanted to press his mouth to the indentation between her collarbone and her neck. He wanted to kneel before her and lick his way into her soft heat, claiming her and tearing her apart in the only way he could.

"I took a great many vows that day," she said quietly, when he had begun to think that she would not answer him. Though she did not meet his gaze, and he hated that. "But I do not recall agreeing to stop doing the things that bring me joy. On the contrary, I seem to recall *you* promising me that I could continue them. That was the reason I married you."

"That is *one* of the reasons," he could not seem to keep himself from growling.

She shrugged again, but it seemed a jerkier motion than before. As if she was not so nonchalant as she wished to pretend. "I could have called you my temptation and repented at leisure in the convent, Asterion. You know full well I married you so I would not need to give up the hills and the trees and the wild things that live there."

"It is unacceptable," he began, all thunder and doom. "Why?"

Brita still didn't look at him as she asked this, as if she was so unimpressed with any storm that he might be gathering that she didn't notice—but he couldn't quite believe that. Or maybe he wished to believe it, but she still seemed not quite her nonchalant self. She leaned forward and was helping herself to the food heaped high on the platters before them, but he was sure he saw her hand tremble and her throat convulse, if slightly.

"You are a Teras wife now," he said, though he did not know why he bothered. He had said the same thing many times and it never seemed to land. Not the way he needed it to land. And he did not wish to interrogate this need, only her obstinance. "You knew this when you married me. Whether you like it or not, there are certain expectations of a man in my position."

"And you knew who I was when you asked me to marry you in the first place." She took a bite of the food she'd piled on her plate and did not look at him as she chewed. Then she took her time swallowing. Only then did she shift her gaze to his, the steadiness of it somehow unnerving. Almost as if she was attempting to hide some kind of *hurt* from him—but he rejected that possibility. "Maybe you can explain something to me. Why is it that people seem to think a marriage will change them? Or more to the point, will change the person they've married? You promised me that you would show me where all those kisses went, and you did. I did not expect that you would transform before my eyes. I don't understand why you thought that I would."

"Because I asked you to."

Her sun and moon eyes seemed perhaps too wise as she gazed back at him. Or perhaps it was something else—but he rejected that, too. "Did you ask me such a thing?"

"Every day," he threw at her.

She studied him. "You have thundered on about a great many things and I have assumed that you simply wished to express those things into the ether. Because if people talk to me like that, I ignore them. And you know this. I was sneaking in and out of my own father's house because I was tired of having similar conversations with him. Why would you think I would behave any differently now?"

"I know you are not comparing me to your father."

"What has changed since our wedding?" Brita was still looking at him, too intently, as if he was a puzzle to solve. He disliked it. He was no such thing. He was made entirely of reason and logic. "Why are you so determined to exert your control?"

"It is not about exerting control. It is about safety. Security. And like it or not, the Teras legacy itself." But he found he did not care for the way those familiar words sat so bitterly on his tongue tonight.

"I've stood with you on hillsides bathed in the magic of the sky, watching the sunset, with no other thought in my head." She shook her head at him. "Why would you think I would give that up? Why would you want to give it up yourself?"

"There are standards," he told her. But he couldn't understand what was happening inside him. He felt as if something in him was tearing apart, ripping wide-open at the seams, though that made no sense. "We are *married* now."

Brita only looked at him in that same, sad way that got deep beneath his skin. "So you keep reminding me."

And inside him, those fragile seams broke.

"The man I was willing to pretend I was while getting to know you is not the man I am," he hurled at her, aware as he did that he was aiming for her as surely as she'd aimed that arrow of hers at him. He intended it to land. "The man I am has a certain station in life. And there are a set of expectations that go along with that. Not the world's expectations, Brita. Mine. I could not change that if I wanted to, and I do not want to. This is who I am."

He expected her to go pale. To blanch at his words, and the truth he had not imagined he would need to tell her—that the man she'd met and spoken to in the moonlight was not him at all.

But instead, this confounding wife of his merely gazed at him, steady and sure.

And less sad than before.

"I never pretended to be someone else," she said, quiet and direct. "So if someone must change now that we are married, Asterion, I don't see why it would be me."

And when he started to argue the point, she simply

stood and slipped out of the shirt given her, so she was naked before him once again. Because he'd taught her how to use these weapons, and she did. Oh, how joyfully she used them.

Tonight she took it nuclear, sinking down onto her knees before him.

And no matter how many times he told himself he would not, could not, lose his head with these games she played, he couldn't seem to help it.

All she had to do was look at him with that fire in her eyes.

Then touch him—with her hands, her mouth, her flesh pressed to his.

So easily, every time, he was lost.

And it never mattered, in those moments, that he knew better. It never mattered what promises he'd made to himself. It never mattered that he'd vowed that he would not allow her to make him little more than cannon fodder.

Much later, after they'd torn each other apart again and again, on the terrace and in the bedroom and then again in the great shower in their suite, he watched her brush out her long, raven black hair.

Even when she did not mean to be a sensual feast for his eyes, she was.

All she had to do was breathe and his gaze began to trace her perfect form, from her lush breasts to her tiny waist, to the flare of her hips—

But tonight, something else dawned on him.

"You're staring at me again," she said, though her eyes were soft when they found his in the mirror. She did not stop her brushing. "The casual observer might conclude that for all your brooding, you quite like me."

"Brita." But something else dawned on him. "It's been six weeks."

"So you keep reminding me, when you must realize I care little about time. I prefer to count seasons."

He ignored that nonsense with the strength of his purpose and his dawning suspicion. "We have been together every day, usually several times a day."

"We have."

She smiled then, in that way she did sometimes, so smug and satisfied that she made him hard all over again.

He did not usually let that pass without taking the opportunity to make her sob out his name a few times, as penance.

Tonight he had something else working in him. Call it forewarning. Or a premonition. Or perhaps a simple, deep *knowing,* in the way he sometimes knew things. He usually called it instinct, though this felt far more primitive than that. "Yet you have not bled."

She blinked, and her hands slowed in her hair. She let the brush drop to her lap and looked down at it, and her voice sounded odd when she replied. "No. I have not. I don't know why I didn't notice that before now."

And what washed over him, through him, then was far more complicated than simple triumph, or even fear.

Though in the moment, it felt like *light.*

He strode to the door of the bedroom and bellowed out an order.

And so it was that within the hour, there was a test at the door, and an answer.

She was pregnant. Brita was *pregnant*.

His wife was pregnant with his child, the heir to his fortune and his half of the Teras estate.

And that meant that Asterion was done playing games.

CHAPTER TEN

BRITA HAD NEVER thought about being a mother.

Her own mother had been such a nonevent in her life, notable only for her absence, and she'd always thought of the island itself as the true maternal influence in her life. Maybe it made sense that, having never wanted to marry in the first place, it had never occurred to her to consider what it might be like to have her own children.

After all, there were so many creatures who needed her.

But all it took were two blue lines on a stick and she rather thought that motherhood sounded like exactly the kind of magical experience she could get behind.

Besides, she had always liked baby creatures of any description. Surely she would love her own even more.

Brita knew she would. She knew instantly. She felt all the love she'd kept inside her expand and glow every time she thought of the baby. And every time she thought of the baby's father. She felt herself grow big and swollen with it, all that love, when her body had yet to change much at all.

She was *ripening* with all that terrible, wonderful, marvelous love that seemed to weave its way into her bones until she felt that even the way she walked and talked and *breathed* was different. And she might not have known much love from people in her life, but she could no longer be afraid of it. She could no longer run away from it.

Because this time it was happening from the inside out, an earthquake that went on and on and on.

It was beautiful. It was so magically, marvelously *perfect*.

But she did not share these thoughts with her husband.

Not that night, when he went thin lipped and glittery eyed.

And not in the days that followed, when everything changed. And not just inside her.

Suddenly there was more staff, everywhere. And more requests from them for her thoughts on domestic affairs that interested her not at all. When she woke up in the morning, she was greeted at the door of the bedroom by happy, smiling members of Asterion's heretofore unseen staff, who would chatter at her as they led her from one thing to the next. There were wardrobe fittings, which were tedious. There were social calls, which were even more tedious, and worse, usually involved the kind of arch, snide conversation that she had always disliked the most.

It reminded her too much of treacherous evenings in the Martis villa, trying to make herself invisible while her family sniped on all around her, sinking deeper and deeper into their cups and gripes and endless conspiracies.

Brita had made herself into a woman she could admire, who knew how to use a bow. She saw her target and she shot it. She did not dance around it, using innuendo or a perfectly placed rolled eye instead of the words she meant.

These social calls reminded her of too many forced interactions with her stepmother, and if she'd wanted that, she could have stayed in the villa instead of escaping to the convent and the far reaches of the island.

But it was not until they were driving back up the drive one night, not long after she'd taken that pregnancy test, that she realized that there was a method to all of this that she'd missed. Likely because she was used to being required to do things she did not wish to do by people who were chaotic, if single-minded.

Of course, Asterion did not have the same goals that her family had always had for her.

"Has a threat been made against you?" she asked Asterion in the car.

"There are always threats," he replied, which was not an answer.

But she understood then. He was being nicer about it. He was neither drunk nor disorderly. It was wrapped up in elegance and requests for her opinions and yet in the end, Asterion was doing exactly the same thing that her family had done back in the day.

He was attempting to imprison her.

And unlike back then, she was letting him.

Because when he touched her, it felt like magic. And she had found so little magic in her life, where people were concerned. She wanted to bask in it longer. She wanted to tell herself stories about why he was behaving the way he did.

She spent hours trying to build good reasons for everything he did, to convince herself. That legacy of his, like a rope held taut around his neck. His grandmother's interference in his affairs, however well-meant.

The tragedy of losing his parents so young.

Brita tried and she tried.

But later that night she waited for him to fall asleep beside her, as he always did. And then, even though she took such a deep, intense pleasure in curling her body up with his and breathing him in as she slept, she got up.

Because she had to.

Because there was something inside her, like a drumbeat, letting her know that if she did not—if she let herself be swallowed up in whatever this was he was doing—she would not emerge whole.

It turned out that there could be too much feeling, and she thought she might succumb to it entirely if she didn't *move*.

For the first time in her life, she thought that perhaps, she understood her own mother's need to run a little.

She dressed silently and then set about seeking her way past the new set of guards he had imported for this new phase of his. Brita moved quietly and carefully, aware that the kind of guards that Asterion was likely to hire were obviously going to be better trained than her own drunken family members.

Still, it was quite late when she finally made it into the hills she loved, collected her bow from the place where she normally stashed it, and felt Heracles lean once more against her legs.

He panted a little. The stars were bright.

Brita told herself she was content.

She did her usual rounds and told herself that, too, was as it always had been. And that it was good. She decided it was fine with her if things were as they'd been when she'd been nominally a resident of her father's house. At least this way, she could carry on making her own world as she liked it.

Every night then, she waited as Asterion fell asleep beside her. She dressed silently and amused herself with various escapes from the house, thankful for her years of tracking wild animals that, it turned out, made her excellent at avoiding guards.

Who, in fairness, were more focused on keeping people out than keeping her in.

Or so she assumed.

She assured herself that she could live a whole life like this, close enough to perfectly happy—or closer than she'd ever been when her family were involved in her daily life. But when she would find herself cupping her belly, wondering about the child she carried, she would very carefully not think about how this would work when there was a baby in the mix. Because though she might have come to a place of peace when it came to thoughts about her own mother, she did not intend to act like her mother had.

Over my dead body, she thought instead.

And then, one night, she found herself out on that same viewpoint where Asterion had once joined her.

Maybe she'd been avoiding it.

Because it was here where the moon sat high above the sea and looked as if it was making a silvery pathway across the water, she had to face a fact she'd been avoiding.

It just wasn't the same.

When she'd snuck away from the old Martis villa, she'd felt her burdens disappear the moment the dark welcomed her into its embrace. She had felt free and unfettered. The hills had felt like home, before the convent and even more during the last year. She didn't think about her family or their demands at all while she was out in the hills.

But these days, no matter what she was doing out here, the only thing she could think about was Asterion.

It was maddening.

She went and sat out on the edge of the cliffs, the way she always had. She stared out at the sea, which she had used to do for hours, and all she could see was Asterion.

Asterion with his head thrown back, taking his pleasure in her body and sweeping her right along with him. Asterion laughing the way he had in those early days, out here with her, though he never did that any longer. Him smiling in that way he had that every nun she knew would call sinful, that lit every single part of her on fire.

And Asterion the night they had discovered she was pregnant.

You will be a mother, he had told her, sounding grimmer than she had ever heard him, while she was still trying to wrestle with all the many emotions fighting for purchase inside her. *That changes everything.*

Perhaps, she had replied, still trying to take in the news. And the notion that she was carrying a new life *inside* of her. *But not for many months.*

And he had looked at her as if she had betrayed him.

As if she had struck him with one of her arrows in truth, piercing him to the bone.

Brita did not like it at all when Asterion looked at her like that.

It would be the same as if Heracles, panting softly beside her, suddenly turned his head and snapped his teeth in her direction.

She would feel…hurt, yes. But she would wonder if he was hurt, too, that he should act so unlike himself.

She frowned, no longer seeing the glorious view before her because all she could seem to concentrate on now was Asterion.

Every member of her family had accused her of betraying them at one point or another, and she had never cared at all. Because she hadn't, and she didn't think they believed most of the absurd things they said anyway. Asterion had not accused her of anything at all, yet here she was, all these days later, still worrying that moment over and over in her head.

And none of her made-up stories helped her feel any better.

She blew out a breath, and wondered why everything couldn't be as simple as it seemed when they were both naked together. That was when everything felt like music. That was when every part of her seemed to work in perfect concert with every part of him.

As if they had been put on this earth to make such songs together that it could put the moon and sun to shame.

She suddenly understood all those mournful tracks the people she knew at university had played in the pubs when they were feeling maudlin. All the conversations she'd overheard in those days that she hadn't been able to make any sense of, knowing as little as she did of men. Or sex.

Or all these inconvenient *feelings*.

Even when he was at his darkest, smirkiest, and grimmest, all she wanted was to put her hands on him. To be near him. Not only to have sex with him, though it was true that she adored that.

It had used to be the only time she knew peace was when she was out in these hills.

But here she was, right now, and she didn't feel at peace at all. What she longed to do, instead, was go back to his house and twine herself around him once more. Because sleeping with him felt safe. Warm.

Like home, something in her whispered.

The sex was like dessert. And Brita had always liked dessert. But it was the *home* part that made her ache…

And everything in her shifted as the implications of that seemed to wind their way into her, because she'd never really had a home. Thinking of him that way felt the way the moonlight did, dancing over the water, making a bridge—

And that was when she knew.

All that love that ripened within her. All that love that

infused her with light. All that *love* was not just for the baby she carried.

How had she missed the truth of it?

She was in love with him.

She was in love with him, she thought in amazement, as the words bubbled up inside of her like joy. She must have made some noise because Heracles whined softly, then trailed behind her as she leaped to her feet and started back for the house.

Because she could not exist a moment more without sharing this extraordinary news with the one person it affected most.

It was so *huge*. It made everything make sense. It made it easy to turn around and run toward him rather than away.

It was why he felt like home.

The only home she'd ever had.

Surely, Brita thought, this was what had been missing all along.

How marvelous that she could fix it now that she'd figured it out. And maybe Asterion might find his way back to the man he'd been when she'd met him. He could tell her he'd been pretending, but she'd been there. And she knew liars and pretenders better than she'd have preferred. He wasn't one of them.

Maybe he'd felt as free out there as she always had. Maybe they could find it again, together.

Brita didn't bother slinking back in the labyrinth, covered in stealth and shadows. She stowed her bow and arrow in the trees where she always did and then walked onto the grounds of Asterion's grand estate, smiling when the guards surrounded her. She raised her hands over her head while Heracles howled out his disapproval in the distance, such a dangerous sound it made the men look around as if a pack of wolves might come tearing over the cliff at any moment.

There was a great deal of radioing and muttering into mouthpieces, and the men escorted her—a bit dramatically, she thought—into the glass dome of light. Only then did they leave her to descend the great central stair by herself.

This was a house of many stairs and she loved them all. But this one was her favorite, as it wound around and around, all the way down to the very lowest level of the house, like something lovely floating down toward the sea, buoyed by the breeze. And she was still learning the ins and outs of this new home of hers. The place was a kind of inevitable slide of glass-enclosed rooms with steel girders that led inexorably down to the wing of the tangled labyrinth where Asterion plotted out how to rule more of the world. A pageant of power, someone at one of the endless parade of parties had murmured in her hearing.

But the spiral stair felt like art, not commerce. Walking on it felt like soaring, dancing, all decked in light.

She floated down one level into the next, around and around, until she reached the level she knew best. The sprawling bedroom and living area, where Asterion was waiting for her.

Dark and grim, as if he was actively attempting to black out everything else.

But she knew the moon better than he did, didn't she?

Brita glanced back up the stair, but the guards were nowhere in sight. She stopped moving a few steps up from where he waited and looked down at Asterion.

This man she had married. This man she had let inside her body. This man who had made a child with her.

This man she wondered if she'd loved all along, ever since she'd looked up to see him appear like a dream in the door to the villa's old kitchen. A dream that felt like one she'd had forever, never seeing his face.

Until he walked in and it was as if she'd never seen anything but that face.

Tonight he looked as if he'd risen directly from the bed, and only moments ago. He looked as close to *rumpled* as she had ever seen him, his dark hair defying his usual insistence that it resemble a military evenness, and that was all the evidence she could need that he was not quite himself.

There was also that betrayed look about him again.

She hated that.

And in case Brita had any doubt, it made her heart hurt to look at him. She wanted to run to him. She wanted to throw herself into his arms—

She would have, she nearly did, but something about the way he studied her stopped her. It held her fast where she stood, as if she was facing down a creature with teeth and a terrible wound out there in the dark.

"You are leaving me no choice," he gritted out to her,

his voice like gravel. "You cannot leave your protection to chance."

Her heart ached in her chest, even as it worked overtime, and she felt overripe and bruised with the need to tell him all of the feelings that she'd discovered.

But she paused at that.

"Protection?" she asked softly. "Surely you are aware that I have been protecting myself for a very long time, Asterion."

He seemed to grow darker. Grimmer. "Things are different now, little as you seem able to accept it. You carry not only my name, my child, but the heir to everything I have built and half of everything my family has made."

She wanted to laugh, because why should any of those things matter when the world waited *right there* on the other side of that glass? When there were flowers that only bloomed at night that most people never knew were there? Wonders required the freedom to explore them, not locked up rooms and guards on the perimeter, no matter how many windows he'd built to let the light in.

It wasn't the same.

Why didn't he want to give their child those things?

"I will protect that heir, and *my* child, and I suppose your name as well, the same way I have protected myself." She smiled, though it felt fake. Like it belonged on the face of one of those women at her wedding, or the parties he took her to. As if she wanted the smile to *do something,* instead of simply letting it be what it was. "Or have you forgotten that I'm the one who pinned you to a tree and could have done much worse?"

"I haven't forgotten anything." But it sounded like an accusation.

"I don't understand any of this."

Brita drifted down another step. She studied him, standing there before her in all of his masculine splendor. He had not bothered to do more than throw on a pair of trousers. They were unbuttoned, there over his narrow hips where that flat, low, furred plane below his navel made her feel shivery. All the rest of him was the same golden shade and it was all more of that lean, whipcord strength that defined him.

She had put her mouth on almost every part of this man, and she still hungered for more. He'd been inside her only hours ago, and yet she felt empty, needy.

She'd never felt such greed in her life.

"I have told you," Asterion said in that low, *betrayed* sort of voice. "I have told you time and again, Brita. This is not a *request*. Things cannot continue as they have. You certainly cannot keep up these…childish pursuits of yours. You can either do as I have asked or be swept up in it anyway. The choice is yours, but I promise you, this gallivanting about, risking yourself and *our child,* is at an end."

She wanted to lash out at that, and she nearly did, but she had grown up in a hard school. She knew better. And besides, she didn't want to argue with him, no matter what bizarre things he was saying.

Brita was more interested in why he was acting like this, but she didn't think he'd tell her if she asked.

Because she had asked. And asked.

So instead, she told him the only thing that really mattered. "Tonight I sat on the edge of the cliff where you and I once stood together. It's where I go to think of nothing but the beauty of this island and the world. But I realized you are the only thing I could think about."

He did not look as if there were tides of joy inside him, yearning to break free, at that statement.

She tried again. "I realized that nothing else, and no one else, has ever intruded on my time in the wilderness."

Brita really thought he might understand then, but he only stared back at her, his gaze dark and opaque.

She sighed. "I love you, Asterion."

And she expected everything to change then, the way it had when he'd kissed her. When everything had been turned on its head and nothing was as it had been before.

She expected it would feel the same—that sudden, shocking acknowledgment that her life was not at all what she'd thought it was. That all the while, there had been another truth waiting for her, just out of reach.

But if anything, he looked as if those words...*hurt* him.

As if she might as well have bitten him and sunk her teeth in deep until she found the bone.

For the first time, possibly ever, Brita did not feel steady on her own two feet.

"That is the worst thing you could possibly have said to me," he told her, as if he was a man condemned. There was nothing but dread all over him. It was in his voice. It was in that gaze of his. She could feel it, hanging all around her like a heavy cloak. "You might as well have consigned us to our doom. I hope you're happy."

Brita felt the way she thought it must feel to be on the receiving end of one of her own arrows—steel shot straight through the heart, an inarguable death sentence.

She didn't know how she was still standing.

She didn't know why she could still draw breath.

And Brita had always thought that dead things died on impact, but here she was. Still upright. Still breathing no matter how little she wished to. She could still feel her pulse in her veins.

She could still feel exactly how much those words had hurt.

"Do you hear me?" he asked then, ruthlessly, and at least that was different. There was a little more heat in his voice then, even as he glared at her. "I promised you endless kisses and sex. And a wildlife refuge. It was never meant to be about *love*. Ever. That is the bargain we made."

"But the bargain has changed," she heard herself say, when she had no plan to speak.

She felt as if she was acting on some kind of autopilot when she was used to being a woman of intention and focus—or maybe it was simply that there was no need to pretend. There was no need for anything but these deep truths she hadn't even known were inside her.

Having never loved anyone before in her life, not a human anyway, it wasn't that she'd expected it to be *easy*. Maybe it was always hard. Maybe it always made you feel as if love and grief were the same, depending on the moment.

But it wasn't as if she could go back and *unsay* it.

Much less *unfeel* it.

"I have changed," she clarified. "You have changed me. There's no going back, Asterion. I couldn't go back if I wanted to, and I don't. I won't."

"Then you're doomed," he told her in that same voice of dark and dread, as if he was delivering them both a life sentence. "And you might as well consider yourself in prison, Brita, because you are. Until such a time as you come to your senses."

CHAPTER ELEVEN

FOR A MOMENT she looked devastated, and it nearly killed him.

But Asterion decided that he must have imagined it.

Because her chin tilted up. Something that looked like battle blazed in her eyes.

She was every inch the huntress of his wildest fantasies.

So it was his own perversities—his not so inner monster, he supposed—that made him almost wish that she really had been devastated by him. That he could reach her that way.

What kind of man was he to wish such a thing on his own wife?

"I am not the one who needs to come to her senses," she said after a moment, and there was a huskiness in her voice, but no other hint that she was discussing anything more emotionally fraught than the endlessly beautiful weather. "You can imprison me for a thousand years, Asterion. I will love you all the while." She inclined her head then, just slightly. "I will also try to murder you, but I'm beginning to understand that those two things can be the same, if necessary."

"*You cannot love me*," he thundered at her then, the

words coming from some terrible place deep within him. "I forbid it."

And when she laughed, it was as if something simply crumbled into ash inside of him. It was like losing himself all over again. It was like the sudden, shocking impact, steel against steel, the jolting and the rolling, and then waking into horror.

It was like a darkness that spread through him, eating everything whole and spinning him around again.

"You cannot forbid me to do anything," she was telling him, still laughing, when nothing had ever been less funny. "I'm your wife. Not one of your domestic staff. Or one of your little corporate underlings. *I* do not race about, desperate for your approval. It does not matter to *me* if you issue lists upon lists of orders. I will only follow them if I wish to." Her laughter faded, and her gaze were something like solemn. "I'm sorry if you don't like it. But not sorry enough to act as if I work for you, or anyone."

"You need to listen to me," he growled, and then he was advancing on her, though surely he should know better by now. There was nothing to be gained by putting his hands on her and too much to lose, but he did it.

There was that heat, as always. There was that terrible longing. There was the sure knowledge that he was already in too deep with her—but wasn't that the trouble? She was quicksand and he couldn't fight his way out, but he kept trying.

Because he was determined that this marriage would end better than his parents had.

There was a part of him, that terrible monster that

he knew lurked within him, that understood things he had always condemned. Like seeing his father shake his mother. Was that the near-electric urge that raced through him then? Was that why his skin prickled? Did he want to simply cross that line once and for all and stop pretending he could make himself any better?

Besides, he doubted very much that Brita would respond the way his mother had, merely issuing a ringing slap before falling into his father's arms. Kissing him madly until the two of them had started shouting at each other all over again, because such was the carousel they lived on. Such was the ride everyone near them was forced to partake in, like it or not.

But none of that mattered. What mattered was that he felt the urge at all.

This was why he had always lived his life so committed to keeping such tight control of everything. His feelings. His thoughts. The whole of his world.

Because he knew.

The intensity in his blood led to darkness and death.

He had witnessed it himself.

"This thing between us is like a fever," he growled.

She dared to look amused. "You told me it was nothing of the kind."

"It is like a fever, we are both infected, and you think that we can survive this, Brita, but I know better." He gripped her, not hard, and even that felt like a bridge too far over a very old, very dark abyss. "I know where this ends. It will consume us whole."

She did not fight him. She did not pull away. She

melted into him, her eyes imploring on his. "Isn't it supposed to?"

"It is like a cancer," he seethed at her. "You can try this therapy or that, but it always gets worse. It always grows bigger. And then, soon enough, you become heedless of your surroundings. Incapable of controlling yourself. Your evil lies inside you, until it explodes, and it will. It always does. And there's no telling who we will take with us when we go."

There was some new shine in her eyes then, making them more silver than gold, as if she needed to be more luminous. "I don't understand."

He wanted to shout, to throw things through walls, to shatter all the glass in this house.

But that was why he had built this house *of* glass. So that he couldn't risk that kind of tantrum. So that he couldn't start behaving the way his parents had, unless he wished to fall off into the sea with the shards.

Asterion fought to remember who he was.

It was distressingly difficult.

He forced himself to step back. "My parents called their relationship *tempestuous*. But in reality, it was torture. They tortured each other, day in and day out. There were always accusations, fights, shouting matches. They threw vases at each other's heads. They threw furniture through windows. They screamed and cried and clawed at each other, and then they called it passion and disappeared into the bedroom for days, and this rolled into everything. It consumed them whole, and then us, too."

Brita searched his face. "I assure you, there were no

relationships in the house I grew up in that anyone would wish to emulate. But that doesn't mean—"

"They were in one of their fights," he gritted out, because he couldn't seem to stop himself. He never told this story. He had lived it, and then there were the versions the media liked to spin, and he'd never spoken of it to anyone but his brother, in the most oblique terms. "Poseidon and I were twelve. We waited with our grandfather for them, in the foyer of the house my grandmother still claims, and we all stood there listening to the splintering of furniture above. When they came down, they were both glittery eyed and disheveled, and it was never easy to tell what, exactly they had been doing. All of their passions had a price, you see. They called their bruises *souvenirs*."

Brita only seemed to melt into him more, when she wasn't even touching him just then.

Asterion regretted that he had ever started down the path of this story, but he couldn't seem to stop. "My father insisted on driving. My mother soundly abused him for this arrogance because she preferred to take a car with a driver, so that she could have my father's full attention. Perhaps you remember the road down from my grandmother's house, with all its twists and turns." Brita nodded, and he swallowed. He found his throat appallingly dry, but even this did not stop him. "In the rain, it is treacherous. But they were too busy shouting at each other to care. As always."

Brita looked something like sad. Terribly sad, and she lifted a hand, as if to touch him—but he couldn't allow that. "Asterion…"

"We were all in the car when it took the last curve too fast to see the sedan coming in the opposite direction. There was no possibility of avoiding the impact. Someone screamed, I remember that."

She whispered his name again.

That helped. He had forgotten the screaming—he wanted to forget it again, and how it had been choked off so abruptly. He swallowed again. "Somehow, Poseidon and I survived. But we had the bad luck of remembering our parents as they were, not as they were eulogized. And there was never any doubt that the same demons lurked within us. We both vowed that we would never become what they were."

"You cannot think…" she began, frowning.

"I had no worries on that score, Brita," he gritted out at her. "I enjoy sex. I like women. It is only you that has made me doubt my own control. Only you that has made me wonder if all this time, I have been lying to myself."

"About something that happened when you were twelve years old? And are in no way responsible?"

He felt something else snap, deep inside, as if it was a fragile thing he had been hiding all along.

"Don't you see?" he demanded. "I have always been destined to be the very same monster. The reality of me is as dark and as twisted as the people who made me. The Monster of the Mediterranean is no joke. It is who I am. This man you see? This Asterion Teras, who has made such a name for himself? This has always been a mask."

That was far more difficult to say than perhaps it should have been.

Still, it was the truth, no matter how unwelcome. His chest hurt, as if he'd run straight up the side of a mountain. Everything hurt, he realized, as if he was waking up in that mangled mess of a car again—but the only thing he could seem to do was keep his gaze trained on Brita.

Who for some reason did not look as horrified as she should.

If anything, her eyes were soft.

Soft enough that something in him seemed to sing out in response—

But then she lifted her chin in that same belligerent way of hers that he could not understand why he found so alluring. The next moment, her eyes were not soft at all.

Instead, she simply gazed back at him, challenge written all over her.

"Take it off then," she said.

He felt all the wind leave his body. "I beg your pardon?"

She waved a hand in a manner so peremptory that it reminded him of his grandmother. "Take it off," she said again. She made a low noise. "I want both, Asterion. The monster as well as the man. Don't you see? I want everything."

Something in him jumped at that, painfully, but he could not allow it. He could not permit anything that felt like hope when he had already lived through the wreckage of a relationship like this once. The literal wreckage. He could not do it again.

"You should run from this, from me. I mean it, Brita. It can only end in disaster." He hated saying these things. It was as if his own body rebelled as he spoke. But he forced himself to keep going. "You should take our child and go to one of those wild places you love so much, where I can never find you."

But Brita only laughed.

And this time, she tossed her head back, as if calling down the gods of old to laugh with her.

Asterion couldn't decide if he was thrilled or incensed. It didn't seem to matter. It hurt him and he wanted her all the same.

"If I run," she said, tilting her head slightly to one side, "will you catch me? Or will I catch you in the end?"

Something in him began to beat, low and hard, like a drum.

"That's not what I meant at all."

She moved then, putting her face entirely too close to his. "Because if I do catch you, there will be a cost to you, *agapi mu.* And of the two of us, I have to say that I like my chances when it comes to a hunt."

"I don't have the slightest idea what you're talking about. There is no *hunt,* Brita."

But if that was true, why did he feel a strange, new kind of lightning inside of him at the thought?

"You have hunted me from the start," she said. "And I have hunted you in return. But we have circled around each other all the while, pretending we were not doing the very thing we have been doing all along. What if we both stopped pretending?"

Asterion thought his heartbeat was so loud it might shatter the windows.

"You cannot take such a risk," he growled.

And he saw something crack then, there on her lovely face. He could see, for a dizzying sort of moment, that this was far harder for her than he had imagined. That she *felt* all these storms just as he did.

That neither one of them was alone in this.

But then she blinked, and the light of battle was back.

As if she knew, somehow, he needed a challenge, not a cuddle. Not when the monster in him was in control.

"If I win," she told him, very deliberately, her gaze steady, "I win you. All of you."

This was not what Asterion had intended. He didn't even know what this was.

But he did know one thing. He was not a man accustomed to losing. And somehow, all his talk of cancers and fevers seemed to wrap up and tangle inside him, then wash away as he got closer to her, too.

"You cannot win," he growled at her. "You won't."

They stayed like that for far too long, suspended in the force of the way they gazed at each other. Asterion wasn't sure which one of them was breathing heavily—he only knew that he could hear it.

He could very nearly taste it.

Brita let her smile flash like quicksilver, there for an instant, then gone.

"I wish you good luck," she said, as formally as a vow. Then she laughed again. "You will need it."

Before he could process those words, she whirled around and was gone. Flying back up that stair, moving faster than should have been possible.

And he was so stunned that, for moment, he simply… watched.

It was a sight that would be stamped into his bones for the rest of his life. He knew this too well. His huntress, his Brita, charging up the stairs at full speed, all that thick and inky hair streaming behind her like a train.

He had the presence of mind to call off his guards, but then he took after her.

He assumed she would head straight up toward the entrance to the house, but she didn't. She feinted left, then took a hard right, running through this house he'd built as if she knew it better than he did.

Then it was like they were both lost in the same maze. A maze he had created and should have known like the back of his own hands, but it was different tonight.

It was different because he felt haunted by the woman he saw only in glimpses as they both ran. She was a little bit here, a little bit there. When he thought he had her cornered, there was only the impression of her on an empty landing.

There was the sound of her laughter down a curving hall. There was her reflection, always dancing away, out of reach.

It was almost as if he'd made her up.

Yet as he hit one dead end after another, he never once thought of giving up. Or letting her run off as she liked.

As she should.

Because he was Asterion Teras. He did not give up. He won.

No matter what, he won—

But still it felt like something of a relief when he saw her start back to the grand spiral stair and finally rush for the glass globe that would lead her to the outdoors.

He did not stop to think. He did not question himself.

He burst out into the night and he charged for her, chasing her as she ran flat out for the woods that lurked on the far side of the cliff.

Then the game began again in earnest.

And here, in these hills where Brita had always been a part of the same wilderness that surrounded him now on all sides, Asterion felt the last vestiges of the man he'd tried so hard to become fall away.

Until there was nothing left but *this*.

His feet against the earth. The pounding of his heart. The heat in his sex and the fire in his blood and her name all over him, like rain.

And this was no car crash. This was no tempest.

This was elemental. This was blood and bone.

She was the song the night sang around him, other-worldly and astonishing, and most of all, his.

I love you, she had said. And had meant it. He had seen that she meant it.

And somehow, this hunt of theirs, this game that wasn't a game at all, seemed to bring those words into him with every breath.

With every step, and her laughter on the breeze, she loved him.

She loved him, and she hadn't said it that first night, after the kiss. The way women had before, angling for his money, his fame.

She hadn't said it at their wedding, when anyone might have been swept away by the vows and the pageantry.

She hadn't said it on their wedding night, when he'd

made her sob over and over again as he'd taught her things about her body she hadn't known.

Instead, she'd said it tonight.

When he'd been nothing but dark and grim for weeks.

She'd said it, knowing full well that she carried his child, and if she wished, she could take him for his fortune and his protection for at least the next eighteen years.

Because she had not only signed all those documents he'd put before her, he had watched as she'd read each and every one of them.

She loved him, and still they ran.

Again and again, he nearly caught her—but only nearly.

And he began to feel that she knew all of this too well. Not just the island they raced through, though she was clearly a part of it in a way he never would be. It was as if they had danced this dance before.

Brita had somehow navigated his own maze better than him. And now they were out here, in these hills she knew better than most knew their own bedrooms, and she was nimble and fleet of foot.

Every now and again he saw the shadow of that wolf of hers, always at his flank, but never attacking him.

Asterion had to think that meant something.

He could not have said how long they played this game. But finally, as perhaps he'd always known they would, they ended up on that same cliff once again, where they had once watched the moon like a ladder over the sea.

The cliff where, she had only told him earlier tonight, she had understood she was in love with him.

And now he knew that he had never wanted anything more, in all his life, than to hear her say those words again.

He chased her out into the clearing, then stopped, because when she turned to face him, she was holding that bow.

"You won't shoot me," he said, in a low, thick voice he did not recognize as his own.

As if the monster had taken him over at last, but tonight he could not seem to mind that as he should.

"Wrong again," Brita murmured.

And then, even as he took a breath to order her to stop, she let loose the arrow.

He felt the impact a scant moment later.

It punched at him, knocking him off his feet until he found himself flat on his back.

Asterion waited for the searing pain. For the agony to catch up with him, and the strangest part was, he couldn't even blame her—

But the pain didn't come.

Brita did.

She moved over him and stood above him, another arrow notched into her bow as she looked down at him. He saw the steel of her gaze and the curve of her lips, and then another arrow flew.

Asterion didn't flinch, and he thought he deserved far more congratulations for that than he received.

For a moment, he thought that maybe it was the power of that gaze of hers, sun and moon together, that made him imagine he wasn't wounded.

But when she lowered her bow and he tried to test what was left of his body, he understood.

She'd shot the arrow at his hips, but not to his flesh. Each one hammered straight into the ground, right on the seams of the loose trousers he wore.

Pinning him there, unless he wished to tear off his trousers and rise.

Which he might have done, but Brita still stood there above him. She considered him for a moment, then tossed her bow and her quiver to the side.

As he watched, she smiled at him and shrugged out of her clothes. One garment after the next, revealing herself to him with that efficiency that made his sex pound with need.

When she was naked, she moved to kneel between his legs and looked up at him, her naked skin gleaming like marble in the moonlight.

But he knew better. He knew exactly how warm she was, how soft and supple.

"I love you," she told him, almost sternly. "And better yet, I have won you. You are mine now, Asterion Teras, *agapi mu*. For as long as we both shall live. And you will not imprison me. Or this child. Or any other children we have. We will all run wild when we like, and we will go into society and put on our masks when we must, but all the while we will know, deep in our hearts, who we really are."

"Brita," he grated out, "I don't want to hurt you."

"I don't intend to let you," she whispered back.

She reached out between them and freed him from his

trousers, torn as they were. And the first thing she did was lean down and take him in her mouth, licking him long and sweet and deep.

Because he had taught her, she knew how to tease him. How to make him groan and sink his fists in her hair.

She brought him to the edge again and again, until he would have pierced his own flesh with one of her damned arrows if she would just—

But she eased back and studied him, looking entirely too pleased with her handiwork.

"Brita…" he managed to say, but it sounded like a wild thing.

And she took far too long for his liking, but she smiled. Then she climbed up onto him and settled herself there, taking the laziest route imaginable before sinking down on him, taking him deep into her heat.

"I already know you love me," she whispered as she rocked her hips and made him see stars. "I suspect I'm the only woman you have ever chased, both in service to your grandmother and tonight. There is only one reason why you would do such a thing."

"Brita—" he growled.

"And you will tell me, soon enough," she told him, and her eyes were narrow as she worked herself over him, but he could see the sun and the moon and all that heat. "Because I will not imprison you, either. And I will always see you, no matter what you wear. We will stand in stuffy ballrooms where no one eats and everyone drinks too much, and everything is fake and brittle, and I will know exactly how wild you are, deep within you, where only I get to see it."

"Brita," he managed to get out. "I—"

"I already know," she told him, there beneath the stars. And he knew then.

He did not need to control her. She did not need to run. They needed this.

The magic here. The moon.

The two of them, when the chase was done, right back where they'd begun.

Freedom was what they found together. Love was what they made it. Passion was only dangerous when it turned toxic, and they could control that without having to control each other.

She was no myth and he was no monster. They were flesh and blood.

And they belonged together, just like this.

Brita took him straight out into the cosmos then, in a glorious rush that he could do nothing at all to stop, and the truth was, he didn't want to.

And all the while he whispered, "I am yours, my huntress. I am yours forever."

The second time he said it, there in her ear, after he took his time returning her the favor of that tease. That torment.

A torment that made them shatter, but nothing else.

And the third time, he shouted it.

So loud that later, Brita would swear the moon shouted it right back. That night, and every night after.

CHAPTER TWELVE

EVERYTHING REALLY DID change that night, and Asterion was glad of it.

It wasn't that he stopped being who he was, protective and overbearing and occasionally grim and stern straight through, as his wife had no trouble pointing out to him. But the core of who they were had changed because of that hunt. Because of that moon.

Because she had loved him enough to fight for him.

And every day that passed that led into months, that turned into years, there was a little less despair in him. And a little more joy.

Because he loved her enough to fight for them.

After she delivered him one perfect daughter, as wild as her mother though named for his grandmother—who inclined her head as if accepting an expected tribute, then wiped away a tear from her cheek—they decided it was time to look for the refuge she wanted.

But it quickly became clear that there was one such place already, and it had been taken over by the wilderness already. And so even though Asterion had paid off her family when he'd married her, and given them far more than they deserved, he went back to that crumbling old villa once more.

And this time he took Brita with him to give them one final offer.

"You are to move out," Brita said, in that calm way of hers that he got to watch work its magic on her family. Meaning it drove them into rages, and she knew it. She depended on it, this not entirely civilized wife of his. "The villa will be mine eventually, of course, when you are all dead." She smiled in a bloodthirsty way at her father, when she said that, making Asterion proud. Vasilis only glowered in response. "All I would need to do is wait you out, but I don't want to. I would like you all to leave, and give me the estate when you do."

"As you have already pointed out so impolitely, it will one day be yours. Why should we give you anything?" her stepmother asked icily.

"Because I will give you whatever home you wish," Asterion said then. And he did not put any parameters on that. He barely raised a brow as he watched high value real estate dance through their heads like sugarplums. "The only stipulation is that it cannot be here. The entire Martis estate, this entire part of the island, will be Brita's alone. And if you're caught here, let me be clear, you will be arrested for trespassing. Just so we understand each other."

And so it was that he rehoused the lot of his unpleasant in-laws, sending them off to whatever far-distant place they desired, and Brita was able to make her refuge a reality. She spent two solid years renovating the old villa, honoring its history, and making sure to continue to keep the staff who had always been her only friends. Or pay for the retirement they deserved if that was their preference.

When their eldest daughter was nearly three and Brita was big and round with their second child, the refuge was opened at last.

"I am a man who keeps my promises," he told her at the gala that evening, there in the villa restored to its former glory that served as the home of the wilderness foundation Brita had formed.

"Those were the easy promises," she replied airily, though her eyes gleamed. "There will be a lifetime to work on the others."

And she kissed him, there in public, the way she always did.

As if she wanted everyone else to see the wildness in him that was never too far from the surface.

As if she wanted to bring it out.

One night, years later, he came back from a business trip to find the labyrinth house shockingly empty of his wife and their children and Dimitra, who was hale and hearty and would likely live forever. She liked to spend time here with all five of her local grandchildren, the three older girls and the twin boys who'd come after, all of whom made certain that the maze of glass and steel was filled with their particular brand of joyful chaos.

Asterion barely recognized the place without them in it, making the glass and steel warm.

He showered off his work and climbed up that spiral stair that he could never use without thinking of that night. When his beloved had led him on a merry chase, then took him to an actual, literal cliff before loving him into submission.

With an arrow or two, for emphasis.

Asterion knew that he was far happier than most.

And he worked as hard as he was able to keep it so.

He wandered into the trees the way he had so many years ago. And by now there was an easy path between the house and Brita's favorite spots, so there was no need to crash about as he had that fateful night—though just like then, he caught sight of that same watchful wolf that his children liked to say watched over them at night.

Heracles had never quite taken to Asterion, but he watched over his mistress's love all the same.

He made his way over the hill to the cliffs he would always think of as theirs alone, and he stopped at the edge of the clearing as he had long ago, when he thought he was merely pretending to be besotted with this woman.

The sun was making a kind of ladder across the sea. And his wife, his goddess, the mother of his children and his eternal huntress, stood at the edge, with five little bodies pressed in all around her.

"Make room," he ordered his family as he walked to the cliff's edge and pulled his babies into his arms as they squealed in delight that he was home. "You know I don't like to miss the sunset."

He didn't like to miss a moment of this. He missed as few as he could.

Asterion would teach his children how to rule the world he'd made for them. He couldn't wait to see what they made of it.

But Brita was already teaching them how to love it.

The way she'd taught him how to love her and them and everything else that mattered.

The way he planned to do until the moon took them back.

But not anytime soon.

Not if he, Asterion Teras, had anything to say about it.

And he usually did.

* * * * *

COMING SOON!

We really hope you enjoyed reading this book.
If you're looking for more romance
be sure to head to the shops when
new books are available on

Thursday 11th
April

To see which titles are coming soon, please visit
millsandboon.co.uk/nextmonth

MILLS & BOON

MILLS & BOON ®

Coming next month

ACCIDENTALLY WEARING THE ARGENTINIAN'S RING
Maya Blake

Abstractedly, Mareka registered that they'd cleared the building, that they were out in the square with a handful of people milling around them.

But she couldn't break the traction of Cayetano's stare. His heavenly masculine scent was in her nose. The powerful thud of his heartbeat danced beneath her fingers, his breathing a touch erratic again after his gaze dropped to linger on her mouth, his own lips parted to reveal a hint of even white teeth.

And just like that she was once again thrown to that night in Abruzzo when this foolish crush had taken a deeper hold. When the only thing she'd yearned for, more than anything else in existence, was to kiss Cayetano Figueroa. Who cared that she'd sworn to be rid of this madness a mere…half an hour ago?

Half an hour ago…while she'd been choosing the engagement ring he intended to give to another woman.

Her eyes started to widen. He sucked in a sharp breath.

A camera flash went off, dancing off the diamond ring she'd forgotten to take off and illuminating their expressions for a nanosecond before immortalizing it in life-altering pixels.

Continue reading
**ACCIDENTALLY WEARING THE
ARGENTINIAN'S RING**
Maya Blake

Available next month
millsandboon.co.uk

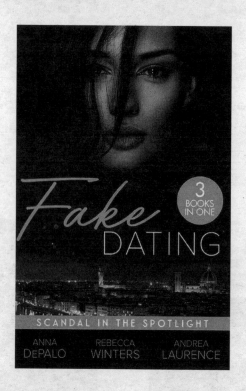

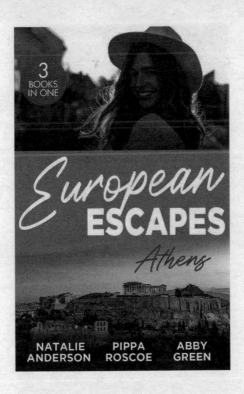

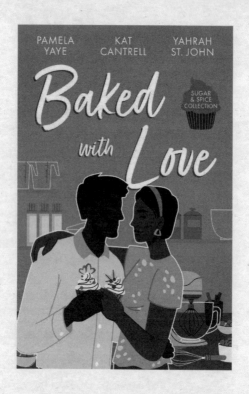

LET'S TALK

Romance

For exclusive extracts, competitions and special offers, find us online:

f MillsandBoon

X @MillsandBoon

◯ @MillsandBoonUK

♪ @MillsandBoonUK

Get in touch on 01413 063 232

MILLS & BOON

THE HEART OF ROMANCE

A ROMANCE FOR EVERY READER

MODERN

Prepare to be swept off your feet by sophisticated, sexy and seductive heroes, in some of the world's most glamourous and romantic locations, where power and passion collide.

HISTORICAL

Escape with historical heroes from time gone by. Whether your passion is for wicked Regency Rakes, muscled Vikings or rugged Highlanders, awaken the romance of the past.

MEDICAL

Set your pulse racing with dedicated, delectable doctors in the high-pressure world of medicine, where emotions run high and passion, comfort and love are the best medicine.

True Love

Celebrate true love with tender stories of heartfelt romance, from the rush of falling in love to the joy a new baby can bring, and a focus on the emotional heart of a relationship.

HEROES

The excitement of a gripping thriller, with intense romance at its heart. Resourceful, true-to-life women and strong, fearless men face danger and desire - a killer combination!

From showing up to glowing up, these characters are on the path to leading their best lives and finding romance along the way – with plenty of sizzling spice!

To see which titles are coming soon, please visit

millsandboon.co.uk/nextmonth